W9-CXY-749

Nunn

Nunn, Kem
Tapping the source

URCE

DATE DUE		
APR 15 1997		
APR 24 1997		
MAY 15 1997		
MAY 28 1997		
JUL 12 1997		
AUG 29 1997		
JUL 24 2000		

Williamstown Public Library
Williamstown, MA 01267
(413) 458-5369

1. Library materials may be kept three weeks with a renewal of one week. Magazines may circulate for two weeks.

2. A fine of $.05/day is charged for each day library materials are kept beyond the due date. No book will be issued to any person with unpaid fines.

3. Books and other library materials damaged beyond reasonable wear shall be paid for.

4. Each borrower is responsible for all library materials charged on their card.

TAPPING THE SOURCE

KEM NUNN

A Laurel Trade Paperback
Published by
Dell Publishing
a division of
The Bantam Doubleday Dell Publishing Group, Inc.
1 Dag Hammarskjold Plaza
New York, New York 10017

FOR MY PARENTS

Acknowledgment

*A special thanks to Oakley Hall for his
perseverance on my behalf.*

Reprinted by arrangement with Delacorte Press

Printed in the United States of America

One Previous Edition

April 1988

10 9 8 7 6 5 4 3 2 1

W

PART
ONE

1

Ike Tucker was adjusting the Knuckle's chain the day the stranger came asking for him. It was a sunny day and the patch of dirt in back of the Texaco was hot beneath his feet. The sun was straight overhead and dancing in the polished metal.

"Got a visitor," Gordon told him.

Ike put down the wrench and looked at his uncle. Gordon was wearing a greasy pair of coveralls and a Giants baseball cap. He was leaning on a doorjamb and staring across the dirt from the back porch. "Gone deaf on me now too?" he asked. He meant deaf as well as dumb. "I said you got a visitor, somebody wants to talk about Ellen."

Ike brushed his hands on his pants and went up the step, past Gordon and into the building, which was both a gas station and a small market. He could feel Gordon behind him, tall and round, hard as a stump, following past the shelves of canned goods and the counter where half a dozen old men twisted on their stools to stare after him, and he knew that when he was gone they would still be watching, their sorry faces turned toward the screen doors and the cool sagging porch where the flies found shelter from the heat.

There was a kid waiting for him in the gravel drive that circled the pumps, leaning against the side of a white Camaro. Ike guessed the kid was close to his own age, maybe seventeen, or eighteen. Ike was eighteen. He would be nineteen before the summer ended, but people often took him for being younger. He was not tall, maybe five eight, and skinny.

Only a month before, a highway patrolman had stopped him on the way into King City and asked to see his driver's license. He had not been out of the desert since he was a boy and outsiders generally made him self-conscious. The kid in the drive was an outsider. He wore a pair of pale blue cord jeans and a white shirt. A pair of expensive-looking dark glasses had been pushed back to rest above his brow in a mass of blond curls. There were two surfboards strapped to the roof of the Camaro.

Ike picked a rag off the stack of newspapers by the front door and finished wiping his hands. The stranger had already managed to draw a small crowd. There were a couple of young boys, Hank's kids from across the street, looking over the car, together with Gordon's two dogs, a pair of large rust-colored mongrels that had come to sniff the tires. Some of the old men from the counter had followed Ike outside and were lining up on the porch behind him, staring into the heat.

The kid did not look comfortable. He stepped away from the car as Ike came down the steps, Gordon following. "I'm looking for Ellen Tucker's family," he said.

"You found it. Here he is, the whole shootin' match." It was Gordon who spoke.

Ike could hear a couple of the old men behind him chuckle. Someone else cleared his throat and spat into the gravel lot.

Ike and the kid stared at one another. The kid had a bit of a blond mustache and there was a thin gold chain around his neck. "Ellen said something about a brother."

"I'm her brother." Ike still held the rag. He was aware that his palms had begun to sweat. Ellen had been gone for nearly two years now and Ike had not heard from her or seen her since the day she left. It was not the first time she had run away, but she was of age now, a year older than Ike; it had not figured that she would return to San Arco.

The kid stared at Ike as if he was confused about something. "She said that her brother was into bikes, that he owned a chopper."

Gordon laughed out loud at that. "He's got a bike," he said. "Right out there in back; shiniest damn bike in the county." He paused to chortle at his own joke. "Hasn't been ridden but once, though. Go on an' tell him about that one, Low Boy." He was addressing himself to Ike.

Gordon's younger brother had a bike shop in King City where Ike worked on the weekends. Ike's bike was a '36 Knucklehead he'd put together on his own, from scratch. On his only attempt to ride it, however, he had dumped it in the gravel lot and driven a foot peg halfway through his ankle.

Ike ignored Gordon's request. He continued to watch the kid, thinking that it was like Ellen to make up some damn story. She never could tell anything straight. Things were too boring that way, she had said. And she was a good storyteller, but then she had always been good at just about everything except staying out of trouble.

"You're her only brother?" the kid asked, still looking somewhat dismayed. He watched as one of Gordon's dogs raised a leg to piss on a rear tire, then looked back at Ike.

"I told you he's the whole shootin' match," Gordon said. "If you've got something to say about Ellen Tucker, let's hear it."

The kid rested his hands on his hips. He stared for a moment back down that stretch of two-lane that led away from town, back toward the interstate. It was the direction Ike had looked the day he saw his sister go, and he stared in that direction now, as if perhaps Ellen Tucker would suddenly materialize out of the dust and sunlight, a suitcase tugging at her arm, and walk back to him from the edge of town.

"Your sister was in Huntington Beach," the kid said at last, as if he'd just made up his mind about something. "Last summer she went to Mexico. She went down there with some guys from Huntington. The guys came back. Your sister didn't. I tried to find out what happened." He paused, looking at Ike. "I couldn't. What I'm saying is the guys your sister went with are not the type of people you want to fuck around with. I was beginning to pick up some bad vibes."

"Just what do you mean by bad vibes?" Gordon asked.

The kid paused again but allowed Gordon's question to go unanswered. "I split," he said. "I was afraid to wait around any longer, but I knew Ellen had family out here. I'd heard her talk about a brother who was into bikes and I thought . . ." He let his voice trail off and ended with a shrug of the shoulders.

"Shit." The word came from Gordon, spat into the dust. "And you thought her big bad brother was going to do something about it. You came to the wrong place, pardner. Maybe you should take your story to the cops."

The kid shook his head. "Not hardly." He pulled the shades down over his eyes and turned to get into his car. One of the dogs jumped up, putting its paws on the door, and the kid shooed it down.

Ike left Gordon behind and walked across the gravel to the open window of the car. The heat on his back and shoulders was intense. He stood at the window and found himself reflected in the kid's shades. "Is that all," he asked. "Is that all you were going to say?"

The glasses swung away and the kid stared at his dashboard. Then he reached for the glove box and pulled out a scrap of paper. "I was going to give somebody this," he said. "The names of the guys she went with." He looked at the scrap for a moment and shook his head, then passed it to Ike. "I guess you may as well have it."

Ike glanced at the paper. The sunlight made it hard to read. "And how would I find these people?"

"They surf the pier, in the mornings. But look, man, you'd be stupid to go by yourself. I mean, you start asking around and you're liable to get yourself in trouble. These are not lightweight people, all right? And whatever you do, don't let that old guy talk you into calling the police. They won't do shit, and you'll regret it." He stopped and Ike could see small lines of perspiration beneath the dark glasses. "Look," the kid said once more. "I'm sorry. I mean I probably shouldn't have even come out here. I just thought that from what your sister said . . ." His voice faded.

"You thought things would be different."

The kid started his engine. "You'd probably be better off to just wait it out. Maybe she will turn up."

"Do you think so?"

"Who knows? But unless you can get some real help . . ." He shrugged again. And then he was gone and Ike was standing in the Camaro's dust, watching the white shape of the car shrinking against the heat waves. And when there was nothing left but that patch of sunlight and dust, the ever-present mirage that marked the edge of town, he turned and walked back across the gravel to the store.

The old men were all out on the porch now, whispering in the shade and sucking down Budweisers. Gordon caught Ike's arm as he started past. "I've known all along something like this was coming," he said. "That girl's been headed for a bad end since she learned how to walk. Shit, the way she lit outta here, hitchhiking, wearing those tight jeans all up her ass. What the hell can you expect? We won't see her again, boy. Make up your mind to it."

Gordon released his grip and Ike jerked away. He went through the store and stood on the back porch, looking down into the yard where he and his sister once scratched their names into the ground. They had dug out the letters with sticks and then Ellen had poured gas into the letters and set them on fire and the fire had gotten away from them and burned down Gordon's pepper tree and scorched the back of the store before it was put out. But his sister had said that it was all right, that her only regret had been that the fire had not taken the store and the rest of the fucking town along with it. He could hear her saying that, like it was yesterday, and when he closed his eyes he could still feel the heat from those flames upon his skin. He went down the steps, into the grease-stained dirt, and began to collect his tools.

2

He told them that night that he was leaving, that he was going to look for Ellen. "What'll you go on?" Gordon wanted to know. "The Harley?"

They were seated at the kitchen table. Ike listened to Gordon's laughter, to the incessant rattle of the ancient Sears, Roebuck cooler. The greasy scent of fried chicken circled his head. "Someone should go," he said.

His grandmother squinted at him over a pair of rhine-stone-studded glasses. She was a frail, shrunken woman. She was not well. Each year she seemed to grow smaller. "I don't know why," she said, making it plain by the tone of her voice that she thought otherwise. Ike did not meet her eyes. He pushed himself away from the table and retired to his room to count his money.

Nearly seven hundred dollars there, crammed into a rusted coffee can. But what had it been? Three years now of working on bikes, and there had not been many places to spend it. The bookstore in King City, the lone theater that two thirds of the time ran films in Spanish instead of English, the pinball machine Hank had gotten for the Texaco. And lately he had begun giving the old lady something for rent. There would have been a lot more if he had not sunk so much into the Harley. He spread the money on his bed, counting it several times in the dim yellow light. He packed a single suitcase and went out the back way.

It was dark outside now. He walked along that strip of barbed-wire fence that separated the town from the desert. There was country music spilling out a window at Hank's place together with a wedge of soft yellow light and when he looked past the fence and into the dark shape of the hills, he could smell summer waiting in the desert. One of Gordon's dogs came out from under the house and followed him to the store.

His plan was to drink a six-pack, get sleepy, and wait for the bus out of King City. He took a six-pack of tall cans, left some money and a note by the register, and went into the backyard. He pulled the canvas tarp off of the Knuckle and sat with his back against the wall of the market, watching the bike gleam in the moonlight. He supposed he could trust Gordon to keep an eye on it until he came back. Christ, he didn't have the slightest idea of what he was going to do, or how long it would take. He supposed that when someone took your sister you did something about it. He supposed that was what families were for. Ellen's bad luck was that he was the only family she had.

It was quiet in back of the market, the music out of Hank's sounding soft and far away. He shut his eyes and waited and he was able to pick out the distant clanking of a freight as it climbed the grade into King City and he thought of the times he and Ellen had sat in this same spot, listening to the same sounds, imagining there was some promise in the sound of those trains, because it was the sound of motion, of going places, and he imagined her sitting with him now, head thrown back against the wall, eyes half-closed, beer can resting on a skinny leg. He thought about how it had always pissed off the old woman that Gordon had let them drink beer, but then most things pissed off the old woman.

As he listened the train sounds grew faint and disappeared and someone shut off the music so there was just the silence, that special kind of silence that comes to the desert, and he knew that if he waited there would come a time, stars fading, slim band of light creeping on the horizon, when the silence would grow until it was unbearable, until it was as if the land itself were about to break it, to give up some secret of its own. He remembered the first time that feeling had come to him. It was summer and he had been sick with a summer cold, feverish and in bed, and he had gotten up somewhere in the middle of the night and gone outside, in bedclothes and sneakers, to stand at the strip of barbed wire that marked the edge of Gordon's land. He had been hoping for a breeze, but there was none to be had. There was only the emptiness, the black shapes of distant mountains hard against a black sky, and an overpowering stillness that was suddenly like some living thing pressing down upon him, something that belonged to the night and to the land, something to run from. And he had, back into the house, to Ellen's room instead of his own. But when he had tried to tell her, she had only laughed and said it was his fever, that he was afraid of too many things, afraid of the desert, afraid of the night, afraid of the other boys in King City.

On another occasion she had told him that he would rot in the desert, freeze up here like some rusted engine, like the old woman herself, his nose stuck in a fucking book. And he guessed now that he had always been afraid of that, afraid of staying and yet afraid of going, too, just like he was still afraid of that crazy time of night and a voice he had never heard. Jesus. It was like him to be a chickenshit and her not to be. It was ass-backward that he should be going after her and not the other way around.

He got about half of the six-pack down before quitting, replacing the tarp, and making the walk down the strip of two-lane toward the edge of town, toward that place where he'd seen the white Camaro vanish in the mirage of high noon, where his sister had vanished as well, swallowed by that patch of sunlight and dust and never seen again.

There was no mirage waiting for him that night. There were only the edges of the desert, flat and hard in the moonlight, and the road that was like some asphalt ribbon at his feet, and the sound of his own blood pumping in his ears. And then he was aware of the approaching figure, Gordon, lumbering up the old road, visible for a moment in the last of the town's two streetlights, then fading into shadow, but his footsteps getting louder until at last he stood alongside his nephew, and the two of them, both half drunk, squinted at one another in the moonlight.

Gordon had a fresh bottle of Jim Beam with him. He pulled it out of his hip pocket and brought it down hard on the heel of his hand, his customary way of cracking the seal.

"So you're really going."

Ike nodded.

Gordon nodded too, squinted down his nose at Ike like he wanted a good look at him, then took a drink from the bottle. "Well, maybe it's time," he said. "You're out of school, and you've got a trade. Hell, that's more than I had when I was your age. Kind of figured you might stick with those bikes, though. Jerry says he's never seen a kid pick up tools the way you have. What do you want me to tell him?"

"I'll be back."

Gordon laughed and took another drink. The laughter had a "like hell you will" ring to it. "Last place I saw your old lady was right here. You know that?" Gordon asked, then tore up a bit of dirt with the toe of his boot while Ike shook his head and mentally added his mother to the list of those swallowed by that patch of sunlight. "Yeah. Said she would be back for you kids in the fall. Shit, I took one look at that candy ass she was leavin' with and knew that was a lie."

Ike had been five years old that summer. He'd never known his father at all, just some guy his mother had lived with off and on for a couple of years.

"I'm not your old man," Gordon said. "And I've never tried to be, but I've given you kids a roof, and it's still here if you want to come back. But I wouldn't get my hopes up about that sister of yours. She was wild, Ike, like her old lady. She could've gotten herself into anything. You understand? Don't stick your neck out too far looking for her."

Ike waited. He was not used to Gordon taking an interest in what he did. There had been a time when that was what he wanted. Now? He guessed maybe that time had passed. Still, Gordon had come. The trouble was, Ike could think of nothing to say. He watched Gordon take another drink, and then looked toward that place where the lights of King City barely managed to put a pale frosting on a piece of desert sky.

As he waited he thought about what Gordon had said, about Ellen being wild, like her old lady had been wild, and he thought about their mother. He could not remember much about her now. There was one picture—what he was certain was the only one of all of them, together. They were seated on the steps of his grandmother's house, himself on one side, Ellen on the other, Ellen with one stick of an arm bent over their mother's shoulders, the other raised and extended to give the bird to the camera, all of them squinting into the sun so that it was hard to see their faces. What he mainly remembered about the picture—aside from Ellen flipping off Gordon, was his mother's hair, thick and black, alive in the sunlight. He seemed to remember that she was given to sitting for long periods of time, brushing it in rhythmic strokes, or arranging it with a pair of combs that were made of ivory and carved into the shapes of long slender alligators. And that summer, before she left, she had given the combs to Ellen—the only things she had ever given either of them, as far as he could remember. The combs had become one of Ellen's prize possessions, even up until the time she left. And it seemed to him now that she had worn them that day as well, that they had gone with her into the heat waves. He shut his eyes to remember and the beer made him dizzy. He was suddenly sorry that he had begun dredging for memories. It was generally a depressing exercise and he should have known better. Others came now, but he fought them off. He focused his attention on the gravel between his feet and waited for the hum of a Greyhound to fill the silence.

He was still waiting when he became aware that one more person had joined them on the street. Gordon must have noticed as well because he turned once to look back over his shoulder toward that place where the streetlamp began to fail among the oaks. She would not step into the light but remained among the shadows, and there was something about seeing her there, in just that way, that made him think of them all together—his grandmother, his mother, his sister. For there had been times when he had seen both his mother and his

sister in the old woman's face, in the certain way she sometimes turned her head, in the line of her jaw. The likeness was
generally very fleeting, like a shadow passing over barren
ground. Just what had made it barren—time, sickness—he
could not say. He supposed that getting religion had not
helped.

She waited until the headlights of the bus were swimming
among the stunted branches before coming forward—small
and stiff, like she had been whittled out of something hard, like
she belonged with the wind-bent trees that had been planted
there to mark the edge of town. And her voice, when she
raised it, was like a weapon, the jagged edge of a broken bottle.
The voice seemed to cut easily through the cool air, the deep
drone of the engines. But Ike was not inclined to stay and
listen. He moved quickly up the steps and then back along the
narrow aisle, sucking down great lungfuls of stale recycled air,
avoiding the eyes of the other passengers, some of whom had
begun craning their necks for a look at the commotion outside.
But it seemed to him as he waited, even as they began to roll
away and the lights began to move and darken, that he could
still hear her very clearly, and that she was cursing them both,
him for going, Gordon for letting him, that she was bearing
witness and quoting Scripture. What was it? Something like
Leviticus 20:17, perhaps—that being one of her favorites:
"And if a man shall take his sister, his father's daughter, or his
mother's daughter, and see her nakedness, and she see his
nakedness; it is a wicked thing; and they shall be cut off in the
sight of their people."

3

It was five hours by bus from the desert to L.A., another one and a half to Huntington Beach. The beers had not been a particularly good idea. He had put them down on an empty stomach and they left him stranded in a place that was neither sleep nor consciousness. There were dreams, but they were all bad and pulling himself out of them was like climbing out of deep holes. And when they finally wore off somewhere in the dizzy neon glare of some bus stop bar and grill on the north side of Los Angeles, he was left with a headache and a knot in his stomach.

Now, his suitcase checked at the bus depot because it was still too early to look for a room, he stood at the rail of the Huntington Beach pier and found it hard to believe that he had actually come. But he had. The concrete beneath his feet was the real thing and beneath that there was an ocean. Twenty-four hours ago he had only been able to imagine what an ocean might look like, might smell like. Now he stood above one and its immensity was breathtaking. Its surface rose and fell under his feet, stretching in three directions like some great liquid desert, and the town behind him, hard, flat, color-less, surprising him in its similarity to some desert town, squat-ted at the edge of the sea in much the same way that San Arco squatted at the edge of the desert, dwarfed by the immense thing that lay before it.

Hound Adams, Terry Jacobs, Frank Baker. Those were the names the kid had written on the scrap of paper. "They surf the pier," the kid had said. "In the mornings." And there were surfers below him now. He watched as they jockeyed for posi-tion among the swell lines. He had never guessed that waves were so much like hills, moving hills, of water. And he was fascinated by the way the surfers moved across the faces of the waves, dropping and climbing, shaping their bodies to the shapes of the waves until it was like some dance with the sea. He thought of what the kid had told him, that it would be stupid to come by himself, that he would only get into trouble asking too many questions. So that was all right. He would not ask any. He had come to look at it this way: First of all, it seemed smart to him to assume the worst, to assume that something bad had happened to his sister and that the guys she had gone with wanted to keep it quiet. He also guessed it would be wise to take the kid's warning seriously: these were not lightweight people.

Given those two assumptions, he did not want to barge into town asking a lot of questions. It had occurred to him that his sister may have made other friends, that finding someone who had known her could prove helpful. But how would he find them? Suppose he mentioned her name to the wrong person? And if there were friends here who could be of help, why would that kid have found it necessary to drive all the way to San Arco looking for Ellen's bad-ass brother? No. He kept coming back to the idea that his first step was to find out who these guys were without them knowing who he was. Once he had them spotted, had some idea of what they were like, he would have a better idea of how to proceed. And that, the proceeding, would of course be the tricky part. What would happen if he found that the worst was true, that she was dead? Would he go to the cops then? Would he look for revenge? Or would he find that he was helpless? He remembered the way that kid had stared at him in the heat of the gravel lot. Is that the way it would be? He would find out what had happened and then find out there was not a fucking thing he could do about it? The fear of that discovery was like a shadow above him and even the rising sun could not burn it away.

He did not know how long he stood at the rail, somewhat transfixed by the contemplation of both his fear and this new sport below him, but after a while he was aware of the sun's warmth on his shoulders and of the increased activity around him. He had heard the surfers' voices, heard them calling to one another, but had not been able to pick out any names; he was too far from them on the boardwalk. At last he turned from the rail and started back in the direction of the town.

The sun was climbing fast now, high above the hard square shapes of the buildings that lined the Coast Highway. And with the coming of the sun any similarities to desert towns he had noted earlier were fast disappearing. For Huntington Beach was waking up and there were people in the streets, lines of cars stacking up behind red lights and crosswalks, and there were skateboards humming on the concrete and gulls crying, and old men feeding pigeons in front of the brick rest rooms. There were guys carrying surfboards, and girls, more girls here than he had ever seen in one place. Girls on roller skates and on foot, a blur of tanned legs and sun-streaked hair, and there were girls younger than himself sitting on the railing at the entrance to the pier, smoking cigarettes, looking bored and tired and washed out in the early light, and when he passed they looked right through him.

It was on the inland side of the highway, headed back toward the depot, that he saw the bikes: a couple of Harleys, an 834 Honda Hardtail. First things he'd seen all morning that made him feel at home. One of the Harleys, in fact, was an old Knuckle in full chop, almost identical to his own. He decided to cross the street for a better look. The bikes were drawn up alongside the curb, engines running, riders straddling oversize valves, talking to a couple of girls. He noted that one of the engines (it sounded like the Knuckle) was missing, and propped himself on the wall of a liquor store to listen.

"You got a problem?" a voice wanted to know. It was the first time anyone had spoken to him since the waitress had taken his order at the bus stop north of L.A. He blinked into the sunlight, and into the sullen stare of one of the bikers. He peeled himself from the wall and started away. He could hear them laughing behind him. He nearly collided with some old wino in the crosswalk and the man stopped to curse him, holding up traffic, so there were horns blaring and tires squealing by the time he made the curb on the other side of the street, and that was where he caught sight of his reflection in the plate glass windows of the depot. He examined the faded Budweiser T-shirt, the grease-stained jeans, the home-cut crop of brown curls, the hundred and thirty-five pound frame, and he looked even skinnier and more useless than he had imagined. Low Boy, that was what Gordon had called him, and he felt like the runt now. The bikers' laughter rang in his ears and the voice of the old man had somehow become the voice of the old woman, as if her words had followed him through the night. Then for some damn reason he started thinking of the lines to this song, just one line actually, all he could remember: "Suckers always make mistakes when they're far away from home." And it struck him there in the street, sunlight hot, air full of exhaust and noise and a funny haze like fine gray dust settling over everything, that this would be an easy place to screw up in, and he knew once more he would have to be careful.

By midafternoon he had found a place to stay. The room was part of a drab-looking structure called the Sea View apartments, a large square building covered in a sort of turd-brown stucco. The front of the building sat close to the street, separated from it by a sidewalk and a thin rectangle of weedy grass. There was another ragged patch of grass in back, together with a couple of stunted palms and a lone oil well. The oil well sat by itself in a corner of the lot, fenced off in a square of gritty chain link.

Ike's room was on the west end of the building, upstairs with a view of the oil well and the vacant lot beyond it. If it hadn't been for the backsides of the buildings along the Coast Highway, the Sea View would have lived up to its name and he could have seen the Pacific Ocean, but the view would have probably run him another hundred a month and he could not have afforded it anyway. He had spent the better part of the day looking at rooms and had absorbed his first lesson in beach economics. Rooms that would have rented for a hundred a month in the desert rented for fifty a week in Huntington Beach, and the Sea View, with its two dimly lit hallways, one above the other, its dirty walls, and its alcoholic landlady in her dirty blue bathrobe, had been the cheapest place he could find. It had not taken him long to see that his money would not go as far as he had hoped.

He had planned to get some sleep that afternoon, but sleep would not come and he wound up sitting on the floor near the pay phone in the upstairs hallway, poring over names in the thick white book. There were a lot of Bakers, Jacobses, and Adamses, but no Terry Jacobs, no Hound Adams. There was one Frank Baker, not in Huntington Beach, however, but in some place called Fountain Valley. He had assumed from what the kid had told him that the people he was looking for lived in Huntington Beach. Still, the kid had not said that, he had said only that they surfed the pier. Shit, he had been stupid not to ask more questions, to stand there like the village idiot while the sun scrambled his brains. And Hound Adams? Hound was certainly some sort of nickname. But there were two H. Adamses listed in the book, and one of them lived in Huntington Beach, on Ocean Ave. He sat for a while eyeing the name, cursing himself for not having asked questions when he had had the chance. At last he copied down the address, found a gas station and a map, then rode the bus to Ocean Avenue; it was something to do. It was several miles inland and the address was across the street from an elementary school. He sat out in front of the school on a cold brick wall, uncertain about what to do next. He figured maybe he would just hang around in front and see what kind of people went in and out. But nobody went in and out for at least two hours, and the sun was getting low and a chilly wind had come up by the time a light went on in one of the windows. Crossing the street for a better look, he could see an old woman against a yellowish background, framed by a set of flowered curtains.

It looked as if she was standing over a kitchen sink. It occurred to him that there might of course be other people living there —a son perhaps. But somehow the signs were not encouraging, and for the moment it was getting colder. He turned away from the house and walked back to the corner to wait for a bus.

So ended his first day in Huntington Beach. It was dark by the time he got back to the Sea View apartments. And if the town had come to life with the rising of the sun, then the Sea View apartments had come to life with its setting. The place had been quiet as a morgue when he'd left; now there was apparently some sort of party going on. Many of the doors stood propped open above the stained linoleum floors. A kind of music he was not used to hearing, but what he took to be punk rock, spilled from the guts of the old building and swirled around him as he climbed the stairs. He went straight to his room and closed the door, collapsed on his bed. He had been on the bed for about five minutes, hovering at the edge of sleep, when someone knocked at his door.

He opened it to find two girls standing in the hallway. One was short and dark, with short black hair. The other was tall, athletic-looking. She had strawberry-blond hair that came to her shoulders. It was the dark-haired girl who did the talking. The blonde leaned against a wall and scratched her leg with her foot. They both looked drunk and happy, slightly stupid. They wanted to know if he had any papers. The music was louder now with the door open and he could hear other voices farther down the hall. They looked disappointed when he said no. The dark one sort of stuck her head in his room and looked around. She wanted to know if he was a jarhead or something. He said he wasn't.

The girls giggled and went away. Ike closed the door behind them and walked into his bathroom. The moonlight was coming through the small rectangular window now, glancing off the porcelain and the silver slab of the mirror so he could still see a dark reflection of himself in the glass. But the reflection was hard to recognize. It seemed to change

shape and expression as he watched it until he could not be
sure that it was his own and then it came to him that the
feeling he got from that dark glass was not unlike the feeling
he'd gotten from the overpowering silence of the desert and
he turned away from it quickly, heart thumping high and fast,
and looked instead down into the yard where a lonesome oil
well jerked itself off in the moonlight.

4

He wasted one more day staking out the Adams house on
Ocean, still thinking that perhaps there were other people
living there besides the old woman. There were not. The *H*
turned out to stand for Hazel, and Hazel Adams lived alone.
Her husband was dead and there was a son in Tulsa and a
daughter in Chicago who never called. Ike learned all of this
because he happened to be sitting around in front of the elementary school when Mrs. Adams crashed the three-wheel
electric cart she drove. She was coming home from the market
and rolled the machine trying to get it in the driveway. Ike
saw it all and ran across the street to see if he could help. The
old woman had escaped unscathed, however, and invited him
in for a piece of banana bread. And that was how he learned
about her family. Old Mrs. Adams, it seemed, was starved for
affection. She spent her days thinking about her lost husband,
her daughter who did not call, the son she never saw, baking
banana bread for visitors who never came. She spoke of noise
and pollution, of blue skies gone the color of coffee grounds, of
elementary school children who smoked weed and fornicated
beneath the shrubbery in her front yard. She warned Ike
against the dangers of hitchhiking along the Coast Highway. A
wealth of gruesome facts lay at her fingertips.

There were punk gangs, she said, high on angel dust and

strange music waiting in the alleys to catch young girls, and
boys like him, force them to carve swastikas into their own
arms and legs, or set them on fire. Ike sat and listened. He
watched as one more day slipped past him, melting with the
sun beyond the dark wood of an antique dining table.

That evening, riding home on the bus, he was struck by a
particularly depressing thought: He suddenly saw himself
learning nothing. His savings would go for greasy food, a
crummy room. His trip to Huntington Beach would turn out to
be no more than some grotesque holiday, and in the end the
desert would reclaim him. Had to be. He did not fit in here.
Like it was not even close, and everything was moving much
more slowly, and awkwardly, than he had imagined. This was
not San Arco, not even King City.

He discovered a small cafe across the street from the pier,
a strange sort of place frequented by both bikers and surfers.
Inside, the two groups kept to separate ends of the building,
glaring at one another over short white coffee mugs. The cafe
made him nervous. He was very much aware of not belonging
to either camp, but it was a good place to eavesdrop and the
food was cheap. And it was in the cafe that he got his first
break.

It was his fifth morning in the town and, as on the other
mornings following his bus ride from H. Adams's house, it had
been hard to force himself out of bed, to fight a growing desire
to give it up and split, to accept the fact that his coming had
been a sham, that the kid in the Camaro had been right. But he
had managed it. He had dragged his ass out of bed with the
first light, then down to the Coast Highway and the cafe,
looking for something, a word, a name, anything. And that was
what he found, a name. He had just finished a breakfast of
coffee and doughnuts and had gone to the head to take a leak,
and that was where it happened, standing at the damn urinal,
his dick in his hand, absently reading over the filth scratched
into the walls, when two words suddenly jumped out at him. A
name: Hound Adams, the letters scratched out of the metal

partition that separated the urinal from the sink. There was nothing else, just the name.

Admittedly it was not a lot. But there was still a thin film of sweat on his forehead as he left the cafe and crossed the street. There was something about just seeing that name someplace besides the scrap of paper. It meant there really was a Hound Adams, somewhere. And with that discovery came a fresh idea. It hit him as he walked along the boardwalk, headed out to sea on the pier: What if he could surf? He wouldn't have to do it well, just enough to hang out in the water. It made sense. He was too far away from things on the pier, and hanging out on the beach in street clothes didn't work either. He had tried that, tried getting close to certain groups as they came out of the water, but he was too conspicuous, always collecting too many stares if he got too close. But if he could surf? If he was in the water with them, with a board to sit on, the whole shot? Shit yes. It was something to think about.

He thought about it all that morning, watching the small peaks take shape and break, and the more he thought about it, the more he liked the idea, until at last he admitted to himself that there was more to it than just getting closer to the action. There was something in the shape and movement of the waves, something in the polished green faces laced with silver while the moon hung still visible above the town. A person could lose himself there, he guessed, and imagined cool green caverns carved from the hollow of some liquid barrel. The thought seemed to add to the excitement he already felt, and he walked home quickly, with a new attention for the multitude of surf shops that lined the street, the new boards that seemed to him like sticks of colored candy shining behind sheets of plate glass.

He thought about it again that night. He remembered the time he had tried to ride the Knuckle. He remembered lying there in the sunlight, his blood forming a dark pool in the gravel while Gordon went for the pickup. He had not tried anything like it since, but there were no machines here, just the boards and the waves.

It was a long night, filled with half dreams and crazy images while the music of the apartment house shook the walls of his room and the oil well squeaked below him, and at some point he became aware of a new fear creeping among the others, something he had not considered before. It was his fifth night in town and the fear was connected to a new understanding of what giving up would mean, of what it would mean to blow his money, to slink back into San Arco. Because whatever else was here, there was along with it a certain energy that was unlike anything he had felt in the desert. There was a hunger in the air. At night he heard their parties. Girls smiled at him now along the boardwalk, above the sand where couples fucked in the shadows of the pier. And he did not want to leave. He wanted to belong. He thought of his uncle's store, the busted-out screen door, the music that spilled from the radio and into the gravel lot, one country song after another until it was the same song, as long and tiresome as the wind out of King City and the desolate high places beyond, and he felt suddenly that perhaps he understood something now about that woman Gordon had once seen go, arm in arm with some candy ass, hooked on a promise.

As he remembered it, they had moved back to the desert, to his grandmother's house, because his mother had gotten sick and needed a place to rest. What he could recall now of that time before San Arco was not much, a more or less shapeless set of memories connected to numerous apartments and cheap motels. Gordon had once told him that she had been trying to sell real estate or some damn thing. He didn't know; but he knew they had lived out of a car for a while there, a beat-up old station wagon. What he remembered the most was the waiting. In the car. In countless offices. In the homes of strangers. In his mind the places they waited all had certain things in common. They were invariably hot and stuffy; they smelled. The odor had something to do with butt-choked ashtrays and air conditioning. It was Ellen who made the waiting bearable. She had always been there with him, had kept him entertained with games of her own invention, with stunts designed to annoy whatever adult was around to keep an eye on them. She was good that way. The waiting, he thought, had been easier for her. But later, the desert had been harder. He could still see her pacing up and down that hot dusty yard in back of the market like some caged cat and saying things like she hoped the woman was dead, that the dude had dumped her and that she had at last drunk herself to death in some foul room—this after they realized she was not coming back. Ellen had never forgiven their mother for that. She had never forgiven her for San Arco. "Of all the damn places," she used to say. "Of all the fucking one-horse dead-end suckass places to be stuck."

As for himself, the desert had been easier, he thought, at least in the beginning. In regard to his mother, however, his feelings were not so easy to sort out. There had been at first something like plain astonishment at the magnitude of her betrayal—an astonishment so large that somehow hatred did not enter in. Later there was a kind of embarrassment, a vague notion that some flaw in his own character had somehow made that betrayal possible in the first place. He was not certain what the flaw was, but he was sure others saw it, that for them his mother's leaving was less of a mystery. He had never known much about that candy ass Gordon had spoken of, or where they had gone in that new convertible, but he guessed he could see now, in the darkness of this room, with this new place throbbing around him, how going back could be like dying. It was the first time he had seen it that way; and from that angle, the betrayal was somehow not so huge.

5

It was hot and sticky when he opened his eyes. He sat up in bed and immediately began to think of reasons for putting off his decision to buy a board. Then he took a look around the room. The place was a mess. His clothes stank. It was like the grotesque holiday he had imagined was taking shape around him, and the new fear swept back over him, blotting out everything else.

He was not sure how much a used board would cost. He slipped four twenties into his pocket and left the room.

It was a hot day, smell of summer in the air, sky clear, ocean flat and blue. In the distance he could make out the white cliffs of the island someone told him was twenty-six miles away. The wind was light, slightly offshore, standing up the waves, which were small and clean, like jewels in the sunlight.

The town was full of surf shops. Surf shops, thrift stores, and beer bars, in fact, seemed the principal enterprises of downtown Huntington Beach. He hung around the windows of half a dozen shops before picking one and going inside. The shop was quiet. The walls were covered with various kinds of surfing memorabilia: old wooden surfboards, trophies, photographs. There was a kid out front wiping down the new boards with a rag. Apart from the kid and Ike, the place seemed deserted. The kid ignored him and finally he drifted back outside and into another shop closer to the highway.

The second shop was filled with the same kind of music that he heard around the hotel: a hard, frantic sort of sound that was so different from anything he had ever heard in the desert. There were no memorabilia in this shop. The walls were covered with posters of punk bands. There was a pale

blue board covered with small red swastikas hanging at the
back of the shop. Near the front was a counter. There were a
couple of young girls in very small bathing suits sitting up on
the glass top and a couple of boys sitting behind it. They all
looked at Ike as he walked in, but no one said anything. They
all looked alike to Ike: sunburned noses, tanned bodies, sun-
streaked hair. He went to the back of the shop and began
looking over the used boards. Pretty soon one of the kids he
had seen behind the counter walked up to him.

"Lookin' for a board?" the kid asked.

"Something I can learn on," Ike told him.

The kid nodded. He was wearing a thin string of white
shells around his neck. He turned and headed down the rack,
stopped and pulled out a board, laid it on the floor. Ike followed.

The kid knelt beside the board, tilted it up on one edge. "I
can make you a good deal on this one."

Ike looked at the board. The board looked like it had once
been white, but was now a kind of yellow. It was long and thin,
pointed at both ends. The kid stood up. "How do you like it?"

Ike knelt beside the board as the kid had done and tried to
pretend he knew what he was looking for. Around him the
frantic beat of the music filled the shop. He was aware of one
of the girls dancing near the plate glass, her small tight ass
wiggling beneath a bikini bottom. "This would be good to
learn on?"

"Sure, man. This is a hot stick. And I can make you a good
deal on it. You got cash?"

Ike nodded.

"Fifty bucks," the kid said. "It's yours."

Ike ran his fingers along the side of the board. On the deck
there was a small decal: a silhouette of a wave within a circle—
the wave's crest turning to flame—and beneath it, the words
Tapping the Source. Ike looked up at the kid. The kid looked
fairly bored with it all. He was staring back toward the front of
the shop, watching the girl. "Fifty bucks," he said again without looking at Ike. "You won't find a better deal than that."

It was the cheapest board Ike had yet seen. "All right," he said, "I'll take it."

"All right." The kid picked up the board and headed for the counter.

Ike stood by the cash register as the kid rang up the sale. He was very much aware of one of the girls staring at him, a kind of half smile on her face. The music was loud. The sunlight was coming through the glass and the open door, burning the side of his face. When the kid had stuffed Ike's money into a box, he pulled a couple of colored cubes out from under the counter and pushed them at Ike.

"What are these?"

"Wax."

The girl on the glass made a face. "You gave him Cool Waters," she said. "I think he needs Sex Wax."

The other boy chuckled. The kid who had made the sale pulled out a round piece of wax and thumped it down on top of the cubes. "You rub it on the board before you go out," he said.

Ike nodded. He had remembered seeing surfers wax their boards. He slipped the wax into the pocket of his jeans and picked up the board. "Rip 'em up," he heard one of the girls say as he went back outside, into the brilliant light. He heard one of the boys laugh, and he had not guessed that buying a board could turn out to be such a humiliating experience. Well, fuck them, he thought; the price had still been good. He adjusted the board beneath his arm and headed up the sidewalk, deciding as he went that the din of traffic was preferable to the music of the shop.

Back in his room he used a pair of scissors on one of his two pair of jeans. He cut them off just above the knees and put them on. He picked up his board, which barely fit into the small room, and tried to get a look at himself in the mirror. One thing was certain and that was he didn't look like many of the other surfers he'd seen around town. His hair was too short, and his body looked white and frail against the dark material of the jeans. He shrugged, swung a towel around his neck, nursed the board out of the room, and headed down the hall.

He was coming down the steps and onto the shabby strip of grass when he nearly bumped into one of the girls who had come to his room looking for papers. It was the tall, athletic-looking one, and the sunlight was dancing off her strawberry-blond hair and her white tank top. He felt somewhat embarrassed, naked, in the brilliant light. He tried to hide as much of himself as possible behind the board.

"You a surfer?" she asked him.

He shrugged. "Trying to learn." He studied her face for signs of a put-down. Her cheekbones were rather high and wide, her brows delicate and nicely arched. There was something about her face, perhaps it was the arch of the brows, that gave her something of a bored, haughty look. But somehow that expression did not carry over into her eyes, which seemed rather small and bright and looked directly into his own. There was a bit of a smile on her face and he decided that it was not like the smiles on the girls in the shop. He went down the sidewalk and turned to look back. She was still standing in the same spot, watching him. "Have fun," she called. He smiled at her and started away, headed for Main Street and the Pacific Ocean.

6

The beach was crowded, the sun bright, but the breeze at his back was cool, and as he stood in the wet sand and felt the Pacific Ocean touch his feet for the first time, sending ribbons of coldness up his legs, he began to see why many of the surfers wore wet suits. Still, he did not hesitate. He had this feeling that every person on the beach was watching. He waded into the white water, stepped almost at once into some kind of hole and felt his nuts shrivel as the water rushed past his waist. He pulled himself onto his board and began to paddle.

It didn't take him long to discover that waves which looked small from the pier got much bigger when you were looking at them from sea level. Getting out was harder than he had expected. For one thing, he kept sliding off the fucking board. He was trying to paddle as he had seen the others do, stroking one arm at a time, but just when he would get himself going in a straight line, a wall of white water would hit him, knock the board sideways, and he would slip off and have to start all over again. His arms and shoulders tired quickly, and when he turned back to the beach to see what kind of progress he was making, it appeared he was no farther out than when he had started.

The point at which the waves rose in smooth hills was growing more elusive by the moment. Still, he kept digging away, his breath coming harder, his strokes becoming weaker. Suddenly, however, the ocean seemed to smooth out, to spread itself in front of him like a huge lake. He dug in for all he was worth and before long he was bobbing with the other surfers in the lineup.

His face tingled from the exertion and his lungs ached. Other surfers sat straddling their boards, looking toward the horizon. Some regarded him with what seemed a quizzical eye. It was amazing how different things were out here compared with what it was like inside. It was peaceful and smooth, the way he had imagined it. A gentle ground swell lifted and lowered them. A pelican flew nearby, skimming the surface of the water. A gull cried above him and the sunlight moved on the water. In the distance he could make out the white flecks of sails and the colors on the distant cliffs of the island.

He tried sitting up and straddling the board the way most of the other surfers were doing. His, however, seemed to tip drastically at the slightest movement. He fell off twice, making loud splashes and drawing looks from those sitting closest to him.

Suddenly, from all along the line of surfers, he began to hear hoots and whistles. He looked outside to see a new group of waves rolling up into long smooth lines. These waves seemed much bigger to him than the others. He struck out for the horizon, paddling now out of fear, afraid the waves would break on top of him, that he would lose his board; he felt too tired out and cold to swim for it. The first wave reached him. He paddled up the face, popped over the crest only to see a second wave even larger than the first rolling toward him. He dug in once more, paddling with arms gone to rubber. To his left and slightly ahead of him another surfer suddenly stopped paddling and swung his board around, pointing it back toward the beach. Ike didn't know what to do. Not only was he apparently going to be hit by the wave, the other guy was now sliding down the face straight toward him.

At the last second, just as the wave was beginning to lift his board, he tried swinging it around, too. Out of the rush and spray of exploding white water, he heard the other surfer yell. Somehow he'd gotten caught sideways in the top of the wave and he was going over.

He came up gasping for air, his arms flailing about him. He was sure his board had gone into the beach, but when he looked over his shoulder he saw it floating only a few yards behind him. How that had happened was a mystery, but he was greatly relieved and began to swim toward it. As he reached the board he noticed the other surfer paddling toward him, the same guy he'd been caught in the wave with.

Ike clung to the side of his board. Maybe the other guy was checking to see if he was all right. He tried to muster some kind of grin but his face felt cold and numb and then he got a good look at the surfer's face and realized something was very wrong. He tried to say something, but he never got the chance. He'd no sooner opened his mouth than the guy hit him. The other surfer was lying on the deck of his board, so the punch didn't have a lot of leverage but it stung anyway. Ike tried to pull himself up on his board, but the guy was punching at him again. One punch landed on Ike's shoulder, another caught him flush on the ear. Everything seemed to be happening at once. He was disoriented from his spill, the cold water seemed to swim in his head, the other surfer was everywhere. Later, when Ike tried to remember exactly what the guy had looked like, it was all just a blur, a red face, white fists, the pain in his ear. And then a wave rescued him. A wall of white water caught him and swept him toward the beach. The board tipped over again, but he hung on. When he resurfaced, he found himself practically on the beach and the other surfer gone.

He didn't know how many people were watching him as he trudged out of the shallows; he supposed they all were. He supposed everyone on the beach had seen him make a fool of himself, had seen him get punched out and washed in like a drowned rat. He sat in the wet sand, his back to the beach, his eyes fixed on the horizon where the waves still sparkled in the sunlight. He had certainly blown that, blown it damn near as badly as he'd blown trying to ride the Knuckle. But he was too worn-out even to think much about it. He felt somehow betrayed but was not exactly sure by what.

He sat that way for some time, afraid to turn around, to walk back through the people who may have seen what happened. He tried to get his body to stop shaking. And yet he was afraid to stay there too long. He was worried the guy in the water was going to come in and finish kicking his ass. So finally he got up. He took one more look out to sea, where others glided effortlessly, dropping and climbing on the faces of the small waves, a fraternity whose membership he had been denied.

The board was heavy beneath his arm, but he tried to assume some semblance of dignity as he plodded through the warm sand. At last the board grew too heavy to carry and so he let the nose drop to drag along in the sand behind him, no longer giving a shit about how he looked. And by the time he got to the asphalt near the pier, he had begun to feel like he was going to puke, or pass out; he could not tell which. He sat

to rest on a curbstone in the sun, and that was when he saw the
bikes for the second time.

He was certain it was the same group of bikes he had seen
on his first day in town. There were more of them now, but he
recognized the Knuckle, and the engine was still missing. He
was sitting only a few yards away from them. The sunlight was
blinding as it jumped off chromed forks and sissy bars. He
could still feel his pulse in his ear. He dabbed at it with his
fingers and found a little blood, but everything was still pretty
numb. He didn't suppose he was hurt very badly.

He had been sitting there for a couple of minutes, his
board at his feet, when he began to pick out the voices above
the roar of the engines. "I thought you fucking tuned it," one
yelled, and Ike saw the owner of the Knuckle swinging himself
off the bike to stand in the parking lot.

"I did tune it, man."

"Then why is it still fucking up?" the rider wanted to
know. He moved around to the side of the bike, away from the
others, and Ike got a better look at him. He was big, taller even
than Gordon, not so thick perhaps, but wider across the shoulders. And his arms were sure as hell bigger. Biggest damn arms
Ike had seen, bigger than any of the guys around Jerry's shop.
And he had more tattoos than anyone around the shop, too.
There was a big American eagle tattooed on one shoulder with
a coiled snake coming out of it some way and winding its way
clear down to his forearm, where it wrapped itself around his
wrist like a bracelet. On the other arm there was a man's head,
like maybe the head of a Christ because it wore what looked
like a crown of thorns, and there were rays coming out of the
thorns and spreading up into his shoulder, where they turned
into lizards and birds. And along his forearms and hands, in
between the tattoos that had come out of parlors, there were
others, what he'd heard Jerry call jailhouse tattoos, the kind
you did yourself with a penknife and ink. The guy was dressed
in a grimy pair of jeans and had on a set of black broken-down
motorcycle boots that looked thick and heavy enough to kick

even a Harley to pieces. Up top he wore a faded tan-colored tank top that looked too small and above that he wore a pair of gold-rimmed aviator shades and a red work bandanna tied around his head. His hair was black, combed straight back and long enough to cover a collar, held in place by the bandanna, and there was a diamond stickpin in one ear. Ike could see it catching the light along with the thin gold rims of the shades.

The biker was standing only a few yards away from where Ike sat and when he bent down to take a look at the engine, Ike could see how the dark hair was beginning to recede just a bit above the red cloth. The guy squatted down, peering into the engine, but Ike could tell by the way he moved that he didn't really know what he was looking for. The other bikers sat on their machines and watched. Suddenly the guy stood up. He did it a bit too fast, though, and wobbled around some so that Ike could see he was fairly well pasted. "God damn it," he shouted at no one in particular, and Ike could see a couple of the other bikers wearing grins. All of a sudden, though, the guy raised his fist and brought it down on the fuel tank. The blow didn't look like it had traveled very far, but a good-sized dent appeared in the black-lacquered tank and the smiles Ike had noticed only moments before disappeared. He heard somebody say, "Shit," and the biker closest to the Knuckle walked his own bike farther away, as if he were expecting some sort of explosion. "God damn it to hell." The owner of the Knuckle shook his head, swayed a bit, then paced back to the far side of the bike and stood staring down on it, his aviator shades flashing in Ike's direction, so that for a moment Ike had the feeling that the biker was looking past the bike and staring right at him.

"It's the carburetor," Ike said, and was surprised at the sound of his own voice. There followed a moment of silence in which half a dozen shaggy heads swiveled in his direction.

"The what?"

"The carburetor."

The biker put his hands on his hips and walked back around the bike to get a better look. He sort of turned his face up into the sun and laughed out loud. He pointed at Ike, then looked back toward his friends. "What's this, Morris, your brother?"

The others laughed.

Ike shifted his butt on the curb. "I can fix it for you if you've got a screwdriver."

The biker just looked at him. He pushed his shades up and over the bandanna so they rested on his hair.

"Shit," somebody said. "I wouldn't let him near it."

The owner of the Knuckle raised his hand. "What if I do have a screwdriver?" he asked. "What are you going to do if you fuck it up?"

"I won't fuck it up."

The biker grinned. "Come over here, Morris. Bring your screwdriver and see how it's done."

A bulky-looking biker with blond hair walked over and tossed Ike a screwdriver. He tossed him a sullen look, too. "Don't fuck nothin'," he said.

Ike left his board at the curb and knelt alongside the big engine, inhaled the familiar hot odors of fuel and metal. It took him about three minutes to adjust the mixture. "There it is," he said. "And I can take that dent out of the tank for you, too."

The biker stared at him and Ike could not tell if he was pissed or not. He swung himself up on the bike and roared off down the stretch of asphalt that ran away from the pier. Ike waited with the others. He was feeling better now; he had stopped shaking. He did not look at the other bikers, but stared into the heat waves at the end of the lot and waited for the Knuckle to come back. A few minutes later it returned. Ike listened for the miss but couldn't pick it out.

"Fuck me in the ass," the biker yelled above the engine. "It's runnin' like a charm. The kid's a better mechanic than you are, Morris."

Morris just walked over and got his screwdriver. He spat on the ground dangerously close to Ike's foot and swaggered back to his bike.

The Knuckle's owner shut down his engine and got off. "About that dent," he said, "how much?"

"The bodywork, the paint, the whole shot," Ike figured quickly. "Fifty bucks."

The biker looked back at the others. "Not bad." He turned back to Ike. "You live around here?"

"I'm staying over on Second Street, at the Sea View. It's at the corner of . . ."

"That dump? Yeah, I know where it is. Where you from?"

"You ever hear of San Arco?"

"That dump? Yeah, I heard of San Arco. Fucking one-horse desert town in the middle of nothin'. Where'd you learn to work on bikes?"

"I've got an uncle with a shop."

The biker was silent for a moment, then took a couple of steps toward Ike. "What the fuck happened to your ear?"

Ike shrugged. "I got hit."

"Yeah. Fist city, huh." The guy bent down for a closer look and Ike suddenly found himself staring into this big square face only about a foot away from his own and he was noticing all sorts of details: the half-dozen small scars scattered above one eyebrow, three-day beard you could see would be dark black like his hair, and thick, if he let it grow, nose a little flat and crooked from being broken too many times. It was a tough face, the kind of face you'd expect to go with those tattooed arms and heavy boots, but there was something else there he had not expected. It was the kind of face you'd expect to hold a set of eyes like black marbles, dead and mean like a snake's, the kind of eyes that could smoke you on the spot. But the eyes were all wrong somehow, as if they'd lost track of the body they were in. They were this very pale shade of blue, not flat and hard at all, and there was something disconcerting about it. There was something about the expression that went with them that was not quite right either, but he could not put his finger on what it was.

The biker looked from Ike to the surfboard. He knelt beside it and put a hand on the deck. "This your board?"

Ike said that it was. He could smell the sour scent of whiskey on the guy's breath, and it seemed to him that as the biker looked over the board a new expression crept into his face, an odd expression, as if he were about to ask something else but changed his mind, and then the expression was gone. "So you're a pretty hot surfer?" the biker asked.

"I'm just trying to learn."

"On this?"

"What's wrong with it?"

"It's a gun, that's what's wrong with it. You don't learn to surf on a gun, it's like a very specialized board. Shit, you could tackle twenty-foot Sunset on this thing. Where'd you get it?"

Ike pointed across the street. Behind the biker he could sense some of the others starting to get restless. "Come on, Preston," somebody said. "Let's split, man."

Preston ignored them. He stood up and squinted across the street. "That shop next door to Tom's?"

Ike nodded.

"It figures. The fucking punks." He raised his hands over his head and shouted toward the highway. "The stinking town is full of fucking punks."

"Come on, Preston," one of the bikers said once more. "Let's split. I told Marv we'd be over there by one."

"Pisses me off," Preston said. "Town's full of fucking jive-ass punks."

"Fuck it, let's go."

Suddenly Preston whirled on the others. "You fuck it, man, you go. I got some business to attend to."

"Man . . ."

"I said split."

"Come on, man, he's on his ass."

"Fuck it if I'm on my ass. You go, I'll meet you over there."

There were some more words, more grins, a few groans. The bikes circled around in the lot and zoomed off into the highway, the roar of their engines soon lost in the hum of traffic. Preston watched them go, then looked back at Ike. "What's your name?" he asked.

"Ike."

"Okay, Ike. You did me a favor today. Now I'm gonna do you one."

About fifteen minutes later Ike was standing on the sidewalk at the intersection of the Coast Highway and Main with a brand-new surfboard tucked under his arm. He wouldn't quickly forget the feeling he had walking back into that surf shop with Preston by his side. And he wouldn't quickly forget the expression on the kid's face when he saw them coming. It was the same kid who had sold Ike the board, only this time he wasn't grinning. He wasn't grinning when he saw them come in and he sure as hell wasn't grinning when they left. What he was doing when they left was picking up all the boards Preston had piled all over the floor in his search for just the right one. That and probably trying to figure out how he would explain to his boss how he had come to sell a two hundred dollar board for fifty.

Back at the Sea View apartments, Preston hung around for a few minutes explaining to Ike why his new board was the kind he wanted to learn on. "See how wide it is. See how it's wide here in the tail block, too. That gives it stability. This one won't keep wanting to tip on you like the other one did."

"You must surf a lot," Ike said.

"Shit." Preston stood up and pulled his shades back over his eyes. "Once upon a time," he said. "No more. I used to surf the pier year round. No leashes, no wet suits. A good winter swell and maybe six guys in the water. Place is a zoo now. Every faggot punk and his brother's out there and they all want to be hot." He suddenly turned and sauntered off toward his bike. He swung himself down on the stick and kicked the big engine to life. "What about my fuel tank?" he asked over the noise. "When do you want to do it? I'll fix it so you can use Morris's compressor."

Ike shrugged. "Anytime."

Preston nodded. "Later," he said, and spun the Knuckle in a kind of a brodie across what was left of the Sea View's lawn, chunks of dirt and tiny yellow flowers flying into the air behind him. Ike watched the muscles bulging beneath those jailhouse tattoos, the dark hair and red bandanna rising on the wind, the sunlight on metal. He could hear the engine for a long time after the bike was out of sight. He looked down the street past the short drab buildings and weedy lots, the palm trees just beginning to stir in the wind that had shifted, was no longer offshore but from the sea and carried with it the smell of salt. He walked back to his new board. He knelt beside it as Preston had done, running his fingers along the smoothly rounded rails. It was probably silly, he thought, but there was something about that first board that he sort of missed. This board was flat and round, like a big ice-cream stick. The first had been lean and mean. He had liked that decal, too, the wave with its flaming crest and the words *Tapping the Source*. He didn't know what that was supposed to mean, but he liked the way it sounded.

7

The first time Ellen ran away, she was ten years old. She took Ike with her. They started out in the morning with lunches she had packed in brown paper bags, headed in what she guessed was the general direction of San Francisco. They got as far as the ruins of an old glass factory somewhere on the far side of King City. They spent the night among hills of sand and walls of corrugated tin. It was summer and the air was warm. They sat up all night, watching the sky. Ellen talked. Later, when he thought about that night, what he thought about was her voice, how it mixed with the breezes that came at them off the salt flats and stayed with them until the first light. In the morning it was hot early with heat waves swarming among clouds of red dust. Ike was hungry and tired. He followed her out to the road, where the asphalt was so hot it burned right through their shoes. They walked on the shoulder. There was no water and Ike was not sorry when they heard a car slow behind them and turned to see Gordon behind the wheel of his pickup. Ike thought Gordon would be pissed, but he wasn't. He told them that he would let the old lady give them hell. He even let Ellen sit beside him and steer. He told them there were all kinds of derelicts and drifters apt to spend the night in the glass factory and that they were damn lucky they hadn't run into any. Ike remembered how Ellen had to tilt her head to see over the dash and how Gordon put his big arm over her shoulders and rested his hand on her leg.

It was almost five years later when they ran away again. She came to his room one night and he could see right away that something was wrong. She kept walking back and forth at the foot of his bed with her arms folded across her chest, her hands squeezing her arms. He could see the knuckles go white when she squeezed. Then she turned out the lights and sat next to him on the bed. She said she couldn't tell him in the light. She sat close to him and he could feel her body trembling against his own. In all the time he had known her, he had not seen her cry—that trembling was as close as he'd seen her come. Gordon, she said, had been in her room, drunk and putting his hands on her. Ike could still remember sitting up cold and stiff when she told him that, feeling sick and thinking about that day in the truck, Gordon's beefy hand on Ellen's leg. She was almost fifteen the night she came to his room, and men were starting to notice her. Ike had seen that, seen the way they looked at her when they went to town. She had a skinny, almost boyish figure, but her ass was tight and round and when she wore those tight faded jeans and the cowboy boots she had saved for and bought herself—there was just something about her. There was something about the way her hips moved when she walked, and about the way she would toss her head to shake back that thick black hair, or the way she would fix it with the combs, like their mother had once fixed hers.

Gordon had two cars. He owned an old Pontiac coupe and a Dodge truck with a camper shell. Ike and Ellen took the truck because it was what Gordon had taught her to drive. The wind was coming up as they left and soon it was hard to see. They spent the night not far from the glass factory, on the outskirts of another small town at the edge of the flats. They slept beneath the shell on an old mattress Gordon kept in the bed. The truck rocked in the wind and they could hear the sand hitting the truck as it rocked and shuddered in the darkness. There was only one blanket and they pulled it over them, pressed close together against the cold that was riding in the wind. She trembled in his arms and he felt her breath on his neck, heard her whispering, asking if he was afraid. He said that he wasn't. She held his hand to her chest so he could feel her heart. "It's going like crazy," she said. She was wearing jeans and an old flannel shirt and holding his hand against her between the folds of material so that he could feel her heart like it was in the palm of his hand. And he could feel her breast, too, round and firm and so soft and her skin hot and slightly damp as if she were feverish and when he moved his hand he felt the hardness of her nipple pass beneath his fingers. In the blackness he could see the dark shapes of her boots catching a bit of moonlight near the tailgate. And he could feel himself trembling now too, both of them trembling and holding each other, her face pressed close to his and her fingers on the back of his neck and when he inhaled he could taste her breath, could pull it down into his own lungs as if he were taking her into himself. He loved her so much. He kissed her neck and her face. He tried to find her mouth. But then suddenly, as if some current had passed through her body, she stiffened and jerked away. "No," she said. "Ike, we can't." And her voice had a kind of wounded sound to it that he had not heard before. She twisted away from him until she was lying with her face to the metal side of the truck. He didn't say anything. He covered her with the blanket and then sat shivering at her side, watching her boots and the blackness outside and waiting for the light.

In the morning the wind was still so bad you couldn't see much. There was sand all across the road and tumbleweeds big as cars passing ghostlike in the sand. He guessed it was one of those weeds that made them crash. They were driving through the town when one hit the glass by Ellen's head and she jerked the wheel, too hard, sent them jumping over a curb and right into the side of a building. He could still remember the sound those bricks made coming down on the hood, Ellen's skinny arms fighting the wheel. And he could remember how he felt that morning, light-headed and numb, so that he was hardly aware of cracking the windshield with his head.

Gordon came for them once more, as he had the other time. Only this time he was in the car and the old lady was riding in the backseat. Ike sat in the car with his grandmother while Gordon and Ellen talked to the sheriff and the store owner and Gordon signed some papers. Later there was some kind of hearing. The ride home was very quiet. The wind dropped away to nothing and it was clear—the way the desert is after a storm, with every bit of color sharp and hard so it hurts your eyes to look. The sky was huge and blue and there were great white drifts of sand left by the wind across the black asphalt of the road. The sand rose in white clouds as they passed through the drifts and then danced on the road like tiny hailstorms behind them.

He remembered Gordon didn't drink for some time after that. It had all happened during Christmas vacation and when the vacation was over they went back to school. One day on his way home Ike passed the store and saw that Gordon was out front, passing a bottle with some of his friends. He went home and told Ellen. She took him to her room and pulled open a drawer. There was a handgun there. He remembered how the barrel looked long and hard, catching some of the afternoon light that cut through the blinds. "He gave it to me," Ellen told him. "Said if he ever gave me cause, I should shoot him." After that sometimes in the afternoons he would hear them practic-

ing out in back of the market, Gordon and Ellen, blowing
empty pop bottles into glass splinters that afterward lay glittering in the red dust.

Those were some of the things Ike thought about the
week after he met Preston, after Preston had brought the tank
by for him to work on, and fixed it so he could work at Morris's
shop. There was something about the way Morris's compressor
popped on and off in the sheet-metal spray booth that reminded him of those gunshots, that made him think of the
desert.

He was glad for the work; not only would it bring in a few
bucks, it would keep him in touch with Preston. He kept
thinking about what that kid had said to him in San Arco, just
before he pulled away, that business about finding some real
help. He kept thinking Preston would not be a bad guy to have
on your side. What he hadn't counted on with the work was
the way it gave him time to think.

He guessed that Gordon had never given Ellen cause to
use her gun. And he and Ellen did not talk about that night on
the flats. But it was not long afterward that things began to
change, and that he began to lose her. She began to see other
guys. Not just boys from school, but older guys from King City,
guys with cars. The old lady didn't like it, but she was pretty
sick by then so about all she could do was yell at Ellen from
that chair she kept out on the porch, tell her she was no better
than her mother, a tramp and a common whore, and threaten
to send her away, to one of those homes where there had been
talk of sending her after she wrecked the truck. The threats
did not have much substance, as it was really Gordon who was
looking after things now, and footing the bill. Gordon had
been married once, Ike had heard, after the war. But then the
woman had left him and he had come back to the desert to
take over the market and the station. Gordon was a strange
guy. He never said a lot about anything, and when Ellen began

to run around, he didn't say much about that, either, but then Ike guessed it would have been hard for him to say too much.

By the time summer came, Ellen was staying out late and keeping all kinds of crazy hours. She was going out a lot with this guy named Ruben who worked at a garage in King City and drove a customized '56 Mercury. Ike saw them together one afternoon on his way home—he was working then himself, just starting at the shop. They were hanging out in this ball field with a few other people on the outskirts of town. It was the first time he had really seen her with someone else. Ruben had the car pulled up on the grass and Ellen was stretched out near the front fender, leaning against Ruben. Her hair was bright black in the sun. She was wearing a white summer dress with blue stripes and the dress too seemed to shimmer in the hot light. Ike went to a piece of chain link fence and watched them for a long time. Finally Ellen got up and walked across the grass to where he stood. Her hair was loose and there was something a bit wild and flushed about her face. She put her hand up to the fence and their fingers touched through the chain link. He wanted her to come with him, but she wouldn't do it. She said that she was with her friends, and then her fingers had squeezed his against the cool steel and she had gone back. But he had continued to stand there. He watched until they left. He watched Ellen get into the front seat from the passenger side and then slide way over, turning as she did so to let another couple push the seat forward and climb into the back, and he could see the summer dress riding way up high on her brown thighs.

She often came home late, but that night she didn't come home at all. It was the first time. And he lay awake in the moonlight, hating them and hating himself for feeling like he did, hating himself for that night on the flats, hating his own twisted jealousy. In the morning she was still not there and he went outside, up that little hill back of Gordon's yard, and he waited.

Finally he saw a dust cloud moving at the edge of town and then the dark blue of the Mercury, like a huge insect

moving in the dust. The car let her out by the store and he
knew she was trying to avoid the old lady. She was still wearing
the blue and white dress, but she was carrying her shoes. He
watched her come around to the back of the house and he
could see her bare feet kicking up little clouds of red dust. She
didn't go into the house but went instead to the cellar. She
went down the steps and she pulled the door closed behind
her—leaving him to stare into the blistered sun-gray wood. He
stood and went down the hill after her. He felt like he was
drunk, as if the ground were playing tricks beneath his feet.
He could feel the sun on his neck, and his throat hot and dry.

The cellar door was unlocked; he opened it and went
down, and even now, standing in the ragged back lot behind
Morris's shop, with flattened beer cans and broken bottles
winking at him from among the weeds and the smooth metal
of Preston's tank beneath his hand, there was not a single
detail of that moment he could not recall: the rush of sunlight
upon the stairs, the look on Ellen's face as she saw him, surprised and at the same time pissed at herself for not locking
the damn door behind her, even that pattern of dust caught
swirling upon the light.

There was an old workbench down there and a washbasin.
Ellen was standing at the basin. Her shoes were on the bench
and she was naked except for a bra. She wasn't tall, but she was
slender and her legs looked long and brown except up high
where her bathing suit had left a white pattern. Her hair was
loose, shining beneath the light of a dim bulb strung above the
bench, and the way she was standing made it hang forward to
hide her face. She turned once and looked at him for a moment and then went back to what she was doing, which was
bending over the sink trying to work some kind of stain out of
the dress. Ike didn't say anything. He was still feeling half
drunk and dizzy and kind of sick from sitting too long in the
sun. He'd left his shirt on the hill and his shoulders felt hot and
raw. The cellar floor was cold beneath his bare feet. Ellen just
kept working at the spot, but when he was close enough and
she stopped to look at him once more, he could see that her

eyes were red and full and that her makeup had run, leaving dark tracks on her cheeks. He wanted to say something but he couldn't. What he did was just put his arms around her and she dropped the dress and they stood there together, her breasts pushed flat against his bare chest through the flimsy white material, her legs against his. He kissed her forehead and her eyes, even her mouth, but he just wanted to hold her, to squeeze her tight and to tell her—something, words half-forming in his mouth, when, suddenly, it was over and the old lady had found them. She was standing up there at the top of the stairs with the door thrown back and the sunlight rushing in once more—the only consolation being that she had for once been shocked into silence so that all she seemed able to do was to teeter there above them, black and bent before the blueness of the sky.

It was, of course, unbearable for them there after that. Ike had work and school. Ellen had her friends and they did not really see that much of each other. The drifting apart that had begun shortly after that night on the flats continued. Ellen lasted out the winter, but she was gone by summer, by herself this time, and for good. In close to two years he had heard nothing, not until the afternoon that kid came driving into town in his white Camaro with two surfboards strapped to the roof.

Preston stopped by Ike's apartment at the end of the week to pick up his tank. Ike could hear the heavy boots pounding the stairwell so it felt like the whole place might come down and he knew who it was before he answered the door.

Preston looked like he'd just climbed out of a shower. His hair was still wet and combed back flat against his head. He was dressed in the same grimy-looking tank top and jeans, but the look on his face was different and Ike could see that he was sober. He didn't say anything to Ike but walked right in and started looking around for his tank. He couldn't believe Ike's job. "Jesus," he kept saying, "it's beautiful. I mean it, man, you did a hell of a job." He carried the tank to the window to examine it in the morning light.

Ike watched him standing by the window, admiring the tank, absurdly pleased with himself. In spite of the fact that he knew he did good work, he was not used to praise. Jerry had always taken everything for granted. "You're a fuckin' artist," Preston told him.

Suddenly Preston turned away from the window and looked straight at Ike. The sunlight was coming in behind him, making him look even bigger than usual, and flashing in that little diamond stud he wore in one ear. "What are you doing here?" he asked. "Living in this dump? This isn't your scene, you're just a kid. Why aren't you back in the desert working on bikes?"

Ike was surprised by the questions, by the fact that Preston was even interested. For a moment he hesitated. He had planned to tell no one why he was in Huntington Beach. But Preston seemed different to him this morning, more like somebody he could trust, and in the back of his mind there was still that notion of getting help. Maybe now was the time. He walked to the card table and picked up the scrap of paper with the names on it. He handed the paper to Preston, and while Preston looked it over he told him about the kid in the desert, the story of a trip to Mexico, three Huntington Beach surfers who had crossed the border with a girl and come back alone.

Ike was standing only a few feet away from Preston as he spoke and it seemed to him that a certain expression passed over Preston's face, a kind of dark scowl that was not unlike that shadow of a look Ike had noticed the day Preston saw his old board. "Is this what you were doing in the water?" Preston asked. "Trying to find Hound Adams?"

Ike nodded, thinking it strange that Preston had mentioned only one name.

"Shit." Preston looked angry about something now. "And what were you going to do when you found these people?"

"I don't know, really. Hang around, see what I could find out."

"Hang around with Hound Adams?"

Ike shrugged.

"Man, you're hurtin'. Look, if you take my advice, you'll hang it up and split right now. Go back to San Arco and work on bikes. If you don't do that, at least stay away from the pier. If you want to surf, do it farther north at the cliffs. The pier's a local spot."

"But what about Hound Adams?"

Preston handed him the paper. "Like I said, if you're smart, you'll go back to your uncle's shop."

"It's my sister," Ike said. "I'm the only family she's got."

"What about your uncle?"

"He doesn't give a shit, that's why I came. My uncle just says that she was wild, that if she got into trouble, it was her own fault."

"Maybe he was right."

"And maybe he was wrong. I mean, somebody should at least find out."

Preston just stared at him for a moment. "Yeah. Well, suit yourself, ace, but take my advice about the pier. Stay away from it. You don't want to meet Hound Adams in the water." With that, Preston tucked his fuel tank under his arm and started out the door.

Ike followed him into the hall. "Wait a minute," he said.

Preston turned.

"Hound Adams. Who is he?"

Preston waited in the hall. He looked down the floor toward that bit of sunlight coming up from the staircase and shook his head. Then he looked back at Ike. "That's your problem, ace. Can you dig it?" Then he was off and stomping down the hallway, down the wooden flight of stairs and into the street.

Ike followed him as far as the top of the stairs. He was torn between running after him and regret that he had even opened his mouth in the first place. It was just that Preston had taken him off guard with those damn questions. He thought back to the line in that song, that business about how suckers

always make mistakes when they're far from home. He felt
like the sucker now, the dumb-ass country boy. Shit, where did
he get off thinking somebody like Preston was going to want to
help him? And now he had put his foot in it. What if Preston
and Hound Adams were even friends or something? But then
Preston hadn't acted like they were friends; he had acted like
the whole thing pissed him off for some reason. The trouble
with Preston was, he was the kind of guy you didn't want to
press. You couldn't. He was too damn close to the edge all the
time. Ike ground his teeth and walked back to his room. He
slammed the door behind him and leaned up against it. He
shut his eyes and when he squeezed them hard enough, what
he saw was a thin pair of dusty legs kicking hot red clouds out
of a desert afternoon and it was not likely that he would forget.

8

It got bad again after that, after his conversation with Preston.
In a way it was even worse than before. He knew now that
Hound Adams was real, that he was around, and that Preston
knew who he was. But Preston's words had revived all of his
uncertainties. He had this feeling that whatever move he
made next was bound to be the wrong one.

He spent the following day alone in his room and that
evening he went out for a walk, thinking that perhaps he
would run into Preston, that they could talk. It didn't happen
and he wound up at the very end of the old pier seated with a
handful of Mexican fishermen as the night turned cool and
damp beneath a heavy mist. The iron rails and painted
benches grew wet and the yellow lights that lined the boardwalk drew lines upon their slick surfaces. Still, Ike remained
there for some time, staring back toward the highway and the
town, which from here had been reduced to a thin band of

lights beneath a moonless sky. He kept thinking about Preston, of the way he had grown angry over Ike's story. He was puzzled by the anger and yet, in an odd way, comforted by it as well. It was perhaps selfish of him to think so, but the anger, it seemed to him, was like some tool just resting there, waiting to be used, if only it could be better understood. And though he could see that doing so would require time, he was against blowing Preston off too soon. The best course, he felt, was to be patient a bit longer. And in the meantime he could continue with his own idea of learning to surf. But he would take Preston's advice on avoiding the pier, at least until he was better. For the present, he would trust in what Preston had said.

He took some comfort in thinking through these things, in deciding on something. His sister perhaps, or Gordon, might have said he was too cautious, and perhaps he was. It was just that he did not want to blow it from the very beginning.

It was late when he left the pier. He crossed Coast Highway and headed inland on Main. He did not know how late it was but noticed that the bars had closed and the streets were empty. As he neared the intersection of Main and Walnut a lowered Chevy rolled past on chromed rims, its tires making a soft swishing sound on the wet asphalt. He could not see how many people were in the car, as the windows were tinted, but it cruised through the intersection a few yards ahead of him and seemed to slow a bit, as if someone was checking him out. He had been about to turn on Walnut, but that would have put him walking in the same direction as the car and he decided against it, thinking suddenly of Hazel Adams's warning. He crossed instead behind it and continued up Main, walking quickly with his hands jammed down into the pockets of his jeans.

There was a vacant lot at the top of the next block, and some trees. He waited there a moment in the shadows just to make sure the car was not circling around. It did not appear to be and he was just about to leave when something else caught his eye. There was an alley that ran parallel to Main, just

behind the buildings that faced the street, and from his position at the end of the block he could look back across the lot
and see down the alley for a fair distance. And that was how he
happened to see the bike.

He moved out from beneath the trees and walked slowly
along the eastern end of the lot. The bike was a big one, and
drawing closer to the mouth of the alley, Ike could see that it
was Preston's Knuckle. Then he saw Preston as well. He was
standing at the side of the alley, in what looked to be the
beginnings of a driveway, only there was no driveway there,
just the back of a building—rough, darkened bricks and a
naked bulb maybe ten feet off the ground. The bulb was lit and
cast a pale light onto the broken asphalt and gravel beneath it.

Preston was leaning, his arm out and braced against the
wall, talking to another guy. Ike could not see much of what
the other guy looked like because Preston was quite a bit
bigger and was blocking Ike's view. All that Ike could really
see of the other man was a bright spot of blond hair above
Preston's outstretched arm. Ike got the idea, however, that
Preston was doing the talking, the other guy the listening.
There was something about the way in which the blond head
appeared to be cocked a bit to one side and tilted down, that
gave Ike this idea. But he was too far away to hear and he could
not take the chance of moving closer, nor did he want to stand
for long at the mouth of the alley where either man might turn
and see him. There was something in the scene, he thought,
that suggested he keep his distance. What was most bother-
some, however, was the location of the building behind which
they stood. As near as Ike could tell, it was the back of the first
surf shop he had gone into that day he'd gotten his board.

The implications of this could of course be interpreted in
more than one way and the task of doing so was enough to
disturb the peace he had found at the end of the pier. It had
him guessing as he moved away from the alley and into the
night, and it kept him that way far into the first gray hours of
morning. For the present, however, his resolve held and he
was up with the dawn, dressed in cutoff jeans and a ragged

sweat shirt, a towel slung over his shoulders, his board beneath
his arm. A sleepless night behind him, he was headed for the
Coast Highway and the beaches north of town.

It was different at the north end of town. There was not
the sense of light and movement one got around the pier.
From the beach you could not see the highway or the town.
There were only the cliffs, which were bare and rocky, capped
by the gray squeaking forest of oil wells and by the black oil-
spattered earth. It was a landscape of grays and blues, dull
browns and yellow ochres, of blackened fire rings and litter.
And on every available chunk of rock and concrete there were
spray-painted messages, swastikas, Chicano names, for he had
been told that the northern beaches were the domain of the
inland gangs when the sun went down, gangs out of the land-
locked badlands back of Long Beach and Santa Ana. It was a
strip of beach the cops did not even bother with at night, and
there were grisly tales told by surfers of ghastly early-morning
finds. One surfer Ike spoke to claimed to have found a human
leg, bloated and discolored, floating in the shallows. But the
beaches were empty in the mornings. There were only the
painted messages, the litter, the blackened fire rings like stone
altars, and Ike made no terrible finds.

He was growing accustomed to a kind of dichotomy he
had discovered here, a contradiction between the bleakness of
the landscape and the beauty of the sea. There were times
when the sea was like the land, flat, barren, the color of concrete. But there were other times when its surface was alive
with light, times when the wave faces were like polished
stones and the white water seemed on fire with the setting
sun. And nowhere was this contradiction more apparent than
along the beaches below the cliffs. In spite of the stories he had
heard and the evidence of human filth in the sand, he came to
love those stretches of beach, empty in the first light, silent
except for the sounds of the surf and the cries of the gulls. He
went there for the first time the morning after he saw Preston

in the alley, and then every other morning for the rest of the week. He took great pleasure in the mornings, in walking along the cliffs, close to the edge, the ocean smooth and glassy beneath, the air still and soft against his face and yet laced with the salty dampness of the sea. But what he found most pleasure in was that certain rush that began as he picked a trail and started down, watching the swell lines as he went, anticipating that first explosion of cold, the first line of white water breaking over him, washing away everything save the moment itself.

The waves beneath the cliffs had a way of breaking far outside. The white water would then roll toward the beach in long, churning lines. There was a point, however, where the white water began to re-form, to swell up into a new wave that would go on to break only yards from shore. It was in this second, inside break that Ike did his practicing. He would paddle out just beyond the shore break, let the wall of white water catch his board, and then try to stand up as the wave was re-forming. He usually fell off shortly after the inside wave had begun to form. His board would shoot straight down the small wave and he would fly off the front, or he would catch a rail trying to turn and slip off the side. Then one morning something happened that was different. Ike got into a wall of white water from a large outside wave. It grabbed his board, sent it skimming across the surface of the water. Ike got to his feet. He was carrying more speed than he was used to, but he found the speed actually made it easier to stand. The wall slowed slightly, began to re-form. Ike leaned into the wave and the board swung easily beneath him. A wall of water rose ahead of him, its face glassy and smooth, streaked with white. He was angling across it. The bumpiness of his rides in the white water was gone, it was smooth, fast. He was riding a wave. The wall rose rapidly, began to pitch out, his inside rail caught and over he went, headfirst into the shore break, his board sailing into the air after him.

He had to swim back into the shore to get his board. But

all the time he was swimming, he wanted to stop and shout, to raise his arms over his head and shake his fists. He knew now what the hoots and screams he had heard from the surfers beneath the pier were all about. He had gotten into a wave. He ran through the shallows, kicking up great rooster tails of water with his feet. He didn't go back out right away. He sat down on the nose of his board in the wet sand and stared out into the lines of white water just now turning a kind of gold in the rising sun and tried to remember every detail of how it had felt.

He thought about it for the rest of the day, going over each sensation as he strolled past the empty lots and scarred palms. Fences formed ahead of him like green walls. He performed imaginary maneuvers of great skill, ducking now and then beneath the lip of an occasional hedge, his hand raised to ward off invisible spray.

He felt like talking to somebody about it and so decided to look for Preston. He still had not seen him since that night in the alley.

He found him at Morris's shop. Morris was out and Preston was alone in the back lot. He was sitting on the wheel of an old flatbed bike trailer, staring at the alley. His back was turned to the drive and as Ike came up it he could see a sixer of tall cans at Preston's side.

Preston looked up as Ike came around the fence that separated the drive from the lot. He watched Ike come around the fence and then stared back toward the alley. "Look here," he said. "It's Billy the Kid." Ike passed behind the spray booth and came up to the trailer. He noticed there was already a six-pack's worth of empties at Preston's feet. "Thirsty?" Preston asked him, and then tossed him a can without waiting for a reply. Ike caught it and pulled the ring. Beer foamed out white and cold, running down the sides of the can and over his fingers. He took a drink and then looked at Preston. Preston was still watching the alley.

"I took your advice," Ike told him. "I've been going farther north, by the cliffs."

"My advice was that you leave town."

Ike took another drink and looked down on that head of Christ that covered Preston's forearm, at the bloody crown of thorns radiating birds and lizards. He felt the beer burning in his throat. "I got a ride today, man. I mean, a fairly decent one."

"Yeah?" Preston looked up at him with one eye. He poured the rest of his beer down his throat. He had a way of doing it, of opening his mouth and holding the can about two or three inches away and just pouring it in, like dumping oil into a crank. When he was done, he dropped the can and stomped it with his boot, added it to the pile at his feet and reached for another.

"You were right about that board, it's a lot more stable."

Preston just nodded again and sat looking across the lot. Ike stood beside him. He was tempted to say something about seeing Preston in the alley, but he didn't. It was Preston's business and Ike did not guess Preston was the type to appreciate prying.

"So you really like it out there," Preston said at last. He made it more of a statement than a question, but Ike answered anyway. "Yeah, I do. It's different. I think about it a lot. Like when I'm working, or doing something else, I find myself wondering about conditions, about what the tide's doing, thinking about what to work on next time I'm out. I need some new stuff. I want to get a wet suit and a leash for my board."

"Buy a wet suit. Fuck the leash. Learn how to hang on to your board."

"It's hard."

"Come on, man. I thought you were Billy the Kid. I thought you were here to take on Hound Adams. It's hard," he added, mimicking Ike but making his voice high and whiny. He looked up at Ike after he said it, sort of one-eyed, like he had before. He was squinting because the sun was in his face, but it looked to Ike like he was grinning some too. "You ready for another beer?"

Ike shook his head. "I still have some." He took another drink. "Christ," he heard Preston say. "So what about Hound Adams?" Ike said. He worked at making his voice as conversational as possible. "You known him long?"

"Long enough. I happen to know he never uses a leash." Preston seemed to find that amusing for some reason. He chuckled and poured some more beer down his throat—what looked to be half the can. "So you're really gonna hang around. You're serious about all this shit?"

Ike nodded. He tilted his head back and chugged what was left of his beer. He folded his can and squashed it, tossed it into the pile at Preston's feet. Preston passed him a fresh one.

"So what're you going to live on? You gonna get a job?"

"I guess."

"What?"

Ike shrugged. "Anything."

"Yeah, well, shit. There's work. You go to work on bikes in this town and you just might put More Ass here out of business. Course, More Ass might not appreciate it. But then, come to think of it, he's not too crazy about your ass anyway."

Ike shrugged once more.

"Tell you what," Preston told him, but was interrupted before he could say more by the sound of a bike—Morris pulling into the drive. "Here's his highness now," Preston said. He stood up and finished his beer, chucked the can and hitched up his dirty jeans. He picked his shades off the trailer and slipped them back on. "Who knows," he said, and tapped Ike in the chest with the back of his hand. "Maybe I can say something to the treacherous old pig-fucker myself. Put in a good word for you, as it were." He winked and walked away.

Ike watched him go, sauntering in an exaggerated sort of way over to where Morris was kneeling near his scooter, unwrapping a handful of small parts he had apparently been out for. Ike could hear them talking for a few seconds in muffled tones. Then he could hear Preston's voice clearly. "I know you got to tear down that Shovel."

Finally Morris straightened up and wiped his hands. He said something to Preston and then walked over to the fence and spoke to Ike through the chain link. "I'm gonna pull a bike apart next week," he said. "You interested?"

Ike nodded. "Sure," he said. "Sure thing."

Morris just looked at him for a minute, like he was trying to decide if he'd made a mistake or not, then he turned and walked back to his bike. Preston said something else that Ike could not catch and then turned himself and moved to meet Ike coming around the fence.

"Thanks," Ike said.

Preston held up a hand. "Just don't turn your back on him," he said, and then laughed out loud at the prospect of this new partnership.

Ike stood there for a moment, waiting. There was a stiff wind kicking down the drive and when Ike spoke again, it was of the surf. "Be blown out now," he said.

Preston nodded and as Ike watched him he could see the sky reflected in Preston's shades. "What you need's a good point break," Preston told him. "Some kelp beds out there to cut the chop. Huntington's not the only place with surf, you know. Shit. You don't know the kinds of places I've seen." He looked off toward the alley. "Was a time I'd never let a day go by without checking it out." He stretched and flexed the muscles in his arms—holding the pose like he was waiting for a picture. "Shit, I ought to walk down there with you and have a look," he said, but made no move to leave the drive. Ike guessed that it was time for him to move on. He did not really want to talk in front of Morris. For the moment he was content to know that Preston was still on his side, that they could talk again. He said good-bye and started toward the street, but Preston called to him and he turned back.

"You won't tell anybody else what you told me, will you?"

"No. I won't. I haven't."

"Good," Preston said. "Don't."

Ike stood for a moment and waited, to see perhaps if Preston would say more, or decide to walk down to the pier after all, but Preston showed no sign of leaving. He stayed with Morris near the entrance of the shop. Morris had peeled off his shirt and slipped on his spray mask. The mask hung down around his neck and his big hairy gut was hanging out over his belt, twisting the buckle so it pointed at the ground. Preston tapped Morris on the chest with the back of his hand, as he had tapped Ike a short while before. "The kid got his first ride today, Morris. What do you think of that?"

"Right in the shore break," Ike put in. He was still feeling somewhat elated about the ride.

Morris had already pulled his mask up to his face. He now jerked it back down and glared at Ike across the top of it. "Big fucking deal," he said.

9

Morris put him to work in the afternoons, leaving his mornings free to surf. They spent the first few days on the Shovel. The work and getting along with Morris required concentration and by nightfall he was beat. He went home tired and slept. He had looked forward to talking some more with Preston, but the week passed and Preston did not come around. Toward the middle of the second week he began to worry once more.

There was more work and he spent his afternoons staring into the oversize valves of Shovelheads and Panheads, laboring over Fat Bob tanks with Morris's new Badger airbrush, leaving in his wake a rainbow of imron cobwebbing, pearl-silver lace, and candy-blue flames. Mornings were still spent in the water. But he was thinking about time now—two weeks since he'd talked to Preston in his room, a month in town and he still did not even know what Hound Adams, Frank Baker, or Terry Jacobs looked like. He had told Preston he would keep his mouth shut, but now—nothing was happening. It was getting harder to think about the work. He needed another break. And then came the fifth week—twenty-nine days since he'd stood on the gravel at the edge of the road and said good-bye to Gordon. It was the fifth week that brought the swell.

It began with the sound, a distant thunder repeating itself at regular intervals somewhere beyond the hum of the high-way, waking him in the night so that he turned for a moment to listen, to wonder, before slipping back into sleep. But in the morning, when the sound was still there, louder than before in the first gray light, he did not have to wonder again. He pulled on his clothes and ran from the room, down the wooden stairs and across the lawn, past the oil well and down the alley, south on Main so he was running toward the ocean and he could see the white water even before he crossed the highway.

The first thing that struck him about the swell was how different it made everything look. He might have been in another town, on a different pier, staring out at a stretch of beach he had never seen before.

The waves did not just rise up out of the ocean in rolling lines, as they normally did. These seemed to come in off the horizon, as if they had marched the whole breadth of the Pacific to pound this stretch of beach. The surface was angry, gray and black, streaked with white. Paddling out appeared an impossibility. The first fifty yards of water looked as if it had been poured from a washing machine. Flecks of foam lay across the wet sand like snowdrifts. As he ran onto the board-walk, the whole structure seemed to shudder beneath him with each new wave.

He was alone with the swell. Far down the beach he could see the yellow Jeep of the lifeguards. The morning was still and gray, the sun wrapped in a heavy overcast. He walked farther out onto the pier, and that was when he saw them; he wasn't alone after all. At first he couldn't believe it; no one could have gotten outside in this kind of surf. He ran farther.

He lost track of them, then found them again. There was no doubt about it. He picked out one, then two more, a fourth and a fifth. The size of the swell made them hard to see. At times they disappeared completely behind the waves. He gripped the rail, damp with spray beneath his hands. They were out there, but as yet, he was pretty sure there had been no rides.

He was nearly even with them now and could see them more clearly: six surfers on the south side of the pier. They stayed together, darting about like a school of fish, apparently trying to get themselves set up amid the huge swells. Occasionally one of them would look as if he were going to take off, only to pull back at the last moment, allowing the wave to peak and pour over, to thunder on through the pier and toward the beach unridden.

The surfers seemed to be having a hard time getting themselves in position. Wave after wave passed them, lifted them and hid them, threw curtains of spray twenty feet in the air as it wrapped around the pilings. And each new set seemed to come from farther outside, forcing them to paddle out farther. Ike was wondering if any of them would be able to take off at all when he noticed one surfer paddling again just ahead of a mountain of gray water. He was paddling hard. The board began to rise, lifted on the wave. And suddenly the surfer was on his feet. It was hard to say how high the waves actually were, but the crest of this one was well over the surfer's head.

The rider sped down the face, drove off the bottom in a powerful turn that sent water spraying in a wide arc from the tail of his board. He drove back up into the face, was nearly covered by a rapidly peeling section. Then he was out of the tunnel, high on the lip, working his board in small rapid turns, racing the wave toward the pier. And then it was over, he had driven through the lip at the last second, just before it met the piling. For a moment Ike lost him in the spray and then he saw him again, flat on his board, paddling hard for the horizon.

By the time the sun had burnt its way through the overcast, there were maybe another half-dozen surfers in the

water. They made it outside by staying on the north side of the
pier, using the pilings to help shield them from the swell that
was moving in from the south. Still, it was risky and Ike saw
more than one surfer turned back, more than one board broken on the pilings.

Though few went into the water, many came to watch,
and soon the railings were lined with a noisy cheering crowd.
The people hooted and cheered for rides. Ike soon found himself cheering along with them. There were cameras set up
along the pier now too, a dozen of them, some manned by
crews in matching T-shirts that advertised various surf shops
and board manufacturers. There were more cameras on the
beach, and more spectators, more yellow Jeeps, so that by late
morning a kind of circus atmosphere had taken over that strip
of the town which huddled about the pier and lined the white
strip of sand.

Ike saw the blond-haired surfer, the same he'd seen get
the first wave, time and again getting spectacular rides, which
drew cheers from the crowd. He had been watching for perhaps an hour when a familiar voice took his attention away
from the surf. He turned and found Preston behind him. He
was wearing that grimy tank top and the old red bandanna. He
looked out of place among the camera crews and surfers who
lined the pier. It was a crowd of sun-streaked hair and clean
limbs. Preston, with his huge tattooed arms and square upper
body, looked more like an extension of the machine gleaming
between his legs. The aviator shades were flashing in the sunlight, so that Ike couldn't see his eyes, but his mouth was bent
into a large shit-eating grin, as if there was some joke in progress of which Ike was not aware, of which, perhaps, he was the
butt. "Thought I told you to leave town," Preston said. Ike felt
himself grinning back, not sure about what to say, but glad that
Preston had shown up. He supposed that since he'd come to
Huntington Beach, Preston was the closest thing to a friend he
had. Preston knew why he had come, and that created a link
between them, at least in Ike's mind.

"It's big," Ike said.

Preston just looked past him at the waves. "First south of the season," he said. "Takes a day like this to get a wave to yourself anymore; the punks can't get out."

"You ever seen it this big before?"

"Sure. Bigger. I've surfed it bigger. But it's a good swell." Ike was suddenly aware of another sound rising now above the din of the crowd and the thunder of the surf. The tower had apparently spotted Preston and the mechanical voice had begun to whine. "No motorcycles allowed on the pier," the voice said. "Please turn your bike around and walk it off the pier." Preston leaned out into the boardwalk and extended his middle finger toward the tower. The voice went on in its tinny fashion: "Please turn your bike around and walk it off the pier."

Preston just shook his head and began to turn the machine around. The spectators nearest them turned to stare but made sure Preston had plenty of room for the maneuver. "Voice of reason," Preston said. "I think there's been one guy in there for about twenty years. It's always sounded like the same voice to me."

Ike looked up at the tinted windows high above the boardwalk. He decided to start back himself and get some breakfast. Still, it was difficult to tear himself away from the railing and he turned back once more toward the ocean—in time to see the surfer he'd been watching get still one more wave. The guy was easy to spot. He was tall and blond and while most of the others wore full wet suits, he wore only a swimsuit and a vest. "That one guy's really good," Ike said, pointing him out to Preston.

"Your hero, huh?" Preston asked, and the grin had given way to a slightly crooked smile. A moment passed while Ike looked out to sea then back at Preston. "Just don't go getting too sweet on him," Preston said. "He's your man. And that other guy"—he waved toward a dark figure in a full black wet suit with what looked to be red stripes down the sides, sitting farther to the south and way outside—"there's another one for you. Terry Jacobs. He's a Samoan, usually the biggest dude out there." Preston thumped at the pier with his heavy boots and began to walk the bike away, back down the center of the boardwalk, the people spreading to let him pass.

Ike went after him. Preston didn't say anything else; he just kept walking the bike through the crowd. When he had gotten down next to the tower he pulled himself up and came down on the stick. The engine didn't catch and he hauled himself up once more. Ike reached out and grabbed his arm. He grabbed him right on the biceps, on top of that coiled serpent, and it was like grabbing hold of a large pipe. Preston let himself back down and looked at his arm, at Ike's hand. He did it real slow and Ike released his grip. He stared into Preston's shades. "Wait a minute," he said. "You can't let it go at that."

Preston just looked at him. "I can't?"

Ike hesitated. "Well, what about them?" he asked at last.

"What do you mean, what about them? That's them, ace. Two of them, anyway. What do you want me to do, swim out there and have a word with them?" Preston kicked hard and the big engine jumped to life. Just above them the speakers had begun another order—something about *walking* the bike off the pier, but the voice was lost in the roar of the engine. A cloud of pale smoke hung in the air and Ike stood in the midst of it, watching Preston.

"Look," Preston yelled at him. "Let's get something straight. I've been thinking about what you told me. You let me think about it some more. In the meantime, do like I told you, keep your story to yourself. If I come up with anything I think you ought to know, I'll tell you. But remember something. This is not your scene. Can you dig that? You don't know what the fuck goes on around here. And one more thing. Don't ever come runnin' up and grabbin' at me like that. I might pinch your fucking head off." With that he popped the big bike's clutch and was off, right down the middle of the boardwalk with pipes blasting and chrome bars burning and people scattering in front of him like leaves in a wind.

10

The swell ran through the rest of the week. Each day, however, the sea grew a bit calmer. And as the spectators on the pier went back to the beach and the circus atmosphere began to dissipate, the number of surfers entering the water grew. By the end of the week the waves were down to a consistent and well-shaped six feet and more crowded than Ike had yet seen them. Fistfights were not that uncommon, both in the water and out. Ike went to watch. At first it had been too big for him, and now that he had at last put faces to two of the names on the scrap of paper, he wanted to get a better look. If his surfing had been further along, he might have ventured out near the pier; as it was, he stood on it, watching from above.

The two men Preston had pointed out to him were there each morning: Hound Adams and Terry Jacobs. Hound Adams was tall, lean but well built. And Preston had been right about the Samoan; he was always, it appeared, the biggest dude out there—maybe just a bit shorter than Hound, but with a chest like a refrigerator. They were both excellent surfers, particularly Hound Adams. Terry seemed to surf effortlessly enough, but with none of Hound's fluid brilliance. His was not a dance with the ocean but a contest of strengths. He could drive through incredible sections of breaking waves, like a fullback pounding through a line, looking simply too heavy and too well planted to be knocked from his board. He was awesome on the beach as well, wearing his hair in a great puffball of an Afro that bounced as he walked.

As a rule they surfed with the first light, with the dawn patrol, as the kid in the desert had told him. But with the swell running they surfed in the evenings as well, so Ike made it a practice to go there after work. He had taken note of the direction they took upon leaving the beach and he had it in mind to follow them. He was certain it was an idea of which Preston would not approve, but then Preston had not been around again since the first day of the swell.

He watched from the pier until the sun slipped into the sea and the lights began to flutter and buzz above the boardwalk, then he turned and walked quickly back to the highway. They usually crossed the street in front of Tom's and then turned left, moving away toward the north end of town. He waited at Tom's. When they passed, he fell in behind them.

He stayed too far back to pick up anything of their conversation, but he could see them gesturing and laughing. For a time their bare feet left wet prints across the dirty pavement. In front of the Capri Room the neon lights cast a pink glow on the concrete and flashed in the chrome of the half-dozen choppers that lined the curb. He saw Hound gesture once in the direction of the bikes and heard Terry Jacobs laugh.

People parted in front of them as they passed. They turned right at Del Taco and walked along a dimly lit street. Ike stayed behind them. He could feel his pulse now, up in his throat, a dampness in the palms of his hands. They were the only people on the street besides him. He slowed some and let them stretch their lead.

They went on for another three blocks before turning into the lawn of a two-story house. There was a light on in an upstairs window and it made a yellow circle on the dark grass, caught in the whispering fronds of an old palm that grew in the front yard. Ike could hear them talking again, pulling off wet suits. He had meant to go on by, do his best to look casual, but suddenly he wanted more. The house next door was dark, its lawn black with the shadow of old trees. A thick hedge separated the pieces of property and Ike ducked behind it. And then he was moving along the hedge, ducked down in a kind of crouch, thinking how stupid it would be to get caught. But the house was dark and silent, the windows shaded.

Through the hedge he could hear them talking, running a hose. He got to his knees and crawled, found a spot in the hedge where he could see through.

They were stripped to their trunks in the front yard. Hound was hosing down wet suits. As Ike watched another man came out on the porch. He was dressed in shorts and a T-shirt. He was shorter than either Hound or the Samoan, rather thin but wiry. He had wavy blond hair that was combed straight back, and looked wet, as if he'd just gotten out of the water. He put his hand to his mouth, taking a toke off something, it appeared, cocking his head a bit when he did, and there was something about that gesture, the angle at which he held his head, perhaps, or the light on his hair, that made Ike think of the alley in back of the shop. He was almost certain that this was the guy he had seen there talking to Preston, and a name formed on his lips. He whispered it to himself.

"You shoulda come back out, brah." It was Terry who spoke to the man on the porch. The guy shrugged and passed Terry the joint. "Tomorrow," he said. Terry nodded and went up the steps and into the house. The new man and Hound Adams were left alone in the front yard. The two men were silent for a time. Hound hung the wet suits to dry on a small line that had been run from the porch out to a tree in the yard. It was finally Hound Adams who spoke, and Ike heard his voice clearly for the first time. "It's a good swell," Hound said. He had a smooth, even voice. "Should be a good summer. I can feel it. You know what I mean?" The blond man nodded, then sat down on the porch. Hound moved to stand in front of him, taking the joint from him and then passing it back. They continued to talk about the surf, about storms and swells, and how they ran in cycles, and how this was the year. Ike listened. The ground was slightly damp beneath his hand and knees and he could smell the musty green of the old hedge. A car passed on the street, but its lights were too far away to find him. And then he started thinking about something. It was a strange thing to think about, perhaps, but he thought about it anyway. He couldn't help himself. He started thinking about how good

they were, especially Hound, how they knew about these cycles and storms and a distant energy and how they had been
alone in the big swell when he had thought no one could've
gotten out and how Hound Adams had ridden the first wave.
He thought back to those names scribbled on a scrap of paper
and he wondered for a moment—why did it have to be them?

Someone killed the light in the upstairs window and the
patterns of shadow died on the grass. But Ike could still make
them out through the hedge: Hound standing up now, the
other guy taking the boards beneath the cover of the porch.
Hound stood for a moment alone, his hands on his hips, staring
into the dark yard, then he turned and went inside. The front
door banged shut in the blackness. Ike waited for a few minutes and then straightened up. The knees of his pants had
circles of wetness on them and he brushed at them with his
hands. He walked slowly back along the hedge and turned on
the sidewalk.

There was another light on in the house now, in what
looked like the kitchen, and he could see them through the
glass: Hound Adams and Terry Jacobs seated at what must
have been a table, although it was too low for him to see. They
were still bare-chested, their faces turned down, intent on
whatever was before them. For a moment Ike flashed back to
what he had thought of behind the hedge, but then it was gone
and there was just the oddly metallic taste of fear far back in
his mouth and throat. As he moved along the sidewalk, passing
in front of the house, he turned once more to look. It was a
different angle and he could see them even better. The two
men were bent slightly forward, their faces hard and chiseled-
looking in the yellow light, faces that seemed suddenly both
arrogant and cunning; murderers beneath the eaves.

A sudden spasm seemed to pass through him and he
moved away, into the darkness of the street. But later, alone in
his room, he thought it all through again. He thought, too, of
Ellen Tucker. Though there was not a day in which he did not
think of her, the work and the swell had managed to fill his
mind with other things. But not tonight. Tonight it was all

right there, like it had been that second week, working on Preston's tank. Only now he had seen them, had put faces to the names on that scrap of paper, and he thought again about what the kid had told him—that they were not lightweight people, that unless he could find some real help . . . And for the first time since he'd come, he found himself fighting in a new way against what Gordon had told him, that part about making up his mind to it, that he would not see her again. He could hear those words now, like the walls were telling him, and he fought against them all night long, until the first gray light was swimming on the cracked plaster ceiling. And it was like finally, somewhere at the edge of a troubled sleep, his eyes hot and scratchy as if he'd been staring into a desert wind, he knew the words were true. He knew it with a terrible certainty, and with a fresh rush of anxiety he thought about that man he'd seen Preston talking to in the alley—the same man he'd seen tonight: Frank Baker. Had to be. And he wondered what they had said to one another that night in the alley, behind the shop.

11

He awoke sometime later to the sound of boots on the stairs. The boots belonged to Preston and he didn't bother to knock but barged right in and right away Ike could see there was something different about him. He propped himself up on one elbow and rubbed his face with his hand. The main thing that was different, he decided, was the shirt. It was a ridiculous shirt, covered with bright blue pelicans and flying fish, the kind of shirt you would expect to see on some flabby, camera-toting tourist and it was the first time Ike had ever seen Preston dressed in anything besides a dirty tank top. He was still wearing motorcycle boots and greasy jeans, but that shirt made a new man out of him.

But then Ike could see that it was more than the shirt. His face looked clear and sober, the way it had that day he'd come for his tank, and his hair was wet again too, like he'd just showered, and it was combed back flat against his skull. He was rubbing his hands together and pacing back and forth in front of Ike's bed. "Well, don't just lay there diddling yourself," Preston told him, "let's get some waves."

Ike hauled himself out of bed and touched his feet to the cold floor. The memory of last night was still with him. He felt washed out in the gray light, hung over, though he'd had nothing to drink. He blinked hard and tried to adjust to Preston's enthusiasm, which seemed not to mesh well with the rest of the morning but was rather forced and just a bit mechanical. He pinched his nose with his fingers, between his eyes. The room was full of blue pelicans and flying fish.

"Well, come on," Preston was saying. He had stopped pacing now and was standing at the front of Ike's bed. He was standing with his hands on his hips—a stance that reminded Ike of Hound Adams. It was the way Hound Adams had stood on his porch the night before, staring into a dark yard. He thought for a moment about telling Preston about it, but then decided against it. He decided to go along with whatever Preston was up to and see where it led. Besides that, forced or not, it was the most jovial he had ever seen the guy and he hated to put an end to this new mood so soon. He got up and started looking around the room for his cutoffs. Then he remembered he was supposed to help Morris overhaul Moon's Shovelhead. "I promised Morris I'd help him on another Shovel," he said.

Preston stared at him, pushed his shades up into his hair. "I thought you wanted to learn how to surf."

"I do."

"Then fuck Morris. Let him tear down his own Shovelhead. You wanna be somebody's nigger for the rest of your life?"

"It's Moon's Shovelhead," Ike said. He seated himself on the edge of his bed to pull on his cutoffs. But he was finally waking up now, and some of Preston's enthusiasm was beginning to rub off on him. He grinned back up at Preston. "I thought you were retired."

"Shit. I'll retire your ass if you don't make up your mind. I'm gonna get some waves. You wanna come with me or what?"

Ike stood up and buttoned his pants. "Where we going?" he asked.

Preston grinned and pulled his shades back over his eyes. "Where it's good, ace, where it's good."

At the foot of the stairs Ike was surprised to find an old Chevy pickup. The truck was primer gray. There were signs of body work on the front fenders. A homemade camper shell covered the bed and a set of Harley-Davidson wings decorated the window at the back of the camper. Preston lifted the rear door so Ike could slide his board in and that was when Ike saw the other board and the camping equipment. Preston's board looked old, a little yellowed around the edges, but before sliding his own in on top, Ike noticed the decal on the deck of Preston's board, a wave within a circle, and the words *Tapping the Source*.

They drove all morning and Ike didn't ask any more questions about where they were going. He climbed into the cab beside Preston and they headed north, out through the oil wells, above the cliffs where Ike had caught his first wave. Preston rolled down his window and let the morning air in to whip about their ears. The air was clean and cool and Ike was happy for it. He began to feel really awake now, and to wonder about where they were headed and what Preston was up to, and he thought as well about that board he'd seen in the back. But he didn't ask any more questions. He watched the road as it rushed toward them, as the first bright rays of sunlight began to pierce the grayness.

They stopped once for coffee at a small doughnut stand on

the seaward side of Coast Highway. They stood in back of the
stand with Styrofoam cups in their hands and watched the
swell lines moving across the ocean far below them. When
they were back in the truck, Preston leaned out the window
and hooted. "It's going to be good, ace," he said, and then
leaned over and jabbed at Ike's knee. Ike felt his leg pop under
the blow and even though he know Preston was just kidding
around, it still hurt some. He looked at the coiled serpent
running along Preston's arm, disappearing beneath the sleeve
of his crazy shirt, and he couldn't help but wonder why they
were doing this. It still seemed to him that there was something out of sync in Preston's enthusiasm. He wanted to talk
about Hound Adams. He wanted to ask Preston about that
blond-haired guy he'd seen him talking to in the alley. But he
restrained himself, as he had earlier in his room. He did not
want to disturb the delicate balance of the morning. So he
kept his mouth shut and stared into the dashboard, where a
rusted key swung on a rawhide cord from one of the knobs. He
watched the morning as it slipped past them and he began to
enjoy himself. This was, now that he thought about it, practically the first time in his life that anyone had ever taken him
along on something—aside from all the driving around he had
done with his mother when he and Ellen were small, but he
figured you couldn't count that. He thought back to those
hunting trips Gordon used to make once in a while, how he
had always wanted to go but had always been left behind—
Gordon saying he was too young, or too small. He wondered
what Gordon would say now, if he could see him riding shotgun in an old pickup with a set of Harley-Davidson wings on
the back and a guy like Preston at the wheel. He pulled himself up straight in the seat and rested an arm out the window,
like Preston. He guessed maybe he didn't give a fuck where
they were headed or why, at least for the moment. It was still a
trip, God damn it. Just kick back and listen to the highway
hum.

By noon they were in Santa Barbara. The sun was slanting off red tile roofs and whitewashed walls on a street called South State. There were a lot of Mexicans and winos taking in the sun and hitchhikers sitting Indian style on the green strip of grass that ran along the highway.

Preston found a rundown-looking Mexican cafe where they ate burritos and rice. Preston ordered a pitcher of beer and an old Mexican woman brought two glasses without asking Ike for an ID.

"We'll kill the afternoon in town," Preston said. "I don't want to go in till after dark."

"After dark?"

"The one thing about this place. The waves are great but it's all on private property. They'll shoot your ass if they catch you surfing it."

Ike felt the beans lumping up in his throat and used a long drink of beer to wash them down. Preston grinned at him and killed the pitcher without bothering to pour it in a glass.

Later they went to a pool hall Preston knew about and then out to a grassy hill with a six-pack to watch the sun slip into the ocean. Finally Preston stood up and brushed his hands off on his pants. He sailed a bottle off the side of the hill. They waited for the sound of breaking glass, but it never came; it was lost somewhere in the breeze and the distant sound of the sea. Preston took off his shades, folded them, and slipped them into the pocket of his shirt. "All right," he said. "Let's do it."

They wound through a series of grassy hills, bouncing along a dirt road that skirted the crests. The moon came up fat and yellow and trailed them among the hilltops. Abruptly they rounded a curve and stopped in front of a long iron gate. Preston snatched the key from the dashboard. Ike could see him wink and for a moment Preston held the key up in front of Ike's face. "Take a look at a real heirloom," Preston told him. "There's been blood spilled over keys like this one. You're lucky to know a cat who's still got one."

"How did you get it?"

Preston jerked at the key and snapped it up in his big fist. "That's for me to know and you to find out." He jumped outside and Ike could hear him chuckling to himself in the moonlight.

Past the gate, they drove for another ten minutes, then pulled the truck off the road and into a kind of gully where a few sparse trees twisted into the darkness. The grass was tall. It rustled about their hips in a light breeze that smelled of the ocean. "We walk from here," Preston said.

The night was not particularly cold, but Ike found himself shivering at the back of the truck as Preston unloaded their gear. There were two packs filled with canned goods and bottled water, plus the wet suits and boards. Preston loaded them down and they started off through the high grass. At the road, Ike turned to look back and found that the truck was completely hidden from view.

The night was filled with the songs of insects, the earthy scents of grass and sage, the damp salt smell of the sea. The moon lit the road and threw a silver light upon the blades of grass, the polished rails of the boards. They walked for what seemed to Ike a long time. His arms ached and each felt about a foot longer when they finally put everything down. They rolled the bags out between the roots of some thick trees on the side of a hill. The ground fell away into darkness, more trees. The moon was straight overhead now. In the distance Ike could hear the sound of surf. "Waves," Preston whispered. "It's been a long time." And it was the first thing Ike had heard him say that day that did not sound like part of an act.

In the morning Ike saw that the hillside was higher and steeper than he had guessed in the night. A clump of trees obscured the view directly in front of them, but off to the left the ground dropped away to reveal other hills, great patches of mustard and wild flowers, green grass and dark trees, and below it all, the sea.

The beaches here were different from those Ike had gotten used to. The beaches in Huntington were wide and flat, colors kept to a minimum. Here the scenery was wild, the colors lush, varied. Long lines of hills rolled toward the sea then broke into steep tumbling cliffs, patchworks of reds and browns. Below the cliffs were thin white crescents and rocky points that reached into the Pacific. There were no traffic noises here, no voices. There were only the calls of the birds, the breeze in the grass, and the surf cracking far below them.

They pulled on trunks and wet suits in the crisp morning air. They knelt on the rocky soil beneath the trees and waxed their boards. The smells of rubber and coconut mixed with the smells of the earth and grass. "We'll get some morning glass," Preston told him. "Surf till ten or eleven, then back here for some food and sleep, surf again around sunset."

They stashed the bags and gear and started down the slope. Ike could see a set of railroad tracks winding through the hills below them at the edge of the sand.

"It's a ranch," Preston said, waving at the hills. "The owners don't like trespassers, but there's usually no one around except a few of the cowboys that work the place. At least that's the way it used to be, in the old days." He looked at Ike and grinned, and it seemed to Ike that some of Preston's biker traits had fallen away from him this morning. Perhaps it was just that he was wearing a wet suit and carrying a board, but it was suddenly hard to imagine that he was the same wild man Ike had seen punch out a fuel tank. He seemed younger this morning, more like a kid himself as he led Ike down through the tall grass, talking of cowboys and perfect waves. "The cowboys can be unpredictable," Preston was saying. "Sometimes they won't do shit and sometimes they will. Had a friend once who lost his board and had to swim in to get it. Turned out there was a bunch of cowboys waiting for him on the beach." Preston paused. "It was a bad scene," he said. Ike waited for him to say more but they walked on in silence.

When they had cleared the trees, they stopped and looked down. "Look at that," Preston told him, and he did: the unmarked crescent of white sand, the rocky point, the perfect liquid lines waiting to be ridden, and he figured that perhaps he knew after all why they had come. He touched Preston's arm as they started down. "Thanks," he said. "Thanks for bringing me." Preston just laughed and led the way, and his laughter rang among the hills.

They entered the water near the middle of the crescent-shaped beach. Ike followed Preston, and when they had pushed through the shore break, Preston angled his board toward the point. Ahead of them the horizon was a straight blue line. The sun sparkled on the water and the water was like glass, smooth and clear so you could look down and see small schools of fish and tendrils of seaweed reaching for the sun. Soon they were paddling over shoulders, the waves lifting and lowering them, and Ike could feel his heart beginning to thump against the deck of his board. He had never paddled out this far or been in waves like these.

At last Preston dug his legs into the water and drew himself up to straddle the board. Ike did the same and together they looked back at the green hills, the white strip of beach. It all seemed very far away. They could see much more of the coastline from here and Ike picked out an area where the vegetation seemed the thickest. The spot was well back into the hills and at first all he noticed was the vegetation. Then he saw the house, not a complete house for most of it was hidden, just a corner of red-tiled roof above a brilliant flash of white. He was about to ask Preston about the house, but Preston spoke first.

"This is what it's all about," Preston said. "You know, there used to be places like this all up and down the coast. Surf 'em with your friends. They're gone now. Fucking developers. People. Fuckers'll all drown in their own garbage before it's over, wait and see." He seemed a little winded from the paddle, as if it was something he had not done in a long time. He swung his arms and rolled his thick neck, then squinted out to sea as the next outside set began to build. Ike forgot about the coastline and began to paddle. It looked to him like they were still too far inside, but Preston called him back: "Just stick with me, hot shot; set up like I tell you to."

Ike did set up as Preston told him. The set was moving past them now and Preston began paddling hard to the left, paddling closer toward the center of the peaks. Ike paddled after him. As each wave reached them it lifted them high into the air and as it passed there was a fine white spray blown back from the lip and there were rainbows caught in the spray. Suddenly Preston turned to him and shouted: "Your wave, ace. Dig for it."

Ike swung the board around and began to paddle and almost at once, without time for a second thought, he was in the grip of the wave. He could hear Preston yell behind him. He could hear the wind and a funny kind of swishing sound. He gripped his rails and swung himself up and there he was, at the top, the wave a great moving hill beneath him, and he was amazed at the height, amazed at how different this was from the short, steep faces he had ridden at Huntington. He was dropping and picking up speed. His stomach rose in his chest. The wave face grew steeper, a green wall that went on forever. The board pushed against his feet. There was a feeling of compression, as if he stood on the floor of a speeding elevator. And then it was over. He made a bit of a turn at the bottom, but it was not enough. A rail caught and the board seemed to come to a dead stop. He left the deck as if catapulted, skidded once on his face and stomach before going under and that was when the whole Pacific Ocean came down on top of him. He had no idea of where he was in relation to the surface. His head filled with salt water. He could feel the leash that connected his ankle to his board dragging him beneath the water. He tried to relax, to go limp, but what he kept seeing was the way Preston would find his body, bloated and discolored, half eaten by crabs, caught between the rocks. He began to claw with both hands, to fight for the surface, and suddenly he was there, the sea a mass of swirling white water all around him, the sunlight dancing in the foam, and he was sucking in great lungfuls of air and blinking the salt out of his eyes and marveling at the beauty of the sky.

He floated for some time in the shallows, just outside the shore break, clinging to his board, torn between the fear of hidden cowboys waiting to beat his brains out if he went in, and drowning if he paddled back out. He could see Preston sitting far outside and he guessed maybe it was the fear of Preston that won out. He was afraid of what Preston would think of him if he gave up. He pointed his board toward the horizon and began to paddle.

He watched Preston take a wave and though it seemed at times that there was a little jerkiness to his moves, he rode the wave well, dropping and carving, getting high and fast, and he thought that there must have been a time when Preston was very good, as good perhaps as Hound Adams was now. Preston at last went up and over the shoulder so that he was back outside and waiting when Ike arrived. He took in a mouthful of water as Ike paddled up next to him and squirted it high in the air like some baby whale, laughed and made a face at Ike. "You'll make it," he said. "Just remember to turn next time. Lean in up at the top, drive off your back foot."

They surfed until the sun was overhead and Ike's arms were so weary he could barely lift them out of the water. But he had begun to catch waves, to paddle for them, make the drop, the turn. He was also beginning to see that the wipe-outs wouldn't kill him, not these waves, not today.

They did as Preston had suggested, surfed until noon then returned to the camp, where they ate canned peaches and drank water, slept in the shade of the trees with the hills and ocean spread out below them. Near sunset they surfed again. The water passed like polished glass beneath their boards. Once Ike turned to see Preston sitting on his board maybe fifty yards away. The sea was dark and all around him slivers of sunlight shimmered and vanished like darting schools of fish. On the horizon, the sun had begun to melt, had gone red above a purple sea. The tide was low and the waves turned crisp black faces toward the shore while trails of mist rose from their feathering lips in fine golden arcs. The arcs rose into the sky, spreading and then falling back into the sea, scattering their light across the surface like shards of flame. There was a cyclical quality in all of this, in the play of light, in the movement of the swell. It was an incredible moment and he felt suddenly that he was plugged into all, was part of it in some organic way. The feeling created an awareness of a new set of possibilities, a new rhythm. He wanted to laugh, or to shout. He put his hand in the air and waved at Preston across the dark expanse. It was a crazy kind of wave—done with the whole arm, his hand swinging at the end of it, full of childish exuberance. And as he watched, Preston raised his own arm and waved back.

12

The sun went down behind them. It was dark as they reached the beach. Ike knelt in the shallows to remove his leash. The water felt warm now, gentle as it slapped against his legs. He could see Preston grinning down at him. Ike wanted to say something, to talk about how he felt, perhaps would have tried, but was silenced quickly by the sound of a truck somewhere on the beach.

"Cowboys," Preston whispered. They ducked down, stretched out on their stomachs in the black water. First they heard the engine. The sound seemed to come from several directions at once, then they saw the lights. There was a single pickup bouncing along the beach up near the tracks at the base of the cliff. Ike could hear Preston's breathing at his side. They watched in silence. The truck went by without stopping or turning. When it was gone, they slipped back into the darkness of the hill, and up to their place.

They made a small fire, heated beans and hot dog buns, talked about waves. Preston talked about big days, and hollow perfect days. He spoke of places like Cotton's Point, Swamies, Lunada Bay, the Huntington pier. He talked about the distant places he had never surfed, the point breaks of Queensland and South Africa, the reefs of New Zealand. He told Ike there were some guys who made a life out of it, traveling, surfing; they surfed places like the ranch all the time; they didn't bother with crowds.

"What about the pros?" Ike asked, because he had seen lists of contests in the magazines.

"Yeah, the pros travel. That's one way to do it. But then that's a whole other scene, too. The thing you've got going for you is a trade. You could make a living just about anywhere, move where it's good, travel. That's how you get good, anyway, surfing a lot of different spots. Think about it."

Ike did think about it and it suddenly occurred to him that Preston was not trying to talk him into something, he was trying to talk him out of something. He was trying to talk him out of looking for Ellen. The feeling came on him quickly and was very strong and he sensed that Preston was aware of it too, aware of what he was saying. Ike was quiet and a silence grew up between them.

It was Preston who finally spoke. "We may as well talk about it," he said, and pulled himself upright. He had been stretched out, propped on one arm. Now he seated himself Indian style and stared into the flames. He acted as if it were a thing requiring great effort. "I've thought about what you told me," he said, speaking slowly, still watching the fire. "And there's a couple of things that bother me. The first is this kid's story. He said your sister went to Mexico, with Hound Adams and Frank and Terry, that they went last summer. That right?"

Ike nodded, the smoke drifting into his eyes now and making them water after a day in the sunlight and salt.

"Okay. Maybe. But I've been around H.B. for a while and Hound Adams usually makes that kind of trip in the winter, around Christmastime. Locks the shop up, splits for about a month. So why would this kid have it in the summer? It could've been there was another trip, but it could have been something else, too. Think about this: I happen to know Hound Adams deals a lot of dope. And he's not above burning somebody, especially some kid. So suppose that's what happened. What's the kid going to do about it? He's not going to go kick Hound Adams's ass. Most likely he wouldn't do shit. But suppose he knew this chick, had heard her talking about her bad-ass brother, and what if the chick split and this kid thinks he sees a way to make some trouble for Hound Adams. You see what I'm driving at?"

Ike thought about it. He thought about the kid making the whole thing up. Preston's idea sounded pretty shaky to him. "I don't know," he said. "I mean, wouldn't this kid think that . . ."

"Wait a minute, man, wait a minute," Preston said, getting impatient, talking faster now, like he was going to get himself pissed off again. "You're missing my point. I'm not saying that's what happened. How the fuck do I know what happened? What I'm trying to tell you is that there is something screwy about this kid's story. I say he's got the date wrong. What I'm trying to tell you is not to believe every damn thing you hear. People will play any number of games with your head. Dig it? Especially in this town." He jerked his thumb toward the trees, south, in the direction of Huntington Beach. "Everybody's got a scam. If all you've got to go on is this kid's story— it's not much."

"But what if there was another trip? What if the kid was telling the truth?"

"All right, suppose he was. That brings me to a second thing that bothers me. You told me that day in your room that all you were going to do was hang out, see if you could locate Hound Adams, then see if you could get close enough to him to find out something. Well, no offense, ace, but that whole idea sucks. The way I see it, you've got two possibilities. Either your sister just moved on, which is very possible, or something bad happened. But suppose the worst. Suppose she's dead and you find out about it. What are you going to do then? You're gonna have to have some real evidence to get the cops in on it, and that may be hard to do. I mean, I hate to scare you, but if she really did go to Mexico with these guys . . ." He paused for a moment and brushed at the side of his face with his thumb. "She could be dead and buried in the middle of some desert, man. No one will ever know. You see what I'm driving at. You may hang out in Huntington Beach, and you may even hear something, but unless you actually find her you're not going to know. You might hear all kinds of shit, but it would just be stories, rumors, nothing you could ever go to the cops with. I also happen to know that Hound Adams has some big friends, people with bucks, the kind of bucks that can shut people up." Preston stopped once more and shifted his butt beneath him. Ike could see there was a dark smudge of dirt where he had brushed his face. "The point," he said, "is that if the worst happened, you'll probably never know it, and even if you did, there wouldn't be much you could do. Oh, you could go after him yourself. I mean, hide out on a roof some night and throw a brick through Hound Adams's head. Probably the best that would get you would be some time in the can." Preston paused and looked at Ike through the fire. "I been in the can," he said. "You wouldn't like it."

Ike didn't say anything right away. Preston picked up a stick and began poking the fire with it. "There's another thing, too," he said. "One more thing just in case you haven't thought of it yourself—then I'll shut up. You said your sister ran away. So if she ran away, how do you even know she would want you out looking for her? It's a loser, man, all the way around. Either your sister's out there someplace, on her own, and doesn't want you along, or she's dead and there's damn little you can do about it. I realize it's a bummer, but that's the way I see it. And either way, if your sister's not in Huntington Beach, then what the hell is? I mean, H.B.'s a damn sewer, man, you hang out in it long enough and you might just drown in it.

"You see what I'm trying to tell you? I'm not trying to

sound like your old man; I'm just trying to run something down for you." Preston had managed by this time to catch the end of the stick on fire and he had begun to play with it, seeing how close he could hold his hand to the flame. "Look," he said, after a few moments of singeing his palm. "The smartest fucking thing you could do would just be to split. You sure as hell don't have to worry about that job with Morris. Shit, I should never have talked him into it in the first place. I think I was half in the bag that day." He stopped and made a kind of shrugging motion with one arm. "I'm not going anywhere. You could keep in touch with me; anything turns up, I can let you know. What did you say her name was?"

"Ellen."

"Ellen." Preston repeated the name, then tossed the stick back into the fire.

Ike lay back flat on the ground and closed his eyes, feeling the way his sister's name hung there, in the night air, above the orange flames. What was there beneath the surface of Preston's words? Preston himself had said that everyone had a scam. So what was his? Why had he taken an interest in Ike? Brought him here? Was it as simple as he had said: Ike had done him a favor and he wanted to return it, that he was simply trying to turn Ike on to something that would get him away from Huntington Beach and off a bum trip? He would have liked to believe that. But it was not that simple for him— even if everything Preston said was true, it was not that simple. He owed something to Ellen. She'd been all he'd had for a long time. And finally, when she'd needed him, he had not really been there—not in the right way. When she'd needed him that night on the flats, he let some other need in himself come between them and it had never been quite the same afterward. Maybe if he'd been different then, things would not have worked out as they had. And maybe that was really why he'd come—not what the old lady had thought, and not even because she was family, but because he'd let her down and he owed her. He could not quit that easily. And yet, for the moment, he was not sure what else to say to Preston. His guilt, he felt, was a private thing.

He lay there for some time without talking, or commenting further on Preston's offer. He thought again of what he had seen in the alley—Preston talking to the blond-haired surfer. But somehow, bringing that up just now seemed pointless. Preston had stated his position. She'd moved on or she was dead. Either way there was not much he could do. It was, of course, all ground he had been over in his own mind. But it struck him now as particularly depressing, perhaps because he was hearing someone else say it, out loud for the first time. He closed his eyes and he fought to hang on to some of that plugged-in feeling he had gotten back to the beach with, to remember the waves, the rush of smooth faces in the last light, the sense of camaraderie that had grown out of the shared day. He turned his head and watched Preston still seated near the remains of the fire. The reddish light of the embers crept up his tattooed arms and into his face, which was bent down toward the coals. He was not like the other biker types Ike had met around Jerry's shop. He could be loud and violent, as Ike had seen that first day in the lot, but there was something else there too, something that, like the eyes, did not quite fit with the rest of the disguise, and he found himself wanting to say one more thing. "Why'd you quit?" Ike asked him. "Why don't you go to some of those places you were telling me about? You still could."

Preston seemed to think about it for a minute. "I guess it has to do with wanting something to be a certain way," he said. "And if it can't be that way, then you don't want it at all."

Ike thought about it. He would have liked to ask what had changed it, but he didn't. He supposed it was not the kind of thing you should ask, that it was private like his guilt.

"It's just different now," Preston went on. "I've got too many good memories, too many good waves." He poked at the coals with a fresh stick. Ike watched him, hunched up, squinting into the ashes, and somehow he didn't get the idea that Preston was thinking back on good times. He looked to Ike more like someone who had lost something and couldn't see the way to get it back. Maybe he was just tired, but Ike didn't think that was all there was to it. And then it came to him what there was in the face, in the eyes that did not seem right, what he'd noticed that first day—a kind of desperate quality, almost as if Preston was afraid of something. And maybe that was what was wrong. Fear did not belong in that body any more than the eyes did. But there it was. Or perhaps it was only in Ike's mind, a product of his overworked imagination, but he did not think so and he suddenly found himself wondering what Preston would think if he tried to tell him about that feeling, that certain time of day when the silence grows too great and it is as if the land itself is about to cry out. And though he did not tell him, because it did not really seem like the kind of thing you could put into words, he did not think that Preston would laugh as Ellen had done. He had this crazy notion that Preston would know. He flattened back out and watched the sky, cut by dark branches above his face. He closed his eyes and saw countless lines of waves moving toward him from a distant horizon and he waited for them to rock him to sleep.

Sometime in the night he woke with a start. He could not say what had disturbed him or how long he had slept. The fire had gone out; the ashes looked cold and dead in the moonlight. Ike sat up in his bag and looked around. Preston's bag had been unrolled and lay on the ground maybe ten yards away, but Preston was not in it. Ike stared hard into the darkness that surrounded the camp. He listened, but there were only the sounds of the forest, the beating of his own heart. For a moment he felt something like panic rising in his chest. He lay back down, forced his breathing into a regular pattern. He was certain Preston would be back. Perhaps he had only gone to take a leak. He forced his eyes to close and at last he slipped into sleep once more. When he woke again, the sky was gray and Preston was asleep near the circle of ashes.

The second day passed much as the first: surf until late morning, sleep and eat in the afternoon, surf again at sunset. They saw cowboys again, this time from the water, a red pickup truck at the edge of the cliff. They paddled back around the point, out of sight, and waited until the truck had gone.

On the second afternoon, while Preston slept, Ike explored a section of trail they had passed on their way down to the beach. There was a place where the trail forked, one branch going down, the other up, toward what Ike guessed would be the edge of the cliff overlooking the point. He was not sure that Preston would approve of his looking around, but he did not plan to be gone for long and the trail was not anywhere near where they had seen the truck.

It was a warm afternoon. Insects sang in the brush. A light breeze whispered in the high grass and the hills seemed to move in the wind, to ripple as if they were alive. Wild mustard cut yellow slashes across great fields of green. He moved along the narrow trail, the ground hot against his bare feet where it was smooth and exposed to the sun, cool and damp where it wound beneath the twisted limbs of the squat dark trees that grew in clumps throughout the hills.

The trail did not go on for long and soon, emerging from a thicket of trees, he found himself in a large clearing at the edge of a cliff. He at first stepped into the clearing but then drew back among the trees. There was something unusual here, a sudden feeling that he had violated some private space. He stood in the shade and looked out at the circular patch of smooth hard-packed dirt. In the center of the clearing there was a stone ring. The smooth dirt, the slight rise of the ground, made it seem as if the earth rose here to cut a great half circle out of the sky. The stone ring was blackened with soot and ash. A series of strange symbols had been scratched into the stone and he was reminded of the fire rings beneath the cliffs, the graffiti of the inland gangs. Those rings, however, were made of concrete. This ring was made from individual stones, and as he inspected it more carefully he saw that the stones were held together with mortar, which in spots still had a rough, almost new look to it, as if the ring was of recent construction. Looking farther around the circle, he saw that along the far edge, closest to the cliff and the sea, there was also evidence of some recent digging—some kind of trench, with mounds of dark earth heaped to the side of it.

He stepped into the clearing once more, intent on examining this work in progress. As he did so, however, he happened to look back over his shoulder and discovered that he could once again see the house he'd glimpsed that first morning from the point. It was a better view from here, and he stood looking back at it, listening to the heat moving in the brush, the sound of the surf drifting up from the beaches below. The house was still very far away, but he could see windows and what appeared to be a balcony. And as he watched he became aware of a tiny speck moving on the balcony. A figure dressed in white? Yes, he was certain of it. There was a person there. He ducked quickly back into the trail, hoping he had not been visible to them as well. He waited for a few moments, listening to the surf below him. It was hard to see much from the trail, but he did not want to risk going back into the clearing now. At last he turned and started down, back toward the camp.

Preston was awake when he returned and Ike told him about the clearing. He told him about the house and the tiny figure in white. Preston listened, a scowl on his face, eyes turned toward the ground as he scratched circular lines with a pointed stick. "It's been a long time since I was here last," Preston said. "Things have changed. Maybe there are more people around now."

Ike wondered how smart it was to stay. They had seen ranch hands both days now. There was someone in the house.

"Swell's still good," Preston said. "One more day. We'll give it one more day."

13

By the end of the third day, Ike felt that they had been there forever. His skin was burned dark and his hair was tangled with salt, streaked almost blond at the ends. His back and shoulders ached from the long paddles, but that plugged-in feeling had not deserted him. He felt alive in a new way, and more confident now than at any time he could remember. He still had occasional doubts about why they had come. Perhaps it was as simple as Preston had said: They had come for the waves.

The third day passed without incident. It was agreed that they would spend one more night, leave in the morning. Ike went to sleep quickly after eating; the last he saw of Preston, he was seated by the fire, a joint held to his lips, his dark hair loose, resting on his shoulders, so that he reminded Ike of certain airbrushed drawings he'd seen on the fuel tanks of bikes, the covers of magazines: the dark scowl beneath the long hair, the heavy tattooed shoulders and arms lit by the orange light of the fire. He looked like a figure out of some remote past, a slayer of dragons.

And once again, as had happened on the first night, Ike woke in the blackness to find that he was alone, the fire dead, Preston's bag unrolled but empty. This time, however, Ike had the feeling that he had been disturbed, that there had been a sound. He strained his ears against the silence, the distant buzz of insects, the far-off crash of waves. Then he heard it again: the barking of a dog. He pulled himself out of his bag and stood in the center of the small clearing. He was uncertain about what to do. He put on sneakers and stepped to the edge of the camp, staring down the trail that led to the beach, that forked off toward the clearing. Could Preston have gone to check out

the clearing for himself? Would it be foolish to leave the camp?
A half-moon melted down on one side rested far above the
trees. He heard the dog again. It would not take him long to
reach the clearing. He had just started down the trail when
suddenly there was a new sound: a voice. A man's voice ripping the night. He began to run.

Somehow the trail seemed longer in the night. The
branches often blocked what light there was and in one place
he collided with a low branch that jutted across the trail. He
turned his face at the last second and caught the blow across
his jaw, driving the skin of his cheek into his teeth. The taste of
blood crept into his mouth. He paused to rest, his hands on his
knees, his head ringing. The voice came again. Was it the same
voice? Or had this one come from behind him, cutting him off?
He was uncertain. His head ached. He heard the dog again, a
first voice and then a second, and suddenly the night seemed
full of sounds, of violence. A light flashed somewhere among
the trees that lay on the inland side of the trail, a single white
spot jumping, appearing and disappearing, someone running.
Ike put his head down and began to run once more, running
now out of panic, afraid to cut back toward camp, his breath
like flame. He ran up a steep section of trail he could not
remember and suddenly he was back at the edge of the cliff,
the clearing, and Preston was there, but he was not alone.

Preston was nearly facing Ike, the cliff edge at his back.
And between Ike and Preston there was another man, a big
man with a wide back and a huge head of black hair and there
was one crazy moment in which Ike stood there, struck dumb,
like a rabbit caught in a light, eyes wide and stupid, as he tried
to remember where he had seen that back and hair before,
then realizing it was the same back he had followed through
the streets of Huntington Beach just three nights ago. And
even as he stood there, remembering, making the connection,
Terry Jacobs and Preston collided near the center of the
empty space. There was a great dull thud, a cursing and groan-
ing as the two men fell to one side. And then they were up,

Jacobs bent at the waist, Preston holding him in a kind of headlock, one arm under Terry's chin, trying to cut off air, the other across the back of his neck, Terry making huge efforts to break the hold. In one such effort he brought Preston completely off the ground, driving him against the stone ring. Preston's back slapped against the stone with a heaviness that made Ike wince. But Preston did not let go and now Ike could see him pulling, arching his back, forcing that forearm up into Jacobs's throat. He could hear Jacobs gasping and spitting, fighting for air, and then he could hear something else as well: voices, on the trail now below him, and though it looked like Preston might win, it was all happening too slowly. There would not be time.

As far as Ike knew, he had gone completely unnoticed by the men in the clearing. He now ran closer, toward the ring, trying to warn Preston, afraid to shout. He saw Preston turn to him over the great rounded hump of Terry's back. His face was twisted and there was blood streaked across one side; one eye was badly swollen. "Well, do something, then, God damn it," Preston hissed at him between clenched teeth. "A rock, anything." The voices were closer. Ike looked wildly around and that was when he saw the dog. It was on its side near the edge of the cliff, and it was dead. Its mouth hung open, the dark tongue spilling over teeth that were white in the moonlight. Blood lay in a dark pool beneath its skull. The broken piece of a shovel lay nearby. Ike looked at the dog, the shovel. For some ridiculous reason he was afraid to go near the dog. One dead eye watched him in the moonlight. He heard Preston curse him. He heard voices. He heard the sound of surf swept up out of the darkness beyond the cliffs. He saw that there were rocks near the edge of the ring—black charred rocks the size of softballs and larger. He picked one up. It was heavy in his hands. It was the first time in his life that he had tried to hurt someone. Where did you hit him? He raised the rock over his head with both hands and threw it against Terry's hip. It landed with a soft thud and dropped to the ground. Terry Jacobs grunted and went down on one knee.

Suddenly Preston released his grip and stepped to one side. He punched with both hands, fast, one punch landing high on the side of Jacobs's head, the second behind his ear. Sharp cracking sounds. Terry pitched forward, caught himself against the edge of the ring, but made no effort to pull himself up. He leaned against it, breathing hard, and then Preston was across the clearing, had Ike by one arm and was driving him into the high grass, down through a steep ravine, dancing and sliding, cutting arms and hands on sharp rocks and branches. At last they were on the ground, side by side, flat with the smell of dirt and grass in their faces, and they could hear the voices above them, see a white shaft of light cutting lines out of the night, finding the branches above their heads.

They began to inch their way down, clutching at anything to keep from sliding too fast, to keep from making too much noise. Finally they were on a thin rocky trail and Ike was aware of Preston's voice in his ear. "Okay," Preston was saying, and his breath was coming hard. "It's just like out on the point now. You stick behind me. Do what I tell you. We've got to forget about the stuff, understand?" Preston's face was close to his, the pale eyes held his own. "Do you think you could find the truck again, alone?"

He began to say he didn't know, but Preston waved him silent. "Forget it," he said, his voice a quiet hiss in the darkness. "Just stay with me, and stay close."

Ike could not say how long it took them to reach the truck. They seemed to make good time and the voices grew more distant, were finally lost altogether. The engine kicked over with what seemed like an inordinate amount of noise, but at last they were bouncing along the twisting dirt road, lights out, jumping through unseen potholes, Preston swerving and cursing, his big arms spinning the wheel first one way and then the other, trying to see out of one good eye, checking his rearview mirror. "Damn," Ike heard him say. "I think I just saw some headlights back there. I think they're behind us." He reached down and pulled on the switch. The lights lit up the road and

Preston picked up speed, jumping and sliding. Ike banged his knees on the dashboard and poked a hole in what was left of the headlining with his head. He rolled his window down for a better grip on the door and hung on. At last they were on a straight piece of road and Ike heard Preston suck in his breath. Ike squinted through the windshield, across the bouncing hood, and he could see the gate. It was wide open, swung back to one side, and the road was clear. They were through. Another five minutes and they were back on paved road, no one behind them and Preston cursing himself now. "So fucking stupid," he said. "Fucking stupid. I practically walked right into Jacobs and that fucking dog. Fucking moron stupid." By dawn they were on the highway and headed home.

14

The drive home had been accomplished in near silence, and Ike stared once again into the drab landscape of Huntington Beach, even flatter and more colorless than he had remembered after a few days at the ranch. Beyond the highway, the Pacific was like a sea of lead in the midday glare. The surf was blown out, thick and gray, and angry with whitecaps churning in the glare.

All the way back he had thought about the fight and tried to figure it. Still, it took him until the outskirts of Huntington Beach to work up enough nerve to say anything about it to Preston. Preston had been in an understandably foul mood on the way back. Ike's own jaw still hurt from running into that branch and he was certain Preston's face was hurting much worse than his own. He had offered to drive once, but Preston only shook his head. And now, when Ike asked him about Terry Jacobs, about what he had been doing at the ranch, all

Preston had to say was that he didn't know, and that Ike should not worry his fucking head over it.

"What you'd better start thinking about is getting the fuck out," Preston told him. They were swerving through midday traffic, too fast, Preston with one hand on the wheel, the other out the window to flip off some guy with a carload of kids who had pulled out in front of them. "I don't know if Jacobs saw you up there or not. But I can tell you he's not one to let something like this slide. More shit will hit the fan. Count on it. If Jacobs sees your ass on the street, he's gonna hang it, ace, and I might not be around to stop him."

Ike thought back to the fight. He tried to remember if Jacobs had seen him or not. He was pretty sure that he hadn't. It had been dark and Terry's head had been down. He said as much to Preston.

"Suit yourself," Preston said. "It's your funeral."

Preston had called the Sea View a dump, but his place did not look much better to Ike. He got his first look at it as Preston pulled up in front of a small set of duplexes. There were two scrubby-looking palms and a beat-up square of grass in front. The two apartments were identical stucco affairs—a sun-bleached shade of turquoise that clashed badly with some sort of large orangeish industrial building that rose up behind them from the other side of a narrow alley.

Ike decided to try one more time. "Just tell me one thing," he said. "At the ranch. What were you looking for?"

They were parked now, in front of the duplexes. Preston sat with both wrists on top of the wheel. He turned to face Ike and Ike got his first good look at the side of Preston's head. The sight made him wince. Preston looked dead tired and in a way Ike was sorry he had asked.

"You're a persistent little motherfucker, aren't you? I took you to the ranch because I wanted to lay something out for you. That's it," he said. He cut the air with his hand. "Anything else is my business. But I'll tell you this. I don't know what Terry Jacobs was doing up there. But it's not that unusual to see people from down here up there. I mean, people sneak in from time to time to surf. They have for a long time. But I don't know what that big asshole was doing. I got up to take a leak and decided to have a look at that place you told me about. I fucking walked right into him on the trail. Him and that damn dog." Preston held one arm up now, away from the wheel so Ike could see it, and Ike could see that he had been bitten on the arm. The bite was already looking nasty, swollen and discolored.

"Shit. You should have somebody look at that."

Preston put the arm down and opened his door. "Look," he said. "You got a problem. I can dig it. But I told you what I would do. So that's it, man. You understand?"

Ike waited a moment before replying. He felt dead tired himself and the pain in his jaw was filling the rest of his head. "She's my sister" was what he finally said.

Preston just looked away and opened his door. "Yeah," Ike heard him say. "She's your fuckin' sister."

Ike guessed that he was meant to walk back to the Sea View, Preston having done all the driving he was about to for one day. He got out and stood in the lumpy grass, letting the door swing shut behind him. He went to the sidewalk and watched Preston moving away, walking slow and stiff, the way Gordon used to walk sometimes after a bad night. Preston was headed down the skinny concrete walk toward the duplexes, but then he stopped and looked around. His eye was swollen shut and the skin around it seemed to give off a kind of blue light. "Sorry you had to leave your stick," he said.

Ike shrugged.

Preston's face seemed to move into a more or less lopsided grin. "Glad you finally came through with that fucking rock," he said. "I thought for a minute there you were going to go fruit on me."

"No," Ike said. "I wouldn't do that."

Preston nodded and started away once more. Ike watched him go. He was almost to the door when a slim brown-haired girl Ike had not seen before came out of one of the apartments.

She stopped when she saw Preston. Ike was too far away to hear what was said, but he could see that words passed between them. He saw the girl raise her hand to her head. He saw Preston brush past her and then heard the front door slam. It was the same door the girl had come out of. For a moment Ike and the girl stood looking at each other, then Ike turned and headed away. He had not quite reached the corner when he heard someone calling to him. He looked back and saw it was the girl. She was jogging across a corner of the lawn.

He watched her slow to a walk and come toward him. She was not very tall and her thinness made her seem young, but as she drew closer he could see that she was probably in her late twenties. Her hair was straight and fine, and the afternoon breeze lifted it from her shoulders. Ike felt uncomfortable waiting for her; he was certain she would begin asking questions about what had happened.

"You must be Ike," she said as she reached him.

"Yes."

"My name's Barbara."

Ike nodded. They stood for a moment looking one another over. Her eyes were dark, nearly the same shade of brown as her hair, and he guessed maybe it was the mouth, hard straight line without makeup, that added a certain toughness to her features. Still, she was not unattractive. She put one hand on her hip, as if to catch her breath after the short run, and smiled a bit. She had on a pale blue tank top and he could see her breasts clearly outlined beneath it. He supposed she looked like the kind of girl who "had been around," as the old lady would have put it.

"Come on," she said. "Let me give you a ride home. I have to park the truck anyway."

Ike did not much care whether he had a ride or not. He would have preferred to be alone, but somehow he did not have the energy to refuse. He turned and followed her back toward the truck. She wore a pair of white shorts beneath the blue top. Her legs were thin but shapely and well tanned, dark against the white cloth, legs that reminded him of his sister's.

"You're at the Sea View, aren't you?"

"Yes."

"Preston's mentioned you. You did a nice job on his bike."

Ike climbed back into the truck beside her. It seemed strange seeing her behind the wheel after Preston. Her arms were slender. There was a silver bracelet around one forearm. He noticed she had a funny way of tilting her head up when she drove, as if she were too short to see over the top of the wheel, although she was not.

"Preston says you're a good mechanic, too," she said. Ike made an effort to smile; he put his hands on his knees and watched the houses slide by in the sunlight. It was hard to believe that only a few hours before, he had been sitting in this same seat, bouncing along a dirt road, afraid for his life.

It was not until they were parked at the curb in front of Ike's apartment that Barbara got around to asking what Ike knew she would. "Was it a fight?" she asked.

Ike nodded. He didn't know what Preston would have wanted him to say.

She shook her head. She sat with both hands on top of the wheel. Ike reached down and unlatched the door. He put one leg outside, one foot on the running board. "I knew it," she said. "Damn." She turned to Ike and he could see that she was upset. "You don't know how that made me feel when he said he was going surfing. I mean, it seemed like a good sign. He hasn't done anything like that in a long time. I was hoping it would go all right."

"It did go all right for a while, the first couple of days. It wasn't Preston's fault. Some guys jumped us."

"At the ranch?"

"You know about the ranch?"

"The Trax Ranch. Sure. The place has been there forever. I remember guys going up to surf when I was in school. You had to sneak in or something. I didn't know people still went, though, until I heard Preston talk about it the other day." She paused and looked at him. "I was real surprised, I'm not sure how to say this, but it made me curious to get a look at you. I mean, no one has gotten Preston out on a board in a long time. And he seemed hot to go." She stopped again and shook her head. "I might have known something would fuck it up."

Ike squirmed at the edge of his seat. He watched a couple of small blackbirds pecking away at the Sea View's lawn. "It wasn't his fault," he said again. He thought about asking her something else about the ranch, but then thought better of it. Perhaps it would be better to wait until he had talked again to Preston.

"I'm sorry," she said. "I didn't mean to keep you."

Ike stepped out of the truck. He felt that there should be something more to say, but nothing came to mind. "It's all right," he said. "And thanks for the ride."

She nodded. "Maybe you can get him to go surfing again," she said. "It would be nice to see him get interested in something besides his bike. He used to be hot, you know."

"He's still pretty good, I was watching him at the ranch."

"Yeah, but I mean really good. He used to win contests. He used to own that surf shop on Main Street. He ever tell you that?"

"No, he didn't."

She shrugged. "He wouldn't. He never tells anybody anything. But he did own the shop, he and Hound Adams."

Ike blinked back into the cab of the truck. He felt a little like he did that first day he hit town, as if the sunlight were going right through him, as if he were in danger of disappearing. "Preston and Hound Adams?" He repeated the names slowly, wanting to make sure he had heard correctly. Apparently Preston had not told her why he was in town, or about the scrap of paper with the names on it.

"The first of the local surf heros," she said. "Come by sometime and I'll show you his scrapbook." She stopped to look at him. "But listen, I know you're beat. Just come by, okay?" She pushed in the clutch and put the truck in gear.

"Okay," he said. "I will." He stood at the curb and watched her drive away. Going up the stairs was hard work. Once back in his room, he lay down on the bed, but he

couldn't stop thinking about what Barbara had said, and when
he closed his eyes he was back at the ranch, the weight of that
rock pulling at his hands, wondering all over again what it had
been about.

15

Three days later he still did not know what it was about and he
had seen nothing of Preston. It was late afternoon, hot but
with a good breeze coming off the ocean. Ike was sitting on the
porch of the Sea View and talking to the two girls, the short
brunette and the tall blonde who had once come to his room
looking for papers. Their names were Jill and Michelle, and
now that Ike had grown his hair out and went surfing with the
likes of Preston, he assumed that he looked less like a jarhead
and was consequently a more acceptable person to be seen
talking to. Conversation with Michelle and Jill was a little thin,
however. They mainly seemed interested in meeting cute
guys and scoring dope. Ike suspected they were sharing a
brain. Still, he was mildly intrigued by Michelle, the blonde he
had spoken to that day he bought the board. For one thing, she
had these very long sexy legs, and he liked how she smiled at
him, always meeting his eyes with her own. Her eyes were
green, flecked with yellow, and there was a dark mark on one
eye which she told him had come from getting hit with a stick
when she was small. But of even more interest to Ike was the
fact that both Jill and Michelle knew Hound Adams, or at least
knew who he was. They knew, for instance, that he was a
dealer. They also knew where he lived. They were both runaways, in town, as it turned out, only a few weeks longer than
Ike himself, but they seemed to have gotten around. They had
in fact already been to one party at Hound Adams's house,
where they were fairly certain Hound had given Michelle the

eye. It was a source of endless speculation between them and they seemed to thrive on an audience. Ike was more than happy to oblige. He had learned more about Hound Adams from Jill and Michelle in only a few minutes of casual conversation than he had learned from Preston after days of prying. And with them it had all been accidental; he had just happened to be standing there when Jill mentioned the name. The ease with which the rest had come about was fairly mind-boggling. And there was even now the fair chance that when Hound Adams gave his next party, Jill and Michelle would be invited, that Ike might come as well. He was determined to go if he got the chance. And so that was what he was doing the afternoon of the fight, providing an audience for Jill and Michelle, and fishing for more information.

He heard Preston's truck before he actually saw it. He heard the gears grinding and the tires sliding. He looked up to find it skidding to a stop in front of the Sea View. Then it lurched forward a little bit; the engine died, and Barbara got out. She came running toward him across the grass. She looked white and scared. "Preston's been in a fight," she said. "Downtown." She sounded out of breath. "I didn't want to go down by myself.

"Morris called," she said as they got back into the truck. "He's been in a fight with a knife or something and the cops are there already." She was halfway crying and Ike was afraid she was going to run into something. She blew the stop sign at Main and finally parked out in front of some beer bar called the Club Tahiti.

There was a crowd on the sidewalk. Two police cars sat in the street and in the distance they could hear the growing wail of a siren. Barbara jumped out of the truck and ran into the crowd. Ike followed. He felt scared and useless. For a moment he lost sight of Barbara. When he spotted her, she had pushed her way through most of the crowd and was standing near the door, where a cop had grabbed her by the arm. Ike pushed his way to her and managed to get her other arm. The cop was telling her she had to stay outside. "It's all right," Ike said. He tried to say it loud so the cop would hear him too. He put his arm around Barbara's shoulders. The cop let go and turned back toward the door. Ike could feel her trembling against him.

Later he would remember being aware of a lot of things at once. He was aware of his own legs shaking beneath him, of the sour feeling at the pit of his stomach, of the feeling of dread, and yet at the same time he was acutely aware of Barbara at his side, of the cool smoothness of her thigh as she pressed against him, of the scent of her hair. And then there was more commotion from inside and suddenly he could see Preston's head. There was a helmeted cop on either side of him and they all seemed to jostle one another as they came through the doors. Ike could see Preston's face was bleeding again around his still discolored eye. He had on his tank top and jeans, but the shades were gone. His hands were cuffed behind him. Ike and Barbara were pushed aside as the small group exited the bar. Preston passed within a few feet of them, but he did not turn his head; his eyes seemed pointed straight ahead and slightly skyward. Ike did not know if he'd seen them or not.

The siren was piercing now and was mixed with the squeal of tires as an ambulance pulled up into the middle of Main Street. The sun dipped behind the buildings. The breeze picked up and there was a patch of late afternoon fog rolling up the sidewalks from the ocean. The crowd had swollen, though Ike and Barbara were in the front now, part of the semicircle at the door. A couple of medics pushed past them into the bar. For a moment the door stood open, but it was too dark to see much inside. The cool stale odors of spilt beer and tobacco drifted outside. Ike was able to make out the colored lights of a jukebox, the corner of a pool table, a number of dark figures scurrying about, and then the door closed in their faces. It was a heavy wooden door, scarred and beaten. A small sign up near the top said NO ONE UNDER 21 ALLOWED.

For a while nothing happened. Ike could hear the crowd milling and murmuring around him. He could feel Barbara still trembling at his side. He did not know why they were still standing there, really. He'd looked once out toward the street, but Preston was lost somewhere on the other side of the crowd. He'd seen the red light of a police car start off down Main, however, and suspected they had already taken Preston away. But it was hard to move back through the crowd and so they waited with the others. Behind them he could hear more cops working to disperse the people. The crowd was mainly kids off the street, people on their way home from the beaches, a few bikers. People stood around holding beach towels and canvas backrests. Many were barefoot and bare-chested. Ike and Barbara were beginning to move back when the door swung open once more. This time it stayed open and people began to come outside. The first person through the door was Morris. He had a cop on one arm and looked at Ike and Barbara once, shook his head as if to say it was bad, and then moved away. Next came the medics. They were bent low and moving quickly. Between them was a stretcher and suspended over it Ike could see a bottle of liquid. The hum of the crowd picked up and people pushed back for a look and the cops shouted for them to clear a path. A cop pushed Ike in the chest, shoving him back into the crowd as the stretcher flashed by, but he'd seen enough to know who it was. He'd seen the great black puffball of Terry Jacobs's head as it made a fierce contrast with the whiteness of the sheets and the coats of the medics, and they were gone, and the cops were breaking up the crowd and all around him Ike could pick up bits and pieces of conversation. "He's cut bad, man . . ." someone said, and Ike looked back once more toward the still open door. Several more people walked outside and among them Ike recognized another face: sharp straight lines cut out of rock. Straight nose and mouth. Eyes set deep and a bit too close together, dark and quick, blond hair pulled back into a ponytail, stretching that tanned skin, pulling it over the bones until it was too tight somehow. And he was tall, too, so the face was above most of the others around it, not as tall as Preston, and not as wide, but lean the way a good light heavyweight is lean.

Hound Adams stood framed for a moment in the doorway and then stepped onto the sidewalk. Several people at once seemed to be trying to talk to him, but he was ignoring them, staring past them into the crowd after his friend. Ike could not make out what they were saying. He still had Barbara at his side. He was holding her hand and knew without looking that she was weeping. Suddenly one of Hound's friends started away from him and Ike saw Hound's hand reach out to grab the guy by the arm. His words were harsh and clear. "Keep your motherfucking mouth shut," he said. "I want his ass on the street." Ike could not hear much more. "But he jumped bad on him," someone said, and Hound called for quiet. Ike strained to get closer, to hear more. He could feel Barbara pulling at his arm and then it was like he was aware of someone looking at him and he turned his head.

Hound Adams was standing with his back to the dirty brick wall. The fog was sweeping up through the streets and above them the purple letters of the Club Tahiti had begun to buzz. For a moment their eyes met; Ike met Hound Adams's stare with his own. But it was only for an instant, and it was Ike who looked away, back into the crowded street.

16

Barbara did not want to go home, and she did not want to be alone. On the way back to the Sea View they picked up a six-pack of beer. The drank it seated on the floor of Ike's room, their backs against the bed. Actually Barbara drank most of it. Ike had two beers and Barbara drank the other four. "You know the funny thing," she said. "When I first moved in with Preston, I thought I was without hope; I mean, my life was pretty screwed up then. But I'm not. That's what I've learned, living with Preston. Preston is without hope. I'm not. It took a while, but I'm beginning to understand that."

Ike felt that he should respond but was not sure about what to say. "You said you've been with him just over a year?"

"Almost two."

"But you've known him longer?"

"Not known him. I knew who he was. This town was different back when he and Hound owned the shop. I mean, everything was smaller. There was only one high school; everybody knew everybody else. I think I was in the seventh grade when Preston moved to Huntington, but I used to spend a lot of time at the beach. Most people who hung out around the beach knew who Hound and Preston were."

Ike took a drink of beer and stared at a slice of moonlight on the glass.

"I remember the day he won that big contest, the nationals or whatever it was. I remember standing on the pier and watching. It's strange to think back to that now. I haven't thought of it in a long time. But I didn't meet Preston until recently, maybe two years ago." She stopped. "You don't have to listen to this," she said. "I can shut up."

"No. I'm interested."

"Are you sure?"

"Yes." Ike watched her take another drink and then rest the bottle on her knee. "I haven't drunk this much beer in a while," she told him. "Not since the night I met Preston, maybe." She seemed to find that amusing in a sad sort of way and smiled at the floor. "We met in a bar, that place that's the punk club now. I can't even remember what it was called then, the Beachcomber or something. I had just gotten out of the hospital and wasn't supposed to be drinking, though; I remember that. I'd gotten pregnant that summer and it turned out to be a tubular pregnancy. I almost died. They wound up having to take everything out. Everything." She said it in a flat voice, the bottle resting on her bare leg, the moonlight finding one side of her face. Ike had not turned on any lights; the room seemed better in the dark.

"Anyway," she continued. "That was where I was at the summer Preston came home. I'd just done two years at a local J.C. I had been planning to apply to this photography school up north, and all of a sudden it was like everything was over. I mean, I just couldn't see the point anymore. Then Preston showed up. He'd been gone for years. First the war, then jail. He came back like he is now. That's the only way you have ever seen him, so it probably doesn't mean that much to you, but nobody else could believe it. He was a different person, completely." She paused and took a drink of beer.

"But I guess I saw us as having something in common," she said. "At least that was how I felt at the beginning, like the whole thing was without hope." She stopped for a moment and looked at Ike. "But that wasn't it really, now that I've had time to think, to be with him. I mean, I don't know if I can say it very well, but what was really going on was that I was looking at Preston and I was seeing this tragic figure, but I was seeing something else, too; I was still seeing that young guy on the beach holding a big silver trophy over his head, and somehow I was still trying to be the girl on the pier. That might sound stupid, but the thing is, I was working at something. I was really believing that if Preston and I loved each other we could help each other, we could get back some of what had been lost, both of us. But what I've begun to see in the last year is that I'm the only one working at it." She stopped. "Preston doesn't care," she said slowly. "About anything. So maybe you can see why I was surprised when he started talking about taking this kid he had met up to the ranch. I mean, he acted like he really wanted to do it. I don't know." She stopped again and shook her head.

"What do you know about the ranch?"

"Nothing. Just what I told you in the truck." Ike was staring at the wall, but he could feel her turning her face to look at him. "Do you think this, tonight, had something to do with what happened up there?"

Ike didn't answer right away. For some reason, he was reluctant to tell her. He supposed, however, that she would find it out on her own sooner or later. Perhaps it was better that she hear it from him. It had all come to seem clear enough. Barbara had told him that Preston and Hound had been partners. Preston had told him that Hound Adams had friends with bucks. Certainly whoever owned the ranch had money. And Preston had not had to break down any fences—he'd had his own fucking key. It seemed plain that Preston once had free access to the ranch, and that now he was no longer welcome there. When he and Jacobs had run into each other, they'd fought over it. And that was how it had started. This afternoon, at the Club Tahiti, they'd met again, and they had ended it. As for Preston's willingness to risk it—to take Ike there, he had evidently miscalculated. It was just as he'd said to Ike that day Ike had seen the figure in white from the clearing, he had not expected so many people to be around. Ike worked his way through these ideas now, with Barbara. She looked away from him as he spoke. When he was finished, she sat with her eyes closed, her forehead on the heel of her hand. "Assholes" was what she finally said.

They both sat in silence for some time after that, until Barbara said she had to use the head. Ike watched her cross the room. When she came back, she asked him if he was ready to go to sleep. He shrugged. "Whatever you want," he said. She put a hand on his arm. "It's okay," she told him. "And thanks."

It was a strange night. Ike let Barbara have the bed. He slept on the floor below it, but he slept fitfully, waking time and again to think that she had spoken to him, that she was awake. But each time he sat up to look, he found her asleep. And at last he slept himself, soundly, he supposed, because when he woke he found her already dressed and poking through the cupboard above what passed for his kitchen sink. "No coffee?" she asked.

"Sorry."

"It's okay. Come home with me and I'll make us some."

Though he did not much care for coffee, he said okay. It seemed like the right thing to do. He pulled on his shirt and they went down the steps. There was a heavy overcast outside. The air was cool and smelled of the sea. It felt earlier than he had first thought and on the drive to her house they passed only a couple of cars.

When they got to the duplexes, the first thing he noticed was Morris's bike standing at the curb. Morris was just coming down the walkway as they pulled up and got out of the truck. Ike thought that Morris stared at him for a moment with some surprise, then he looked back at Barbara. "The only thing they got him on now is drunk and disorderly," Morris said. "They want him on the knifing, but nobody seems to be talking. I didn't see it myself. I was at the other end of the bar. Frank and Hound were right there, but they ain't said a word to the pigs." He shook his shaggy head. "I don't know," he said. He looked tired and hung over. The sun was starting to burn through the overcast and it was starting to turn sticky. Ike could see the lines of sweat making trails across Morris's big greasy face. There was a moment of slightly awkward silence. "I was going to make some coffee," Barbara said. "Do you want any, Morris?"

Morris shook his head. "Just come by to let you know what was goin' on," he said. "Just thought you might be interested." Ike thought he noticed a slightly sarcastic tone in Morris's voice and he was beginning to get the idea that Morris thought there was something funny about Ike and Barbara being together at this time of day. Morris stood for a moment longer, then turned and swaggered off in the direction of his bike. Ike watched him go, then walked the rest of the way to Barbara's door. But all of a sudden he just felt too funny being there. He didn't want to go inside. "I think I'll skip it this time," he said. "I should check with Morris, see if he needs any help at the shop."

She shrugged. "Okay," she said. "But thanks. I needed to be around someone last night, somebody I could trust." Then she went inside and closed the door.

He ran back down the sidewalk to see if he could catch up with Morris. He was too late; Morris was already pulling away as Ike reached the street. Ike suddenly felt very grimy and tired, as if he hadn't slept at all. He decided to skip the shop and walked instead back to the Sea View apartments. The mailman was just leaving as Ike got there and Ike found that there was a letter in his box. It was the first piece of mail he had gotten and it was from San Arco. He carried it up to his room and read it seated by the window. The letter was from Gordon. Ike recognized the big, familiar scrawl right away. Gordon had apparently written a couple of letters, one to Washington, D.C., and the other to the American embassy in Mexico. Apparently there were no records of an Ellen Tucker having been found, either dead or in jail. Gordon wasn't sure what this meant, but he said he figured Ike might want to know. That was it; Gordon not being much for small talk. Near the bottom of the page he told Ike to take care of himself.

Ike read the letter several times. When he was done, he folded it, slipped it back into the torn envelope and placed it near the scrap of paper with the three names on it. After that he walked to the window and rested his fingertips against the glass. He looked toward the ugly line of buildings that hid the sea and he imagined her here, in this town, walking the streets he walked now, seeing the same things, and thinking . . . what? He might have guessed that once. Because they were so alike then. It had been in fact one of their games—guessing what the other was thinking. Only it was somehow more than guessing, it was knowing and it was a special thing. He thought, as he had so many times before, how things had changed after that night on the flats. And how, when she'd left for the last time without bothering to say good-bye, he had by chance come to the front of the market and seen her go, in broad daylight, a ragged suitcase at the end of one arm, sun-bleached denims and red boots wading into those ribbons of dust and heat while he'd stood there on Gordon's sagging porch, scared shitless of the loneliness to come.

He stood for a long time by the window, his fingers against the glass until the glass had gone warm and moist beneath them. He was struck by a sense of something he could not quite articulate. But it was connected to the way he had once felt in the desert, with Ellen, that he had helped to set something in motion—a chain of events he was linked to but unable to control. And it was like that again now, he thought, here, and he knew that Gordon's letter had changed nothing, that he would not do as Preston had asked. He was reminded of those desert windstorms, a whirlwind kicked across the desert floor, only he could not say if the storm was outside himself, pulling him in, or inside himself driving him forward, just that he was locked in and that there was suddenly something more at stake here than his search for his sister. He could see that now for the first time. It was not only Ellen Tucker he pursued. It was himself as well. He stared out the window, across the small yard toward the ragged skyline of Huntington Beach, hearing once more in the dark recesses of his own mind the high electric whine of those neon letters above the Club Tahiti. And he saw again that dark stare he had been unable to meet.

PART
TWO

17

Mazatlán, San Blas, Puerto Vallarta, Cabo San Lucas. The names had magic in them. They hung in the smoke-filled air like some religious chant. Ike listened. He imagined tropical waters, steaming jungles split by rutted roads where green lizards curled in the shade.

When he opened his eyes, Hound Adams was looking at him. They were seated around a map spread on the living room floor. Michelle was by his side. She had locked her hands around his arm and was resting her chin on his shoulder. Hound Adams had at last thrown his party, and Michelle and Jill had been invited. Michelle had brought Ike. Now it was very late, or very early. Beyond the window Ike could see the sky beginning to lighten.

It had been a noisy party, but by now most of the guests had gone, leaving a small circle of admirers to sit on Hound's living room floor, around the map upon which he outlined plans for the winter's surf trip. The winter, like Preston had said.

Terry Jacobs was not at the party. He was still, after nearly a week, in intensive care at the Huntington Beach Community Hospital. The fight, however, had been a prominent topic of conversation during the party, and there seemed to be some confusion as to how it had started. Every story Ike heard was different. The only thing certain was that Preston Marsh was a marked man. Apparently Terry Jacobs had a bad family, some of whom had already arrived in Huntington Beach from the

islands. Ike had had them pointed out to him, several hulking
strangers in flowered shirts, quiet and dark.

Ike had seen Barbara only once since the night of the
fight. She had stopped by briefly one afternoon to let him
know Preston was still in jail, that there were still no witnesses
to the knifing. Ike had thought then about Hound's words,
what he had said about wanting Preston on the street, and he
thought about them again now as he observed one of Terry's
ominous-looking relatives draped over the couch.

He had not seen Morris since the morning after the fight,
and he had put off going by the shop. He'd spent most of the
week keeping to himself, thinking, watching the oil well, the
dead grass, and the small brown birds beneath his window.
And then Michelle had come by and invited him to the party.

The party had provided Ike with his first chance to ob-
serve Hound Adams at close range, and he had watched as
Hound circulated among his guests, greeting some with a soul-
brother handshake or an embrace, others with a cool nod.
Hound seemed pleased that Michelle had come and more
than once Ike had noticed Hound putting his hand on
Michelle's shoulder or back as he passed, or paused to say a few
words, and Ike was beginning to believe that maybe Jill and
Michelle had been right; Hound did have an eye for Michelle.
Also, more than once Ike had looked up to find Hound Adams
staring at him. He did not think it was his own paranoia. And
now, sitting Indian style above the spread maps, his yellow
hair gleaming in the dim light, Hound Adams was staring at
him again.

"Todos son hermanos del mar." Hound was looking at Ike
as he spoke. Ike had no idea of what was said. There was a
silence and Ike did not know how to fill it, though it seemed to
be expected of him. At his side he could feel Michelle pressing
against his arm. He could feel the sweat prickling at his neck
and down the center of his back. Hound was smiling at him
with his mouth, but his eyes were like stones.

Ike grinned back and shrugged, trying to say he did not understand.

Hound laughed. "We are brothers of the sea, no? It is what the people of the village say." His finger rested on a spot of the map. Ike felt some relief. He looked with great interest at the map.

"It is a small fishing village," Hound continued. "A beautiful spot."

When Ike looked up, he found Hound still looking at him. "I hear you're a surfer," Hound said. Ike did not know if it was a question.

"I'm just learning."

"We are all just learning."

Ike looked into the dark, humorless eyes and he did not get the idea that Hound was joking with him. For a moment, as he had done on the street outside the club, Ike held the stare, studied the face. He had noticed in the course of the evening that it was a face that seemed to vary in age depending upon the distance from which you viewed it. Hound's hair was more like a boy's, or a young woman's, rich, yellow, in places bleached white by the sun. The combination of flashy hair, the tanned skin, the athletic build, gave Hound the appearance of many of the young surf jocks you found around the pier, in the shops along Main. From a distance you might have thought he was in his late teens or early twenties. But when you saw him close up, you noticed other things, the wrinkles that spread around the eyes, the thin white scar above the bridge of the nose, the slightly yellowed teeth. Up close it was not a young man's face. It was serious and cunning and more than once tonight Ike had felt that he was being toyed with.

"I hear you've got a good teacher," Hound said.

Ike stopped short. The tone of Hound's voice, like his eyes, gave nothing away. Was this it? Had Hound been baiting him for this? On the couch one of the big Samoans pushed himself upright and pulled the ring on a can of beer. Ike shifted his weight, thinking of a way to reply.

But it was Hound Adams who broke the silence with a

short laugh. "That's all right," he said. "Everybody needs a teacher. The trick is in choosing the right one." There was a pause. "Where are you from, Ike?" Hound asked. It was such an abrupt turn in the conversation that Ike felt suddenly off the hook. "The desert . . ." he began, then let his voice trail away, waving with his hand toward the far side of the room, as if the desert were just beyond the wall. "There is an energy in the desert," he heard Hound say after a period of silence, "as there is an energy in the sea."

Later, they stood outside on the wooden porch as the sun rose above the town. Hound had already gotten into his trunks and vest. One of the Samoans was waxing a board in the front yard. After a night of partying they were going down to surf the pier. Ike stood with Michelle at his side. It was funny how he'd gotten used to her being there in the course of the night, funnier still how it made him feel. She had been uncharacteristically quiet, supportive in some important way, and he was both grateful and puzzled at the same time. He was also bone tired and hung over. He did not understand where Hound Adams found the energy to surf.

"Maybe you would like to join us?" Hound asked suddenly, jerking Ike out of the daze he had slipped into. And for a moment Ike was at a loss for words. "I would like to," he said, "but I can't."

"He lost his board," Michelle put in. "Somebody ripped it off."

Hound nodded, head slightly cocked, staring once again at Ike. "There are other boards here."

"I guess not this morning. I've got to work in a few hours. But thanks."

Hound Adams nodded. "Another time," he said. "Come back, both of you."

Ike and Michelle were nearly back to the sidewalk when Hound called Ike's name. Ike stopped and looked back. Hound Adams was standing at the edge of his porch. He looked tall and hard, like one of the columns that supported the roof above the house. "Why don't you come by the shop," he said to Ike. "You shouldn't be without a stick. Maybe we can work something out."

Ike felt slightly numb as they walked back along the deserted sidewalks. His head still rang with the beer and dope, and the concrete beneath his feet seemed at times to be very far away. He glanced at Michelle and could not help but think how different she seemed to him after the party. It was very puzzling.

The morning was cool, drenched in a rosy light. A few scattered clouds, luminous and metallic, floated like great airships far above them. The sky was turquoise streaked with orange and red. "This sunrise reminds me of the desert," Ike said.

"I've never been to the desert."

"That's hard to believe."

"It's true. My dad left us when I was small. My mother never goes anywhere. I haven't been anywhere. It was one of the reasons I ran away."

"Well, imagine the ground as empty as the sky, as full of color." He stopped and looked at Michelle. They were practically the same height and he looked directly into her eyes. He could see she was paying attention, but he did not go on. He shrugged it off. "It's best in the spring," he told her.

"You're different," she said. He met her eyes for a moment, then looked away.

"I mean it. You're not like the other guys around here."

"Maybe it's because I'm not from around here."

"So tell me about the desert."

He shrugged again. "There's not that much to tell."

"What about your school? What were the other kids like?"

He laughed, thinking about the single row of white portable buildings that had served as the school, small tinny rooms so hot there were days when the instructors ran sprinklers on the roof to cool them down. "Most of the kids there were

Mexicans," he said. "But I didn't make a lot of friends. I don't know what they were like, to tell you the truth."

"You didn't have any friends?"

"My sister. We were friends."

"Your sister?"

"Yeah." He hesitated, it always made him uncomfortable talking about it, about his family—if that was what you could call it. "You see, my old lady just dropped my sister and me off one summer and split, left us with her mother and her brother and never came back."

"What about your father?"

"I never knew him at all."

She seemed to think about this for a moment. "So it was just you and your sister," she said. He thought that now she would ask something more, about his sister, but she didn't. They had been holding hands as they walked and he was aware of her palm, damp and warm against his own. "Maybe we can go there sometime," she said. "You can show me what it's like."

"Maybe," he said, though he felt funny saying it and was not sure why.

Back at the Sea View apartments, they climbed the stairs and he stood with her in front of her door. The door was open and inside he could see Jill sprawled on the couch, still clothed. Michelle looked in at her roommate then back at Ike. She wrinkled her nose and smiled. "You could come in," she said. "I have my own corner. Or do you have to go to work?"

Ike stood looking into the small cluttered room. "I lied. I have to go to bed. I'm really tired right now."

"Will you surf with them sometime?"

He shrugged.

She stood with her back to the door, her hand resting on the knob. He looked at her and he could see she was waiting, that he was expected to do something besides say good night. He would have liked that as well. There was an odd kind of charged moment as her eyes held his in which he might have moved toward her, touched her, but he allowed it to pass, or rather he waited too long so that to have gone to her would have seemed awkward and clumsy. He turned back toward his own door, and then turned to face her again from a safer distance. "Maybe we could do something tomorrow," he said. "Go to a show or something."

"Okay," she said. "Come by after I get home from work." She waved at him and he waved back.

Once in his room, he sat on the bed and thought back over the evening. As he undressed he kept thinking about those questions Hound Adams had asked him. The questions implied a certain amount of knowledge on Hound's part, and yet Ike had the impression that he was fishing a bit too. What did Hound Adams know? And what about that offer to come to the shop? It was a tricky proposition, he thought, no matter how you looked at it.

18

Ike did not feel very refreshed when he finally got out of bed. He showered and decided to go for a walk downtown. The shower made him feel better and there was a good breeze off the ocean. He walked by the Curl Theater to check out the movies. He thought maybe Michelle would want to see a surf movie with him. He had never taken a girl out before. It made him feel strange, a little nervous. He still could not get over how different Michelle seemed to him after the party. Jill had been there too and had seemed a lot more like her old self, loud and dumb. But Michelle had been different. He suddenly found himself trying to imagine what it would be like to have a real girl friend—a wife, even. He tried to imagine himself driving a station wagon full of boogie boards and sandy kids down Coast Highway on a Sunday afternoon. He tried, but he couldn't quite do it. As far as he knew, no one in his family had turned out normal yet and he didn't see why he should be the first.

The Curl was a crusty-looking old building with peeling paint, bordered on both sides by vacant lots. It ran surf films nearly every week. This week it had one called *Standing Room Only*. He stood for a while examining the posters before deciding they should go. Then he walked down to the Del Taco, where Michelle worked, to get a Coke.

She seemed surprised to see him. He'd never been there when she was working. She was wearing an orange and brown uniform with a little white name tag pinned over her breast. He hung around the counter for a while, sipping his Coke from a straw and talking to her. When he told her about the movie, she said, "Far out."

All the time he was talking to her, he kept noticing this other girl, about Michelle's age, staring at him. She was working the drive-thru window, but she kept looking over at Ike, staring at him like she was trying to decide if she knew him or not. Ike had never seen her before in his life. He met her stare a couple of times and each time she looked away. He would have hung around awhile longer. It was pleasant enough to stand there, talking to Michelle, the wind at his back, but finally some people started to line up behind him and so he said good-bye. "I'll see you tonight," she told him. "It will be fun." Ike walked down the steps to the sidewalk and then turned to look back. Michelle smiled at him through the glass. Behind her, he could see that the girl at the drive-thru was looking at him again.

He made two stops on his way back up Main Street. He stopped first at the travel agency and picked up some maps of Mexico. He wanted to see if he could remember the names and trace out the same lines that Hound Adams had drawn the night before. And then he went on to the Main Street Surf Shop.

He did not see Hound Adams. In fact he did not see anyone and the shop, as it had been on his first visit, was empty and quiet. He pushed his fingers into the pockets of his jeans and walked inside. He was not really certain what he had come to see. He supposed it had something to do with what Barbara had told him, that the shop had once belonged to Preston.

In tennis shoes, he moved silently across the dark rectangle of carpet in the showroom and onto the concrete. It was odd, the silence in the shop, giving him the sensation that any loud noises would be out of place. That feeling was enhanced, he guessed, by the memorabilia on the walls, the trophies and old posters, the faded photographs, some of which had writing across the bottoms of the mattings in which they were framed. He paid closer attention to what was around him now than he had on his first visit and he noticed one thing right away, was surprised in fact that he had not remembered it from his first visit. On the deck of one of the old balsa wood boards that hung suspended from the ceiling, he saw a decal. The ceiling in the shop was high, as if the room had once served another purpose, but he could easily make out the shape of the decal: a flaming wave within a circle. He began to study some of the photographs and he saw that there were other boards in the photographs with the same decal, the logo repeated perhaps a dozen times throughout the pictures.

The shop consisted of two rooms. There was the large room with the carpet and the raised ceiling in front and another smaller room in back where the used boards and wet suits were kept. Ike walked into the back portion of the shop. He smelled the distinctive rubbery odor of the new wet suits, the sharp, rather sweet scent of fresh resin. It was on the wall above the wet suits at the east end of the small room that he found what was to him the most remarkable of the photographs. It was an enlargement done on what looked to be a cheap paper, for the picture had once been in color but was now faded and full of light. The sky was the palest of blues and the color was completely gone from the faces of the people: a middle-aged man, two younger men, and a girl. It took Ike a moment or two to be certain, but certain he was, even before finding the very thin, spidery handwriting that traveled along the photo's bottom edge: the two young men were Hound Adams and Preston Marsh. They both had short haircuts, were dressed in swimsuits and matching sweat shirts. They stood propped against an old Ford station wagon with wood on the sides and surfboards protruding from the back. The girl was between them, standing on the running board, one arm over Hound's shoulders, the other over Preston's. She was a very good-looking girl with fine curved brows, a straight nose, and even teeth, a face that might have been in the movies, and she was smiling, laughing almost. Preston and Hound were smiling.

The middle-aged man did not seem to fit with the others somehow. He was dressed in slacks and a T-shirt. A sport coat hung draped over one arm. His hair was very short and dark, combed straight back, and he wore a pair of small round shades. His mouth was thin, straight, turned up at the corners in what might have been a smile. The writing across the bottom said: *Mexico, Labor Day, 1965. Hound, Preston, Janet, Milo.*

The shop was still and quiet and Ike stood before the picture for a long time. It was surprising how much alike Hound and Preston seemed then. Preston was nearly a head taller, a bit wider and thicker through the shoulders, but with a leaner look than he had now, built more like Hound. His nose was straighter then too, and with the similar haircuts, the matching sweat shirts, the similarity was striking. But there was something else that kept him before the picture. What was there about it? Perhaps the girl, something about the way she laughed, her hair caught in the wind. For some reason, he imagined the picture had been taken at the end of the day, but not just any day, it had been a good one, and it was the kind of picture that made you wish the people in it were your friends, and having to settle for just looking at it made you feel left out of something and lonesome. That was what he was thinking when a voice jerked him around, asking him if he needed help. The voice came from behind him, and when he turned, he saw that it was the same blond-haired man he had seen Preston talking to in the alley, whom he had noticed that night he followed Hound and Terry, the man he had so far taken to be Frank Baker—though of this he was still not certain.

The man's words were loud in the silence of the shop and Ike was a moment in replying. "No. No, thanks," Ike said, "just looking around."

The man walked into the room and stood just a few steps behind Ike, his arms folded across his chest. He seemed to be looking at the picture as well. Ike spent a few moments pretending to examine the wet suits that hung beneath the photographs, made a remark about the need to save bread, then left the shop. He left the young blond-haired man still standing before the picture.

It was on his way out of the small room that Ike noticed another photograph, one of the man he had just seen—the older dark-haired man. Ike recognized the same thin smile, the small shades. This time the man was alone on an empty stretch of beach. Ike did not take the time to look at the photograph for long, but before he left he was able to read the name written on the mat. The name was Milo Trax.

19

The wind stung his eyes, blowing them dry as he passed the Greyhound bus depot and headed north toward the Sea View apartments. He thought about the man he'd just seen in the photographs. And he thought of the small figure dressed in white that he'd glimpsed from the clearing above the point. The man with the bucks. And it might be interesting, he thought, to talk to Barbara again, to have a look at that scrapbook she had mentioned.

Michelle was waiting for him when he reached his apartment. She was sitting in front of her door, dressed in jeans and
a T-shirt. She had brought him some food from work. He sat at
the card table by a window and ate. Michelle watched.

"Where's Jill?" he asked, looking for something to say, for
a way to get his mind off the surf shop and the ranch.

"Getting her hair done. This girl we met is going to do it
for her. Punk."

He nodded, looking around the room. It was small and
cluttered, like his own. The apartment consisted of one room
together with a tiny kitchenette and a bathroom. The girls had
rigged up a curtain to divide the main room. Jill apparently
slept on a large, ragged couch, while Michelle had a mattress
on the floor. Some pictures from pornographic magazines had
been stuck to the wall over Michelle's mattress. She noticed
him looking at the pictures and smiled. She took a file from the
windowsill and began to fiddle with her nails. He saw that her
nails had been painted a bright red and all of a sudden she was
beginning to seem more like the Michelle he had known before the party. He couldn't think of a fucking thing to say. A
long evening filled with awkward silences was beginning to
yawn before him.

"Got any dope?" Michelle wanted to know.

Ike shook his head.

"I'm growing a plant. Want to see it?"

Ike said that he did. He finished eating and got up to rinse
his hands at the sink.

Michelle led him past the curtain, to a windowsill near her
mattress where several tiny marijuana plants grew in plastic
cups. She touched one of the frail green leaves with her finger
and laughed. Ike tried to look interested.

There was a rattling at the front door and Ike turned to
see Jill walk into the room. She had gotten her hair done, all
right. It was shorter than Ike's. He suspected for a moment
that she had driven to San Arco and let his grandmother do it.
It looked shorter on one side than on the other and a patch of it
had been bleached out to an ugly shade of orange. Michelle

said it looked all right, though. The two girls stood in the bathroom inspecting it from all angles in the light of a naked bulb. Jill had heard about a party somewhere and she was hot to go try out her new haircut. "They're gonna have a live band," she told them, and Ike could see that Michelle wanted to go too. She looked at him, but he pretended not to notice. Finally she told Jill that they were going to a movie. Jill shrugged. "Suit yourself," she said, but made it plain she considered it a very boring thing to do.

They left the apartments in silence and started for the theater. Ike had the feeling that Michelle was somewhat pissed about missing out on the party. They didn't hold hands as they had done the night before and he felt slightly awkward walking beside her, unable to think of anything to say, beginning to wonder if she was the one who was different tonight or if it was him. Last night he had been half drunk, and stoned. Perhaps his judgment had been impaired. Or maybe it was like the line in that song—one of the many country songs he had been forced to listen to again and again in back of Gordon's market—the part about how the girls all get prettier at closing time. It was a depressing thought.

"Marsha says she knows you from someplace," Michelle said. They were about halfway between the Sea View apartments and the Curl Theater.

"Marsha?"

"She works with me. She was there today, when you came by. She says she's seen you before."

Ike thought now of the girl he had seen at the drive-thru window, the one who'd been staring. Somehow, going to the shop had made him forget about her. "I don't see how," he said. "Was she ever in San Arco?"

"I don't know. I don't think so. She thinks she knows you from around here."

"Can't be."

"Then you look like somebody. She says she either knows you or you look like somebody."

"Who?"

"She didn't say."

There was a small line at the Curl. Ike and Michelle waited, standing in silence once more. Ike thought about the girl at the taco stand. Michelle walked away from him to look over the posters for coming attractions posted behind the glass frames at the front of the building. Ike wished there were a way he could split right now, go see that girl again, ask her who it was he looked like. And he wanted to see Barbara, too. He began to get nervous standing there, like he was wasting time, like maybe he and Michelle did not belong together anyway and that asking her out had been a mistake.

The funny thing was, the film was so good that after it began he practically forgot about everything. He might have even forgotten he was with Michelle, except that she kept saying things out loud. It was a very annoying habit. In any other theater it would have been even worse, but the Curl was a fairly noisy place anyway, the crowd hooting and cheering for the more spectacular rides. Still, Ike found Michelle's talking annoying. She acted as if no one had ever taken her to a damn theater before.

Ike didn't say anything. He kept his mouth shut and watched the screen. He had never seen anything like some of the waves in the film. There was footage from all over the world, places like Australia, New Zealand, Bali. The waves were like those he had seen at the ranch, empty, perfect, and he thought back to that plugged-in feeling he had found there. He recalled the sight of Preston seated above a black sea, arm raised in greeting. A liquid barrel gone amber in the setting sun filled the screen, gone hollow and riderless, blowing spray thirty feet in the air. And there was no way to explain it to someone who didn't know.

He had planned, toward the end of the film, to take Michelle directly home, to turn in early and see Barbara the first thing in the morning. They were on their way out of the lobby when Michelle spotted Hound Adams. He was with the blond-haired man Ike had seen just that afternoon, in the shop. Michelle went to them before Ike could stop her, and began to talk. Hound Adams, of course, had dope and Ike soon found himself out on the sidewalk, headed toward the north end of town. They took a route almost identical to the one Hound took the night Ike followed him home from the beach. Before leaving the theater, however, Hound Adams introduced Michelle and Ike to the man he was with and Ike shook hands with Frank Baker.

Hound and Michelle did most of the talking on the way home. Ike had the feeling that Frank was not particularly pleased to have company. He went off to some other part of the house when they got there and Ike did not see him again. Ike and Michelle wound up seated once more on Hound's living room floor. And once again Ike got the feeling that Hound was coming on to Michelle. He seemed to find reasons for touching her, for putting his hand on her forearm or knee. And Ike felt himself growing angry about it. It was crazy. Only a short while before, he'd been telling himself he would not ask her out again and now he was jealous. It didn't make sense.

Hound talked about the movie, and about Mexico. "Remember what I told you?" he asked, turning to Ike. "About the desert, how there is an energy there, just as there is an energy in the sea, a rhythm? It's like surfing can plug you into that rhythm if you learn to let it. But notice I said learn. We're taught to think with our heads too much of the time. We get out of touch with other areas of perception, other ways of seeing." He paused for a moment and took a hit off the pipe. "That's one of the good things about Mexico," he continued. "A combination of both, the desert and the sea, a blend of rhythms. It always seems strange at first, when I go there from here. It takes me a few days to adjust, two or three; but it's a necessary adjustment. Mexico is also a great place for doing mushrooms. Have you ever done any?" He looked at both Michelle and Ike, then shifted his weight and smiled. "They have two kinds in this village. Derumba and San Ysidro, those are the names. San Ysidro is the stronger of the two."

Hound paused for another toke on the pipe and Ike glanced at Michelle. He could see that she was hanging on every word. Hound Adams went on to relate a number of mystical experiences with the powerful San Ysidro. He spoke of the morning he both surfed and watched himself surf, and of the time he looked into the sea through the transparency of his own flesh.

"I want to go," Michelle said suddenly, interrupting Hound in one of his stories. Hound smiled and leaned forward to place the pipe in the middle of the circle, holding his hair back from his face with one hand as he did so. "You should. And so should you," he said, looking at Ike. "You can learn things about surfing down there it would take you years to learn up here."

Ike nodded. Michelle had put her hand on his leg and he could feel the heat of her palm burning through his jeans. He was thinking now about the ranch, about how he had felt up there and how it was like there was some crazy bit of truth in the things Hound Adams said, but that somehow talking about it didn't seem to work. It was as if Hound was putting on a show for them, and Ike couldn't help but wonder what Preston would think of it, or even if Hound would say the same kinds of things if he weren't talking to a couple of kids half his age.

"By the way," Hound said. "You found your stick yet, Ike?"

Ike said that he hadn't.

"You remember my offer?"

Ike said that he did, and Hound had launched himself into another description of Mexico when he was cut short by the ringing of a phone. He was gone for several minutes and when he returned, Ike could see right away that something was wrong. Hound was no longer smiling and the skin seemed to

be stretched tighter across the bones of his face. He looked
suddenly older and harder than he had looked only moments
before. "That was Terry Jacobs's brother," he said in a flat
voice. "Terry just died."

20

Ike and Michelle stood in the hallway, as they had the night
before. It seemed to Ike that the building was spinning
slightly, tilting first one way and then the other, the naked
bulbs throwing narrow shafts of light into the hot, spinning
darkness. His knees felt weak and he could not tell if it was
because he was nervous with Michelle or because he could not
forget the look on Hound's face as he announced Terry's
death.

Once again she invited him in, and once again he hesitated. "Okay," she said, "I'll come to your room, then. You
can't get away two nights in a row." She laughed. Her face
appeared flushed, perhaps a trifle wild. He noticed a small
drop of perspiration near her upper lip. She was standing with
one hand on the doorknob, the other on her hip. Her hands
were rather large, and strong, like a boy's, except that the skin
was smooth and soft to the touch. He watched her hands
because it was easier than meeting her eyes, and he thought
about his room, the pile of dirty clothes, the sack of garbage he
had forgotten to take out.

"There's beer in the refrigerator," she said. "Come on."

He followed her into the room, which seemed even
smaller and stuffier now than it had earlier. Jill was not around.

"You have to sit on the bed," she told him. "It's the only
comfortable spot."

He seated himself at one end of the mattress and watched
as Michelle went to the refrigerator for the beer. When she

returned, she sat the bottles on the floor near his feet. She then walked past him and took a candle from the windowsill. She placed the candle on the floor and lit it, killed the overhead light, and drew the curtain that divided the room. Immediately everything was changed. The room seemed close and hot. The soft yellow flame jumped in the darkness, creating strange shifting patterns of shadow and light, dancing in the black glass of the window. She sat close beside him so that their shoulders were just touching and he could feel the heat from her body. He drank the beer quickly. It was cold and he could feel it burn all the way down. He put his hand on the bed, just behind her, his arm held straight, and she leaned back against it. He looked into her face, at her small, perfectly shaped mouth, the high cheekbones. She held his eyes with her own and he could see the light of the candle in her eyes, in the small dark spot that was the scar left by the stick. He focused on that dark spot, watched it moving ever so slightly, growing suddenly larger as she leaned toward him, and then her lips were against his. He tasted her breath, her tongue. They lay back together on the mattress and he felt like he was falling. He felt the way he had felt going down the face of that first wave at the ranch. Out of control. It was crazy to think about this being the same girl he had been so annoyed with at the show. He lay beside her, kissing her, her mouth, her neck, her eyelids, and then suddenly it was like the fall was over and he was just there, beside her, freezing up. He lay very still and he could hear her heart, feel his own beating against her arm. A long moment passed before she began to squirm at his side. She took him by the shoulder and rolled him away from her, as if she wanted to get a good look at him from arm's length. "I've never met a boy like you," she said.

"I'm sorry."

"Why?"

"Well . . ." He paused. "I mean, I know what you want but I don't think I can."

"Why not?"

"I don't know."

She pulled him back down beside her. "I guess there weren't many girls out there in the desert," she said.

He shook his head. "No."

"And so you've never had a girl friend?"

He hesitated. He could feel the blood in his face and when he closed his eyes it was like the red dust of San Arco lay in back of his lids, making them dry and scratchy. "One," he said. "There was this one girl. But she moved away." He could feel her watching him, feel her not believing his story.

"It must have been lonely when she left."

He nodded again. "Yes," he said, "it was." He was looking at the ceiling now and he could not remember feeling this miserable in some time, useless, the way he had felt that first day in town when the bikers laughed at him. Shit. If he couldn't fuck and couldn't fight, he didn't see how he was ever going to amount to anything. He imagined Gordon staring down on him from where the sky should be, his big red face wagging from side to side, then turning to spit in the dust.

Michelle was propped up on one arm now, her jaw resting in her hand. "I guess it was just the opposite for me. I mean, I was like getting it on before I was thirteen." She seemed to think about that for a moment. "Didn't you and this girl ever mess around?"

He shrugged. "Once."

"Once?" He could hear her laugh. "I'm sorry," she said. "I mean, I'm not making fun of you. But once?"

"She moved away."

"That's right. And then it was just you and your sister again. Out there in the middle of all that nothing.

"Well," she asked him after another pause, "did you like it?"

"What?"

"What you did. With your long-lost love?"

He turned his face to look at her and saw that she was smiling, but it was the way she had smiled at him that day he passed her on the lawn, not snotty but real.

"Maybe you just need some more practice," she said. "And you know what?"

He said he didn't.

"I'm not going to let you get out of here until you fuck me."

She slipped off the mattress and bent to blow out the candle, then straightened to pull her T-shirt up and over her head, to toss it away. And when she stood up to unbutton her pants, there was just the moonlight coming through the ancient glass of the window, finding one side of her face, her breasts that were small and round, and incredibly white where the bathing suit had kept them from the sun, and after she had stepped out of her pants and lay back down beside him, he could have sworn that she looked as pure as any angel in that soft light coming through the glass. He ran his hands along her legs, across the cool places beneath her thighs, and later, when he lay down between them and she guided him inside and he felt the heat of her body and her arms closing around him, he shut his eyes and felt the hot red dust of the desert rising to choke him and he thought that somewhere, out of a musty past, while his body rocked on in the present to some rhythm of its own, he could hear the old woman call his name. And the voice was filled with surprise, with pain and anger.

21

She slept for a while. Her skin was warm and soft next to his own and it was very nice just to lie there, in the darkness, listening to her breathing beside him. He must have dozed himself, for a time, because he was aware of waking, of having to remind himself that it had really happened, that he was in fact here, her leg thrown out to cover both of his, her breath against his neck, her fingers on his chest. It was a pleasant discovery. He shifted his weight some and she stirred beside him. "Are you awake?" she whispered. He said that he was. She laughed at something. Her fingers slipped down to his stomach.

"Will you do me a favor?" he asked.

"Like what?" He could hear a certain amount of amusement in her voice.

"Like finding out from your friend who it is that I'm supposed to look like."

"Are you serious?"

He said that he was.

He felt her fingers pressing against him. "You're a funny boy," she said. He turned toward her, finding her mouth with his own.

He woke again early. Michelle was still asleep, on her back now, her mouth open, one arm swung up above her head, one breast peeking out of the sheet into the gray light. The contentment he had experienced earlier came back easily and he devoted some time to watching her, and to a study of the room. It was, he decided, one of the strangest rooms he had seen. Half of it was like something you might expect to find in a whorehouse, the other half belonged to a young girl. The closet was a good example, tall and narrow with a series of narrow shelves, one above the other. On one shelf a pair of black fishnet stockings lay piled on top of a catcher's mitt. On another a pair of red high-heeled shoes sat next to a pair of white tennis shoes with faded initials on the backs. There was a tiny dresser next to the bed that held a small collection of perfume bottles and makeup jars, as well as a picture of a girl's softball team. Above the dresser there was a photograph of two people getting it on, and beneath the picture were a series of cutout letters that said *Sooooo Hot.* Near the curtain was a decal that read *Chaste Makes Waste.*

In a way, she was like the room, a crazy mix. It had made her difficult to judge. She could change quickly. She could seem very young one minute—younger even than her sixteen years—and the next minute she could appear very strong, and more knowledgeable than he had guessed. And it wasn't just that she was more sexually experienced. It was more than that. It was something deeper. It was what made him feel good about being with her.

He continued to look over the room for some time, to think about the night. Michelle continued to sleep. He tried to imagine what it would be like if this were all there was: sun-baked days in the cool shadows of the pier. Clean lefts. Fine nights in Michelle's bed. And it seemed to him that for just a moment he achieved that—or something like it. It seemed to him that for an instant he was totally alone with this moment, immersed in it, free of the confusion of the desert. It was a fleeting perception, and when it was gone the contentment of only moments before seemed to vanish as well. What replaced it was an image of Hound Adams's face—as it had been when he announced Terry's death. The face seemed to enter with the sunlight through a single narrow window and spread until it had filled the room.

At last Ike slipped from the bed and began to look for his clothes. He shivered above the cold linoleum as he dressed, then went to the sink and washed his face—as quietly as possible, so as not to wake Michelle. When he was done, he came back to look at her once more. She was still asleep, but turned on her side now, leaving her hair spread out behind her, a delicate fan upon the sheet. He would have liked to touch her, to smooth the hair where it curled about her temples with his fingers, but something stopped him. He went instead to the door and let himself out, closing it softly behind him.

It was cold and still dark in the hallway. A draft entered from the stairwell and traveled the length of the building. He stopped at his own room long enough to change shirts and then he was back outside, warming as he walked, on his way to Preston's duplex. He was thinking hard this morning about that mansion above the point, its connection with the surf shop on Main Street. And Barbara had once mentioned something about a scrapbook. He wanted a look. He walked quickly, his eyes glued to the pale concrete before him, still trying to shake that image of Hound Adams's face that had destroyed his morning.

Preston's duplex faced the east and it was bright and warm on the porch when he got there. Barbara did not look good. Her face was pale and somewhat blotched; there were dark circles under her eyes. She did not look particularly pleased to see him, but then she didn't look pissed about it either. She mainly just looked tired. She invited him in. She was dressed in what he guessed was one of Preston's flannel shirts. The shirt came down to just above her knees and the sleeves were rolled into big wads above her elbows. He sat in the kitchen while she made coffee. She looked tired and small and there was something about sitting there watching her that made him feel guilty about having come. He thought of his night with Michelle and he wondered if it had ever been that way for Barbara and Preston too.

Barbara had already heard about Terry's death. He asked her about Preston and she told him that there were still no witnesses. Apparently, Hound Adams had even told the police he did not think Preston had done the knifing, that someone else had been involved and had escaped out the back. She also said that the police had been unable to find a weapon, and that Preston should be out soon. "He may be out already," she told him, "for all I know."

"But wouldn't he have come by here?"

"Not necessarily; he might be at the shop."

"I'm afraid they just want him on the street," he said, and he told her about seeing some of Terry's family. She seemed shocked by the news, as if she hadn't guessed why no one was talking, and he immediately felt stupid for having mentioned it.

They sat for a while in silence, Ike staring at the scarred linoleum beneath his feet. "Listen," he said. "One of the reasons I came by this morning was because I wanted to ask you about something." He looked at her, and she stared back, her elbow resting on the table, a coffee cup in her hand. "You told me once about Hound and Preston having been partners. What do you know about that? I mean, do you know what happened between them?"

She got up and went to a cupboard over the refrigerator. She moved some things around and finally stepped back with a large, beat-up book, a kind of folder with cardboard covers, held together with a dark ribbon. "His scrapbook," she said. "He cleaned out a bunch of stuff when I moved in here with him and I found this in the trash." She placed the book on the table in front of Ike. "I don't know if you'll find anything in there that interests you, but you're welcome to look, because I really don't know anything about what you're asking. I don't know what happened, with Hound, with the business. I know they don't speak to one another now. I've been with Preston a couple of times when Hound Adams has showed up, I mean like on the street or something. They go by each other without even looking, like they're trying to pretend the other one is not there. It's strange, but I don't know what it's about."

Ike opened the cover and began leafing through the book. "You said Preston wasn't from around here, that he moved here by himself."

. She nodded. "He grew up someplace back of Long Beach, I believe. At least that's where his parents live now. His old man's a minister of some sort, if you can believe that."

"He tell you that?"

"Not voluntarily. When I moved in with him, he told me his parents were dead. Then one time this old lady called up here asking for him, saying she was his mother. I pestered him about it for a whole day and he finally admitted that his parents were alive. That was when he told me about his father being a minister. I asked him why he had told me they were dead and he just shrugged. You can't keep asking him about anything or he gets pissed off."

"I know," Ike said. There was some interesting stuff in the scrapbook. There were a few old pictures of the shop and he

could see that it had once been about half its present size—the
brick wall that now separated the showroom from the rest of
the building having once served as the storefront. In one photograph the wall was bare, in another it had been painted and
bore the shop's old logo—the wave within the circle and the
words *Tapping the Source.*

The book was also filled with shots of Preston, many cut
from the pages of surfing magazines, the same dark young
man Ike had seen in the photograph at the shop, and he could
understand now what Barbara had told him, that everyone
used to know who Preston was, and he guessed he could see
too why people had been surprised by the way he had
changed. Clean limbs and graceful moves. Mr. Southern California. There were no tattoos in the scrapbook. He was about
to turn one more page when a name caught his eye. The name
appeared in an ad for a surf film, an ad that read: *Senior
Nationals champ, Preston Marsh, in* Wavetrains, *a Milo Trax
surf film.* "This guy," Ike said, "Milo Trax. Is it the Trax who
owns the Trax Ranch?"

Barbara leaned over the table and stared at the name. "I
don't know. I don't think I ever noticed that before."

He told her about the photographs in the shop, described
Milo Trax as he looked in the pictures. She shrugged. "Doesn't
ring a bell, but then there was a time when a lot of weird
people started hanging out around that shop. I mean older
guys, city types, people who looked like they were from L.A.,
not the beach. I remember the place got to have a bad reputa-
tion. That was back when a lot of people were just getting into
drugs, that was part of it. Hound and Preston supposedly did a
lot of dealing then, made a lot of money. Like you would see
the two of them riding around town in brand new Porsches
and all that. I think Hound's still into it. He owns a number of
houses around here from what I've heard, and you don't make
that kind of money running a shop."

"What about Preston?"

"His money? I don't know. Pissed it away. I think I told
you he was in the service. I remember that surprised a lot of

people. I think everybody figured Hound and Preston would be smart enough to get out of it, but I remember standing on the pier one day and hearing some girl say that Preston had gone into the Marines, that he was going to fight and that no one could believe how stupid that was. Then he was gone, and then he came home and that was when I met him and it was like I told you." She had been talking rather quickly and paused now for a breath, a sip of coffee. Ike continued to stare at the book. "There's a picture in the shop," he said. "A picture of Hound and Preston together, and there's a girl with them. Her name's Janet."

"Her name *was* Janet."

He raised an eyebrow.

"I'm assuming it was Janet Adams. Was she nice-looking?"

He nodded. "Hound's sister?"

"She's dead. It happened quite a while ago. I was still in high school at the time and I didn't know her. But I believe she OD'd or something. I remember it was drug-related and that was supposed to be a big deal."

Ike was silent for a moment. He found it an oddly disturbing piece of information. He thought back to the photograph at the shop, thinking of the girl's laughter, her hair caught on a breeze and swept to one side of her face. "Do you know any more about it?"

Barbara shook her head. "No. I didn't know her. It was a long time ago. I just remember the event, that everyone was so shocked to think that a girl like Janet had been on drugs." She paused for a moment, looking at the table. "Do you mind if I ask you something?" she asked. "Why are you so interested in all of this?"

Ike closed the book and shrugged. There was a moment in which he considered telling her, but then the moment passed and he had decided against it. "I don't know," he said, "I guess I'm just curious. I mean, you've talked about how different Preston used to be; haven't you wondered what made him change?"

She gave him a rather sour look, as if it were a stupid

question. "Sure, I've wondered about it. But he was gone a long time, two tours in Vietnam. I mean, a lot of people came back from that place changed."

"I guess I was thinking more about why he went in the first place, why he chucked the business. Maybe it had something to do with Janet Adams. You said he and Hound were into dealing."

Barbara got up and took the scrapbook from his hands, returned it to the cupboard. When she had closed the door, she leaned back against it, turning to face Ike. "Maybe," she said, "maybe it did. Six months ago I might have been more interested in thinking about it. Now it all seems beside the point, somehow. If someone doesn't care about himself, you begin to lose interest after a while."

Ike pushed himself away from the table and stood up. There was suddenly a lot of things he wanted to think about, and he wanted to be alone. Still, he wished there were something he could say to Barbara. There wasn't. He said good-bye, told her he would keep in touch, and she let him out the side door.

The sunlight was dancing on the sidewalk and houses seemed to float in the heat waves, like scraps of colored paper. He walked in the general direction of the town, scarcely paying attention to where he was going, thinking about what Barbara had told him. He kept seeing the girl in the photograph, one arm around Hound Adams, the other around Preston, and he was certain she was the key. The death of the girl was what had come between Preston and Hound. And somehow, though he could scarcely put his finger on a reason, he was certain Janet Adams had been the reason for the strange expression that had passed over Preston's face the day Ike had told him about his sister, shown him the scrap of paper with the names.

He was walking rapidly now, and before he knew it he was already downtown, walking toward Main along some shabby side street, past a collection of weedy lots and stray oil wells, a lone beer bar. He was almost at the entrance of the bar when Morris suddenly stepped out of the doorway and onto the sidewalk. Morris was wearing a trucker's hat with the bill turned around to the back and a set of wire-rimmed shades. He was wearing his sleeveless Levi jacket and looked to be fairly well crocked. He seemed to sway a bit in the bright light as Ike walked toward him, and there was something distinctly belligerent in the way he blocked the sidewalk, in the half-assed grin back of the matted blond beard. Yet somehow it seemed crazy to turn and run away. He knew Morris. He was being overly paranoid. Ike came a couple of steps closer and said hello.

Morris methodically removed the wire-rimmed shades, folded them with great care, and slipped them into the pocket of his jacket. He put his right fist into his left hand and popped a few knuckles. Ike took a step backward. Morris came after him, grinning broadly now, and swung.

It happened very quickly. Getting out of the way was somehow never even an issue. There was just this fist that dropped out of the heat and the sky went dark. Ike realized that he was suddenly on his back, but for a while nothing hurt. Everything was numb. He knew that there was blood on his face. It was very hard to focus his eyes. It was like he couldn't decide whether to be knocked out or not. His vision kept getting dark and then light and then dark again. Morris's big dirty face appeared above him and he was aware of a thick finger aimed at his chest. "I knew you'd fuck up," Morris said. He grabbed Ike by the front of the T-shirt and it looked like he was going to get hit again. He thought of the concrete behind his head. Then he heard someone else talking to Morris. "I thought you said you could knock him out, chump."

"Aw, man, I slipped."

"Bullshit."

Ike's vision had begun to clear slightly and he could now see the other figure standing behind Morris: Preston, dressed in the old tank top, the red bandanna wrapped around his head.

"Give me one more, man," Morris pleaded. "I'll fracture his fucking skull this time."

"Fuck it. You lost. You owe me a beer." Preston turned and went back into the bar. Morris released his hold on Ike's shirt. "Get the picture, queer bait?" Morris asked.

22

Once back in his room, Ike examined himself in the mirror. He'd bled all over everything. The punch had caught him flush over the right eye and there was a nasty-looking cut close to the brow. It was all puckered open and red with a thin piece of white showing. It made him sick looking at it and he puked in the sink. He packed some ice cubes in a towel and lay down, holding the ice to his head, which had at last begun to throb. He was too disoriented to think very hard. Mainly he felt betrayed and he did not know why. Had Morris said something to Preston about Ike and Barbara? Would Preston believe it if he had? But that was not it. There was something else and he did not know what it was.

He must have gone to sleep, because when he jerked his eyes open again he saw that the sky had turned red beyond the window. The room was dark and stuffy and stank of barf. The ice cubes had melted, soaking his shirt and pillow, but the bleeding seemed to have stopped. When he got up to open the window he nearly fell back down. He clutched at the bed and waited and finally got it done on the second attempt. After that he lurched to the door and opened that too, hoping for some kind of cross-ventilation. Then he lay back down. He lay there for what seemed like a long time, thinking, watching the sky go purple and then black, watching the moths flutter about the naked bulb in the hallway. There was something about that bulb, the whir of moths in the yellow light, the darkness beyond. He was reminded of the desert, of the hard-packed dirt back of Gordon's, the run-down porch where the night-light burned a hole out of the darkness, drawing insects from the whole town to ping in the metal shade.

He dozed again, thinking of the desert, and when he opened his eyes it was because Michelle was staring at him. She was standing just inside the doorway, dressed in her uniform. She had her hair pulled back in barrettes and he couldn't remember seeing her wear it that way before. It made her face seem rounder, not so grown up.

"I got hit," he said.

She turned on a light and bent down for a closer look, then she went to his dresser and fished around for a clean T-shirt and a pair of jeans. "Put these on," she said, and tossed them on the bed.

"Why?"

"Because I'm going to get Jill's car and drive you to the hospital."

"I don't have to go to the hospital."

"Yes, you do, you have to get stitches in that."

"I don't need stitches," he said. He was up on his elbows now, watching her heading out the door. She stopped and looked back at him. "Not if you want a big scar. Don't argue, okay? My mother's a nurse."

"Shit. You can't drive."

"I can too. Just get up and get your clothes on. Now." She closed the door behind her and he could hear her walking down the hall. He sat up on the edge of his bed and pulled off his shirt. He was still sitting there when she came back in. She finished dressing him. He took an absurd pleasure in watching her do it, in looking down on her hands, her arms that were just as big around as his own, perhaps stronger. When she had finished, he stood up and followed her outside.

Jill's car turned out to be a '68 Rambler, and Michelle wasn't too good with a stick shift. It was five or six miles to the hospital and she ground gears all the way. She took him to

Huntington Community, the same hospital they'd taken Terry Jacobs to the night of the fight.

The whole process wasn't as bad as Ike had expected. They sat him on a white table in a brilliantly white room and examined his head. When it had been cleaned and stitched, they gave him a shot and a prescription for some Nembutals.

As he stood at the counter waiting for the prescription, he had a clear view of the corridor that led back toward the entrance to the Emergency Room, and that was where he was when they came in. What he saw first was the ragged blend of grease-stained jeans and T-shirts, and that was enough to sap the strength from the backs of his legs. Because somehow, at once, he knew what had happened. And then he saw Barbara. She was holding a handkerchief to her face. He left the counter and started toward her. He walked down the narrow hallway, past gray doors, beneath fluorescent lights, Michelle pulling at his arm, Barbara looking up to see him, her eyes wide and bloodshot, but her voice flat and calm as she gave him the news: The Samoans had caught Preston at the shop, alone. Morris had been out for parts. Someone passing at the mouth of the alley had apparently seen the commotion and called the police. The phone call had probably saved his life, although there was a head injury, the extent of which was still not known. It had not been in time, however, to save his hands. His hands had been pushed into the lathe and he'd lost all his fingers, everything but the thumbs.

Ike felt numb on the way home. He felt paralyzed in the blackness that surrounded him. Michelle helped him out of the car and up to the room. The drug was working on him now too, and he lay on her bed as the room spun slowly around him. She lay down beside him and he felt her fingers, cool on his forehead. He listened to her telling him it would be okay, telling him how much she liked him. And then it was like it all seemed to come down on him at once. He staggered into her bathroom and shut the door. He stayed there, on his knees, until the light had begun to go gray, puking his guts into the sewers of Huntington Beach, giving the place something to remember him by.

23

Ike Tucker hid in his room for a week. He felt like he was the one who had had his head stove in and his fingers chopped off. He lay on his bed and watched the shadows change shapes on the ceiling. He stood at the window and studied the oil well and the birds through dirty panes of glass. Perhaps if he'd had his board, it would have been different. He missed the mornings in the water, and he thought back bitterly now on the trip to the ranch.

His only visitor was Michelle. She brought him food from work and tried to talk him into going outside. By the middle of the week the weather had turned particularly hot. "Why don't you go down to the beach?" she asked him. "You could at least cool off."

Ike shrugged as he stood at the window and watched some neighboring palms, unmoving in the still, hot air.

"You afraid you'll run into Morris?" She didn't ask him in a snotty way. Still, the question made him irritable.

"Those guys are assholes," she said. "Both of them. Morris and Preston."

"Not Preston."

"Jesus. What does it take? Why do you want to make a hero out of that guy? He's just another dumb-ass biker. Can't you see that?"

"No. I can't." He turned away from her to look back into the yard. "You don't know what the fuck you're talking about."

"Me? I don't know what I'm talking about? That's a good

one. Look, I'm sorry he got hurt. But he was standing right there when Morris hit you. You said he was. They were taking bets or something to see if Morris could knock you out."

He wished now he had never told her about seeing Preston at the bar. He just didn't know what to think. Perhaps there was some element of truth in what she said. Maybe he was warped by all that time in the desert, feeding fantasies with books, wanting a father he had never known, even trying for a time to make one of Gordon. Maybe all that was mixed up in it. Maybe he was even a secret faggot or some damn thing. But that was not the end of it; you couldn't just write it off to those kinds of things and it was wrong to try. What he knew for certain was that Preston was not just another dumb biker. She was wrong about that. But he did not try to tell her. He stood silently, staring into the still air until she came and stood beside him.

"Why don't you go downtown and talk to Hound? He told you to. You can get another board."

"Don't you understand?" he asked, turning to face her. "He was in on what they did to Preston."

"No, I don't understand. He let Morris hit you. He stabbed Hound's friend. He's just like all those other asshole bikers. I don't know why you want to hang around with him instead of Hound. And Hound likes you."

He let the remark about Preston go this time. "What makes you think Hound likes me?"

"I can tell. For one thing he calls you brother all the time."

"He calls everybody that."

"No, he doesn't."

Ike watched the oil well below, trying to decide if there was anything to what Michelle had said. She could be a difficult person to talk to sometimes, when she had her mind set on something. But then her stubbornness was connected to her strength, he supposed, and her strength was one of the things about her that he most admired. He thought again of how wrong his first impression of her had been. She was not a mindless chick. She was young. She was on her own. There

were a lot of things no one had ever told her. But she thought
about things. And she was tough. He had never heard her
complain. There was one decent pair of jeans in her closet, one
funky dress she had bought at a local thrift store, and yet she
had been the one to come up with money for Ike's medicine
when he was too fucked up to pay for it himself, never asking
to be paid back. And since he had been laid up he had learned
other things that contributed to his admiration of her toughness. He had gotten a glimpse into the kind of shit that a young
girl out on her own had to put up with—the sexual harassment
of employers, for instance, jerks who knew they could mess
with your head and that nothing would happen, that runaways
were not likely to go to the cops. At one job in particular—an
all-night doughnut shop—the manager had tried to rape her,
had pulled a knife on her and held it between her legs. She had
taken the blade with her hand and turned it away, stabbed at
his eyes with her nails, and run. She had shown Ike the long
white scar across one palm. And sometimes when she told him
things like that, he was reminded of Ellen. Especially that
business with the knife, grabbing the blade, that sounded like
something Ellen might have done. Ellen had been tough too,
he thought.

    This was running through his mind as he stood at the
window and suddenly he wanted Michelle to know about Ellen, about Hound Adams, about why he had come. He turned
from his view of the yard and went to the dresser. The sunlight
was coming through the window, falling across the battered
wood so that the handles on the drawer were hot to the touch.
As he slid the drawer open he saw the white scrap of paper
with the names on it. He looked back over his shoulder at
Michelle. "If I tell you something, can you keep it to yourself? I
mean, don't tell anybody, not Jill, not anyone?" He watched
her nod. He took the scrap from the drawer and passed it to
her. "It's about my sister."

    He told her the story as he had once told it to Preston
Marsh. He told her about the kid in the white Camaro, the trip

to Mexico with Hound Adams. She watched him as he spoke, holding the paper in her hand.

"So far the only person who knows any of this is Preston. I thought he was going to help me."

"You thought?"

He shrugged. "I don't know now. I don't know what he was doing. Preston's a funny guy. He's not always easy to talk to. Now I can't talk to him at all."

"I don't think funny is the right word," she said. After that she was quiet, staring at the floor. "So that's why you want to know who Marsha thinks you look like, who you remind her of?"

He nodded. "She might know something."

"But why would your uncle let you come by yourself? You said he was standing right there when the kid told you. Why didn't he want to do something?"

"Because he thinks Ellen is wild, that whatever happened to her was her own fault. Because he doesn't give a shit."

"Does he give a shit about you?"

"I don't know."

"He raised you."

"He figured out a way to get money from the state for it."

"For real?"

He nodded. "Ellen heard him talking about it once to my grandmother. She told me."

"Shit." Michelle shook her head. "That sounds like something my old lady would pull. He sounds like my old lady. She doesn't give a shit where I am. She thinks I'm wild too. But I'm nothing compared to her. You know what she was doing before I left? She was getting so bad she was trying to put the moves on every guy I brought by the house. When she wasn't working, she was lying around half naked every day. I came home from school one afternoon and caught her fucking this guy I had been going with. Can you believe that?"

Ike stopped to think about it. He thought back to that day Ellen had told him about Gordon getting the money and how it had made him feel. He wondered if it had been anything like the way Michelle had felt.

"So anyway," Michelle said. "Forget that. Screw your uncle and my old lady." She moved closer and leaned against him. "I know one thing," she said. "I like it that you came; I like it that you're like that."

He shifted beneath her arm, wondering just what it was that he was like, because he had, of course, not told her everything about Ellen. "And I will talk to Marsha," she was saying. "I can ask some other people, too. I'll help you." She seemed to be getting almost enthused over the idea.

"And wind up like Preston?"

"But you don't know that's what happened. You're not even sure he was trying to help you."

"Just don't go asking around too much. You know what I mean? Go slow."

"Yes," she said. "Yes. Yes. Yes." She let the words out slowly, with her breath, and rested her head back against his shoulder so that her face was close to his own. He raised a hand, letting his fingers slip through her hair, felt her breathing, inhaled the scent of her skin, and suddenly she was whispering once more, telling him once more that she was glad he had come, and that he was different, and that maybe she could help. And before he could protest again, she was saying some crazy thing about how he should get more exercise and how it was unhealthy just to lay around all day. And he was letting her undress him. Then he let her push him back on the bed and get on top, trying to be very still as she moved above him, to see how still he could be, to sink into the mattress as she pushed him deep into her, to watch the square of sunlight on her bare shoulder, to watch the dark spot on her eye, beneath the sleepy half-closed lid, as if she were rocking herself to sleep, all the time thinking about how crazy it was to be making love when there were so many things to think about, when it was so hot. Finally he put his arms around her and pulled her to him. She buried her face in his neck and he arched himself against her and the only sounds were the sounds their bodies made, pressed against each other, wet with sweat, and the squeaking of the old bed.

When they were finished, she rolled away from him and they lay side by side in the heat. They stayed that way for a long time while the light changed and the room took on the dark yellow glow of late afternoon. It was finally Michelle who spoke. "So what are you going to do," she asked, "after you find your sister? Go back to the desert?"

It seemed strange to hear her voice after the long silence. "I don't know," he said. It was odd, but he suddenly realized he had never given that much thought.

"You must want to do something. Work on bikes. Have your own shop."

"I don't know. Not that, I guess."

"Then what?" She was back up on one elbow now, watching him.

He shrugged, thinking now of what Preston had said at the ranch. "Travel maybe. Surf."

"You like it that much?"

He nodded. "So what about you? What do you want?"

"Traveling would be nice, see things I never have."

"What then?"

She didn't answer right away. She moved her shoulders and lay back down beside him. "You won't laugh?"

"No."

"I'd like to train horses."

He was quiet.

"You think that's dumb?"

"No."

"My mother thought it was dumb."

"Do you know anything about them?"

"I can learn. You think I can't."

He shook his head.

"You sounded like you think I can't."

"No. You can. I think you can. If you want to."

They were both quiet again after that. Ike watched the

light on their bare legs. He felt slightly paralyzed in a pleasant
sort of way. The room turned orange, and then a kind of soft
rose as the sun moved toward the sea somewhere beyond the
window. Michelle left the bed and went to the sink for a drink
of water. When she came back, she sat on the edge. Ike
watched her profile in the soft red light. "It probably is crazy,"
she said.

"What?"

"The horses. That's supposed to be what all little girls
want to do, isn't it? Dumb."

He pulled himself up and took her by the shoulder. Something about the way she said it made him mad. "Screw that,"
he told her. "You're young. You can do whatever you fucking
well want to." Saying that, he reminded himself of Preston. It
was what Preston had said to him.

By the end of the week it was time to get the stitches
pulled and Ike had to leave his room. Michelle was at work and
he rode the bus to the hospital by himself. It was the first time
all week that he had been out and he expected to find Morris
waiting around every corner.

He had planned to see Preston when they were finished
with the stitches, but when it was time his nerve failed him.
Still, he hung around the hospital, hoping perhaps that it
would prove to be only a momentary loss of courage. He went
into the bathroom and looked at himself in the mirror. The
new scar was over his right eye, close to the eyebrow, however, and barely noticeable. He was hoping it would make him
look tougher, less like a goddamn pretty boy, which is exactly
what his sister had once told him he was. His appearance had
changed in other ways, though. His hair was much longer now,
thick and wavy, brown but with places that had been streaked
nearly blond by the sun. He wore it parted in the middle, and
it was long enough to cover his ears. His skin was darker and
he thought that he looked a little heavier in the arms and
shoulders, like maybe all that paddling was doing him some
good. He was still pretty scrawny, there was no getting around

that, but he looked better. Or maybe it was just that he looked more like the rest of Huntington Beach, not so much like a hick anymore, and he wondered if Michelle would've started liking him if he hadn't changed, if he hadn't started looking like every other surfer around the pier. Funny how important those things seemed around here, the necessity to look like something, a punk, a surfer, a biker, anything, so long as it wasn't a fucking hick.

He stood around in the bathroom for a fairly long time. He kept thinking about Preston, standing in the doorway of that bar, behind Morris. He was not angry about it so much as he was confused. He could not shake the feeling that he was at fault in some way, that he had brought all this upon himself, though he could not think of what it was that he had done. At last he walked outside and down the hall to a nurse's station.

The nurse at the counter was a fat woman with brittle red hair sticking out from beneath her cap, and Ike found himself thinking about Michelle's mother as the nurse ran a finger down a list of names, looking for Preston's. He wondered if this one got her kicks out of boozing and putting the moves on sixteen-year-old dudes. "Two fourteen," she said without looking at him, and then led him to the end of the hallway, to a cart covered with dressing gowns and surgical masks. There was a heavy gray door there and a small red light on the wall. "You'll have to put these on before you go in," she told him. "He has an infection in one of his hands. And you'll only be able to stay a short time. He's had surgery, you know. Just the day before yesterday. They had to put a plate in his head."

Ike put the gown on over his T-shirt and jeans, then the mask and gloves. He felt awkward wearing them. It was hot beneath the mask. The nurse opened the door and he walked into the room. It seemed cooler inside and there was much less light. There were three beds in the room, but two of them were empty. Preston was in the bed farthest from the door. He looked asleep. Ike walked quietly across the room. Preston's hands were outside the blankets, palms down alongside his body. One hand was lightly bandaged, the other was wrapped in some kind of plastic and there was a plastic tube running out of the bandages toward the floor on the opposite side of the bed.

There was a pale green cap on Preston's head and there were the white edges of bandages showing beneath the cap. The face was nearly unrecognizable. The skin around both eyes was black and puffy and there were stitch marks across the bridge of his nose. Ike sat down heavily in the stiff green chair nearest the bed. He looked across the body of his friend toward the venetian blinds that covered the window, the faint patterns of light which spread from their edges. The room smelled of medicine, and Ike adjusted the mask. He could feel himself sweating beneath it. When he looked again toward Preston's face, he saw that Preston's head was turned some on the pillow now and he seemed to be watching Ike with one eye. The white of the eye was a dark red, so it was hard to see where the white ended and the pupil began. Ike was suddenly afraid that he was going to burst into tears, or be sick on the floor. His throat felt hot and tight. Before he could say anything, though, Preston had turned his face back toward the ceiling.

Ike stood up. He felt the room spinning slowly around him. He took a step forward and put a hand on Preston's arm. The arm felt thick and hard beneath his palm. The sleeves of Preston's gown had been rolled up just above the elbows and Ike could see the tattoos going down into the bandages. Preston didn't say anything and he didn't turn his head. It was hard to tell if Preston was looking at him or not. Ike squeezed Preston's arm. "I'm sorry," he said.

Preston swallowed. He did it like it was something that took a lot of effort. He blinked and Ike could see there was water at the corners of his eyes. He felt his own eyes getting hot and gritty. There was a lump in his throat and he knew that he was not going to say anything more. "I'll see you," he mumbled. "I'll be around." When he had left the room, he tore off the gloves and mask, wadded them with the gown, and

threw the whole mess against a wall. An orderly watched him
with a disapproving eye but said nothing. Ike stared back, then
stomped off down the hallway, through the heavy doors and
into the blinding sun.

24

"You were right about Marsha," Michelle told him. It was still
midday. He had been home from the hospital for about an
hour. "She says you look like this girl she worked with at a
dress shop. She says the girl's name was Ellen. I asked her if she
knew anything about where Ellen might be. She said no. She
said she'd heard Ellen left town. But I was thinking, maybe we
could go by the dress shop, talk to the . . ."

"Forget the dress shop."

She stopped and looked at him. "What do you mean?"

"I mean fuck it. So we go to the dress shop and the owner
says, 'Oh, yeah, Ellen Tucker. She doesn't work here anymore.
I think she left town.' So big fucking deal. Nobody knows
anything, Michelle. Nobody knows any more than I do. That's
why that kid drove all the way to the desert looking for Ellen's
family, because he couldn't find anything out either, and he
lived here. You see what I mean? It's Hound Adams. Hound
Adams and Frank Baker. The only way I'm ever going to find
out anything is to get close enough to hear it from them.
Everything else is a waste of time."

Michelle had sat down on the edge of the bed. She'd
crossed her legs and was jiggling one foot, staring at the end of
her shoe. "And so how are you going to do it?"

"I'm going to start by taking Hound up on his offer. I'm
going down there and see about a board." He paused. "I don't
know after that." He stopped and popped one fist against an

open palm. "Fucking Hound Adams, man. Why does he want
to give me a board?"

"I told you, maybe he likes you."

"Or maybe he likes you. Or maybe it's something else. I
have this idea that Hound knows damn well I was at the ranch
with Preston. It's like he's playing some fucking game."

He watched her for a moment, but she didn't say anything
and he turned and walked to the window. "Maybe Preston was
right," he heard her say. "Maybe you should just leave." She
paused. "I could go with you."

He shook his head. The trouble was that now, for the first
time since he'd climbed onto that damn bus with the old
woman yelling at him from the darkness, he was something
besides scared. First they'd taken his sister. Now they had
fucked up his friend. It was not right that he should be so
fucking helpless. And he was not going to leave it at that. He
said as much to Michelle. She continued to study her shoe, her
face smooth and pale in the sunlight. Finally she looked up at
him. "Hard guy," she said. "Just be careful."

He went that afternoon. And he found Hound Adams
seated on a bench out in front of the shop, talking to a couple
of young girls. They were dressed in these one-piece suits with
holes and crazy angles in them so you could see a lot of skin.
The girls seemed to be doing most of the talking. Ike could see
their mouths moving, expressions changing. As he got closer
he could hear their laughter. Hound Adams seemed to be
finding some amusement in their company. He was smiling
and when Ike got close enough, Hound turned the smile on
him. He gestured toward the end of the bench, inviting Ike to
sit down. Ike sat. "Got a little business to take care of now with
my man," Hound told the girls after introducing them to Ike.
The girls scampered away. Ike joined Hound in watching their
skinny asses disappear in the heat. When they were gone,
Hound looked back at Ike. "What can I do for you?" he asked.

Ike met Hound's eyes with his own. Hound's eyes were a
deep shade of brown, almost a black. They reminded Ike of

those dark polished stones people sold for souvenirs in the desert—agates, they were called. "You said something about a board."

Hound nodded. The slightly bemused smile seemed to widen almost imperceptibly. He turned a palm toward the open door of the shop, then he rose and went inside. Ike stood and followed.

It was cool in the shop. Frank Baker stood behind the glass counter. He watched them come in without changing expression, then bent to sort through some boxes at his feet. Ike made eye contact but had read nothing there, not even recognition. Now he stood just in back of Hound Adams and slightly to his side as Hound waved toward the rack of new boards. "Take your pick," Hound told him.

The boards were arranged by length, going from the longer boards, the nose riders and rounded pins, down to the twin fins and knee riders. "Check out the used boards, too, if you like," he heard Hound say, and he turned to look across the room. He saw almost at once the nose rider he had used at the ranch. It had been cleaned up and leaned against the wall with the other used boards. He thought back to the conversation he had had with Michelle only a short time ago. Cat and mouse with Hound Adams. He looked away quickly, hoping that his face had not lost its composure. He thought about Preston, on his back in that room that smelled of medicine, and his anger held. He went to the rack and pulled a rounded pintail from it. He placed it on the ground and stepped back, sighted down the tail toward the nose, as he'd seen Preston do the day they got the other board. When he bent at the waist to do the sighting, he noticed that Frank Baker had come out from behind his counter and was watching, standing as he had the last time Ike was in the shop, with his arms folded across his chest.

The board was a single fin, pale blue with white pinstriping on the deck. Hound Adams looked at it with him. "It's a nice stick," Hound said. "But I think you could go for something a little shorter." He walked down the rack and pulled out another single fin, also a rounded pin but with wingers. "This board will still give you some stability in the wave, but it won't be quite as stiff. The blue board is a little bit gunney. But you can try them both, as far as that goes. Take the one you think works the best."

Ike looked at the price tags taped to the rails. Both boards were well over two hundred dollars. "What about the money?" He was getting very low and soon he would have to find something to do.

"I said we could work something out. It's up to you, brah. Hard to learn much without a stick."

"I'm out of work right now," Ike told him.

"So I've heard. The man with the machines. But there are other ways of making a living in this town without having your face stuck in an engine all day long. Look, why don't you take one of the boards now. Come and surf with us tomorrow, see what you think. Then we can talk payment."

It seemed to Ike as he stood in the shop, the boards at his feet, that Hound Adams was different than he had seen him before, somehow more businesslike today, less the guru. He looked down at the board Hound had suggested. It was a clean stick, the more expensive of the two, an airbrush job with a deck that went from bright yellow at the nose, through a nicely blended rainbow of colors, to a red tail. He picked it up and tested the weight beneath his arm and it felt like it belonged there. He looked once more toward the rear of the shop, toward the used boards and wet suits, the photographs that he knew hung there but could not see from this angle, and he found himself wondering when the shop had dropped the *Tapping the Source* logo, for the new boards were marked with a sort of squiggly V shape and the words *Light Moves*.

Ike carried the board to the front of the shop. He was aware of both Frank and Hound watching him. "So let's see you out there with it, brah. Tomorrow. We'll get some waves together." It was Hound who spoke and he was grinning broadly now. He walked Ike to the door and raised a hand in farewell. Ike held up his own free hand as he stepped out onto the sidewalk. He looked past Hound, into the shop, and he could see that Frank Baker was still at the counter, his arms still folded. Frank, Ike noticed, was not smiling.

When Ike reached the Sea View, Michelle had already left for work and the room was empty. He wondered if she would see Marsha today, and if they would talk. And he wondered if he had been right in telling her. But it was done now. And something else was done as well. He had taken the board from Hound Adams. It had begun. He placed the board on his bed and walked around the room, examining it from all angles. It was definitely, with the exception of a big chopped hog waiting for him in the desert, the flashiest thing he had ever owned.

25

Ike was up early the following morning. He passed through the streets of downtown Huntington Beach, his board under his arm, walking to meet the dawn patrol, to surf with them for the first time. Above the Golden Bear and the Wax Factory the beginnings of a sunrise spread into the sky. Thin strips of blue fused with yellow. Hard lines of color against the gray. And he found the sunrise repeated in every thrift-store window, in the dark plate glass of every parked car, until all of Main Street was alive with it.

As he walked he listened to the crack of waves beyond the highway, tried to guess size and swell direction by the sound, counted out the intervals between reports. He passed the Club Tahiti, the wide gaping alleys, at last the highway itself. He paused for a moment at the top of the concrete steps, staring down across the empty reaches of sand, and the rush, as always, was there. It came with his first glimpse of swell lines running from the horizon, the collision of sea and sky, the great pure source against whose edge the town was nothing but a speck, a tiny soiled mark on the face of eternity.

The swell, which had been light and out of the west for the past few days, had given way in the night to a much stronger swell out of the southwest. The waves were overhead, bigger than anything he had surfed at Huntington. He watched them as he came down the steps. He could see the dawn patrol already out, jockeying for position near the pier. The waves were not that much bigger than those he'd surfed with Preston on the first day at the ranch, but it was a different kind of surf. The ranch waves had come off a point. There had been long shoulders and a path to the outside. But this was day one of a strong swell. The waves came in long, pumping lines. Hollow grinders that hit like trucks. He was still without a wet suit and he shivered as he knelt in the wet sand to fasten his leash. He guessed he was ready for it, but he was wrong.

He made his first mistake that morning before even getting in the water. For some strange reason he would later be unable to recall, he crossed beneath the pier and entered the water on the south side, about fifty yards down the beach, having failed to calculate the power with which the swell was pushing from that direction. After about fifteen minutes of hard paddling he was still not outside but getting dangerously close to the pilings. The old pier, for which he had developed a certain affection, was suddenly an ominous presence. He was close enough to see the hairline cracks, the pigeon shit and moss—and the sound of the white water sweeping back through the concrete corridor formed by the pilings was like a barrage of cannon fire.

Far above him he could see the impassive faces of half a dozen fishermen watching his progress. The dawn patrol was still a good thirty yards beyond him and he was profoundly aware of being stuck in this thing alone. And it was just about at that point that he saw what he had been dreading, a full-on clean-up set moving off the horizon and there was no way he was going to make it. He kept his arms going for the simple reason that he didn't know what else to do, but there was no feeling left in his hands. Caught among the pilings, bound to his board by his leash. He could see it all now. They would have to send him back to San Arco in a shoe box.

He was almost beneath the pier when the first wave of the set reached him. He started up the face, watched the lip curling above him as a concrete column rose at his side. He swung out wildly with his left arm and, with his right arm braced against the deck of his board, actually used the piling to push himself through the lip. And then he was down, in the trough between waves still being sucked backward by the first wave, but for the first time that morning doing the right thing and paddling like mad for the north side of the pier, hoping to make it through before the next wave hit him. And he did, barely. He popped out on the north side just in time to get caught in the lip of the second wave and sucked over the falls, driven down with such force he felt like his balls had been kicked up inside him, but he had escaped the pier.

The wave held him down for a long time, and when he finally did resurface, still caught in the white water, moving north and toward the beach, he'd managed to lose most of his enthusiasm for this particular swell. He was back on the beach, seated on the nose of his board, when he caught sight of Hound Adams walking toward him out of the water. Hound was dressed in a pair of blue trunks and the dark vest Ike had never seen him surf without.

Hound put his board down next to Ike's and sat with him. "Chew you up and spit you out?" he asked.

"I guess."

"You started out on the wrong side of the pier, brah. Let's rest a minute, then we'll go out together. I'll show you the way."

Ike came close to refusing the invitation, but it was a little like having Preston waiting for him after that first wave at the ranch. At last they stood and Ike followed Hound back to the water's edge. "It's a state of mind," Hound told him as the white water reached their feet. "These waves demand a certain commitment. Once you've picked a wave, don't let yourself think about anything else, don't doubt what you can do. Paddle as hard and fast as you can. You'll get into the wave faster and with more control. Don't hold back. Be part of it. Understand?"

Ike nodded and followed Hound into the water. The sun was just coming up behind them now, charging the sky with a fine yellow light that seemed to hang above the sand in a golden mist. Above the water, tiny rainbows appeared in the spray blown back from the lips of the waves, and beneath the pier there was an incredible play of light and shadow, a seemingly infinite progression of blues and greens shot through with the rays of the sun.

It was easier getting out this time. Ike stuck in Hound's tracks. They stayed on the north side of the pier—maybe ten yards out, their boards angled toward it at forty-five degrees—and soon Ike was back outside, moving with the rest of the pack, no longer a part of the crowd on the pier, but among the dancers.

Ever since that first day, when the other surfer had punched him, Ike had followed Preston's advice and avoided the pier. But he had stood on it and watched the others often enough. Things were hectic and competitive among the crowds below the pier, surfers always moving, jockeying for position, shouting. And now he was with them, trying to stay on the outside edge so as not to get caught inside. He was able to spot a number of surfers he recognized, Frank Baker and one of the Samoans among them.

Along with the crowded conditions at the pier, however, there was a certain pecking order. He had noticed it before: there might be forty people in the water, but you would still see the same dozen picking up the best waves. Part of that had to do with judgment and skill; part of it had to do with intimidation. And one of the things Ike noticed that morning was

that even though there were other younger surfers who were
just as good, no one got any more waves than Hound Adams.

But for Ike it was a tough session, a morning of freight-
train lefts, of clawing over the top into waves that only closed
out and snuffed him. Perhaps it was, like Hound said, a state of
mind. It was also hard work and so Ike did not give it much
thought when, at one point, he noticed the spot of brightness,
which he identified as sunlight on chrome, moving along the
highway. And later, as the spot grew and contracted so that it
was possible to see that it was not one large object but a
number of smaller ones, he was not watching at all; nor did he
see them make the turn off the highway and into the lot
beneath the pier. It was not, in fact, until Hound had officially
called it a morning and Ike was following him back through
the sand that he noticed the bikes, and in particular the low-
slung Panhead he recognized as belonging to Morris.

Hound and one of the Jacobs brothers were a few steps
ahead of Ike as they came out of the sand and into the lot, the
point at which Ike identified the bike. It was a bad moment,
and Ike was aware of a sinking sensation spreading through his
tired body. He called to Hound, but even as Hound was turning to look back the bikers made their move. It was Morris and
three other bikers Ike did not recognize. Ike figured they
probably wanted the Samoan the worst, but he was definitely
caught in the middle.

There was a brick rest room near the center of the lot and
the bikers had been waiting behind it. They came around now,
two from each side, and they were coming fast. Chains and
wrenches appeared out of nowhere, grabbing scattered bits of
sunlight. A surfboard hit the pavement with the crunching
sound Fiberglas makes when it shatters. Ike thought that it
was the Samoan's board that fell, but for some reason it was
hard to tell. He was trying to see everything at once, to consider all possibilities. He took a few steps backward but did not
run. The strength seemed to have left his legs. It was the way
he had felt earlier, in the water, clawing his way over the face

of that first outside set, staring into the stone jaws of the old pier. For a moment it was hard to register exactly what was happening. There was just all this movement: a blur of grease-stained jeans and tattooed flesh, black boots digging sparks out of the pavement, sunlight on metal. And then the action seemed to arrange itself into two separate battles, one on each side of him.

It was the bikers' play and they had called it two on one, going after Hound and Jacobs first, saving Ike for last. To Ike's left, Hound Adams moved so quickly it was hard to see what was happening, but he seemed to have turned and his board was in the air spinning rail over rail, as if he'd flipped it at the two bikers coming toward him. One biker sidestepped the board, the other knocked it to the ground and then stumbled over it. And it seemed that just as one biker stumbled, Hound crouched and made a move to his left, as if to run. The other biker went for the move, digging bootheels into the lot, spreading arms as if to block an escape. But Hound was not trying to run. He came out of the crouch, moved a half step forward and spun around, catching the biker coming in with a vicious roundhouse kick to the head. Ike saw the biker's jaw go slack, saw him drop to one knee, his mouth dripping blood as he stared into the pavement with a slightly puzzled expression on his face.

To Ike's right, however, the big Samoan was in trouble. He had dropped his board and then, in an effort to set up for the biker's charge, had brought his foot down on the rail and thrown himself off-balance. And Morris had picked up on the slip. He had caught the Samoan with his legs spread, fighting for balance, and kicked him solidly in the groin. Jacobs gasped for air, then went down hard, landing on his shoulder, and instantly the two bikers were on top of him. Someone wrapped a bicycle chain around his head and two pairs of heavy black boots went to work on his rib cage.

Ike himself stumbled backward, though no one had touched him, and banged his board into a parked car. Suddenly there were people running across the lot, fishermen, tourists, a few surfers, everyone coming to watch. Ike clung to his board as if it were going to save him, banged it again into the car. The lot was a place of fear and confusion, dozens of people running from all directions, pigeons scattering and rising like leaves on a wind. Somewhere there was a siren, the red flash of a passing Jeep. But Hound Adams was alone now, circling, kicking, trying desperately to hold three bikers at bay. There had been a moment, earlier, with one biker stumbling, one down, when Hound could have run, but he had stayed and he was now all that stood between Ike and the chromed wrench in Morris's hand.

The bikers, however (and Ike would think of this only later), had been stupid to make their play so close to the pier, in full view of the lifeguard towers. Perhaps they had thought to make it fast, not counting on Hound Adams to slow them down. Or perhaps they had not thought at all. At any rate, there were suddenly black-and-whites skidding across the lot and helmeted cops coming out of the woodwork.

The bikers made no attempt to fight their way out, and suddenly, as suddenly as it had begun, the whole thing was over. It could not have lasted more than a couple of minutes. Ike found himself standing beside Hound Adams as the bikers were spread-eagled over the hoods of the two cars.

Jacobs, though able to get up under his own power, had been taken away in an ambulance, and Ike and Hound now stood alone on the sidewalk that ran above the parking lots. "Stupid," Hound said. "Very stupid. And those are his friends." Hound was not looking at Ike but gazing out at the sea. The strange part was that Ike knew exactly whom Hound was talking about, and he found it strange as well that there was a note of disappointment in Hound's voice, almost the way one would talk about a family member who had gone bad. Hound shook his head and continued to squint out to sea. The delicate lighting of dawn was gone now. The horizon was a straight blue line, the sun high and bright above the water. "The guy used to kill me," Hound said. "He was so fucking innovative, but he never knew what he was doing. Like he had a way of making bottom turns when it was big; he would switch rails, roll to his outside rail a split second before setting the inside edge. It was a way of getting more curve, more projection out of the turn. I picked it out of some films once and mentioned it to him. He didn't know what the fuck I was talking about. He just did it, by instinct or something. I don't think the guy ever knew how good he really was. And he threw it all away, man, chucked the whole thing. Now he's got friends like Morris." By this point, Ike was not certain if Hound Adams was talking to him or to himself. The only thing he was certain of was that it was the first time he had listened to Hound Adams and not gotten the idea that Hound was playing a part or putting him on; it was like he was just talking. The first honest words Ike had heard him say, and they were about Preston.

26

Later that afternoon, Ike sat on the steps of the Sea View apartments, watching the sun dip behind the buildings that lined the highway, waiting for Michelle to come home from work. All day long he had thought about what had happened at the beach, trying not to imagine what might have happened had Hound not slowed the bikers down, had the cops not come when they did.

He was still there when Michelle came home. He followed her to her room while she changed clothes and tended her plants. He told her about the fight, about the way Hound Adams had stood his ground against the bikers.

"Maybe you were wrong about him," she said.

"I don't know. He saved my ass today, though. He could have split. There was this moment when he could have run, but he didn't. He stayed. I know that much."

"I told you, he likes you."

"Why?"

"Have you ever thought about just asking him?"

"It crossed my mind."

"And?"

"Not yet." He went to the mattress and sat on it. "He wants me to come by tonight," he told her. "He says he wants to see me about something, working off that board, I suppose."

"Take me."

"I don't know. I think maybe I should go alone." Michelle had been changing clothes. He watched her pull a faded pair of jeans up over that white triangle of skin that was the mark of her bathing suit on her bare ass, and suddenly what he wanted to do was stay with her. He was certain he didn't want to take her with him, have to watch Hound Adams giving her the eye.

She sat down beside him. "Come on," she said. "I want to go."

"Shit, you just want to get high."

She fell back on the mattress, letting herself bounce. "So what's wrong with that? At least Hound's always got good dope."

"I just think I should go alone, that's all."

"You just don't want to take me to Hound's," she said, "because you're jealous."

"Shit." He got up and went to the window. He hated it when she sounded like a goddamn little kid. He looked back at her spread out on the bed, propped up now on her elbows, hair resting on her shoulders; he wanted to walk over and slap the smile off her face. And one of the reasons he wanted to was because he knew that she was right. He was jealous. Hound Adams was too slick. If he wanted to put the moves on some chick, he was going to make it work. He looked away from her and into the dark glass of the window. Then Michelle was up and standing beside him, her voice softer. "You don't have to be jealous," she said. "I know he likes me. I can tell, but I know what he wants. It's too easy to get hung up on guys like that."

He wished she would shut up. It was crazy how it went.

Sometimes he felt so close to her, like they were so much alike, and other times it was as if they didn't even speak the same language.

"I mean, I've had boyfriends like that and . . ."

"All right, all right." He didn't feel like hearing her get started about all her past boyfriends.

"Why does that make you so mad? You know I've had lots of boyfriends. It's just because we grew up in different kinds of places. You think it means I don't like you?"

She was still beside him and he put his arm around her shoulders. "No. Look, I'm not mad, but I just don't think you should come with me tonight, okay? I didn't mean to make such a big deal out of it."

She turned back to her bed and sat down. "You never ate anything," she said.

"I'll get something later."

"Come by, okay?"

"Okay, if it's not too late."

"Come by anyway."

He stood in the doorway looking at her. She was still on the bed, sitting up straight with her arms out behind her. With her long arms and legs all tanned and her sun-streaked hair, her tank top and cutoff jeans, she looked just like all those girls he saw every day around the pier, sitting on the railings, walking with their transistor radios, but she wasn't just like them; for him she was special, and that could never change.

The house on Fifth Street was dark. He almost turned and left, thinking he was too late, thinking too about Michelle and wanting very much to go back to her. But he figured he should not leave without at least knocking.

To his surprise the door was opened almost at once by a slender brown-haired girl he had not seen before. She let him in without a word and led him to a back room where Frank Baker, Hound Adams, and two of the Jacobs brothers sat on sagging couches, passing a pipe. Ike looked for the brother who had been beaten but did not see him. He stood in the doorway, feeling out of place, awkward.

"Enter," Hound said. "Sit."

Ike took a place on the floor and waited.

They finished what was in the pipe. No one offered any to Ike and he kept quiet, feeling more uncomfortable by the moment.

"How's Michelle?" Hound asked him.

He heard one of the Jacobses chuckle. "Okay."

"Just okay?"

"He means on a scale of one to ten," Frank said. There was another soft chuckle. The dark-haired girl smiled.

Hound Adams stood up. He was wearing turquoise jewelry and a heavy Mexican shirt. "Let's you and I go for a ride," he said. He was looking at Ike.

He led him across the back lawn toward the alley and a small wooden garage. The moon was a sliver high above them. The night was windless and still. There was a Sting-Ray convertible parked in the garage. Ike waited in the alley while Hound started the car and backed it out, then he closed the garage door and got inside.

They cut through the dark residential streets, down to the Coast Highway, then north toward the cliffs and oil wells. The lights of the town were far behind them when Hound swung the car around in a U-turn and parked it on the sea side of the highway. They were among the oil fields here, somewhere above the beaches Ike had seen only during the day, the domain of the inland gangs.

It was quiet in the car, a little stuffy. Ike cracked his window a bit. He could hear the sound of the surf, an occasional bit of music caught on some draft and carried among the oil rigs from the beaches below. Once in a while he could hear voices. He thought of the blackened fire rings he had seen by day, and wondered what they must be like by night, alive with flames. They waited in the car. Hound was silent, checking his watch. Ike could feel the sweat on his back, on the palms of his hands. The air that crept in from the partially open window was tainted with the odors of the fields, the heavy scent of some obnoxious gas. Hound reached across Ike and opened the glove box. Something solid slid across some papers and thumped against the metal of the lid. And in the flicker of light from the box, Ike could see that it was a handgun. Hound said nothing. He picked the gun up and slipped it into the large pocket on the front of his shirt, then snapped the lid closed.

After what seemed a very long time, Ike was aware of movement on the beach side of the car. There were several figures there, moving among the oil rigs and pieces of chain link fence.

"Come on," Hound said, "let's go."

Hound reached behind his seat as they got out of the car and grabbed a large paper bag. The doors slammed shut and they walked toward the edge of the cliffs. There was a handful of people there, among the shadows. Ike counted six, all dressed in white T-shirts and dark pants.

When they had moved closer, he could see that it was a group of boys—maybe high school age, or younger—and that they were Mexicans. They were spread out in a loose half circle. As Hound and Ike reached them they turned and moved closer to the edge of the cliffs. Ike and Hound followed, across a set of railroad tracks and then back behind one of the rigs. They were hidden from the road here, near a ravine that split the cliffs and revealed a section of beach below. Looking down, Ike could see a fire, couples dancing in the orange light, and beyond it, the white lines of breaking waves moving across a black sea.

The boys had money for Hound. Hound gave them the bag. Ike was surprised at how young these guys looked, not at all like the people he had imagined. Somebody had a pipe going. It was passed to Ike and he took a hit, passed it on to Hound Adams. "Hound," one of the boys said. "Tony wants to know can you get more of those pictures, the good ones, man, like this." He flashed a picture toward Hound and Ike. There was a chorus of laughter from the circle. They were squatting in the light of a rig, but still it was hard for Ike to make much of the photograph. He could see that it was some kind of porno shot. He'd seen a set of spread thighs, a dark patch of hair. Hound nodded. "Sure thing, you got the bread."

"You should give them to us free, man, bonus for your customers." There was more laughter.

"Nothing's free," Hound told them. Ike was still thinking about the vanished photograph. What was there? A splash of color across the skin, red like blood? He would have liked another look, but the picture was gone and Hound was standing up to leave. The boys got up too, and soon they were out of sight, vanishing among the shadows of the trail that led through the ravine, back to the beaches. Ike brushed at the knees of his pants, tried to recall a single face from among the group and realized he could not. He could only remember the voices, the white flashes of shirts, and the splashes of light on the black pointed shoes.

When they were back in the car, Hound passed Ike the roll of bills. "Count it," he said. He leaned over and put his handgun back into the glove box as Ike counted the money.

"Not bad for a night's work?"

Ike agreed.

"Now it's your turn."

They drove back toward town with Ike wondering what Hound had meant, back toward the cluster of light that marked the intersection of Main Street and Coast Highway, toward the long, graceful line of light that was the Huntington Beach pier stretching into the Pacific.

They cruised slowly by the pier entrance on their first run, then looped around to come back from the other direction. This time Hound made a left turn off the highway and pulled into one of the long rectangular parking lots beneath the pier, the same lot in which he had fought the bikers. When they had parked, he killed the engine and turned to face Ike, his hand resting on the console between the seats. "How'd that board work for you today?" he asked.

"Okay. I'd like to try it in some easier waves."

"End of the swell."

Ike nodded.

"You've got potential," Hound told him. "You stayed out there today. Surfing is as much a mental activity as it is a physical one." Hound paused and Ike stared across the hood toward the dark stretch of beach. "I brought you with me tonight," Hound said, "because I wanted you to see some things. There's an idea I want you to think about." Hound paused again and Ike looked at him for a moment, finding something disconcerting about the intensity with which Hound Adams seemed to be studying him. "You work on engines," Hound said. "That requires a certain skill, and a certain knowledge. You have to have an understanding of the various systems that make up the engine, how the systems work together. Basically, what you have to understand first are the principles upon which the thing operates, so that it, like surfing, like everything else, is mental as well as physical. There is always this problem of understanding certain underlying principles. Am I right? Are you following me?"

Ike nodded. He was staring back toward the dark beach now, wondering where this new flight of Hound's would lead, how it might connect with the new surfboard he had assumed he was to begin paying for tonight.

"Well, look around you," Hound continued, "I told you there were other ways of making a living around here besides working on bikes. I might have said there are other sorts of machines you can work on, because you can work on this town just like it was an engine. You can make it work for you, make it do what you want it to. And you don't have to get greasy doing it. You don't have to get shoved around by some Neanderthal like Morris. What you do have to do is get a grasp on the underlying principles upon which the machine operates." Hound paused again, waited a moment, and then went on. "Now you've seen one principle in operation tonight. A very simple one: supply and demand. I had what those greasers out by the oil wells wanted. I know what they want and I know how to get it. All they know is what they want. They're in the dark about everything else. They'll bust their asses at some job all day long, always at the mercy of the machine. Now admittedly those guys are at the bottom of a certain process, but the principles apply all the way to the top. That principle of supply and demand is always around. You lose a board and want another. I can give you one. I can give you your pick, in fact, but now you can do something for me."

Hound opened the console between the seats and produced a small plastic bag containing perhaps half a dozen joints. "What you can do tonight," Hound said, "is hang around the pier for a while and find some young girls who want to party."

Ike stared stupidly at the plastic bag. It was somehow a request that did not make much sense. He had never guessed that Hound Adams wanted for girls to party with, and he did not think that was the case now.

Hound seemed to tap into what he was thinking. "The Samoans like young tail." He smiled. "Not an uncommon like. So I could buy it. I could also get girls I already know. But then neither of those possibilities strikes me as being very interesting right now. There is a constant turnover of girls in this town, and I like meeting new ones. It has become another aspect of the machine I've learned how to use, and I can use someone like you, some good-looking young guy who can meet chicks with no problem."

Ike continued to stare at the joints. A thin line of perspiration moved along one temple. For the first time since arriving in Huntington Beach, he felt that he was really close to something, something more than anyone had yet told him, perhaps more than anyone knew. The prospect seemed to hang there before him in an almost palpable way.

"Is something the matter?" Hound asked.

"No, I . . ." Ike was suddenly sweating profusely. "I don't know if I can."

"Nonsense. Let me run something down for you. I've given you the board. It's yours. I don't want it back. Giving it back would mean nothing to me. The board is just an object.

What we're talking about is the spirit behind the giving. Now, I'm asking you for something, a very simple thing, but it's a beginning. Find some girls, bring them to the house. If you can't make that work, maybe you can go get Michelle and her friend. The thing is not to come back alone. But you're making a big thing out of it. It's simple, really. Find a few chicks, do a number with them, tell them you know where there's a party. There's nothing to it." Hound Adams put his hand on Ike's knee. "See you at the house, brah."

27

Ike stood in the parking lot and watched the tail lights of Hound's Sting-Ray vanish into the night, acutely aware of the weight in his shirt pocket. As he began walking slowly toward the pier it seemed to him that he'd reached a moment of decision. He could either do as Hound Adams asked, or he could leave town. There was no in-between now. And yet, wasn't that what he wanted, to get next to Hound Adams, to find out what went on, to find something that could be used against him? Damn. He let his breath out slowly between his teeth as he walked. The strange thing was, that somehow, played off against all of his anxiety, against the slightly gritty feeling that he had been put up to some unwholesome task, there was a part of him that had not gone unmoved by Hound's vision of the town as some great organic machine one might learn to make work to one's own advantage. And there was something else, too, a kind of crazy curiosity about himself. Here he was, Ike Tucker, some hick out of nowhere walking around on the edge of the Pacific Ocean with a pocketful of dope on a mission to deliver girls to some party. There was something about that that was both terrifying and at the same time wildly exhilarating.

He mounted the concrete steps that led to the pier. The boardwalk was crowded: people on skates, couples strolling arm in arm, suntanned young punks leaning on the rails. Music spilled from the fish-and-chips joint at the pier entrance and from a number of transistor radios. Across the highway, the town was a string of light set against the blackness of the sky.

He turned up the pier, walking now out to sea. He felt drunk, but he was not, still a bit high maybe from the dope he had smoked at the oil rig. But it was a different feeling, almost like something in him had snapped and set him free, though free from what he could not say. He did not feel the boardwalk beneath his feet. He felt instead the blood pumping in his arms, in the palms of his hands. Two girls glided past him on skates and he racked his brain for an opening line. He spotted a group of four girls. These were on skates as well and like him were headed toward the dark end of the pier. He fell in behind them. They stopped at a place where the pier widened out, and began leaning over the rail to watch some surfers below them.

Ike walked up and stood beside them. His heart was beating with such force, he was surprised they could not hear it. "Nice swell," he said. This statement seemed to bring all conversation to a halt and all four girls turned to look at him, then at one another. Finally one of them said, "What?"

"I said, it's a nice swell."

There was no response. The girls continued to look at one another as if it was necessary to confer on what he had said.

"Good waves," Ike went on, figuring it was too late to stop now. "I mean, it's pretty big and all."

Still no one responded to him, and he was beginning to feel that something was terribly wrong. Maybe he only thought he was talking, perhaps he was just staring.

The girls stared back. One of them giggled. Now that they were no longer moving targets but standing in one spot, giving him time to look them over, he was beginning to suspect he had misjudged their ages. The biggest of the group looked to be about twelve. He guessed the skates made them look older, or at least taller.

He was rescued from further embarrassment, however, when some old man came walking toward them from the opposite side of the pier. "Come on, girls," the man said, "let's get some food." He gave Ike a dirty look and the four girls rolled off after him. One of them said good-bye as she was leaving.

Ike slumped against the rail. His heart was still pounding and he'd broken into another sweat. He stood at the rail for some time, letting the breeze cool his face, trying to collect his thoughts, watching the machinery of Huntington Beach as it hummed around him.

At some point he became aware of three girls standing at the railing opposite him. These looked like better candidates right away. They looked young, but there were plainly not with their parents. Two of them, dressed in very tight jeans and skimpy tank tops, were leaning against the rail smoking cigarettes. The third, a redhead, was standing with her profile to Ike. She was dressed in a pair of silky running shorts and a light-colored tube top.

Ike walked across the pier and said hello. He walked toward the redhead and it was to her that he spoke. She was the prettiest of the three. Her hair was very red, a dark, blood red, and her skin was very white. Her lips and nails were red as well. The other two might have been sisters. They were thin with blond hair, but it was a peroxided, brittle-looking shade. The redhead smiled and said hello. The other two smiled at each other, as if they knew exactly what he was up to. Ike moved to one side and put his hand on the rail. They were all looking at him now. "You want to get high?" he asked. He had decided not to beat around the bush.

The girls looked at one another. One of the skinny blondes flipped a cigarette butt over the rail. "Maybe," the redhead replied. "Where 'bouts?"

"Anywhere. The beach."

"You got good stuff?"

"Colombian."

The redhead looked at her friends and raised her eyebrows.

"Why not?" somebody asked.

It was like Hound had said, there was nothing to it. They smoked a J and he told them his brother was a dealer, that there was supposed to be a party going on at the house, later. They huddled on it while Ike stood off to the side, waiting, trying to look bored. They were standing in the sand beneath the pier and he could hear their laughter mixing with the sound the white water made as it wrapped around the pilings. They finally decided to go, and he could hear one of them say, "I think he's cute," as they walked toward him from the shadows.

So that's how it's done, he thought. He walked beside the redhead, who would have been quite a bit shorter than him without her shoes. The shoes made her nearly as tall as Michelle, made her legs look long and sexy, and he thought of how Michelle's looked like that all the time, even when she was barefoot. Perhaps it was thinking about Michelle that did it, but suddenly, walking along Coast Highway toward Hound's street, he was set upon by a great wave of guilt. It washed over him in flashes of hot and cold. The excitement he had felt earlier seemed to have vanished completely, leaving only a gritty, unwholesome clammy feeling in the palms of his hands. What was he doing? He had no real idea of what would happen at Hound's. He flashed again on the picture he'd seen in the light of the oil rig. What if something bad happened? He flashed on his sister. Somehow the skinny blondes reminded him of her. She was like that. He could see her at the rail of the old pier, a cigarette between her lips, looking wild, an easy pickup. How had she fit into the great machine, the system of supply and demand? A chill ran up his back and spread across his shoulders, and he was finding it difficult to think of anything to say. What if he should run into Michelle or Jill? He wondered if he was running the risk of blowing everything.

Would Michelle believe that this was what Hound Adams wanted by way of repayment? But he thought of another thing, too, in terms of repaying Hound, and that was the sight of Hound Adams standing his ground against the bikers in the parking lot, standing between him and Morris. Where did you draw the line when someone had saved your fucking life? Or was that only a rationalization, an excuse for his own lack of conviction?

He was feeling fairly miserable by the time they headed up Hound's street. Behind him, the two blondes had begun to bitch about somebody's mother's boyfriend. One of them had begun a rather lengthy story about how the guy tried to get a look at her when she was in the shower or something. She was talking in this very loud voice and Ike got the idea that it was partly for his benefit. The redhead looked at him once and rolled her eyes. Before they reached the house, though, the subject changed and they all started talking about some party they'd been to the night before. Seems some boys had invited them over for a party, except there wasn't a party, just a bunch cf horny guys sitting around waiting for some chicks to show up. "That's all those guys do," one of the girls said. "They just go down to the beach every day and tell a lot of girls there's a big party at their place. Then when you get there, it's just them, sitting around, trying to act cool."

"And it's not even their house," someone said. "It's just a summer rental. They're from Santa Ana, or some dumb place, I heard them say."

"And they never have any decent dope," the redhead added.

Ike was getting a little nervous with this line of conversation. Suppose he got them home and they got scared, or pissed off? What would Hound have to say about that? Would he send him back after Michelle?

The house was dark when they got there. There were just a couple of candles lit in the living room and some music on the stereo, some of the punk sounds Ike heard around the Sea

View but had not until now heard at Hound's. The girls seemed to like the house, though. They could see it wasn't just some summer rental. "You live here?" the redhead wanted to know. Ike said that he did. Hound and Samoans were not in sight. But the girls did not seem to mind. They didn't even ask him about the party. The redhead sat on the couch and the other two started looking through the records.

Ike sat next to the redhead. His palms felt cold and damp. He was still having a hard time thinking of anything to say and he'd used the last of his joints. Then Hound came in. He looked much as he'd looked the night of his party, the night Ike met him. He was decked out in a pair of white cotton pants and one of his fancier Mexican shirts. He wore a necklace of beads and there were more beads on the front of his shirt. His hair looked straight and clean and was held in place with an Indian-looking headband. Ike introduced him as his brother. Hound smiled at the girls and seated himself on the floor. He produced a pipe and a match. He told Ike there were some beers in the kitchen. Ike went to get them, and by the time he got back the other two girls were seated on the floor with Hound and the pipe was making the rounds. Ike rejoined the redhead on the couch and started opening the beers.

The pipe was loaded with hash and soon everybody was pretty stoned. Ike was getting wasted in a hurry. He'd skipped dinner and now he was getting his share of hits off the pipe and pouring beer down fast to cool the burning in his throat. The two girls on the floor got up and started dancing and their bodies were like slender flames licking the walls. The redhead reached across Ike once in a while for the pipe or a beer, pressing her breasts against his arm, and pretty soon he was necking with her. At some point, out of the corner of his eye, he noticed that one of the Samoans had showed up and had started dancing with the skinny blondes. He noticed, too, that Hound Adams had left the room. He'd already forgotten all the girls' names. He'd even forgotten the redhead's name, but he was feeling no pain at the present and the redhead's top had somehow gotten down around her waist and she was grab-

bing at his cock, and nothing had ever happened exactly this
fast for him before. It was like one minute they were just
sitting there, and the next minute they were going after each
other like mad and he had forgotten all about Michelle waiting
for him at the Sea View apartments.

"Come on," he said, whispering in the redhead's ear. He
took her by the hand and pulled her off the couch. She left her
top on the cushions and followed him into one of the back
rooms. It was the room he'd been in earlier that night. The
couches were empty now. The girl sat down hard, pulling him
with her, but he slipped away and knelt in front of her, began
working her shorts down and over her red high-heeled shoes.
And in one part of his mind he kept thinking how crazy it was,
how a few weeks ago this whole scene would have been incon-
ceivable. But here he was pulling down some girl's pants without even knowing her name and he was going to fuck her, and
he knew, with a rather faint twinge of guilt, that it was
Michelle who had taught him how, who had given him the
confidence necessary to make this thing work. But there was
really not time to think of all that at the moment. It was
enough just to know that the two things, what happened with
Michelle and whatever this was, were not the same and had
nothing to do with each other.

He was back on the couch beside the girl now, his hand
between her legs. She was hot and wet, working her ass
around on the couch, pushing herself against his fingers, pushing her tongue into his mouth and moaning all at the same
time. It was like everything was moving at once, the room in
motion around him, hot, dark, panting. A slice of moonlight
broke through the window and touched her breast, cutting
across the nipple. And then he was aware of the hand on his
shoulder. He would later try to remember just how it had
happened. For a moment he thought the hand belonged to the
girl, but then he knew it did not. He straightened a bit on the
couch, the girl still twisting and moaning beside him. He
jerked as he saw it was one of the Samoans who had touched
him. The man was naked, standing just behind him, on the

other side of the couch, then he was moving around it, kneeling on the floor near the girl. He was smiling. Later Ike would remember the whiteness of his teeth in the dark room. It was a confusing moment. He did not even know the Samoan's name. He watched the muscles flexing in the man's chest as he seemed to glide in front of them, to sit on the couch on the other side of the girl. The girl now seemed to be waking up to what was going on. The Samoan pulled her toward him so that her body was twisted, the upper half turned toward him, the lower toward Ike.

To Ike's surprise, the girl did not resist but let the Samoan kiss her. She seemed, in fact, to grow even more excited. Ike's fingers were still inside her and she was still moving on them, harder than before. Then the Samoan was moving again, this time moving the girl as well. Still no word had passed between them, but the man seemed to know just what he wanted. He managed to get the girl on her knees in front of Ike and his hand was on the girl's neck, pushing her toward Ike's cock. Ike's fingers slipped out of her, drying quickly in the dark room. He felt her take him into her mouth and nothing had ever been quite this crazy. It was like his body was on fire, moving on its own, and he could think of nothing else. And then, suddenly, the room was not dark at all, but there was some kind of white strobe light going. Flashes of light pierced his eyes and exited at the base of his skull. And when it was bright, you could see everything. It was like daylight, like one of those electrical storms he had witnessed in the desert. And when it was light, he could see the Samoan only a few feet away from him, fucking the girl from the back, moving behind her in a slow rhythm, his face a mask. And the girl, her red hair flying, going after Ike's cock until that was the only part of him that was alive and he was going to come and that was all that mattered. He took the sides of her face in his hands, pushing himself into her. And when he came it was like it was from so far inside of himself that his eyeballs ached and his head buzzed. There was a moment when he guessed the buzzing was all in his head, and that was followed by another moment when he knew it was not, that it was coming from somewhere in the room. And then he saw the girl.

He saw her by the light of the strobe, so it was like seeing a series of still photographs. It was the slender brunette he'd seen earlier with Frank Baker. She was in the doorway and there was some sort of movie camera in her hands. The camera made a soft whirring sound. Hound Adams was standing behind the girl, his arms folded across his chest, his blond hair and jewelry coming alive in the white light, vanishing in the darkness.

Ike woke up on the floor. The room was already warm and the sunlight was spilling in a window and forming a pool near his head. The minute his eyes opened, the pain began. His eyes burned and his neck felt like someone had stepped on it. He sat up slowly, trying to keep the room from spinning too rapidly. He blinked hard, bringing back the night, and the first thing he thought about was the redhead getting sick.

They had made more movies, smoked more dope. And then one of the Samoans had come in and started doing cocaine. The girls had all sniffed some with him, taking hits out of a tiny silver spoon. Ike had declined. He had begun mixing gin and tonics and had elected to stay with that. Then at some point, later, an hour or two after the first business with the little spoon, Hound Adams had come back into the room and he and the Samoan had started mixing the cocaine with a few drops of water, filling a teaspoon, getting ready to shoot the stuff, and the redhead had wanted in on it. Ike had been sitting right next to her on the couch as the Samoan pushed the needle into her arm. He'd watched the substance disappear, then watched the syringe fill back up with blood, red like the shade of her nails against her white skin, and then that was gone too, shot back inside as the Samoan booted it. And that was what did it, the boot, that blood rushing back in to send it all on its way. All of a sudden she was out, stiff, frozen, as if someone had just shot a bolt of electricity into her body, and Ike was certain she was dead. He was looking right at her and her skin was whiter than it had been all night, so white it was like chalk, and all he could think of was that he had done it and for a moment he was not even drunk, or stoned, just alone with this terrible knowledge and guilt. And then she was not dead anymore, but staring at him, shaking uncontrollably, and then sick, sick all over everything, the couch, his arm, before they could get her into the bathroom off the hall. Damn, he could close his eyes now and bring back that whole scene: Hound and the Samoan trying to figure out what had happened, Hound Adams suddenly looking more scared there, in his own house, than he had ever looked out on the parking lot, standing up to those bikers who had him outnumbered three to one. And when things had quieted down, and there was just the sound of the girl being sick in the other room, they'd decided someone must have crossed the spoons, given her Hound's or the Samoan's instead of the lightweight dose they had made up for her. She'd pulled out of it okay, finally coming out of the bathroom and acting very wired up, still shaking but wired, and that was about the last he could remember, how everybody was wired up except him and how he'd finally crashed on the floor while the rest of them partied around him. And he was there now, the room quiet and warm and smelling still from where the girl had gotten sick. And for some dumb reason, as he was standing up, he remembered her name; it was Debbie. Christ. She had nearly died on top of him and he could just now remember her name.

He found them in the living room, Debbie and the two skinny blondes, all three seated on a couch beneath a huge Indian rug hung on the wall with a quotation from the *Book of Changes* pinned to the middle of it. They still looked slightly wired, staring at him out of blasted eyes while the smell of breakfast drifted back into the room. The scent made him sick.

He walked past the girls without speaking and into the kitchen. The slender brunette was scrambling eggs. "Rise and shine," she said. Ike ignored her. He had in mind going out the back way and slipping out the gate in the side yard.

There was a large screened-in porch off the kitchen, which had to be crossed to get to the yard. But as Ike came out into the porch he saw that Hound Adams was seated on the grass outside the door. He was seated Indian style, his face to the sun, his back to the house, and Frank Baker was standing over him. Neither of them had seen Ike and he stopped in the center of the porch. For a moment he thought that they were talking, but then he saw that it was Frank Baker who was doing the talking, that Hound was just sitting, staring into the yard, and that Frank was angry. "You're fucking blowing it, man," Ike heard him say. "Letting that chick shoot coke. I mean, things are gettin' too loose around here. You know? I thought you said you could keep Terry's family in line."

Frank was dressed in a pair of trunks, and behind him, Ike could see a couple of boards lying in the yard. Frank was standing close to Hound, almost bending over him. His arms were held out, away from his body, with the palms turned up, so that the sun was hitting him in the chest and on the white palms of his hands.

When Hound spoke, his voice was quiet and Ike had to strain to hear. It sounded like only one word, like *later*, or something like it. He could not be sure.

Frank shook his head and it seemed to Ike that he was about to speak again when he looked up and saw Ike on the porch. He turned away then, walked back into the yard to pick up his board. He passed Hound Adams without another word, but stopped as he reached the gate at the fence. He was nearly even with Ike now, slightly shorter due to the elevation of the porch, and he looked up into Ike's face as he reached for the latch. "You get that board paid for last night?" he asked.

The question took Ike by surprise. Frank seemed to be waiting for an answer. He shrugged. "I don't know."

Frank laughed when he said that, a short, barking laugh that ended as quickly as it had begun. "Might take a long time to pay for a board like that one." He went out through the fence, leaving the gate open behind him.

When Ike looked back toward the yard, he saw that

Hound was standing now, that he also was dressed in trunks. He was again amazed, as he had been after Hound's first party, that Hound was able to find the energy to surf after a night like the last one.

Ike stepped out of the porch, into the light. He studied Hound's face for signs of anger, some response to what Frank had said. But his face was empty. He was only squinting against the light as he looked at Ike. "Where's your stick?"

Ike had felt something go out of him with Frank's words about the board, about how it might take a long time to pay it off. He was not sure how many more nights like the last one he had in him.

Hound shook his head. "You spend energy where you don't have to, brah. We'll have to talk about that sometime." Then he went out the gate, leaving Ike alone on the concrete step.

Ike went out through the yard. He stood for a moment watching Hound Adams moving away from him, toward the beach, then he turned and headed for home. The longer he was awake, the worse he felt. For one thing, the longer he was awake the more he remembered, and the more he remembered the more he wanted to forget what had gone on, but he couldn't forget and it was like some vicious circle in his head. And when he thought that all the while Michelle had been waiting, hot waves of guilt swept over him. And yet, somewhere in the midst of all that guilt and disgust, there was this other feeling that was in some way connected to that curiosity about himself he had felt earlier, a dark sense of satisfaction lurking in the gritty morning, a sense of awe almost, at what he had done, him, Low Boy, picking up girls in the heart of surf city and fucking their brains out in the heat of a California night. He had done that. It was like finding some new power suddenly at one's disposal. It was strange. One minute he felt incredibly guilty and the next he felt this crazy elation. It was enough to complicate an already serious hangover and he paused to retch behind a bush at the corner of Fifth and Rose.

The sun was climbing fast by the time he reached the Sea View, heating up the streets, and the machinery of the town was heating up as well, moving into high gear now, the boomer gear, greased with hash oil and cocoa butter, hot-wired with cocaine, chugging to some New Wave anthem, and his heart was beating time, hammering erratically as he reached his room and stepped inside. What he knew for certain, leaning against his doorjamb, staring into the shabby room, was that he was not the same person who had stood there the night before.

PART
THREE

28

"Some like 'em skinny, some like 'em round, can't tell the difference when they're upside down." It was a song Gordon's brother used to sing. Once, at the shop in King City, Ike had walked in on Jerry and one of his friends while they were fucking some girl. It had been out back, in the storage shed, and the girl had been on her knees, Jerry in back, the other guy in front, and Ike could still remember how the shed had been hot and close, charged with a strange odor, and how he'd run, back across the dirt yard and into the shop, his teeth chattering while Jerry's laughter hung on the air. And later that night in the shack back of Gordon's, he had imagined it all over again, certain that what he'd seen that afternoon would be as mysterious forever as it was just then.

Funny how everything had changed, how what was once so strange was now so familiar. What had once seemed a mystery without clues was now a puzzle solved with such pitiful ease that there were times when the whole process just seemed stupid and boring. And there were times when he felt that he was full up with something, some feeling in his guts he could never puke away.

He didn't know. At first, after that night with the redhead, he had tried not to fuck them, just to recruit them for the parties, sad stupid little girls. And he had laughed at himself for ever thinking there was more to it, something magical, even, and he both wished back the magic and sneered at himself for ever having believed it there. And most of the time it turned out to be too hard not to fuck them. When he was skulled, half crocked. He wanted to fuck them then, from the top, the back, the bottom, like putting moves together across the face of a wave.

Frank Baker had been right about paying for the board. It was not a simple thing, locked as it was into the Process, woven into the design of the Machine. "It's not the money," Hound had told him, "but the spirit in the giving." And so even though he was on the payroll now, and Hound paid him well enough, it was hard to know about that board. Mornings were still spent with the dawn patrol, in the shadows of the old pier. Then it was home for breakfast and back into bed, only this time the bed was Michelle's. And then it was back to the shop, or down to the beach with a pocketful of Hound Adams's dope and an eye out for the girls, down in the hot sand and maybe a noseful of coke, because he had discovered where Hound Adams found the energy to party all night and surf all day.

He learned other things about Hound as well. He noticed, for instance, that Hound never made it with any of the girls. He was always there, watching, but never taking part. Still, it was Hound who decided when there would be parties and when there would be movies, and he was fairly picky, Ike learned, about the girls he used for the films. He liked having a lot to choose from, but there was only a handful who were encouraged to stay, or to come back. And if something got started with a girl who didn't like it, or who freaked, Hound would call it quits right away and he would make sure the girl got calmed down before she left. What had happened that first night, with the redhead, was an exception and nothing like it had happened since. But Hound had slipped up that night. He had come close to blowing it very badly and he had been scared, and Ike had seen it.

The incident had proven to Ike that Hound was mortal, that he could screw up, but nothing had come of it. That was an odd word—nothing. There were times when he repeated the word to himself, as if testing it for shape and weight. He would think about it in connection with those weeks he had now spent in the service of Hound Adams. Certain questions presented themselves. The questions were obvious and had to do with his search for Ellen, revenge for Preston's maiming. The answers were more obscure and much of the time it seemed enough for him simply to say that things were not the same. Because for him they were not. Something had gone out of him and with its leaving, something had changed. It was as if those stakes he had once imagined had been tampered with once again. There were days at a time now when he did not even think of his sister, and when he did, he thought of her in new ways. It was like he had seen too many things. He could still not believe the kind of girls he'd met on the pier, and at the parties, girls you could do anything to and watch them crawl back for more, girls who would let the Jacobs brothers slap them around and fuck them in the ass and still be back the next day giving head for a line of coke. It had been two years now since he'd seen Ellen and he would think of that day she had gone, how she'd walked right past him without so much as a good-bye, and how he'd seen her out there on the edge of town in her dust-caked boots and tight jeans, waiting to flag down some trucker, and he would think maybe it was like Gordon had said. He would think about those nights in the desert, alone, Ellen out on a date, partying somewhere beyond the dark boundaries of the town. Partying. The word had a new meaning for him now.

He didn't always like himself for thinking those things, but he thought them anyway. He couldn't help it. Maybe it was her karma. And maybe what had happened to Preston was his karma, too. All he knew for certain was that his perspective had shifted, that the summer was slipping away and that what he had come for was slipping away with it, joining itself to another place and time, a place and time that seemed to him more foreign and more distant by the day, less connected to the person he had become. It was as if some piece of himself had fallen away—or perhaps some former shell; he was like a snake shedding skin.

But then the easiest thing was not to think about it at all.

The easiest thing was just to let it slide, to make it work for you and not let it get you bummed. And so that was what he did. He stayed stoned and he surfed and he watched it all go by. He became a spectator at the zoo, as Preston had once called it, that collection of crazies on land and on sea. And sometimes, on warm summer evenings when the air was soft and laced with the scent of the sea, he would collect young ladies and make movies for Hound Adams. There was, as Hound had once told him, nothing to it. And it might have gone on that way for a long time. It might have gone on that way for too long and the summer might have slipped away altogether had not something come along to end it. Something did. It began when Preston Marsh returned to Huntington Beach.

He had been gone for over a month. There were various wild rumors that had been circulated: He'd lost his hands, his arms from the elbows down. Been brain-damaged and sent to some veteran's home, a vegetable for life. Or that he had just cleared out, had enough of H.B. and split for good. Ike was not sure what to believe. Earlier, toward the middle of July, he'd been back to the hospital and found Preston gone. He had tried a couple of times to get hold of Barbara, but she seemed to have disappeared too. Still, he did not think they were gone for good. On his two visits to the duplex he found a growing stack of yellowed newspapers on the front porch, drawn curtains, and a side yard thick with weeds. Obviously there were no new tenants. So he listened to the rumors, and he wondered, left it to the workings of karma, and went his own way. And then one day there he was, Preston Marsh, standing on the sidewalk and staring into the Main Street Surf Shop.

Ike was in the shop. There was not much of a swell and he was taking care of a few things for Hound. He was putting a leash on a board at the time. He was on his knees near the counter when he happened to look up and see Preston. The change in Preston's appearance was shocking. His skin looked darker somehow, but an unhealthy sort of darkness, the way winos get that dark look that comes from too many broken blood vessels, too much sun and dirt. He wore a beat-up-looking army jacket and a dark cap. There was something about the cap that was familiar, a dark green beret with a small gold shield sewn into one side near the front, and Ike recognized it as the cap Preston was wearing in one of the photos Barbara had shown him, a picture Barbara told him had been taken just before Preston went overseas. Ike noticed too that Preston's hair had been cut very short. Even though it was a hot day, Preston had the jacket zipped to the neck. He was standing with his hands pushed down into the pockets, and he was listing to one side. With the beret and army jacket and unshaven face, he looked like some burnt-out revolutionary. He looked out of sync. And there was something frightening about seeing him there, like a ghost in broad daylight.

Ike did not get up but remained kneeling by the board. He could not tell if Preston saw him or not, or if he did, if he recognized him. He was just standing there, staring into the glass out of his new dark face. Then, as suddenly as he had appeared, he was gone, jerked offstage.

Ike stood up quickly; he felt as if someone had slapped him. He walked to the front door and watched Preston moving down the sidewalk, toward the Greyhound depot and coffee shop. Ike could see there was a whiskey bottle jammed into the hip pocket of Preston's jeans, and that the jacket, which should have hung down to at least keep the bottle covered, was hung up on it, tucked behind it so that the bottle was flashing in the sunlight. And then Ike was aware of someone else standing beside him. He turned to see that Frank Baker had come out from the back room and was standing at the door. Together they watched as Preston lurched toward the corner, zigzagging his way down the sidewalk until at last he collided with a rack of newspapers in front of the depot. There were actually several racks, held together with chains, and Preston seemed to have gotten his leg tangled in one. They could see him cursing and kicking at the racks. People closest to him were moving away, though a few others, at safer distances, stopped to laugh. Then some old man in a white apron came out of the restaurant and started yelling. Ike couldn't hear what he was saying; he couldn't tell if the guy was more pissed off about Preston creating a disturbance in front of his place, or about Preston's cap. Ike could see him point at his head, then back at Preston. And then suddenly, Preston pulled a hand out of the coat and swung at the guy. And even half a block away, Ike could see that it was a strange-looking hand, somehow more like a club than a hand, and that was how Preston seemed to use it, swinging it in an uncharacteristically awkward fashion. More a swat than a punch, the blow caught the old man on the collarbone with enough force to knock him backward into the restaurant. But Preston went down too, apparently from his own momentum, and Ike could hear the whiskey bottle busting up as he hit the pavement. Ike watched a family who had begun to cross the street, moving in the direction of the depot, stop in the middle and go back to the other side. He figured he should do something but was not sure what, and when he turned to look at Frank he was nearly as shocked by the change that had come over Frank's face as he had been by seeing Preston. He did not know when he had seen such a look of disgust, though he was not sure disgust was the word for it; it was more than that. But Frank had apparently seen enough. He shook his head and disappeared into the shop.

When Ike looked back down the street, he saw that Preston had succeeded in getting to his feet, and that the old man had returned with a broom. The man was trying to get close enough to get in a lick without getting hit again. But Preston was not paying much attention to the old guy. He was shooing him away with one arm while staring back up the sidewalk toward the shop. And then, as Ike watched, Preston raised one of his strange-looking hands into the air, the back turned toward Ike as if Preston were flipping him off, except that there were no fingers there to do the job. But somehow, just now, they were not needed. The meaning of Preston's gesture was clear. And then he was gone, around the corner and out of sight, leaving the old man alone at the edge of the street.

Ike walked back into the shop on shaky legs. He found Frank Baker in the back room. He was standing in front of the Labor Day photograph. Ike stopped beside him. Although he had worked with Frank a number of times, Frank had never had much to say and Ike had always assumed that Frank did not think much of him. But now Ike had this odd feeling that they had both been affected by the sight of Preston, that it was all right to ask something he had often wondered about. "Were you the one who took it?" Ike asked.

Frank looked at him for a moment then back into the faded colors of the photograph. "I took all of them, all the photos in this room."

Ike was silent, wondering how much he could ask. He wound up asking about another photograph that had always interested him, a shot of Preston carving a bottom turn from the base of a huge dark wall. It was a good picture in that you could sense the power of the wave, the speed with which he was coming out of the turn, feel the force that was driving him down into a crouch. It was a backside bottom turn and you could see the lines of concentration on his face, the way in which his hair was swept back, as if he were riding into a strong wind, and you could see the great fan of white water thrown back into the face of the wave by his board. "I like this one," Ike said, pointing to the photograph, and he told Frank what Hound had said about Preston's bottom turns.

"Surprised he remembers," Frank said, and Ike was surprised by the bitterness in Frank's voice.

"Hound says he was good."

Frank continued to stare at the wall. "He was good."

"Better than Hound is now?"

"Preston was the man. You know what I mean? He was the guy who won the contests, the guy who made it work."

"Made what work?"

"The business. If you want to make a living out of surfing, you've got to have somebody with a name. That was Preston."

"And Hound?"

"He was good, but he was more into the business end of it.

He was the one who brought in Milo." Frank suddenly stopped talking when he said that, almost in midsentence, as if he'd caught himself actually having a conversation with a wimp like Ike, and answering too many questions. But the added note of bitterness that had crept into his voice at the mention of Milo Trax had not gone unnoticed.

Frank shrugged it off. "Ancient fucking history," he said. "It's over now. You saw what was left of the star today."

Ike did not have the opportunity to ask any more. Frank left him alone with the photographs and walked outside. Ike went to the window. He watched the thin, blond-haired figure of Frank Baker cross Main Street and go into a bar.

29

If Preston's return was the beginning, then what happened with Michelle was the end. She had been, he supposed, the fly in the ointment for some time, the one aspect of his life that did not compute, that was not colored by what went on with Hound Adams—or so he liked to think. The matter of his sister was rarely mentioned, and when Michelle did bring it up, he would just tell her that he was still working on it, still trying to learn something from Hound, and that it would take time. And when she asked him about what he had learned, or what he did, he would get vague, and he would look for ways of changing the subject. Pretty soon she stopped asking. But she had this accusing way of looking at him sometimes, as if she thought he was copping out. But to tell her the whole story, to tell her how what he had really learned from his association with Hound Adams had affected his perception of his own past, seemed an impossible task. It was easier here, too, just to party down, get high on Hound Adams's stash, to make love and lay plans for some distant future when they would be on their own, together, visiting exotic places. And he loved her hard. Because in one part of himself he still believed in their plans. He still believed that Michelle was something special, and that he could still keep their relationship separate from what went on at Hound's, from how he made his living.

This business of keeping the two things separate was, of course, no easy task. Michelle knew about the time he spent with Hound, and even after she quit asking him about it, he knew that his not telling her pissed her off. And Hound Adams, for his part, could see that Ike was keeping Michelle out of it as well. When the subject came up between them, as it did from time to time, Ike would always make some excuse, and Hound would just shrug it off and say, "Later," and Ike would double up on his determination to keep the two things apart. He found at times, however, that he was haunted by a particular image—Preston Marsh seated at a campfire, saying how it was that with some things you either wanted them a certain way, or you didn't want them at all. And by the time he realized just how crazy and impossible and unworkable it all was, it was over. Too bad he hadn't taken the hints along the way.

Like this one morning. It was late and hot and the sheets were wet with their sweat. They'd been making love for a long time. And while he was fucking her he started playing with this fantasy, that they were doing it for the camera, that the Jacobs brothers were standing in line. He was repulsed by it and excited by it at the same time. He wanted to fuck her so it hurt. He slid out of her and got her up on her knees so he could fuck her from behind, but somehow that wasn't quite enough. There was a square of sunlight on her back and the small of her back was slick with sweat, his own as well as hers. He slipped out of her once more. He started working his fingers around in her cunt, then back into her asshole, getting it wet. She started to pull away from him for a moment, to turn, but he held her tightly, pulling her back and then going into her, slowly, painfully at first because it hurt him a little bit too, but he could see that it was hurting her more and that was what he wanted. He fucked her harder, pushing himself as deep as he could until he came and fell against her, panting like a madman, his heart slamming against her back. Then he was off of her, and standing outside on the wooden porch, letting the sun and wind dry his legs and chest. He was naked in the bright light, squinting, hearing the traffic on the highway and beyond that the distant pounding of the surf and all he could think about was that something was wrong. He had never had to fantasize like that before, not with her. The moment itself had always been enough. Now he stared into the dead grass, the oil-spattered machinery of the well, trying to think about it, to clear his head. But it was hard to think, what with that sunlight too bright in the yard and his head wound up tight as a clutch spring after two coked-out days and no sleep. And then Michelle had suddenly appeared on the porch beside him, wrapped in a beach towel, and he could see that she had been crying. She wasn't saying anything, just staring at him out of those green eyes gone glassy and red-rimmed. The sunlight caught on the tracks of tears moving across her cheeks and on the tips of her two front teeth peeking at him from beneath her upper lip. And it was like she was waiting for him to offer some explanation, to explain something that he did not understand himself, at least not in this damn heat with the sunlight gone crazy in the yard, pinstriping everything with neon beads, from the grass and trees right up to Michelle's face, which would not stop staring at him, and asking, until at last he reached out to knock it away, hard, so his open palm rang from the blow. And then he was down on his knees, uncertain of how he got there, pushing his face into the beach towel that circled her waist and crying like a baby while she smoothed his hair.

And then it ended: all the shucking and jiving, the fancy footwork. It ended on a Thursday; he would not forget that, the same week in which Preston had returned to Huntington Beach.

He'd gotten up early to surf a small mushy swell out of the west. Hound Adams had not been in the water. Ike surfed for about an hour, then left for home. He liked waking Michelle in the mornings. He liked the way she looked, all sleepy and warm with the morning light coming through the rippling glass. He liked the way she smiled, still half-asleep, when he slipped beneath the covers to let her warm him with her body. Later they would walk down to the coffee shop for breakfast.

He hung his wet suit off the balcony and slipped into jeans and a T-shirt, then walked down the hallway to her room and tried the door. Normally it was unlocked. Thursday morning, however, was different. He heard voices, bare feet on the wooden floor. He was certain that something had gone wrong, and it was becoming difficult to draw a deep breath in the cramped corridor. The first thing he noticed when she opened the door was the strong scent of grass. The first thing he saw was one of Hound Adams's Mexican shirts draped over one end of the couch. He could not see her bed, but he didn't have to; he could see her face. She looked slightly flushed, he thought, and very beautiful. Her hair appeared mussed and there was a damp strand curled against her skin near the corner of her mouth. He turned without speaking and walked away. The door closed behind him.

And that was it—the end of everything that had been special between them. He couldn't sit still. He couldn't stay in his room. He did not have the desert to walk in, as he had the day his sister had run. He finally put a cold and slimy wet suit on and went back to the beach. The swell, if anything, had gotten worse and he spent the better part of the day scratching for rides in the mushy surf, cursing the waves and anyone reasonably close to his own size who got close enough to crowd him. It was the first time he had ever yelled at anyone in the water. A true local at last.

By late afternoon he was tired and chilled to the point of sickness. He found some guy he knew from the dawn patrol and got him to buy a sixer of Old English 800, the most rotgut stuff he could think of. Then he spent what was left of the afternoon in his room drinking. He waited. He watched the sun go down beyond the buildings that blocked his view of the sea. He waited for the sound of her footsteps in the hall, but they did not come. She should have been home from work by now. Maybe she had not gone. Perhaps she was still with Hound Adams, at his house. Perhaps they were making movies right now.

He was set upon by a nearly uncontrollable compulsion to go there, to find her. All sorts of wanton and perverse acts took shape in his mind. And yet how could he blame her? How could he judge her now when he had been the one who had ruined it? The parties, the movies. He had told himself there was a reason. Was there? Or was it his own selfishness? He should have taken Michelle and run, as far away from Hound Adams as possible, should have given up the charade of looking for his sister, the charade that had become nothing more than a mask for his own lust. Shit, he had stayed because he liked it. The girls, the movies, it was all some sort of crazy ego trip and now he had paid the price. Why was he such a goddamn fuckup? What was wrong with him? Everything had been a lie, his whole stay here. He could see that now. He had simply run away. He had endured the old woman's hateful stare, the silence of the desert, as long as possible and then he had run. It was just that his sister's disappearance, the kid's story, had given him some reason, the necessary push, to do what anyone else with more guts would have done long before. He was twisted in some way, had to be. It was his mother's blood. He had found a good thing here and a bad thing and he had gone after the bad. Maybe the old woman had called it after all. Maybe he was the one who had been wrong at the ranch—all that stuff about responsibility and guilt. Shit. He had left because he didn't want to stay without Ellen; responsibility and guilt had nothing to do with it. Maybe the old woman had been right about all of them, his mother a common whore, his sister no better, and him a goddamn degenerate—the whole bad line of them winding down to him. He'd come to Huntington Beach and he'd found a way to get high, to get laid, to make money without working for it. And he'd gotten off on it. But of course he wanted it all; he wanted Michelle, too. And now he was whining and sniveling because it was all going wrong. Jesus. Crying just like the fucking punk he knew in his heart he was.

He thought along these lines, polishing off the last of the malt liquor, occasionally punching out a chair or kicking the wall, the thought of Michelle's sweet ass in Hound Adams's bed spreading like some cancer through his system until the room was too small to hold him. He was reaching for the door when he saw the fucking board propped against the wall, and was somewhat surprised that he had not turned his attention to it before now. The fucking board. The fucking hot stick with its tucked-under rails and flashy airbrush job. Looking at it made him sick, and he laughed out loud when he remembered his reasons for going to see Hound Adams about it. Shit. It had been like everything else, a lie. He had wanted the board and had found a way to get it. He snatched it away from the wall and lurched out of the room, bashing the board against the doorjamb, running the pointed nose into the wall in the hallway with enough force to create a tiny explosion of plaster. He didn't know if the board had gotten bigger or the hallway smaller, but he couldn't seem to take a step without running into something, and by the time he reached the darkness that waited at the foot of the stairs there were people yelling for quiet and cursing him. He stopped just long enough to yell back, to flip off the whole fucking building, and then he was gone, lurching through the streets of the town, the board tucked beneath his arm, headed for Hound Adams's house.

30

All sorts of grotesque scenes took shape in his mind as he walked, unspeakable perversions that he might interrupt. But he was not in the mood to consider consequences. He did not bother to knock, but dropped the board on the porch and pushed wildly through the door.

The living room was dark, but he could see light coming from one of the back rooms. And that was where he found them. So many crazy scenes had filled his head getting there that it took a moment for the real scene to sink in. He stopped in the doorway and stood looking at them, the single loudest sound the rush of his own blood in his ears.

It was very simple, really. Michelle was seated on the floor near Hound Adams. One of the Jacobs brothers sat on the couch. Everyone was fully clothed. The room smelled of grass and some kind of incense. Everyone seemed to be looking at him; their faces swam before him in a watery haze. He lurched a few steps into the room, fighting to maintain that singleness of purpose that had driven him through the night.

"Come in," he heard Hound Adams say. "Sit."

He looked for a moment at Hound and then at Michelle. He was certain he did not want to sit down. "I want to talk to you," he said to Michelle. His throat felt very tight and he was able to force out the words only with great difficulty.

Michelle seemed to be floating somewhere in front of him, in that thick haze that filled the room. Her face was blank. He could not tell if she was angry or embarrassed.

"What do you want?"

"We have to talk."

"We can talk here."

He saw her look at Hound, then back at him. He wanted

to step forward, to pull her to her feet. It was like the whole situation was slipping away from him, like he was drowning in the thick smoke.

"God damn it." He was aware of his voice being much louder now. "I came here to talk to you. Will you get off your fucking ass or what?"

She didn't get off her ass. She just kept sitting there, floating there, this slightly blasted expression on her face. It was a terrible expression, the sort that needed to be erased with the toe of one's shoe. He started toward her with no real idea of what he was going to do when he got there, only that it would be something she deserved. But he never reached her. Hound Adams was up quickly, standing between them. He put a hand on Ike's shoulder and Ike knocked it away. He was fairly certain that Hound was going to kill him, but the malt liquor had washed away most of his fear; he was determined to go down swinging. Hound, however, only took a step backward, his hands at his side. "Jealousy's a very negative trip, brah. Think about it." His voice was calm.

Ike stood still, watching Hound Adams, never hating him more than at this particular moment.

"What is it?" Hound asked. "You want to jump bad? Spill some blood, maybe? We can fix that." He turned abruptly and stepped to the dresser at the side of the couch, leaving Ike to stand there like he was nailed down, to stare at Michelle, who had turned her face to the wall. Then Hound was back, pushing something into Ike's hand. It was a gun. The metal was cold against his skin and he looked down at it stupidly. It seemed to be sort of dangling from his hand, as if it were attached in some way and he was not really holding on to it. Suddenly Hound snatched it back from him and pointed it at a wall. The gun went off with a deafening explosion. A new odor hung in the room and Ike's ears rang with the sound of the blast. Hound put the gun back into his hand. "You've got the bullets," he said, "and you've got the gun."

Ike felt as if he had a high fever, as if nothing in the room was quite real.

"You think you own me," Michelle said suddenly out of the silence that had come to fill the room. She was looking up at him now, her face twisted with anger. "Boys are so fucking stupid, they think they can own you, that you're supposed to be their property or something while they do any fucking thing they want to. I know all about your little parties. So why don't you take a walk, because you don't own me. Nobody does. Why don't you go back to the sticks where you belong?"

"You fucking cunt." He couldn't keep his voice from shaking now. It was like her words struck too close to home and he wanted to strangle her for them. He called her a fucking whore cunt and she was up on her knees screaming back at him. He didn't know what they said. If there had been nobody else in the room, he would have fought her. They could have rolled on the floor and clawed at each other's eyes. At least Hound's presence spared them that; it was bad enough as it was. His stomach was a knot of pain. The floor spun beneath his feet. He threw the gun at the couch and staggered back through the house, across the wooden porch, and into the night.

There was no relief in sight and no place to go. He stomped through lawns, kicking flowerpots, cursing small yapping dogs. He stumbled down alleys, trash cans tumbling in his wake. People yelled at him: disembodied voices reaching him in the darkness. And he screamed back, his voice going hoarse, losing itself among the run-down buildings.

He finally wound up down by the tattoo parlor on the Coast Highway and a brilliant idea came to him. He suddenly realized why certain people had tattooes all over them. It was because they were fuckups and they knew they were fuckups. He could suddenly see how guys in jails could get into sitting around carving on themselves. They knew they were assholes and they defaced themselves for it. It made perfect sense. He might have gotten into that himself, a little ink, a penknife, but then he figured he probably wouldn't have the guts to go through with it and it would be disastrous to try and fail. No, he would get one from the shop. He would climb into that chair and it would be all over except for the buzzing of the needle. He'd seen how it worked. You just picked the one you wanted and gave the man your money. He checked his pockets to see how much he had. It would be nice to get a large one, preferably a very stupid one to boot, the larger and stupider, the better. A member of the fuckup club for life and there would be no hiding it.

The shop was stuffy and warm, filled with a peculiar odor, a kind of medicine smell, as if he'd stumbled into some third-rate doctor's office. He went up to the wall and examined the selection. He finally settled on a set of Harley-Davidson wings. Only in the middle, instead of that little shield and the word *Motorcycles,* this one had a skull and crossbones, and beneath the bones it said *Harley-Fuckin'-Davidson.* There was another one that was even better. It had the same wings, the same skull and crossbones, only on top of the skull there was a naked woman, her legs spread so you could get a good look at her big hairy snatch. But the price on the second tattoo was too steep. He asked the guy if he could pay him some now and the rest later, but the guy said, "No way." He was an old guy with a bald head and heavily tattooed arms. He stood around chewing a cigar while Ike made his selection, then he sat Ike down, checked once to make sure of the design, and went to work.

Ike was getting it on his shoulder. The way he figured it, he could keep it covered with his T-shirt, then sort of spring it on people as a surprise, just when they were starting to think he was okay. It would be a little like having a secret identity. The old man passed a razor over his shoulder then washed it down with alcohol. He transferred the image with some kind of stencil. Ike felt hot and dizzy. He looked out through the greasy plate glass and into the street. There were a couple of very weird-looking chicks standing outside on the sidewalk now, watching him. They had haircuts sort of like Jill's. One's was very blond and the other's was a strange shade of red, purple almost. The night, the malt liquor, the hot yellow lights, the punk chicks on the other side of the glass. It was like a dream. And the old man was full into it now with that needle. He worked with the needle in one hand and a sponge in the other to wipe away the blood.

At first his shoulder just felt hot and prickly, but the feeling seemed to grow and spread until he could feel the sweat breaking on his forehead and down his back. A wave of nausea hit him and for a moment he thought he was going to be sick. He asked the guy if they could take a break for a minute, but it must have been that the old guy couldn't hear him, because he just kept going. Ike closed his eyes, wondered if he should try to force his voice a little louder, but in the end he just sat there, grimacing, until the old guy spun him around like he was in a barber's chair so he could get a look at the tattoo in a small mirror over the sink. He gave it a quick swipe with the sponge so Ike could see it, before covering it with a piece of gauze and taping the gauze to Ike's shoulder.

Ike had wanted a big one, but he was still a little shocked to see how big the damn thing actually was, it covered his whole fucking shoulder. It had somehow looked smaller than that on the wall. The shock passed, however, into a certain grim satisfaction. He had done it. He had joined the fuckups.

He damn near passed out getting out of the chair. The old guy had to give him a hand. "You all right, pardner?" the old man wanted to know. Ike said he was, that all he needed was a little air.

It was better on the sidewalk. There was a breeze off the ocean laced with the smell of the sea. Then he noticed those chicks again. They were about half a block down now and there were a couple of guys with them. They were hanging around in the shadows of some storefront. He heard one of the chicks say, "That's him." Someone else said, "Hey, man, show us your tattoo."

He told them to fuck off and they all started walking toward him. So he turned and ran, back around the corner of the tattoo shop and down the alley. His legs felt like rubber and his chest burned, but he could have cared less. He had this half-assed plan of leading them down an alley and then ambushing them, beating their faces in with trash-can lids. He was even sort of laughing while he ran, alternately cackling and gasping for breath. They didn't follow him very far, though, a few hundred feet down the alley. He even turned and yelled at them once, but they went back the way they had come. They probably thought he was crazy, or had a gun or something. He remembered Gordon telling him once that if you could make people think you were crazy, really crazy, they would almost never mess with you. He guessed maybe it was true, at least once in a while.

He took a leak in the alley then walked out to Main. He was starting to feel a little less drunk and his shoulder hurt, but he did not think of going home. The night grew cooler and the sweat dried on his face. Where he finally wound up was across the street from Preston's duplex. He could see that there were lights on inside now, but he did not go to the door. Instead he sat down Indian style in the damp patch of grass that bordered the sidewalk, and stared. He was not exactly sure why he had come, or why he could not go to the door. Maybe the fact that he had come had something to do with the tattoo. But, whatever the reasons, he did not want to leave. It was almost as if there were some force holding him there. He stayed until the light went dead behind the curtains, leaving just the porch light, forgotten, drawing moths out of the night to flutter stupidly in its warmth, and even then he did not leave.

31

He must have passed out on the grass, because when he opened his eyes, the sun was bright and hot on his face, and he was still in the same spot. There were cars in the street now and blackbirds singing in the palms above his head. He sat up slowly and looked around. He was a bit amazed that he had actually slept here, like some wino at the edge of the curb, and that he was still breathing, having escaped punk gangs, rape artists, and God knows what other scum that crept from the shadows to prowl the streets of surf city when the sun sank into the sea. He felt a stab of pain in his shoulder and looked down to see some gauze and tape sticking out from beneath his sleeve. It took a moment for the night's events to sweep back over him, and when he thought of what lay beneath the gauze, a sudden feeling of nausea passed through him. But then it was gone and he was thinking that it was what he had wanted, that a certain justice had been served.

He was just in the act of getting to his feet, no simple task, when he saw Barbara coming down the walkway toward the street. For a moment he looked for a place to hide but saw there was none and that it was too late, for she was already crossing the street, moving toward him.

"Jesus." That was the first thing she said when she saw him, putting the back of her hand to her head. "Ike, you look terrible."

"I feel fine."

"I didn't even know if you were still around. You really look bad."

"I feel fine, really," he said, swaying slightly. "I've been by a couple of times, but you were gone." He thought, now that he was getting a closer look at her, that she did not look so good herself. She seemed paler and thinner than he had remembered, and she had been thin to begin with.

"I've been living with my parents. Actually, I moved back in with them, but I'm looking for my own place. I'm just here to help out for a couple of days. Jesus, Ike, what's that on your arm?"

He turned to look at it himself, as if he were noticing it for the first time. "I fell."

She bent some at the waist. "No, you didn't. I've seen enough of those. You got tattooed, Ike." She straightened back up, shaking her head.

He felt that he should apologize for something, but he didn't, and it would have taken too long to explain. So he just stood there, feeling sheepish, staring into the grass at his feet.

"Well, look," she said. "I'm not going to be around very much longer and I've been hoping we could talk. Why don't you come with me? I've got to go to the drugstore and I'll buy you breakfast on the way."

They wound up in the depot restaurant, the seediest place in town, but it was across the street from the drugstore. Ike was feeling dizzy and very washed out by the time they got there. It was hard to concentrate on the present because he kept dredging up some forgotten detail of the night, and his shoulder was hurting. He ordered a cup of coffee and waited to see what Barbara had to say.

"I called you a couple of times at the Sea View," she said, "but couldn't get you. I was hoping you had left town, if you want to know the truth."

"Why?"

"Preston told me why you're here."

He stared into the chipped Formica before him.

Barbara placed her hands on the counter and studied her fingers. When Ike said nothing, she went on. "It's not really like him to talk about things like that. But then he talked about a lot of things while he was in the hospital, particularly during the first few days after the operation. He was pretty doped up."

A waitress came and poured coffee, took their orders. Ike wrapped his fingers around the mug. "What else did he talk about?"

"A lot of things; some pretty crazy things. He didn't always make sense." She paused for a moment. "He mentioned Janet Adams," she began again, slowly. "He called to her. And some of the time I think he thought he was talking to her, thought I was her or something. But I guess it made me start thinking back to what you and I had talked about. Anyway, one day I went to the library. They keep old newspapers there on microfilm and I wanted to see what had been in the papers about Janet Adams. All I had ever heard on the subject was talk; and like I told you, it was some time ago."

Ike took a sip of his coffee and burned his mouth. The waitress showed up with their breakfast. Plates rattled against the counter. The greasy smell of fried eggs hit him in the face.

"I found the articles, one in the local paper and another in the L.A. *Times*. There were a number of things I hadn't known or hadn't remembered. You asked me once about Milo Trax. Well, the article in the *Times* concentrated mainly on him. He is the guy who owns the Trax Ranch. Apparently his father was one of the first Hollywood movie moguls. He was the one who bought the land and had the house built. At any rate, his son Milo owns it now, he's some kind of playboy, I guess, and for a time he was into making surf films. Evidently that was what was going on when Janet died. Milo Trax had taken Preston, Hound, and Janet down to Mexico on his yacht. Then the men came back alone, without Janet. The first story was that she had drowned. Then some Mexican fishermen found the body, and that was when it was discovered that her death had been drug-related. And they found something else out, too, that she had been pregnant."

Ike had not touched his food. He was still staring into the pink Formica. The sunlight was coming through the glass behind them now, heating up his neck, and there were flies buzzing against the glass. Barbara put down her fork. She reached into her purse and pulled out a pack of cigarettes. "I've just started," she told him. "Stupid, isn't it?"

Ike shrugged. The only thing he could think of just now was the similarity of two stories: two trips to Mexico. Two girls who had not returned. When he closed his eyes, he saw the faded photograph in the shop, Janet Adams smiling at him out of the palest of skies. Certainly the similarity had not been lost on Preston. Was that why he had never said more, because to admit that he had a good idea of what had happened to Ellen would be to admit some involvement in the death of Janet

Adams? New questions were forcing their way into his aching head with frightening speed.

"I don't know how you think all of this connects with what may have become of your sister," he heard Barbara say. "But I figured maybe that was why you were so interested in Hound and Preston. Preston said that your sister had been involved with Hound, or so you thought. And that was what you were up to, trying to find out something."

"Is that all he said?"

"Basically. It was a fairly one-sided conversation. I know he thinks it's a bad idea, that you're going to wind up involved in something you may not find it so easy to get out of."

"What's that supposed to mean?" But he knew well enough what it meant.

Barbara shook her head. "I don't know. But I have the feeling he's probably right, for once. I'm frightened for you, Ike. You can't get involved with people like Hound Adams and expect any good to come from it."

The trouble was, he was not even listening now. A new and terrible thought was slowly seeping into his consciousness. If there had been other trips to Mexico, other girls who had not come back, what about the future? What about Michelle? He had already heard Hound talk it up, and he had heard Michelle say she wanted to go. Christ, she would go in a minute now. He was sure of it. And then another thought struck him: the girls, the parties, the movies. Could that have been what Hound was up to, looking for a certain girl, the right girl for some terrible end? He felt his pulse hammering in his temples, and when he thought back on his stupid attempt to talk to her at Hound's, he felt that he might be sick on the counter. He even imagined that he was responsible, that he had driven her to Hound with his own paranoia and erratic behavior. But he was sure of one thing: He would not stay in Huntington Beach and see Michelle leave with Hound Adams. He would not wait for Hound Adams to come back alone. It would not happen like that this time. He would find a way to stop her. He would find a way and he would make it work. It was suddenly all that mattered.

He could scarcely remember what else he and Barbara said to each other on the way home. All he could think about was Michelle, and that he wanted to talk to Preston again, consequences be damned.

They came upon the duplex from the backside this time and stood near a small hedge that separated the yard from the alley. There was a gate in the hedge and Barbara stopped with her hand resting on it.

"I should come in," Ike said. "I should talk to him."

She had taken her shades out of her purse and slipped them on. "Not now," she said. "I'm sure he's sleeping. He had just taken some medication when I left. It always knocks him out for a while. Then he wakes up and starts drinking."

He told her about seeing Preston in front of the shop.

"Happens all the time," she said. She turned away for a moment, then looked back toward him. "I'm leaving him for good, Ike. I've put some applications in at some schools. My father's going to foot the bill. But I'm getting out."

He wasn't sure what to say. He waited.

"You think that's terrible, running out on him when he needs me? Something like that?"

"I don't know."

"I can't handle it anymore. It's like I've woken up to what I told you that night in your room. I'm not going to sit around and watch my life go down the tubes any longer. I'm going to get on with it. And he's killing himself, Ike, for sure now. It's just a question of time. I can't watch any longer."

Ike felt the sunlight on his shoulders. He felt very tired and somehow unmoved by what Barbara was saying. After all, it was his fucking karma, wasn't it? Damn him. All he wanted now was to talk to him once more. Let him live long enough for that, at least. "I'm coming by," he said. "Tonight."

"Not tonight. His parents are supposed to be coming by

later today. And I'm packing. They're going to give me a ride into the city. That should be a scene."

"I'll come by late."

She shrugged. "Suit yourself," she said. "I don't know what to tell you to expect. He's bad, Ike." She dropped her cigarette in the alley and stepped on it. Then she reached into her purse and took out a matchbook and pen. She scribbled a number on the inside cover. "Call me if anything happens. If you're still around. Good-bye, Ike." She put a hand on his forearm, then turned and started down the walkway without looking back.

Ike stood for a moment in the alley, watching her. He felt irritable and slightly dizzy as he walked back toward the Sea View apartments; there were times when he actually thought he was disappearing in the heat waves that rose from the pavement at his feet.

He climbed the stairs to his room, aware now that his shoulder had begun to throb again, and he went to the bathroom to peel the gauze from the still bloody-looking act of madness. He felt the breeze, cool on his hot skin. He wondered what had happened to him. He wondered who he was and was frightened to discover he could not recognize the crazy face and tattooed body caught in the ancient discolored glass above the sink.

32

"The cunt left me" was how Preston greeted him. Ike came in from the alley, through a cluttered kitchen where a single naked bulb provided the only light for the rest of the apartment. He walked between half a dozen bags of trash and into a dark living room where Preston sat, sunk into a sagging couch surrounded by empty beer cans. A slightly medical odor seemed to come from the living room to mix with the sour scent of garbage, the smells of sweat and beer. Ike had waited until late to come. He had been tired and he had done the last of his coke just to keep awake. Now he felt wired, on an edgy kind of high.

Several weeks earlier, while Preston was still in the hospital, Ike had worked out some ideas for converting the Knuckle to a suicide system—a plan he figured would make it easier for someone who had lost his fingers to ride a bike. He had almost come without them, but had at last changed his mind. Perhaps it was a failure of nerve, the drawings providing some excuse for the visit, a buffer between himself and Preston. And now, standing at the entrance to the dark, stuffy room, his head spinning, he was glad he had brought them.

He took a few steps into the room and placed his drawings on a chair near the front door. "Mind if I turn on a light?" he asked. "I want to show you something."

"Suit yourself," Preston told him. "Turn every mother-fucking light in the house on if it makes you happy. But get me another beer while you're at it."

Ike got the beer. He walked back into the living room, flipping on lights as he went. Preston did not look good in the light. His face still had that new dark look about it Ike had noticed at the shop. And the pale blue eyes seemed to have retreated somehow, to have sunk farther into the face until they were like distant chips of ice. There were the reddish tracks of stitch marks across the bridge of his nose, and another thin red scar running across his forehead just below the hairline. He needed both hands to take the beer from Ike, and the hands rose up until they were practically pushed into Ike's face. Ike studied the scarred stumps and he felt more than saw the sneer on Preston's face.

"Pretty, huh? Well, fuck it. It's not a fucking thing. A man sows what he reaps, or some such shit. That's what my old man would say. You know that fucker was here? You know that?"

Ike didn't answer. His resolve to question Preston, the nervous high that had carried him here, were dissipating quickly in the heavy air and he was reminded of what he had thought only the night before, when those punks had chased him into the alley and he had scared them off, that business about people not wanting to mess with a crazy person. He guessed it was that way for him now, because he did not doubt that Preston had at last gone over the edge, that he was as crazy as you would find them.

"Yeah, he was here, the self-righteous bastard." Preston raised the can to his mouth and Ike noticed the open Bible, facedown among the litter on the coffee table at Preston's knees.

"But he showed me something," Preston continued, his head cocked to one side now, those blue chips of ice burning in their deep wells. "What do you do when a thing is rotten?"

Ike stared back, trying to imagine what kind of answer Preston might want.

"Come on, what do you do when something's no good? It's right here." He made a move to pick up the book, but it slipped away from him and fell on the floor. Ike started to retrieve it, but Preston waved him back. "Doesn't matter. Fuck it. I know what it says. 'What communion hath light with darkness?' " He laughed. "Didn't know I could quote Scripture, did you? Shit. You don't know shit. 'If thy hand offend thee, cut it off.' " He held the ragged stump of a hand up to the light. "Cut the beggar off," he said. "Rip it out by the goddamn roots. Get it? If it's rotten, you get rid of it." He rocked back on the couch and sat waiting for some reply.

Ike had taken the seat by the door and he sat there now, fingering the drawings in his lap, knowing it made little sense to show them to Preston. But still he was here, and he had brought them, and he had to say something. "I want you to look at something," he said.

Preston stared dumbly back, as if they were talking in different languages.

Ike walked across the room and knelt at the coffee table. He pushed aside enough trash to make room for the drawings. "You can still ride your bike," he said, and realized as the words left his mouth what a ludicrous thing it was to say. In Preston's condition he would be lucky to make it across the room, much less across town on a bike. But he had started now; he continued: "I figured a way to alter the grips," he said. He tried to force a bit of enthusiasm into his voice, but his throat and mouth were dry as cotton. "With a suicide shifter you can shift with the palm of your hand. All you'll have to do up top is work the throttle." He looked up to see how Preston was taking it.

Preston wasn't even looking at the drawings. He was leaning back on the couch, the beer resting on his thigh, his eyes closed. When Ike was silent, Preston opened one eye and squinted down his nose, across the red tracks. "You dumb shit."

Ike blinked back at him.

"You stupid shit, you think that makes any difference now? You think you've got it all figured out, don't you? Shit. You don't know shit. Working for Hound Adams. You think I don't know what goes down? What're you doing for him, pimping or letting him fuck you in the ass?"

Ike stood up. He felt slightly dizzy and there was this funny screaming sound in his ears.

"You don't know shit," Preston repeated, looking up now.

The screaming continued, like a kettle about to boil over. He reached down to collect his drawings, then flung them back at Preston so they floated in the air all around him. "If I don't know shit, it's because you never told me shit."

For a moment the sneer died on Preston's face. He blinked hard and stared back at Ike. "What's that supposed to mean?"

"Just what I said. You never told me shit. You never told me that you knew Hound Adams, that he was your fucking partner. You never told me there had been another trip to Mexico, another girl who didn't come back. You never told me about Janet Adams, or Milo Trax, or why we went to the ranch."

Preston's face had been getting darker as Ike spoke. Sud-

denly he made an awkward attempt to get up, banged his
knees against the table, and sat back down, managing only to
knock his beer to the floor, where it lay spraying foam onto the
carpet. "You little fucker," he croaked. "You little son of a bitch
whore asshole."

Ike wasn't inclined to stay and listen. He wanted out,
away from the stench, and the screaming in his head. He
leaned over and shook his middle finger in Preston's face. Hell,
Preston couldn't even get off his damn couch; he didn't know
what he'd been so scared of. "Go fuck yourself," he said, and
started away. That screaming sound was going crazy now, but
above it he could hear Preston fighting to get off the couch. He
could hear the coffee table hitting the floor and all the shit
sliding off of it, Preston cursing and kicking his way over it.
And suddenly Ike was running for the kitchen door and Preston's boots were tearing up linoleum to get there ahead of
him.

Actually, Ike did reach the door first, but Preston was just
a split second behind him, punching the door closed as Ike was
trying to pull it open, and Ike saw that stump of a hand hit the
wood with enough force to leave a bloody smear where the
hand slid across the yellowed paint. And then Ike was turned
around and staring up into those crazy eyes and Preston was
holding the door shut, blocking Ike's way with his arm. And
Ike noticed all of a sudden that the screaming sound had
stopped, that there was just the sound of his own breath, and
Preston's, coming hard in the silence. "You little fucker," Preston said, between breaths, leaning against the door. And it
appeared to Ike as if maybe some of that crazy light had gone
out of his eyes, as if the race to the door had sobered him just a
bit. "I said you don't know shit and you don't. Hound Adams.
Milo Trax. What's all that shit supposed to mean? You think
you're really on the trail of something, right?" He paused for
breath and to wipe his forehead on the sleeve of his shirt. "You
wanna know about Janet Adams? I'll tell you. She killed herself. She found out she was pregnant. She took too many drugs
and she fell off the damn boat. She took her own fucking life."

He swung his big head from side to side. "Now what does that tell you about your sister? What does that tell you about anything? I tried to tell you at the ranch, man. You're not going to find out anything around here." He waved at the room with his free arm, but it was a gesture meant to include the town. "Your sister's not here. But what did you do? You hung around, started whoring around for Hound Adams. And what has it gotten you?" Preston paused for more air, sucking it down, suddenly looking more beat than crazy. His question went unanswered.

Preston stepped away from the door. The tattooed arm swung down. He lurched back to the refrigerator for a fresh beer. "You're blowin' it, Jack. You should've left when you had the chance. Now you can get the fuck out of my sight."

Ike put his hand on the doorknob but did not go out. He felt that maybe he had been wrong again, that something was slipping away from him here.

"Hey. I said split, man. You'd better start movin' while you still can."

Ike turned and went out the door, down the walkway and into the alley.

33

Sleep did not come easily. He kept thinking about what Preston had said, that part about him blowing it. Perhaps he had been blowing it for a long time, not just here, but before, as far back as that night on the flats when Ellen had needed him and he had let some need in himself turn it all around.

What Preston had said to him at the ranch seemed to make more sense now, too. About his sister either being gone or being dead, how either way there was little he could do. He had thought then that he had owed her, but what? Perhaps the price for information was too great, had come to involve too many people besides himself. There was already one man dead, another maimed. And now there was Michelle.

Maybe she would have wound up with Hound Adams anyway; she had, after all, known him before Ike had come along. But that would have happened without Ike's knowledge. Whatever Preston had to say about it, the fact remained in Ike's mind that there had been more than one trip to Mexico, more than one girl who had gone and not come back, and what he had promised himself that day with Barbara still held —he would not wait around to see the same thing happen to Michelle. The problem now was how to get her back, or at least how to get her away from Hound Adams. Nothing else seemed to matter anymore. The rest was in the past and he could not change it. Whatever it was that was going to happen with Michelle, though, was still coming down, could still be changed. And maybe that was what he owed his sister, he thought, just that it should not happen again.

He spent the next day looking for her, walking the streets and feeling like a ghost himself, washed out and ill with something besides fatigue. The day passed without results. That evening he went to her door, where Jill informed him—a stupid smirk on her face that he would have liked to remove with the back of his hand—that Michelle was staying with Hound. It was not what he wanted to hear. He went back to his apartment alone. Later he walked downtown and bought a couple of long-sleeved T-shirts. They worked better for hiding his stupid new tattoo.

He woke with a start the next morning, feeling even as he slept that something was wrong. When he opened his eyes, the first thing he saw was his surfboard propped against a wall.

"The board was a gift," Hound told him as their eyes met, "from a friend."

Ike had been sleeping in one of his new T-shirts and a pair of shorts. He got up now and pulled on a pair of jeans, sat back down on the edge of the bed, still without speaking to Hound.

Hound watched him, still seated on the floor, his legs crossed beneath him, his back against the wall.

Ike rubbed at his eyes with the heels of his hands. There was something oppressive about Hound's presence. The prospect of some stupid conversation seemed almost too much to bear. "What do you want?" Ike asked him.

"Brought your stick back, brah. Missed you."

"I gave it back to you. Remember?"

Hound shrugged. "You're confused," he said. "About a lot of things."

Ike shook his head. "Jesus."

"You've also been acting like a real asshole. You know that?"

"Why did you tell her about the parties?"

"Hey, brah, do me a favor. Don't lay your guilt trip on me. Why didn't you tell her? I wasn't under the impression that there was anything to hide."

Ike didn't answer. He was not really in the mood for one of Hound's lectures. Still, there was something in the question that bothered him.

"No answers? Maybe I can run something down for you. You thought what was going down at the house was wrong, something you had to hide from Michelle. Now all of a sudden you think everybody's playing games with you. You think I stole your girl, something like that."

"Didn't you?"

"I didn't know she was yours to steal. I think maybe you're the one who's playing games."

Ike looked away, his face feeling suddenly tight and hot.

"Michelle's a young girl, man, you've got to give her some room. Okay. But that's one thing. The other thing, the bigger thing, is you deciding you had to hide all this other stuff from her, that there was something wrong with it. I would like to know how you reached that conclusion."

Ike shrugged. He had been around Hound Adams long enough now to pick up on his changes of character. Today Hound was the guru. There would no doubt be a lecture on values, on ways of seeing, a lecture that would surely end in some offer of friendship and reconciliation. That was how the game would be played today.

"Still no answers? Well, think about this: I say people have been filling your head with shit. All your life, and you don't even know it. You have a family? They all get along? Everything all right?"

Ike did not answer, but he thought about the desert, the old woman hidden away in the house, Gordon at his station. He thought about his mother and the father he had never seen.

"Fucked up, aren't they? But don't they still know all about what's good and evil? And aren't they always ready to run it all down for you? That's what my family was like. No communication, everybody so cut off from everybody else they couldn't even touch each other. But they still knew what was good, and what was bad, what was acceptable behavior. Bullshit. It took me a while, but I soon began to see they had it all turned around. Almost everything they thought was bad turned out to be all right, and what they thought was acceptable turned out in my mind to be evil of the worst kind, the kind of evil that sucks the life out of people without their even knowing it, leaves 'em shells, fucking lifeless zombies."

Ike had been staring at the floor, braced for the lecture, but he looked up now. There was something in Hound's voice that made him do it. The morning light was coming through the window and striking Hound Adams full in the face so Ike could get a good look at it, at the crow's-feet spreading around the eyes, the uneven pigmentation that betrayed the years of exposure to sunlight and water.

"I don't know about you, little brother," Hound went on, "but I haven't seen anything bad at the house. I haven't seen anyone getting anything other than what they came for. And I've seen some people having a good time, blowing off a little steam, maybe breaking down some barriers. Why hasn't it been the same for you? The guilt you lay on it? But where does the guilt come from? Maybe from those people back home,

those zombies you see driving up and down the Coast Highway on the weekends, screaming at their kids? You beginning
to see my point? I think maybe you're letting other people fix
your values for you, do your thinking. Not uncommon. Most
people go through life that way. I'm trying to get you to start
looking at things for yourself. I want—" Hound suddenly
stopped talking. It was very abrupt, in the middle of a sen-
tence. He brushed his hands on his pants and stood up. "There
anything you want to say?"

Once again Ike had nothing to say, but he was startled
that the lecture was ending so quickly. He had known Hound
Adams to go on forever, whether anyone was listening to him
or not.

Hound took a step toward him and offered a hand. "You
do what you want," he said. "But no bad vibes, okay? *Hermanos del mar,* no?"

Ike took the hand, which was dry and strong.

"Listen," Hound said. "Michelle and I are going sailing
tomorrow. Why don't you come along? I think she would like
for you to. And there's somebody I would like you to meet, an
old friend of mine. What do you think?"

"When?" Ike asked.

"Early. Six. Michelle and I will come by and pick you up."
Hound turned as if to leave, but then stopped and came back.
"There's something else I want to say to you," he said. "Because I know it's on your mind. Frank told me about Preston
coming by the shop. I know you think I had something to do
with all of that." He paused for a moment. "But you're wrong
if you think that. I've seen something like this coming for a
long time. But I took no pleasure in it. It was not my doing, but
his own. Preston has brought this end on himself. It's his
karma, surely you can see that? I would have saved him if I
could."

"Saved him?" Ike met Hound's eyes. He might have been
thrown off-balance a bit by the abrupt end of the lecture, but
he was not going to be taken back in that easily.

"Let me ask you something," Hound said. "Who do you think opened that gate for him at the ranch?"

Ike was ready to say more, but the question stopped him cold. He thought back suddenly to Preston's words that night, his question to Ike about being able to find the truck, and later, his hiss of astonishment when the gate was open.

"Yeah, I saved his ass that night. And yours, too. Right? Some of those cowboys had guns. There were even a couple of guys there who knew Preston. And not everybody is as fond of that big fucker as you and me."

Ike started to say something, but Hound just waved him silent. "What happened here, that was between him and the Samoans. I was hoping he would be smart enough to split. But of course he wasn't. If you want to know the truth, I think maybe that's the way he wanted it—except that he's still alive." He stopped to stare for a moment at Ike, his dark eyes charged with an odd light. Ike stared back. What was there about Hound's expression just now? Something familiar. Something besides his usual cool, or a coked-out high, something a trifle wild, maybe even desperate, and then it came to him where he had seen that look before. It was the same expression he had once seen on the face of Preston Marsh as he sat squinting into the fire at the ranch, what Ike had taken for fear. He was aware of Hound continuing to talk, something about how he had seen all this coming, but how he had taken no pleasure in it. "The man was my friend, Ike," he heard Hound say. "And I loved him."

When Hound had gone, Ike sat for some time, alone in his room. That stuff about the ranch was hard to figure, leaving as it did a number of holes in Ike's theories. Maybe that whole cat-and-mouse business had been something Ike had invented. It didn't make sense. There was the possibility, of course, that Hound was lying, that this was for Ike's benefit. But he had Michelle now, what did he still want with Ike? Ike rose and paced the floor of his room. Beyond the window, the sun was climbing fast, turning the sky hot and blue. It was confusing, but then the confusion was bound up with the past and Ike was done with that. Hound could have his little mysteries, and his games, Preston his karma. All Ike wanted was out, but he wanted Michelle with him. She was the reason he had shaken hands with Hound Adams, the reason he would go tomorrow. Still, as he stood at the window, a cloudless sky spreading above the rooftops before him, he could not help but wonder who that friend with the sailboat would turn out to be. A name seemed to hang there, at the tip of his tongue. But he did not say it.

34

They picked him up the following morning in Hound's Sting-Ray. It was cramped inside the car. Ike and Michelle had to squeeze into the same seat and all the way there he was conscious of her shoulder pressing against his, of her thigh against his own. She wore a pair of white shorts and a light-colored tank top with a seagull on it. He had not seen the clothes before and wondered if they were gifts from Hound Adams. Michelle did not seem particularly pleased to see him. She acted as if he made her uncomfortable, so he wondered if she had really wanted him to come along, as Hound had said.

It was a strange trip. Ike contented himself with looking out the window, watching the beaches slide past. It was the first time he had ever been south of Huntington Beach and he was surprised at how quickly the landscape changed. The oil wells and squat brick buildings of Huntington Beach were soon replaced by large beach-front homes. They passed a sign that said NEWPORT BEACH CITY LIMITS, turned right off the highway and onto a bridge that spanned a huge harbor. The harbor was wide and blue. Its edges were lined with docks, sections of white beach, and high-rise buildings. There were boats everywhere, colored sails brilliant against the blue expanse of the bay. The traffic was thick on the bridge and it gave Ike a chance to take in the view. He could scarcely believe that they were only minutes away from downtown Huntington Beach, that the coastline could change so spectacularly within such a short distance. There was no similarity to any desert town here. This was southern California as he had imagined it: white sails in the sunlight, signs of opulence everywhere, and he found himself thinking back to something else Preston had once told him, something about Hound having friends with bucks.

"Ever seen the harbor before?" Hound asked as they waited in traffic.

Ike and Michelle answered at the same time. Apparently Michelle had not been this far south either.

Hound smiled and nodded toward the water. "Lots of money," he said.

The Sting-Ray crept down the bridge and onto what Hound told them was a peninsula. Two blocks later they turned left and crossed a second bridge. The homes here were unlike any Ike had ever seen, save perhaps the mansion he had glimpsed above the point. Everything was concrete and glass, wood and stone, manicured trees, flashes of white sand and narrow walkways blocked by gates and signs that said PRIVATE BEACH. The walkways led down toward the blue water of the bay.

Hound pulled into a small lot near a guardhouse and parked. It was bright and hot and there were heat waves dancing at the edges of the lot. Ike stood alone at the side of the car while Hound locked the doors. Michelle did not look at him but stood several yards away, watching Hound. When Hound had finished with the doors, he walked to the trunk and removed a cardboard box, then motioned for them to follow.

Michelle walked at Hound's side and Ike brought up the rear as they passed the guardhouse and headed down a long gray finger of dock. They were on the bay now, passing through a forest of masts. Rigging snapped and creaked all

around them. White hulls brushed against rubber bumpers
lining the docks. Across the bay there were more docks, more
boats, more huge homes and private beaches.

At last they came to a large single-masted sailboat with a
white hull bearing a green stripe and the name *Warlock*. The
deck was a maze of glittering chrome gadgets. There was a
white set of boarding steps set up on the dock and Hound led
them up and onto the deck. Ike was last up the steps. He went
over the lifeline and felt the deck roll slightly beneath him.
For a moment they were alone on the deck with the crack of
the rigging, the gentle slap of wind waves against the hull.
Then a man's voice reached them from somewhere beneath
their feet and soon a face appeared in the cockpit.

Ike watched as a body materialized after the face and soon
the man was standing on the deck, walking to meet them. It
was the man Ike had seen in the photographs at the shop. He
recognized at once the small straight mouth and pointed chin.
Certain features were the same and immediately recognizable. But there were changes. The body seemed much thicker
than in the pictures, not fat, but thick and powerful in a way
that did not match up well with the face, which had an almost
elfin quality in its small chiseled features, and small dark eyes.

The man was dressed in a blue shirt and a white pair of
shorts. His legs were well tanned, short, and heavily muscled,
flexing in the sunlight as he came toward them. His height was
deceptive. It was not until Ike stood looking him in the eye
that he noticed that the man was only about half an inch taller
than himself, though probably outweighing him by a good fifty
pounds of muscle.

"Ike, Michelle," Ike heard Hound say. "I would like for
you to meet a friend, Milo Trax."

And though Ike had known it was coming, there was still a
slight chill that ran down his back upon hearing the name. He
thought back to the bitterness in Frank Baker's voice, to his
words: Hound was "the one who brought in Milo," as if that
had been the beginning of the end.

Ike took the offered hand. It was a thick, firm hand, like

the body, and he felt that his own was thin and frail by comparison. He met the eyes, which were very dark and bright, almost boyish, features that had not been apparent in the photographs.

"Yes," Milo said, and there seemed a genuine enthusiasm in his voice. "Ike Tucker, I've heard a lot about you. Pleased to have you aboard." Then he turned to Michelle, leaving Ike to wonder what he possibly could have heard.

They went out of the harbor under power, Milo at the large silver wheel in the cockpit, Michelle at his side, Ike and Hound Adams on the deck. The harbor seemed to go on forever, winding out of waterways into ever-widening channels. The water went from deep green to a blackish blue, and looking over the side, Ike could see small schools of fish darting beneath them, like silver coins cast into the water. They glittered and fell, passed from sight.

The closer they got to the harbor entrance, the bigger everything seemed to get, the size of the beaches, the homes, the yachts, and Milo Trax seemed to know whom everything belonged to. He pointed out a number of famous racing yachts, other boats and houses owned by certain movie stars. Like some wonderland, it slipped past them, a world of money Ike had never even imagined in the desert.

At last they were moving down a channel, passing between two long jetties and then out into open sea. Milo got them all moving now, telling them which line to pull on and when. At last there was a great rattling of rigging, a tremendous explosion of sail as the sky went white and yellow. The hull seemed to leap beneath them, shuddering as it met the ground swell. Suddenly Ike's face was wet, his lungs full of a fresh sharp wind. They were under sail. He scrambled back into the cockpit, where Milo stood grinning and Ike could not help but grin back. The ship heeled. Spray swept the deck.

"You can go anywhere on a boat like this one, Ike," Milo

told him. "Hound says you like to surf. You would be amazed by the places we've seen."

They spent the day far from land, the coastline a distant mirage glittering on the horizon. Around noon they ate sandwiches and beer. When they had finished, Michelle took the things below. Ike volunteered his assistance and followed her down.

She was standing at a small sink in the galley, rinsing plates; the sea had grown calm and the boat rode easily, no longer bucking a ground swell. She looked over her shoulder as Ike came down the steps, then back into the sink.

He stood beside her. She had pulled her hair back into a small ponytail and he studied the wispy strands of hair that curled about the back of her neck. "I've been looking for you all week."

"I've been at Hound's," she said, her voice flat, eyes still turned toward the sink.

"Michelle, look, I'm sorry, about everything."

"I thought you were different," she said. "You're just like all the rest."

"I know it was wrong. I thought it would be a way of finding out something."

"Sure. About your sister." She said this in a sarcastic way.

"I did in the beginning," he said. "I know it probably doesn't look that way to you, but I did in the beginning. And I had already taken that damn board. I had to pay for it."

"With the movies?" Her voice was still sarcastic and she was still staring into the sink, although he noticed she had stopped washing dishes. Her hands were still, floating in the soapy water. He was a little afraid of saying too much, of upsetting her in a way that would let Hound know something was going on. "Look, Michelle, just listen to me a minute, okay?"

She did not answer and he went on. "I was looking for my sister. I wanted to find out what had happened, but I wanted to find out some other things too, about Preston and Hound. And

I got sidetracked. I know that now. I mean, I just got caught up in some things I couldn't handle and it was stupid. I know that. But I never thought you were like those other girls. I mean, it was different with us. It could be that way again. It's what I want, just to be together."

She looked up at him and her eyes were glassy, slightly red. "What you want?"

"We had something special. Don't you see? That's all that matters. And there's other things I can tell you, but not here. We can't really talk here. Just say you'll think about it, that we can talk again, later." He was talking fast now, worried about staying down too long. He put his hand on her shoulder, and she turned to face him, her hands dripping water on the floor between them. She looked him square in the eye and there was something in her stare that made him want to flinch. "I'm all that matters? What about your sister? She doesn't count anymore?"

"No, it's not like that. It's not that simple. Damn it, Michelle, I know I've fucked up. I mean, you don't even know how badly I've fucked up. But I have learned a few things too. Just say we can talk someplace, soon. Tomorrow." He waited, watching her face, but then the silence was broken by the sound of another voice. Milo Trax. He must have been lying on his stomach on the hatch cover, because his head was upside down, hanging into the cabin, grinning. "Whale off the starboard bow," he said. "Come look."

The head disappeared. Ike was silent. He stood watching Michelle at the sink.

"We should go up and see," she said.

He stepped away from her, waiting, when he noticed something lying on the seat near the galley table. It was the cardboard box he'd seen Hound take from the trunk. He went to it and pulled a bit of the cardboard where it was starting to come undone. Film cartridges. The box was full of them. He pointed this out to Michelle.

She looked at the box. "So what?"

"I don't know. I mean, I've always wondered what he did with these things."

"I'm sure I wouldn't know anything about it."

There was something in the way she said it that annoyed him. "Like you never made any yourself."

"That's right," she said, going by him, stopping to look at him with those eyes that still made him want to flinch. "And you want to know something else? I've never even gotten it on with Hound Adams. He's just been really nice to me, nothing else."

She left him standing in the galley, watching her legs disappear into the sky above the hatchway. He looked once more at the box of films on the seat, then followed her into the light to see Milo's whale.

It was near sunset when they returned to the harbor. The sky was red and gold above the huge bay-front homes. It was hard to believe they were only a few miles from downtown Huntington Beach, from the cliffs and oil wells, the graffiti-covered fire rings and the parties of the inland gangs.

After they had hosed down the boat and coiled the lines, they stood above the docks, looking back toward the bay and the lights of the homes. "I own some land north of here," Milo said, looking at Ike. "Some good surf up there. I'm planning a party in another week or so, kind of an end-of-the-summer ritual that I practice with a few friends. I could use some help getting the place ready. How would you and Michelle like to come up and help? You can bring your stick and get some waves."

Ike nodded. He looked at Michelle. "Sure," he said. "Sounds okay." He tried to force the correct amount of enthusiasm into his voice.

"Good," Milo said. "You can all come up together." The idea of that seemed to amuse him for some reason and he clapped his hands together as he laughed.

35

Ike's skin felt hot and tight after a day in the sun and wind. Michelle's shoulder pressed against his once more as the black stretches of beach slipped past them. They rode in silence and soon they were at the west end of Main Street, waiting in traffic, cruising past beer bars and pizza houses, the dark windows of the surf shops.

When they had parked in front of the Sea View, Hound got out to open the trunk. Ike opened his door and put one foot in the street but continued to sit close to Michelle. "I still want to talk," he told her.

She shrugged. "We can talk."

"When?"

"I don't know. Are you coming to Milo's party?"

"Are you?"

"Yes."

"But I want to talk soon."

"It's only a couple of days." Ike eased a little more of himself out of the car. Hound was waiting by the open trunk. Suddenly Michelle covered his hand with her own. "Come to the party," she whispered. "I want you to, okay?"

He watched her, holding her eyes with his own, trying to say more. She looked at him for a moment, then back across the hood.

"Okay," Ike said. "I'll come. So we can talk." He left her in the car and walked back to the trunk. Ike's canvas bag with his extra clothes, the bathing suit he had not needed, was already sitting on the curb. Hound was standing beside it. "Milo doesn't know you've already seen his ranch," Hound said. "I think we should keep it that way."

Ike nodded, somewhat surprised that Hound had felt it

necessary to tell him that. He felt very tired all of a sudden. He was in the act of picking up his bag when Hound Adams seemed to stiffen at his side. It was something he felt more than saw. When he looked up, however, he saw that Hound's face had changed, that he was looking past Ike, staring toward the old building that loomed out of the blackness behind them. Ike turned too, following Hound's gaze, and it was then that he saw the dark figure standing on the steps that led into the building.

The figure was little more than a black shape silhouetted against the yellow background formed by the open door. But it was immediately recognizable as Preston. No one else was quite that big, or stood in just that way. He seemed to be dressed in the same bulky army jacket that Ike had seen him in on the street, and there looked to be the same cap on his head. The elevation of the yard, the height of the step, the way in which he was silhouetted in the light of the hall, all conspired to make him look somehow even bigger than he was, a dark shadow rising above them out of the shadow of the building. It was a strange moment, a moment frozen in time, in which the two men did not speak but stared at each other across the ragged lawn. It was Hound Adams who at last broke the spell. He turned to close the trunk lid, then walked to his door. He looked once more at Preston across the roof of the car, then got in and drove away.

Ike did not know what to expect as he walked across the lawn. He stopped short of the step. Preston was leaning on a doorjamb now, hands pushed down into the deep pockets of the coat. It was too dark to make out the expression on Preston's face. "Stash your gear," Preston told him. His voice sounded steady and sober. "I've got something I want you to see."

It was late and the streets of the residential section were quiet. Preston did not speak again. He walked quickly, his heavy boots ringing on the pavement, and Ike had to work to keep up. They cut across Main Street and into an alley and Ike did not have to ask where they were headed. He could see a light burning in front of the shop and then he spotted the dark shape of Morris propped against a telephone pole near the gravel entrance.

Morris said nothing, but fell in behind them as they walked toward the shed, and the night was full of the sound that boots make sinking into gravel. Preston pushed the door open with his foot and they stepped inside, Preston first, then Ike and Morris.

The shed was small. There was a dirt floor and in the middle of the floor there was a bike. It was not a chopper, not even a Harley, but a BSA Lightning Rocket. It was nearly a stock machine, but not quite. Some lettering had been removed, the tanks lacquered and rubbed out until they sparkled like dark jewels, a kind of gunmetal gray, in the light of the small shed.

"I wanted you to see it," Preston told him. "What do you think?"

"It's all right. He did a good job."

"All right, my ass," Morris said from behind them. "That's a bad motherfucker." And it was—a bike capable of a hundred and twenty plus off the showroom floor. Ike shook his head, walking around the machine for a better look, and getting a better look at Preston now, too. He looked better than the last time Ike had seen him. At least he was relatively sober, and he was on his feet. But there was still a certain wildness about the way those pale eyes had retreated into the dark face. And there was also an abruptness of manner, a hyper quality in the way Preston carried himself, that Ike had not seen before. He did not stand in one place but paced back and forth, from one end of the shop to the other. "I want you to listen to it," he said. "Check it out."

"Shit, man, I checked it out," Morris said. "What do you want?"

"I want him to hear it. I want it right."

Morris had been standing by the door. He now took a

couple of steps toward Ike. "Man, you're crazy. I should waste the little fucker right now."

Preston stopped pacing and looked at Morris across the machine. "Forget it. I want him to hear it."

"But he's with them. He was with Hound and the Samoan on the lot. I want his skinny ass, Prez."

Morris was looking at Ike as he spoke, a sort of glazed, hungry look creeping over his features—almost as if he was working himself into some trance, and Ike had to wonder if Preston would be able to stop him even if he wanted to, in his weakened condition. Ike took his hands out of his pockets and let them fall against his sides, a gesture that was not lost on Morris. "Oh, look at this," Morris said, his voice coming out of a sneer. "He's ready for it this time. Look at him, the little scumbag. I bet he's pissin' his pants right now." He chuckled. "Come on, queer bait, let's see your moves." Morris took a quick step forward and swung, a kind of openhanded round-house designed to rupture Ike's eardrum. But Ike was ready for it this time, after a fashion. He'd never been in a real fistfight in his life, but Gordon had once bought him a pair of gloves and had spent some time knocking him around in back of the market, trying to show him a few things. One of the things Gordon had taught him was that a lot of guys carry their right too low when they throw a left, and that if you come up under it, hooking, you can often land a good punch. And that was what Ike did. He wasn't exactly sure why. He knew he hadn't a prayer of winning a fight with Morris, that he would be smarter to let it end quickly, but there was just something about that fat, greasy face, the half sneer, the memory of lying on the sidewalk in front of that beer joint swallowing his own blood. He stepped under the blow and hooked for all he was worth, throwing it off his hip the way Gordon had taught him, what Gordon would have called hooking from the ankles, and he felt the punch land with a sharp pain and jolt that ran clear up his arm and into his shoulder.

Morris just grinned at him. But he stopped coming forward and looked at him for a moment. "How do you like that?"

he asked. "The little pussy's gone and got himself some balls."
Then he reached into his hip pocket and pulled out a set of
pliers. "Let's see how he likes it when I pinch them off." His
laughter rang in the shed, but Preston was around the bike
now and his voice was a low snarl.

"I said drop it. You're not gonna bust him again."

"Fuck that, man. I want him. You can see he's beggin' for
it. I want his ass so bad I can fuckin' taste it."

Ike stood his ground. He still had his hands up the way
Gordon had taught him and he was staring over them into
Morris's hungry grin.

It looked as if Morris were set to come after him once
more when Preston suddenly shot out a hand, thumping Morris square in the chest and knocking him backward so he had
to backpedal quickly to retain his balance, and Ike was once
again surprised at Preston's strength, in spite of what he had
been through.

"I'm warning you, Morris. You fuck with me right now
and I'll tear your goddamn throat out."

For a moment the two men stood facing each other, Preston's gloved hand still pressed against Morris's chest. Suddenly, though, Morris spun away and threw the pliers. He
threw them more or less in Ike's direction, but the throw was
high and they crashed into the sheet-metal wall. Morris went
to the door and stood looking into the blackness outside. "All
right," he said. "But get that little cocksucker outta my sight."

Preston laughed. He threw back his head and his laughter
had a crazy sound to it. He pulled a set of keys from his pocket
and walked to the bike, swung himself on and looked at Ike.
"Come on," he said. "Get on."

Ike stood staring into the six hundred and fifty cubic
inches of death and destruction. It was not the kind of bike you
wanted to climb on behind just anybody. But with a half-crazy
alcoholic with crippled hands . . . Morris turned from the
door and smiled and Ike could see that he picked up perfectly
on what Ike was thinking. There were two choices: a ride with
Preston. Further conversation with Morris. Ike got on the

bike. He found a certain sense of satisfaction, however, in noticing the mouse that had risen beneath Morris's eye. Gordon would have been proud.

Preston kicked the bike to life and the roar of that power-jumped engine threatened to blow the tin walls of the shed into the sea. Ike put his arms around Preston's waist. He stared into a set of broad shoulders covered in green army cloth and he noticed the same slightly medicinal scent he'd first detected in Preston's apartment. Preston pulled the beret down tighter on his head and walked the bike to the door where Morris stood waiting. " 'Behold a pale horse,' " Preston croaked above the roar of the engine. " 'And his name that sat on him was Death, and Hell followed with him.' " Then he laughed and hooted into the blackness and they were off into the night, ripping the backside of surf city, carving turns out of empty streets, finding the Coast Highway, where they blew past a string of low riders like they were standing still.

They must have been halfway through the oil fields before Preston, taking it all the way out in every gear, jammed it into high. There was nothing for Ike to do but hang on, to think about sand and curves, and he figured that at least at this speed death would come quickly. They found it somewhere on the north side of the oil fields, that place bikers called the edge, and it was black and hollow and silent because the roar of the engine was lost behind them, a memory on the wind.

Then they stopped. They found the edge and left it, stopped at the side of the highway, where the air was warm and the night smelled faintly of tar and machinery and the sea. It was very dark here. The only lights in sight were the distant yellow dots of the offshore rigs, caught between a black ocean and a starless sky. The sound of waves they could not see echoed from the beaches somewhere below them.

They stood on a hard-packed dirt shoulder and Ike tried to adjust to the sensation of stillness. Preston seemed filled with a jumpy enthusiasm, as if the speed of the ride had blown some spark of life back into him. "Hey, what about it, ace?" Preston

wanted to know. "Runs like a champ. Right? I shit you not."
Preston seemed to find that phrase amusing and repeated it
again, cackling to himself as he paced the dirt. He stopped
long enough to pull a bottle from his jacket, and took a long
drink. He passed the bottle to Ike and Ike drank too. Tequila,
burning all the way down, heating up the night, and somehow,
though he had not been glad to see the bottle, he was no
longer scared. It was as if his fear had been blown away, lost
somewhere with the roar of the engine. He even felt a rather
bizarre sense of elation of his own that he supposed only a trip
to the very edge could bring. So he stood there, passing the
bottle, talking engines and speed, letting the tequila burn
away any residue of fear that might have lingered in his guts.

It was too late for questions. He knew that now, at the side
of a dark road; he knew he would not ask Preston again about
the trip to the ranch, or about Terry Jacobs, or Hound Adams.
It was past, and Preston, this Preston, was not the same one
who had taken him to the ranch, who had wanted to show him
what it could be like. Ike suspected that Preston had been
fading for a long time, that the beating in the shop, the operation, the steel plate, were final nails in the coffin, and that
whomever Ike had once sat talking to by a campfire at the end
of one perfect day had passed away and now there was only
this stranger, and the ride back to town.

Preston left him at the curb in front of the Sea View
apartments. It was hard to believe that only a couple of hours
had passed since he stood here last, with Michelle and Hound
Adams.

"I want to tell you one thing," Preston said as Ike stood
waiting. "That time Morris dumped you. I was wrong to let
that happen. You were my partner, man. And I never stood
back and let a partner get dumped on like that before. I was
kind of hoping it would scare your skinny ass out of town. But I
was wrong to let it happen."

"You were right," Ike said, his voice sounding too loud and
hurried. "I should've gone. But it's Michelle, now." He sud-

denly felt that perhaps he had been wrong out on the road, that he could talk, tell Preston everything. He wanted to tell someone, but it was hard to know where to begin. "Michelle's my girl," he said. "Was my girl. Now she wants to go to Mexico with Hound Adams and Milo Trax. . . ." But something made him stop short. He saw that Preston was not really listening, that he was only nodding, and that there was this very distant look on his face, as if what Ike had to say was all beside the point somehow.

When Ike stopped talking, Preston looked at him. "I was wrong," he said again. "I owe you one, Jack. And you're looking at a dude who pays his debts." And then he was gone, the big engine spitting fire into the night, and Ike wondered if there had ever been a time, even in the emptiness of the desert, when he had felt so alone.

He saw Preston once more that week. It was the night before he was supposed to go to the ranch. He could not sleep and he was walking, down along the Coast Highway, past the old tattoo parlor, and that was where he saw Preston. It was very late and all the other stores along the highway were closed, but Ike saw this yellow light coming out of the shop, spreading across the sidewalk, and he stopped to look through the greasy glass as those punk chicks had once stopped to look at him. And he saw with a start the heavy black boots and ragged, fingerless hands hanging from the sides of the chair. Preston was tilted back and staring at the ceiling. The old man was bent over him, his thick back bowed as he concentrated on his work. And he seemed to work very slowly, and it was different somehow from the way he had worked on Ike. He was not sure exactly what the difference was, or what it meant, only that he was not supposed to see it, and he stepped back into the shadows. He thought about waiting for Preston to come out, doubting once again the conclusions he had reached at the side of the highway. But he did not wait. For some crazy reason his teeth had begun to chatter and he hurried back to his room through the streets of Huntington Beach, which he could no longer quite see as part of some smoothly running machine, but which instead had become a labyrinth, a dark maze from which he feared there was no escape.

PART
FOUR

36

The drive to Milo's party was not a pleasant one. The moment Ike got his first look at Hound Adams, he could see that Hound had not been getting much sleep lately. He looked coked out, on edge, and he drove that way. Foot to the floor. Gray concrete ribbons unwinding too fast in the early light. They rode in the Sting-Ray. Frank Baker was going up too, delivering some equipment in the van. Hound stuck the boards and wet suits in there as well and they started out together, but Frank was soon left far behind. At one point Michelle said something to Hound about slowing down and he snapped back at her, told her to stay off his case as the tires left skid marks around a long curve. The incident left Ike wondering just how much Michelle really knew about Hound's habit.

It was still early in the day when they arrived at the small brick house guarding the entrance to the Trax estate. Nothing here to prepare one for the grandeur that lay just beyond: the lush forest that seemed to spring suddenly from the dry hillsides. Huge dark trees. Moss like pale ghosts beneath black limbs. Patches of blue sky, straight up, so you had to crane your neck to see. Sounds of running water. And suddenly, the emergence from the trees. The great circular lawn, stone drive. The huge house with its small Spanish windows, iron-railed balconies, and tiled roofs, patterns of old ivy clinging to the walls, ancient stuff, black with time. And over everything, a silence.

Hound stopped near a fountain and pool. Dark birds, bathing in the water, darted at the sound of the engine, and then returned, their singing mixing with the splash of the fountain, the soft ticking of a hot engine.

They went up a series of stone steps, through a tall wooden door, and into a rose garden. And it was passing through the garden that Ike noticed for the first time, as if the initial impact of the place had been enough to blind him to any imperfections, that the house was in a surprising state of disrepair. The rose garden was spotted with weeds and thick dry grass, among which the few old bushes sprouted a handful of bright petals like points of flame in the sunlight.

They crossed another stone entry and climbed a set of heavily carpeted stairs. They found Milo Trax seated behind a desk, engaged in conversation on the phone. He nodded at them as they entered the room, his small eyes twinkling, but his voice betraying nothing to the party on the other end. Hound led them to a window from which they could admire the view.

They were on the west side of the house here, and looking down through a heavily wooded canyon that Ike realized was the patch of dark vegetation he had once seen from the water, they could see the ocean. A magnificent view, like having the world spread out below them. Green hills. Yellow patches of wild mustard. Distant collision of blues. At his side, Ike could hear Michelle suck in her breath.

"So what do you think?" a voice asked from behind them. Milo Trax had risen from his desk, and was now walking toward the window, the muscles flexing in an odd way in his short thick thighs.

"Beautiful," Michelle said. "I can't believe it. I've never seen anything like it."

"Good," Milo said, putting a hand on her back. "There's plenty of time before the party. Look around. Enjoy. Ike, you brought your board?"

Ike said that he had. He looked past Milo and noticed Hound Adams, now standing back, at the side of Milo's desk, arms folded across his chest, head bowed, face pointed toward the floor, as if he were lost in thought, or asleep on his feet. Ike could not see his face clearly enough to say which.

By midmorning Ike was alone with the waves, Frank having arrived with the boards before disappearing along with Hound Adams somewhere on the grounds. Michelle had stayed at the house to let Milo show her around. She had agreed to meet Ike later, on the beach.

The morning, the surf, could not have been more perfect. A clean swell, three to five feet out of the southwest. Paper-thin walls with long workable faces turned toward the sun. While he surfed, a school of porpoise arrived to join him for a time in the waves, passing in a leisurely fashion, slapping at the water with their bodies, calling to one another with strange sounds. They passed so close he could have reached them in a single stroke. A group of pelicans cruised by in formation, their bodies within inches of the sea. They circled the point and passed him once more, this time just inside the lineup, actually skimming along the faces of the waves, the last bird just ahead of the falling crest so it was like they were surfing, at play on the empty point, and he joined them in the waves, letting jewel-strung faces slip beneath his board, carving lines out of crisp morning glass.

He did not have to rush, to worry about beating anybody back outside, or watch for someone dropping in on him. He could paddle out slowly, take as much pleasure in watching the empty liquid lines as he did in riding them. It was something he had not fully appreciated on his first visit, how surfing was not just about getting rides. It struck him this morning that what he was doing was not separated into different things. Paddling out, catching rides, setting up. Suddenly it was all one act, one fluid series of motions, one motion even. Everything coming together until it was all one thing: the birds, the porpoise, the leaves of seaweed catching sunlight through the water, all one thing and he was one with it. Locked in. Not just tapping the source, but of the source. It must have been what they felt before him, what two young men had felt and given a name to. And he thought of what it must have been like then, beaches like this one scattered up and down the coast like jewels at the edge of the sea. It must have seemed too good to be true, and it must have seemed that it would be that way forever, and yet now it was the wreckage of that dream that lay between them. And he saw too that it was not just Preston and Hound who had lost. He thought of the pier, the crowds fighting for waves, the entire zoo of a town crouched on the sand and what had once passed as hunger and vitality had only a certain desperateness about it now, coked-out fatigue, because they had all lost and it was one great bummer, one long drop with no way back over the top. It was plain now, plainer than it had ever been before, what Preston had wanted him to see here. And he did see it. Preston had been right. There was something here, in this moment, that was worth hanging on to, that was worth building a life around. And he could see it, within reach, if he could only break away now, if he could only go and take Michelle with him.

Michelle was there when he reached the beach, turned on her stomach, eyes closed. He came up through the warm white sand and stopped to watch, quietly, because it looked as if she was asleep.

She wore a white two-piece suit, the top unfastened at the back. Her legs and arms seemed slenderer than he had remembered. Fine golden hairs glistened along the backs of her thighs. Lost moments from Huntington Beach returned to haunt him. Self-pity and desire rose to choke him, like dust on a desert wind. He was dizzy with it. He pulled off his wet suit and lay down beside her.

His body was still cold and damp. Hers was hot, warmed by the sun. She started and then shivered as he pressed against her. She turned to face him, laughing softly. "You're getting good," she whispered. "I was watching." There were small bits of sand stuck to her skin, on the cool white places beneath her breasts where they had been pressed against the towel. He lowered his face and took one of her nipples into his mouth, feeling the tiny grains of sand against his tongue. He moved his mouth across her body, tasting her skin. She arched beneath him and the sun was a fire at his back. He felt her fingers in his hair as he worked the bottom piece of her suit down over her legs and then they were both naked, on the white rectangle of cloth, on the white crescent of sand. He moved his face back toward hers, felt her hand upon him now, guiding him inside, and he felt the heat of her body reaching to swallow him. He came very quickly, and for a long time, shuddering, as if his whole body were emptying itself into hers. He closed his eyes against the ache of it, pressing his face into that sea of light-colored hair, mouth open, lips parted and pressed against her neck, his heart pounding between them. He felt himself still moving a little inside her, still hard, and then he was aware too, for the first time, of a minor distraction, a small sharp pain near his temple as if something was digging at his skin. He opened his eyes and raised his head. Her hair had fallen back, spread in a golden arc across the towel beneath her, and a sudden flash of light caught his eye—a piece of ivory, brilliantly white in the sunlight. The ivory was delicately carved in what looked to be an oriental design—a long slender alligator with jaws running two-thirds the length of its body and holding, now, in a devilish grin, Michelle's strawberry-blond hair as it had once held the coal-black hair of Ellen Tucker.

37

The sight of it stopped him. He lay still in her, but staring, suddenly aware that her eyes had fixed upon him as well, though they were not turned toward his face but rather toward the tattoo that spread itself across his shoulder, and the expression on her face was something between fascination and

horror—much, he imagined, like the expression on his own
face.

Though their eyes met, neither of them spoke. And then
the spell was broken by the sound of loose rock tumbling
somewhere far above them and Ike raised his eyes to see a pair
of boards catching sunlight and two figures picking their way
down the long, crumbling staircase. Hound Adams and Frank
Baker, come to surf the point.

In the time it took Frank and Hound to reach the beach,
Ike was able to pull his wet suit back on. The black and purple
material was still wet and cold and the coldness seemed to
reach him at once, to find its way down and into the bones.
Michelle had begun to move also, replacing her suit and covering the bottoms with a pair of white shorts. And then they
were both dressed, sitting suddenly side by side, in silence, the
magic of only moments before lost. The combs. The tattoo. He
knew that for a few seconds she had watched him, puzzled by
the change that had come over him. But he had not trusted his
voice and had remained silent. And while she watched him, he
had felt her hand, cool upon his own, but still he had been
unable to turn toward her and the hand had slipped away.

He knew now, without looking, that Hound and Frank
were nearly upon them, still moving across the sand. "Those
combs," he said finally, his throat tight around the words.
"Where did you get them?"

"Milo gave them to me," she said. "I think they're pretty."

There was something defensive and rather distant in her
voice, and when he turned to look at her he found that she was
staring toward the sea.

"Tide's dropping," he heard someone say. "Getting better."

It was Hound who spoke. Ike nodded. He saw Frank
Baker already at the water's edge. He watched as Frank
pushed his board ahead of him, then flattened himself on the
deck and began to paddle, quick, efficient strokes that carried
him into the sunlight as it danced upon the water.

Michelle rose suddenly at his side and for a moment blocked the sun. He watched her bend to brush some sand from her legs. "I'm going back to the house," she said. And then, as an afterthought: "You should let him show you around, Ike. I've never seen another house like it. There's a regular movie theater downstairs." Ike felt that her tone of voice was mechanical and forced, as if she was trying to be conversational for Hound's sake. He wondered if Hound noticed it as well. He wondered too just how long Hound and Frank had been at the top of the stairs.

He watched Michelle move across the beach, then looked once to see that Hound was watching her too. When she was gone, Hound knelt beside him, smiling, full of energy now, the tired look Ike had noted earlier, in the study, gone, the eyes jerked open, sandblasted clean and flat like two dark stones. There was something funny in that, though, in the way the eyes rested in the face—as if the eyes were brand-new but the face was still tired, the skin still a bit too pale, and too tight across the bones. "Not calling it a morning, brah?" Hound's voice was flat and even. "See you out there, huh." Ike felt Hound's hand on his shoulder.

And then he watched as Hound left him and walked toward the surf. Ike blinked into the light, following a line of white water as it wrapped around the point. When he stood, he found that his knees were weak from the lovemaking. He was still for a moment, watching as Hound broke through the lip of a wave and disappeared on the other side. Then he picked up his own board and followed, though it was more like he was sleepwalking now, like his body was going on its own while his mind continued to work on the combs he had seen in Michelle's hair. And as he waded into the shallows and felt the stones there, sharp against his feet, he found that he was actually talking out loud, his words spreading and vanishing in the air. "She was here," he said to no one. "And they have known —known everything all along." It was an astonishing phrase and he repeated it once more as he began to paddle, as the first line of white water washed over him, as if it were the only thing he knew.

They surfed for another hour. Hound said that the ranch was like Mexico, that there was a different rhythm here, that it took a while to adjust, to match one's energies to the flow. He said a lot of things, and oddly enough some of them were things that Ike had thought of himself. But they didn't sound right when spoken. Maybe it was because they were beyond words. Or maybe it was that Hound's voice was too flat and hollow, just one more rap, so that Ike was reminded of days in Hound's house—Hound sitting Indian style on the floor, lecturing on some artifact he had found, or some bit of lore, while the people came and went and even dumb little girls stoned on his dope knew it was bullshit. Frank Baker, Ike noted, did not join them but stayed to himself, surfing farther on the inside, and finally Ike himself turned his back on Hound Adams. He left Hound in midsentence and began paddling farther to his left, where he had once sat with Preston Marsh, where he could now be alone to think.

Later they left the water and climbed the stone stairs. They moved in single file, Hound in front with Ike bringing up the rear. The ground turned cool and damp beneath their feet. The scent of flowers drifted down from the gardens.

It was in the first of the terraced gardens that they found Milo Trax and Michelle. Milo was dressed in tennis clothes, his short thick legs propped on a chair. A pair of small wire-rimmed shades hid his eyes. Michelle was dressed in a white summer dress Ike had not seen before. There was a drink on the white wrought-iron table in front of her. Her fingers rested near the glass and she was looking away, into the trees, so he could see her profile, the small straight nose and arched brow he'd always held responsible for her slightly arrogant look. Her hair, he noticed, was pulled back, held in place by the ivory combs. She did not turn to meet his eyes.

"Home from the sea," Milo said. He smiled beneath the

shades and raised the drink in his hand, as if to toast them.
"How were the waves?" he asked.

"Good," Hound said.

Ike said nothing but continued to watch Michelle. Frank
Baker did not stop at all but continued walking and quickly
disappeared among the trees. Then Ike was aware of someone
speaking to him.

"Good that you enjoyed yourself," Milo was saying. "I'm
glad there was surf. Are you ready for some work?"

Ike felt himself nod. He looked for a moment at Michelle
and then down and into the small black holes that were Milo's
shades.

"There's a list in the house," Milo told him. "Some things I
would like done before the guests arrive. There are also some
clothes there I would like for you to wear tonight. Hound will
show you." Ike turned and followed Hound up the path.

38

He spent the rest of the afternoon hosing down driveways and
patios, raking leaves, and sweeping floors. "Milo's been in Eu-
rope," Hound explained. "The place needs some work."

Ike went through the motions, but his mind was still busy
with other things. Had Ellen been here, as he had at first
supposed? Or had the combs been left someplace else—in the
boat, or in Mexico? And why had they been given to Michelle?
Was it some bizarre coincidence? Or were they bait? At one
point in his work, Ike looked up to see Frank Baker and one of
the Samoans from Huntington Beach pushing some boxes on a
small truck. They were headed down through the gardens,
away from the house and out toward the point. Ike stopped
sweeping and rested on his broom. For a moment he thought
of following them and he looked back over his shoulder to see

if anyone else was around. What he saw was Milo Trax standing
on a small balcony, resting against the black iron railing. When
Milo saw Ike's face turn up toward him, he raised a hand. Ike
waved back and then resumed his sweeping, pushing his
broom beneath the sun-bleached walls, the ancient ivy with its
dark leaves and stems thick as branches.

When he was finished in the gardens, he went to Milo's
study and found the clothes that had been placed there for
him, a white long-sleeved shirt with ruffles down the front, a
black pair of pants, dark socks and shoes. He showered and put
on the clothes, which fit him surprisingly well and were fancier than any he had ever owned. Then he stood at the window of Milo's study and watched the sun set over the ocean. It
went down rapidly, beginning as a great red sphere, then
breaking and melting into the sea. There was something hyp-
notic in this movement of light and he was held by it until a
knocking at the door disturbed him. He hoped that it would be
Michelle. But it was Hound Adams who pushed the door open
and walked into the room, then stopped and closed the door
behind him. Ike instinctively tightened a hand on the sill.

There were only the pale jukebox colors of a vanishing
sunset to light the room and Hound did nothing to alter that.
He moved across the carpeted floor toward the window,
where he stopped to face Ike. "Not a bad view, is it?" He
paused for a moment but did not seem to be waiting for a
reply. He seemed rather to be waiting for Ike to turn his head
and look once more down across the purple trees, toward the
sea and the last blood-red sliver of sun. Ike obliged, watching
as Hound spoke. "When Preston and I were in high school, we
used to sneak up here and surf," Hound told him. "I knew
about it before Preston. You should have seen his face the first
time he saw this place. We camped down there on the hillside,
almost the same spot we found the boards, your boards."
Hound paused. Ike waited, watching the last of the sun. "We
used to sit down there and talk about places to go, talk about
what it would be like to own a place like this. What more is

there? Right?" Ike thought about his own first trip to the ranch, his first sight of the empty point. He had thought the same thing.

"It didn't really take us long to meet Milo," Hound said. "As it turned out. I'll tell you how it happened. Preston and I had this escape route all planned out. We'd found a kind of ravine that split the main cliff out near the point, then ran in what was almost a straight line all the way back to the gate and that little dirt road the cowboys use. There was a lot of brush and sage in it and we took the time once to bring up some machetes and clear it out a bit, left it thick down near the beach, though, because we had an idea that maybe the cowboys didn't know about it." Ike thought once more about Preston crouching at the foot of the cliff, asking Ike if he could find the truck.

"And you used it that night."

Hound nodded. "Worked like a charm. But I was telling you about the time we met Milo. We'd come up on a big swell and we were in the water, way outside. I mean, the point must have been a good fifteen feet, almost closed out, and we looked up and saw these cowboys up on the hill, watching us. Then we saw them get in a truck and start down. We started talking about what to do. The road down is fairly long, winding as it does, and we figured that if we could pick off a couple of waves and get back in—in a hurry—we could make it into that ravine. The trouble was, it was damn big and the waves were getting hard to make. Big ledgy drops." He paused here for a moment, as if remembering those drops. Ike worked on imagining them too, on imagining Hound and Preston out there together—like he had seen them in that photograph at the shop.

"Preston was always a shade better than I was," Hound said. "I didn't like admitting it at the time. But he was. He was that day, too. He picked off this fucking wave I couldn't believe. It was getting hard to get into them. Steep faces. You really had to claw. Anyway, Preston got a wave. Finally I saw his head pop up over the lip way on the inside and I knew he had made it. Time was running out and I had to take whatever I could get. I still don't know if the wave I got was makeable or not but I ate it, right at the top." He paused and made a slight motion as if to shrug off the memory. "Maybe I just choked," he said. "Anyway, it was a tough swim back in and it took a long time. When I got back to the beach, there was this pickup and three cowboys waiting for me. One of them had an ax handle. I'd never had any trouble at the ranch, but everybody had heard stories about getting caught there, getting your board stolen and your ass kicked in. I was so tired from the damn swim it was all I could do just to drag my ass out of the water. Preston was nowhere around so I figured he'd made it into the ravine and I would have to take whatever came. I remember I tried getting up and this asshole with the ax handle kicked me back down, caught me in the side of the face with his fucking boot. And then all of a sudden there was Prez. He'd gotten all the way back up to the truck, ditched his board, and come back with a tire iron." Hound paused to chuckle and once again Ike had that feeling that he'd had only a couple other times, that Hound Adams was not bullshitting him, or playing some role, but just talking, and it seemed to Ike now, that at such moments there was something in Hound one could still like. That in spite of everything else, his obvious treachery and many guises, there was still something there— some shadow perhaps of Preston's old friend. "He wasn't the crazy-looking motherfucker he is today," Hound said. "But he was big, and he was a hell of an athlete. He flattened that guy with the ax handle before the guy knew what hit him. I thought for a few minutes he might even have killed him. He hadn't, but nobody knew that just then and all of a sudden the other two guys didn't want any part of either of us. I grabbed the one guy's stick and together we ran these assholes right off the beach. Then we climbed into their own damn truck and started back. By the time we got back to the gate, though, there was this short, stocky guy in a tennis outfit standing there waiting for us with a double-barreled shotgun laid across his arm and a half-dozen more ranch hands waiting behind him.

"That was how we met Milo Trax. The funny part was, we had impressed him. Seems he'd been watching the whole thing with his field glasses and he was not used to seeing his boys run off like that, but then he was not used to seeing the ranch ridden at fifteen feet either—particularly not the way Preston had ridden it. So he invited us up to his place, his crib, man. Right here. In this room. We sat up here looking down over the point and smoking up some dope that Prez and I had in the truck, and then smoking up some of what Milo kept in the house." Hound stopped to wave toward the glass. "One thing led to another," he said. "We left the ranch that night with our own fucking keys. Our keys, Ike. We thought we'd died and gone to heaven."

Ike turned back to the window. The sun was gone now. A single band of reddish light lay on the horizon, beneath a quickly darkening sky. The trees were dark now too, black and wild against a deep purple sea, and from beneath their branches a light mist had begun to rise. He didn't know why Hound was telling him all this. There was always a reason. But Ike was tired of Hound's games, and of his own. "And your sister, Janet," he said, speaking slowly. "You brought her here too?"

Hound Adams was a moment in replying, as if for once Ike had taken him completely by surprise. "Yes," he said at last.

"And then to Mexico?"

"Yes."

"And Ellen Tucker. Did you bring her here too or just to Mexico?" The feeling Ike had as he spoke was not unlike what he'd felt on the highway with Preston—the adrenaline rush of a trip to the edge.

Hound just looked at him but his first slightly stunned expression had begun to shift. There was now the shadow of a smile in his eyes. "I think you've got it all wrong, brah," Hound said. "I didn't take your sister anywhere, though she may have gone to Mexico on her own. She might be there now." He smiled and spread his hands.

"And you've known all along that she was my sister."

"No. Not at first. I had heard her mention a brother, but I had gotten the impression that you were older. Then I got a look at you one morning in that cafe. After that I saw you nosing around down on the beach, sticking out like a goddamn sore thumb. Then I saw you at my party. Bad hick vibes. Lots of paranoia. I began to think that Ellen had lied, or exaggerated, or that there was another brother. Those first questions I asked you that night were intuitive, but you were giving me the right answers. Then there was that bit about somebody ripping off your board. I did a little checking up on the nose rider we found at the ranch, finally ran it down to that kid who had sold it to you." He stopped to laugh. "Preston must have put the fear of God into that kid; he was still sweating the return of the crazed biker."

"So why didn't you ever say anything?"

Hound was still smiling—an obnoxious, knowing sort of smile now. "A good game always makes life a little more interesting. I could see that you were playing one. I decided to let you play your hand. But what makes you think I took your sister to Mexico?"

Ike stared back into Hound's smile, wondering about what to say. Should he mention those combs? Or perhaps the kid in the white Camaro? Cat and mouse one more time. But then he was set upon by the sudden notion that the combs should go unmentioned, at least for the moment. "Someone told us," he said. "A guy drove out to the desert and told us that Ellen had gone to Mexico with some guys from Huntington Beach, that she had not come back."

"He said I took her?"

Ike tried to pick his words carefully. "Just that she went, that you might know what happened."

"Who was he?"

"I don't know."

Hound appeared genuinely puzzled for a moment. "I

would say you were lied to, brah. I don't know why. Your sister
was on the run, Ike, from the desert, from the people who
raised her, from you." He let that last word hang there for a
moment between them, and then went on. "She passed
through," he said. "We had a few laughs."

"Like you had a few laughs with Janet?" Ike could feel
that adrenaline surge building once again, but he didn't like
the way the conversation was going. Hound was simply putting him together, laying down bullshit, as Ike had always
known he would. He just wanted to wipe that smile off Hound
Adams's face one more time.

It worked. Hound came a step closer, so that his chest was
almost touching Ike's, but the smile was gone. "You're pushing
it, aren't you?" he asked. "I don't know what you think you're
hip to about Janet, and I don't know who told you, but I'll tell
you something about her, and about your sister. And about
Preston, too, as far as that goes. They all chose, man. Their own
paths. They chose what they wanted. Your sister could have
stayed. I liked her. She chose differently. Janet chose too."

"And what did she choose?" But even as he was asking he
realized that he had not been specific. Janet or Ellen? He
waited on Hound.

"She chose to die," Hound said. His voice was softer now
and when it fell away the room was very quiet. "Death because she was afraid of life," he added. "You see, things got
complicated for her that time in Mexico. They were not really
that way. Only in her own head." Hound paused and tapped
his temple. "Things were not complicated; they were new, for
all of us. It was a voyage of discovery, brah. I mean that. And
Janet was there with us. She began very free and loving, but
she made the mistake of stopping, of falling back on the
thoughts of others. She stopped listening to her own heart."
He shrugged. "And it killed her." He looked past Ike and into
the blackness of the window. "Now maybe you can see more
about what I was trying to tell you that day in your room—that
business about letting others do your thinking. It's all in here,"
he said, and stabbed at Ike's chest with his hand, hard enough

to be uncomfortable. "You see, most people never make the kind of trip I'm talking about. They never even start out. What they really do is spend their lives hiding from themselves. And because of that—and because they're the ones who set the standards, it's a lonely trip, Jack. You're out there on your own and it can get weird and I've seen people flipped out by it. They get halfway, man, and they lose faith. They can't handle it. Janet couldn't handle it. Preston sure as hell couldn't handle it. With Janet the complications began around something as simple as not knowing who the father of her child was." He stopped and shrugged once more. "But it's what I've been trying to tell you all along. This is your trip, brah. And it's your choice."

Ike waited for Hound to go on, to say more about the choice, but he didn't. Hound turned away from the window in silence and retreated a few steps into the center of the room. When he turned once more, his voice had taken on a more conversational tone. "You know, Milo likes you," he said. "And you've done all right this summer—with one minor exception that need not be mentioned. You've done as well as could be expected. I mean, we've worked pretty well together, haven't we? And I could use someone new around the shop. I don't mean just working there, I mean really looking after things. I want to travel some more, but I want to know things are in good hands when I'm gone."

"What about Frank?"

Hound made that shrugging motion once more. His reply was surprising. "Frank's a loser," Hound said. "I mean, he's around. That's all. Shit. He's always been around. But you want to know something? Frank Baker doesn't even have his own key to that damn gate out there. I could swing that for you. I mean it, brah. Your own goddamn key. You could have it all, man." And he nodded into the blackened window beyond which the forests and ocean were now invisible, so that it seemed to Ike that Hound spoke only of the darkness. "But remember what I told you, brah. You'll have to choose. Think about it."

Hound left then. He went out into the hall and left Ike alone in Milo Trax's study. He left the door ajar and Ike watched a thin shaft of yellow light fall across the carpet to break upon the polished leather of his shoes.

39

Ike walked to Milo's desk and turned on a lamp. The light made mirrors now of the tall arched panes of glass that faced the sea, and in them Ike could see himself reflected, a stranger in expensive clothes. So what, he thought, if he made that choice right now? What if when Milo returned there were two sets of expensive clothes on the floor of his study? And what if by then Ike and Michelle were already gone? Down to the beach and up through the ravine. There was still some money left in Huntington Beach, enough for bus tickets. By morning they could be on their way to another place. Anywhere. It didn't really matter. He would tell Preston, and they would keep in touch, and if anything was ever found, Preston would let him know. It would be as Preston had said. He went out of the room and into the hall.

There were noises in the house now that he had not noticed in the room. Someone was playing music in one of the outside patios, and there were voices—Milo's guests, he supposed. The party had begun.

Most of the voices were indistinct and drifted to him from remote parts of the house. One voice, however, made itself separate and he recognized it as Milo's. The voice was closer than the others, suddenly almost below him, and he stepped to the railing that lined the balcony to look down.

He was above the stone entry upon which he and Hound and Michelle had stood earlier in the day. There were four

men below him now. Hound, Milo, and two other men he had
not seen before. One of the men was wide and dark. He stood
slightly apart from the others with his hands at his sides. The
other man was tall and rather thin, but wiry and tan. He wore
white slacks and a blue blazer jacket. Above the jacket, his hair
was a very fine shade of gray—nearly silver, beneath the lights
of the entry. The two strangers had apparently just arrived
and were being escorted into the house by Milo and Hound.
They passed almost directly below Ike and Milo's voice
reached him once more, clearly enough to be heard distinctly.

"Yes," Milo was saying. "I have some men working on it
right now. It will be ready."

The silver-haired man nodded. When he spoke, his voice
was softer than Milo's, and serious. "These people?" he asked.
"The real thing?"

"Oh, yes. Some, anyway."

"And you can handle them?" The men were turning now,
moving back beneath the railing and out of Ike's sight. "I rely
heavily upon Hound," Milo said. "But don't worry. I think
you'll find it interesting." The silver-haired man said something else, but Ike was unable to make it out. He remained at
the rail a moment longer and was about to leave it when he
saw Milo and Hound once again. The two men were walking
back across the stone floor beneath him. Milo walked with his
hand at Hound's back. It was held there in an odd way, as if he
were guiding Hound across the floor and through the doorway
on the other side, and Ike was struck by the gesture. It was the
way a man might put his hand on the back of a child, he
thought, or a lover.

Ike stepped quickly away from the railing and entered
the doorway at the far end of the balcony. It was dark there
and he waited a moment for his eyes to adjust. He did not
know what to make of the things he had heard. What he found
himself thinking about was that final image of Hound and Milo
as they passed through the door, Milo's hand at Hound's back.
It seemed to connect for him to other things—to those letters

he'd once seen scratched into the metal partition of a bathroom in Huntington Beach, to what Michelle had told him on
the boat, to Hound's abstinence at his own parties. And he
found himself wondering what Hound would have to say
about it. Quite a line of bullshit, no doubt—one more stop
perhaps on the road to discovery. Or maybe Ike was wrong,
maybe it explained nothing.

There was a window open somewhere. He could feel the
damp draft on his face. He could smell the sea and a trace of
bougainvillaea. There were several doors along the hall. One
stood partially open. Ike went to the door and stopped. He
whispered. When there was no answer, he pushed it open and
walked inside.

The room was large, empty, and dark, though saved from
total darkness by a pair of tall French doors that stood open
upon a small balcony. The fog seemed to have lifted a bit and
the doors emitted a pale light. He could make out a few pieces
of furniture—a bed, dresser, a small nightstand, a pair of large
chairs. The scent of the gardens was strong in the room. He
was about to leave when he noticed what appeared to be a
white dress hung against the blackness of the closet. At first
glance he thought that the dress was the one he had seen
Michelle in that afternoon. But moving closer, he saw it was
not. The style was slightly different. And then he noticed a
second dress draped over a chair. This dress was white as well,
also similar in style to Michelle's. He held aside the dress that
hung in the closet's doorway. The small space was filled with
women's clothes—or girls' clothes, because there was something in the general cut and color of the fabrics that suggested
youth. Pushing through them, he was aware of the pulse in his
hand, of the coolness of the fabrics against his skin.

From the closet he moved to the dresser. There were
some toilet articles on top—brushes, a hand mirror. Opening a
drawer, he saw that it was filled with jewelry, with bracelets
and ornaments for the hair. He moved them about with his
fingers, listening to the soft scraping sounds they made upon
the wood, suddenly seeing Milo Trax doing the very same

thing, standing in this same spot, searching for some trinket and selecting the ivory combs—they were, judging by what he saw here now, the nicest, the most expensive. It had been that simple. The combs had not been given to Michelle to bait him. Hound Adams was probably not even aware of them and Ike had been right not to catch him in his lie. His hunch at least had bought him some time. And yet there was something in that now which struck him as little more than a cruel joke. He had entered the trap, and he could not believe now that he had not seen it before, had not sensed the evil of this place from the beginning. He had, he supposed, always been too sidetracked by other things. On this particular trip he had thought only of the chance to talk to Michelle, to save her from some dread trip to Mexico. Save her. Jesus. There had been no trips to Mexico for Ellen Tucker. Preston had been right: the kid in the white car had lied. Or, Ike thought, perhaps he had only been wrong. But then it really made no difference now. He had been right on the beach: Ellen had been here and this is what there was. A party at the ranch. And the ranch was the end of the line.

40

He left the room as he had found it, lit only by the pale light entering through the glass doors. But it felt more like a tomb now, and as he closed the door after him he felt something go out of him, as if some piece of himself had been left there.

He found another set of steps at the far end of the hall, and a door to the outside. He went through it and felt the cool air, damp and heavy on his face. His face, he thought, was very hot, almost feverish, as he moved through a dark garden, around a corner of the house, and into one of the patios where guests were congregating.

A fair-sized group had already arrived. Some had seated themselves in lawn chairs, others on the ground. Ike stood for a moment at the edge of the patio, searching for Michelle, taking in the scene. The ages of the guests appeared mixed, though most looked to be younger than Milo, closer in fact to Hound's age, and Ike was reminded of the conversation he'd recently overheard—the silver-haired man's question about control, Milo's answer that he depended upon Hound.

Many of the people were dressed simply, in Levi jeans, Mexican pullovers, or Levi jackets. Others, however, were decked out more elaborately in a kind of funky evening dress that seemed to Ike to be more costume than anything else. The clothing seemed to have something to do with how the guests were grouped. A circle of those more simply dressed had been formed upon the concrete floor of the patio, and as Ike turned toward them he saw that Hound Adams was there as well, seated at the center of the group, apparently engaged in some conversation, or debate, with a thickly built bald-headed man Ike had not seen before. Ike was too far away to catch anything of what was being said, but he could see both men moving their heads, occasionally gesturing with their hands. The rest of those seated on the ground seemed to be following the conversation with some interest. And though a few of the more elaborately dressed people had come to stand at the edge of the circle, most of the others were scattered about across the garden, forming smaller groups of their own.

Through an open sliding door Ike caught a glimpse of the two men he'd seen earlier, in the entry with Hound and Milo. He could see a bit of light shining off the taller man's hair. Whether or not Milo was with them he could not say. Music drifted from the house and across the gardens—damp now in the fog, so that where the light struck the leaves of the plants the leaves looked slick and wet. Ike stood for a moment longer, making certain that Michelle was not among the guests, then he stepped backward, away from the edge of concrete and into the shadows.

He was desperate to find her now. He did not want to go
back into the house by way of the patio. He did not want to risk
another confrontation with either Hound or Milo, as he still
did not know what was expected of him. He was beginning to
feel rather foolish in the clothes. They were, he decided, a
little like those costumes he'd seen some of the guests in. But
there was something else about them as well, something that
made him feel he had already compromised himself, that he
was Milo's boy.

It was back near the front of the house, looking for the
door he had come out of, that he heard the sound of an engine
starting somewhere in the night. He hurried along a narrow
walkway and up a ragged flight of stone steps. The steps led up
to the great circular lawn and he reached the level of the lawn
in time to see a set of headlights moving toward him out of the
fog. The headlights turned away from him as the drive curved,
and he saw Frank Baker's yellow van move past him. Frank
must have spotted him coming up the steps, because the van
slowed a bit as it went by and he could see Frank's face turned
toward him through the glass. They were not separated by
much, ten or twelve feet perhaps, but it was still too dark to
make out an expression on Frank's face. There were only the
shadows of features, the curly blond hair, slicked back and
wet, catching a bit of light—just as it once had in that alley in
Huntington Beach the night Ike had seen him talking to Preston Marsh.

The van did not slow to a complete stop. The face turned
from the window and it was all gone, nothing left but the red
glow of taillights vanishing among the trees and finally just the
sound of the engine, growing fainter until it too was swallowed
by the forest, by the silence of the ranch.

When he finally found her, she was downstairs in the
theater she had spoken of. It was a small theater, but a theater
nonetheless. There were perhaps three-dozen seats, a screen,
and a small stage. Thick velvet curtains covered the walls, and
where the curtains were parted there were various pieces of

ornamental plaster, scrollwork, prowling cats and lions' heads with soft blue light spilling from their jaws. Michelle was alone in the room. She was seated on an aisle down near the front, one leg over the arm of her chair so that the white dress was pushed back on her thigh. There was a drink in one hand, resting on her knee, and when she turned to look up at him her eyes appeared sleepy and slightly out of focus.

"Don't you like it?" she asked as he knelt beside her. "This room is so great."

"Michelle, we've got to go, now."

She blinked at him in a slightly drunken fashion. "He told me to wait here. What are you talking about?"

He looked instinctively over one shoulder, back toward the heavy wooden doors at the end of the aisle. "I'm talking about leaving, just the two of us, right now." He put a hand on her arm. "Look, just trust me, okay? I can explain it to you on the way. Right now we've just got to get started."

She seemed to sink farther back into the seat. "But why . . ."

"Because something crazy is going on here," he told her. He was talking quickly now, like he was running out of breath. "Remember how we thought my sister went to Mexico, how that was what the kid told me? Well, I came up here because I was afraid you were going to go. I didn't want you to. I wanted to talk you out of it, to tell you what I'd learned. But it's not Mexico, Michelle. Ellen never went to Mexico. They brought her here, to the ranch, and they did something." He was squeezing her arm now and she tried to jerk it away from him. He held on tighter. Finally she just shouted at him to stop, and so he did. He let go of her arm and she sat there rubbing it.

"Jesus," she said. "Slow down a minute. Hound knows why you're here, you know. He knows you're Ellen's brother. And I didn't tell him."

"He's known it since that party at his house. I've just talked to him."

"He says that she was in Huntington Beach but that she's gone, that she was running away and that she didn't want

anyone following her. He says that she didn't want you following her. But that you don't handle it very well so you make up
things."

"And you believe that?"

She was still holding her arm, looking down now at the
floor. "I don't know," she said. "I'm not sure what to believe.
You were right about one thing. You remember that dress shop
Ellen worked in with Marsha? I wanted us to go there but you
said it wouldn't do any good. Well, you were mostly right. The
old lady that owns it says she doesn't know anything about
where Ellen went. But she said she left without picking up
some money the old lady owed her. She said it's not that much,
but that if I could get an address she would mail it. I was going
to tell you but I never got the chance."

Ike was silent for a moment, thinking about Michelle going to check that out, thinking of what she had told him. "But I
just don't know, Ike," Michelle was saying now. "You were
acting like such a jerk. . . ."

Ike reached up suddenly and tore one of the ivory combs
from her hair. She made a small, sharp cry and put one hand to
her head. Ike held the comb in front of her face. "Do you see
this?" he said. "It was hers, Michelle. It was Ellen's goddamn
comb. Our mother gave these to her. And she wouldn't have
gone off without them. Listen to me. I saw this picture once.
Hound had sold it to these guys that buy dope from him. I
didn't get a real good look at it, but it looked like a picture of a
chick who'd been all cut up." He shook his head. "I don't know
exactly how. But all this shit connects. The movies Hound
makes, those runaway girls he's always trying to meet. And
that day on the boat. Hound was delivering movies. I think
Hound spends the summer making those damn things, then
he shows them to Milo. They're looking for something—the
right people, something. And then they come up here. Milo's
summer party. Have you taken a good look at this place? They
could pull any kind of shit they wanted to up here and no one
would know. All I know is that something bad is coming down,
Michelle. Here. Hound was acting very strange—which is not

that unusual, but he was trying to lay this trip on me about choosing, about how if I made the right choice I could be his partner or some damn thing. But I don't want to be his partner, Michelle. I've already chosen, and Hound's not going to like it when he finds out. That's why we've got to leave, both of us, now."

She was really looking at him at last. He was still not sure that she believed what he was telling her, but there was no more time to talk. He got to his feet and pulled her up with him. Her leg swung down off the seat and her drink hit the floor between them, the glass breaking. "Ike." She started to say something but did not finish. She was cut short by the soft swish of a swinging door.

"Not leaving?" The words drifted down to them from the back of the room. Ike turned to see Milo Trax and Hound Adams standing at the top of the aisle. Milo held something in his hand, what looked like a roll of film. Standing behind Milo and Hound were the two men Ike had seen before, the tall man with silver hair and his thick, dark friend. "But they make a fine pair, don't they?" Milo asked. No one answered him.

Ike felt something twisting in his chest. He looked at Michelle. She was still watching him, her eyes wide and clear now. But he had been too late.

The four men came down the aisle. Hound was holding something as well, a dark leather bag. The silver-haired man had his hands pushed into the pockets of the blue blazer jacket. He was smiling. Ike looked at each of the men, then at Hound Adams. Hound met his stare, but his expression did not change—it was in fact a perfect blank and after a moment he looked away, toward the screen and the heavy curtains. And there was something in just that simple movement of the eyes that suggested something, a kind of washing of the hands, perhaps. Hound and Ike had had their little talk. Hound had done what he could; what happened now was between Ike and Milo Trax—or so it seemed.

"I was about to suggest that we do drugs and make a

movie," Milo said. "You ought to be in pictures. And you will, both of you."

The gray-haired man, Ike noticed, was watching Milo and smiling. "I always wondered how you handled these things," he said. Hound Adams unzipped the small leather bag and removed a needle and a syringe, also a light-colored cord.

"What is it?" Michelle asked. "Coke?"

"What the doctor ordered," Milo answered. He was looking at Ike now. "Right?" he asked.

Ike didn't answer. He looked at Milo and then he turned and looked at Hound Adams. He did it very deliberately. He turned his shoulder to Milo and his friends and he waited until Hound raised his eyes from the works in his hands. When he did, his face was still without expression—as if Ike were a perfect stranger. But Ike knew better. He knew what he was going to say; he only hoped that he could say it without his voice cracking. His heart was beating heavily, making it hard to breathe. "We don't want it," he said. "Neither of us. And no more movies." He watched Hound Adams. "And we're going to leave. Now." He knew, of course, that it was not true, but it was something he wanted to say—for the record or some damn thing. He even reached behind him with one hand, as if to take Michelle's, as if the two of them were going to step out into the aisle and go home.

Somewhere at his side, Ike heard Milo making a soft clicking sound with his mouth. He thought that Milo was shaking his head a bit too, sadly, from side to side, but he was not sure; he didn't want to take his eyes off Hound. And Hound's expression was starting to change just a bit now, or so it seemed to Ike; he was beginning to look rather tired again, as he had in Milo's study. He was still not looking at Ike, however. He was very carefully putting his works back in the bag, and then setting the bag on the chair in front of Ike and Michelle. Then he looked up and for a moment their eyes met. And then Hound hit him.

He hit him so fast and hard that for a moment Ike was not even sure where he had been hit, only that something was very wrong, that he had lost his voice and that he was drowning. He was on his knees when Hound took possession of his arm, pinning it between his own bicep and upper body while Milo bent to roll Ike's sleeve. Ike watched Milo—eyes fixed on the needle, mouth pursed in a disapproving fashion. He watched the cord go around his arm, and then he watched the needle slip under the skin. He was not sure what to expect. He waited for a rush but it did not come. There was instead a kind of gradual blurring, a slowing down, a slipping into darkness. The experience was not unlike the time the doctor put him out in King City to work on his leg. And somewhere, going down, he thought he heard Michelle scream and he tried to pull himself back, but it was no use. He was definitely going, going under. He could still see their faces, though—Hound and Milo peering down on him from this great height, cheek to cheek almost, it appeared to Ike, like a pair of surgeons about to lose a patient. Something funny, though, about those faces—Milo's all pinched and dark, his little mouth puckered up like a hole in something. A spoiled child about to throw a tantrum. And given the power-lifter's body that went with the face, Ike was able to take a certain comfort in his distance from it. Hound didn't look angry. He looked something else, worried perhaps, or maybe even scared. But Ike was puzzled, in a curious and detached sort of way, that he should be the object of such concern. And then, and it was the last detail he would remember, he saw that they were not really looking into his face, but rather at his shoulder, at the tattoo that had come snaking out from beneath his rolled-up sleeve. And then Milo reached down—small thick fingers like pegs of iron, cold on Ike's skin, and tore away the rest of the shirt so that they might have a look at the whole thing. And apparently they could not dig it. Imagine that. Ike smiled into Milo's pouting mouth. He smiled into Hound Adams's fear. Harley-Fuckin'-Davidson. The faces went away.

41

He thought there was a movie, though it might have been a dream. When he opened his eyes for the first time after getting the drug, the first thing he saw was fire. One fire was almost directly in front of him, others at either side, and there were more lights above the flames—different, white holes burning out of the night, hurting his eyes. And music, a kind of dull rhythmic drumming like the beat of his own heart and above that a thin, reedy wail. It was too much, really, to take in all at once. He felt sick and disoriented, lost amid the motion and noise—everything pulsing and swaying in time to that slow heartbeat rhythm. He closed his eyes once more and a light breeze kissed his face. The smoke of the fires hung on the breeze and burned behind his closed lids. Also on the breeze were the scents of brush and sage together with the damp rotting odor of a distant shoreline—and then something else as well, the heavy scent of incense rising with the smoke, growing quickly, heavier and sweeter, until it had blotted out all the others and clung to the night in an overpowering way. He felt on the verge of nausea and he opened his eyes.

There was a pole near each fire and from each pole an animal hung butchered. Above the fire nearest him he could make out light-colored fur matted with blood, black jaws and white teeth, a dark tongue. There was more blood on the pole. He looked away. He was seeing more now, taking more in, but it was like he was doing it all in slow motion—in time to that strange slow beat through the odd mix of lights, the smoke and incense. There was also the growing awareness of a dull ache beginning somewhere at the base of his skull, of an incredible weakness in his limbs. He saw that he was seated on the ground and that others were seated around him and that together they formed a great circle. Inside the circle formed by the people there was another circle of stones, and in the center of that circle there was the great stone ring with the flat rock in the middle and he realized for the first time where he was—that place at the edge of the cliff from which he had first glimpsed the house, the spot in which Preston had fought Terry Jacobs, and he remembered there had been a dead animal that night, too—white teeth and black tongue. Dead eyes.

The fires, and he could now see that there were four, burned at what might have been the four points of the compass—one at the edge of the circle nearest the sea, another at the edge closest to the forest, the remaining two at equal distance in between. He also saw that lines had been drawn in the earth. The lines led out, away from the center, connecting the stonework in the middle to the four fires that were between the ring of people and the ring of stones. The lines appeared to have been scratched into the ground, then spattered with blood.

Beyond the ring of people, of which Ike himself was a part, he could just make out the dim shapes of what appeared to be more figures—these, however, wore dark robes and hoods and it was hard to tell how many there were because they blended easily with the night. In places the fire lit patches of flesh—bare chests and faces like his own, but many others had blackened their skin with a dark paste. He looked for the source of the music; it did not seem to be coming from anyone he could see, but rather from the forest, as if the whole place had been wired for sound. At the far side of the clearing there appeared to be some kind of structure to which the brilliant white lights were attached, but the lights made it hard to look in that direction and he could not see much. Nor could he see anything of Milo Trax or Hound Adams. It was at this point, however, that he saw Michelle.

She was carried into the clearing by one of the robed and hooded figures. It must have been a man who carried her because the figure was tall and thick beneath the robes and strong enough to hold Michelle easily away from his chest in his arms. The man passed through the various circles until he stood at the center and there he stopped to place her upon that rectangle of rock that marked the very center of the rings. He placed her on her back and she was immediately bathed in a direct flood of light.

The figure who had brought her now stood at her feet and removed his hood and Ike saw that it was the bald man he had earlier seen talking to Hound Adams in the garden. It was hard to guess the man's age. His head was ringed by a fringe of light-colored hair, but whether the hair was blond or gray, Ike could not say. The man's face appeared smooth and unlined as he stood silently and stared into the trees and music before him. Michelle did not move. She was still clothed in the white dress. After remaining motionless for several seconds, the man suddenly bent forward and with one swift movement ripped the dress apart, letting the white material fall back upon either side of the stone. The stone's surface was slightly convex, so that as Michelle lay upon it her legs curved down and her head was thrown back, her body thrust forward into the night. She was naked now and with the blackness of the rock beneath her, the blackness of the sky above, her body, with arms stretched back as if to reach for the ground beneath her head, and breasts pulled flat, was like some slender white arc. There was something terribly beautiful in it, Ike thought, and something that made his bones numb with horror. He couldn't take his eyes from her. He thought of her on the beach—sun-warm skin, hot beneath his fingers.

Someone now passed the man a large ceramic container and he began to anoint her, spattering what appeared to be the blood of the butchered animals upon her, mostly down the center of her body, until at last he tilted the container and emptied it upon her genitals. Still she did not move. The man placed the container on the ground and bent his face between her legs.

Ike was set upon by a cold flood of nausea. He wanted to move and yet the waves of sickness were like hot lead—like his body was shot through with it, too heavy to budge. He leaned forward, trying to gather himself for some action, to rise, to move toward her, but a hand came from somewhere behind him and pushed him back down. "Watch it," a voice said, and he recognized the voice as Hound Adams's. He thought of that photograph he had once glimpsed on the cliffs of Huntington Beach. Had it been the blood of animals in the picture, or the blood of the girl herself? Who were these people and how far would they go?

But he would never know for sure. For whatever Milo Trax had planned for his summer's party that night, he had not planned the sudden rumble that shook the ground, a kind of dull thunder that seemed to begin somewhere beneath them and then rose, bringing to the night a fresh reddish glow that spread on the sky high above the light of the fires. Ike was aware of the hand leaving his shoulder, of Hound Adams stepping past him and into the clearing. Hound was not dressed in any dark robes, but rather in a pair of white cotton pants and a white Mexican pullover, and he stood now in sharp contrast to the dark figures around him. And then from the opposite side of the circle, Ike saw Milo Trax entering the clearing as well. And if it was true that Hound, in his white pants and pullover, might have stood in contrast to the figures in black, it was also true that the very contrast of black and white might have been taken for some part of the scene. Milo, however, was dressed in a pair of blue shorts and a wildly colored Hawaiian shirt. There was a skipper's hat turned backward on his head and even in the darkness he still wore the small wire-rimmed shades.

The man who had been kneeling before Michelle had raised his head and was looking about him, first at Hound then at Milo, his face smeared now with the dark liquid. His robes had fallen open and Ike could see for the first time a necklace of skulls upon his chest and the flash of something metallic at his waist. Others were beginning to stir as well, looking toward the woods where the music had stopped.

It was an odd moment—like a frozen frame. Ike kept

expecting some movement, but it did not come. Milo, Hound, the man nearest Michelle, all of them seemed locked in place, waiting. And then Milo reached to his face and pulled off the shades. He held them for a moment in his hand and then threw them to the ground in a gesture of disgust. He turned a bit and said something over his shoulder. It sounded like: "No, it's not part of it." And Ike saw that he was speaking to the silver-haired man in the blazer jacket. The man was barely visible, just at the edge of the clearing, beneath the white lights.

Milo looked back toward his house, toward the thunder that had given way to a distant crackling, and Ike saw for the first time that he was holding a small stick in his hand—something like a riding crop. He banged it against his leg, and then he did an odd thing with it. He held it up and shook it toward the trees, almost as if he could change things with it, Ike thought, as if it were a magic wand. And there was something almost comical in the gesture, in the absurd figure cut by Milo Trax—his squat, powerful body, his garish shirt, his little stick. But then the moment was past and the scene had begun to dissolve.

It took a moment for Ike to connect the sharp cracking sounds from the forest with what was happening to Milo. One second he was standing there in the clearing, arm upraised, the next he was on his back in the dirt, and then over on one side and there were holes in his chest—black, ugly places where the shirt was wet and stuck to the flesh—and there was this odd sound, something Ike knew he would not quickly forget, as if the holes were sucking air and blowing back a dark mist. But that moment of silence, in which the strange sound was audible, was short-lived—for suddenly it was not quiet at all, and it was not still. The adrenaline rush of pure fear had finally found the collective nerve and the night was one great circus of motion and sound, of panic and death. And if those hooded figures had come to practice some satanic ritual, or to invoke some devil, then it must have seemed, at least to a few of those demented minds, sailing on whatever twisted combinations of unnatural highs they'd been able to manage, that they had succeeded. For there must have been those who thought the half-naked giant descending upon them from the trees, his body a labyrinth of dark symbols, his hands filled with flame, was Lucifer himself.

It was all mixed up after that. There were people tearing hoods from their heads, looking for a way out. Some ran blindly into the night and disappeared at the cliff's edge. Screams were drowned in the clatter of automatic rifle fire. The main thing Ike would remember later was the incredible effort it took to move, to force himself to his hands and knees, to crawl to where Michelle still lay, her hands over her face now, weeping, and to drag her with him. It took all of his strength and there was little time for other things. But he took with him a collage of images: faces twisted, blurred in flight or frozen in death, of Preston himself, bare-chested, dark pants and beret, wires crisscrossing his chest, like he was plugged into something, the dark box beneath one arm, automatic weapon spitting flame, an odd detail connected to that: Preston's hand not fixed right somehow where one would think the trigger should be, but out a bit to the side. Suicide shifter against the palm of his hand, firing as Ike had told him to shift. There was more—bits and pieces that would not come back to him for some time: like the silver-haired man's dark friend standing near the stone ring and firing a pistol. He was holding the thing with both hands and aiming it toward the trees. The gun made a funny popping sound, as if he were firing off caps. And there on the ground, at the feet of the man with the gun, was the man who had brought Michelle, close enough still to the stone ring that Ike realized he must have had to practically crawl over him to get to her, and yet had not seen him until later, until he was ready to try for the beach. The man was no longer bald—there was nothing there at all, the whole top half of his head having been blown away. He was flat out, on his back but with his legs bent back under him at an impossible angle. His robes had fallen open and Ike could see clearly what he'd only glimpsed before—that flash of metal at the man's waist. It was a long dagger, the handle ornately carved, and gleaming still in the brilliant white light.

As for Hound Adams, he was just about the last person Ike saw before going over the edge. He had his back to Ike, and to the sea. He was facing the rifle fire with his feet slightly spread, his hands at his sides, and Ike was reminded of that day in the lot when Hound had faced the bikers, when he had saved Ike's ass. It was the last Ike saw of him. Hound Adams and that dark-haired guy with the gun—they were the only two not wild with fear, and he often wondered at how it must have ended, the final scene. Had Hound Adams and Preston Marsh at last faced each other there in the clearing? Had there been that one strung-out moment of silence while the invisible surf pounded below them, the last heartbeat of a dream gone bad? "What do you do when a thing is rotten?" Preston had once asked him, and Ike had not answered but Preston had, and was answering still as one final explosion rocked the cliffs above them, sending down showers of dirt and rock, so that it was necessary to stop, to cover up and wait it out. And then back down, toward the beach on legs like rubber, sucking breath gone to flame, moving the way he had often moved in dreams, and there were times, slipping and sliding in the dirt and brush, when he was certain it was a dream, or at least some twisted, drug-induced hallucination from which, in the end, he would awake.

42

Michelle was beginning to come around as they reached the beach, but still unable to walk without support. Ike stayed with her in the black shadows of the cliffs, talking to her, making her keep moving, anything so she would stay awake. At last they undressed, Michelle shedding the remnants of the bloodstained white cloth, and bathed in the cold water. Above them, above the jagged black line of cliffs, they could still see an orange glow on the sky. There were no more voices, however, and no music. The night was very still. They were alone on the beach and there was only the sound of the waves, and then, finally, as if from another world, the distant wail of sirens.

They did not talk about what had happened as they followed the railroad tracks toward town. They talked instead about small things, about how much money it would take to get back, about the length of the walk. Michelle had lost her shoes and Ike let her take his. She was still groggy and was having trouble keeping to the ties. Once she stopped and was sick.

Ike could not say if it was a long walk or a short one. Sometimes it felt as if they had been walking forever, and other times, as if they had just begun. He counted ties, lost count and began again, bare feet thumping against the rough wood, until at last the lights that had begun as a faint glow on the horizon had grown and separated to become the lights of the town.

In a bus depot they went to the bathrooms and tried to make themselves as presentable as possible. Still, Ike wondered what impression they must have made—Michelle wrapped in the black robe he had found for her beneath the cliffs, Ike himself in the soiled black pants and ragged shirt (both sleeves gone now because he figured that looked better than just missing one). He saw people stopping to stare and there was a moment of near panic when he wondered if they would even be let on the bus. In Huntington Beach they might have passed for punks. He had no idea of what they would pass for here but was as polite as possible at the ticket counter, where a fat Mexican woman barely gave him a second glance.

They rode a Greyhound to Los Angeles and transferred to a Freeway Flyer. They were less conspicuous now, Ike thought, in the city. He kept thinking the bus they boarded in Los Angeles was the same one he had ridden the night he had come, the night he had run from the desert. He was not sure why he thought that, being unable to remember the number, but he did. Michelle was able to sleep. Ike could not. He thought about the bus. And he thought about what they should do when they reached Huntington Beach. He pulled Michelle to him and arranged her in such a way that her head rested against his chest. He stroked her hair while she slept.

The bus purred on an empty ribbon. The night slipped past them. Vibrations from the engine spread into his legs, up into the bones of his back, but they did not put him to sleep. He felt stuck in that strange giddy place where sleep would not come, but where he could dream without sleeping, with eyes stuck open, and he dreamed of the desert, of skinny brown legs streaked with dust. He studied the people around him, peering at them from the dream, and he wondered if they were like him, if their lives were as confused. He wondered if there were dark secrets in every heart. He looked around him at their faces, slack-jawed and sleeping, eyes glued shut. He watched an old man in gray work clothes quietly smoking, staring from a window. What did these people know of the world? Did they know that humans still slaughtered animals and drank their blood, performed sacrificial rites on the cliffs overlooking the sea? If they knew, would they care? Or were these faces just clever masks—behind each mask a grinning skull, leering with bloodstained teeth? He shook his head. He was very tired, he thought, and how could he ever know what they were thinking, any of them. He looked at Michelle, her face round and smooth, and he wondered how much she had seen and how much she remembered. All she had told him about, waiting in the bus station, was the rage Milo Trax had flown into after Ike went under in the theater— something about the tattoo, going on about how it was all wrong, and that it spoiled everything, and then they had put her under as well and the last thing she could remember was Milo Trax throwing a canister of film at Hound Adams as Hound turned and walked away. He thought about that for a long time. Had it been the tattoo that kept him at the circle's edge instead of at its center with Michelle? He turned again to Michelle, watching her as she slept, thinking again of what she had been through, but her face betrayed nothing, was as empty as the others around him, as empty as his own, which stared back at him now from the black mirror of the window. It seemed to hang there, at a funny angle, an image of himself watching him watch himself, an image hung on the night sky, suspended above nothing.

He had a terrible time waking her when they reached Huntington Beach. The bus driver finally came back to see what was going on because they were the last people on the bus and there was another terrible moment of near panic as both he and the driver worked to wake her. At last, however, she began coming around and they were able to get her to her feet.

"What's she on, man?" the driver wanted to know. He stood back a few feet now, staring at the two of them. Ike said he didn't know. "Maybe she should see a doctor," the driver suggested.

"No, it's okay. She'll be all right. She's just real tired."

The driver squinted at them down his nose. He was a tall wiry guy with a big western buckle on his belt. Ike saw him study his tattoo. Finally he stepped aside and let them pass, but Ike could feel the guy's eyes burning a hole in his back as they went down the steps. He obviously knew a fuckup when he saw one.

43

It was decided in the morning that Michelle would go back to her mother's, at least for a while, that she would wait there until some word came from Ike. It was mainly Ike's decision, but Michelle went along with it. It was funny how that worked. Not long ago he had been ready to run with her, to go anywhere, as long as they were together. But the night had changed that. Maybe it was that now he had a better idea of what he owed to Preston. Or maybe he just did not like loose ends. There had, after all, been three names on the list: Terry Jacobs, Hound Adams, and Frank Baker.

He walked Michelle back to the station and waited with her for still one more bus. They'd spent the night at the Sea View, in her room. She'd taken a long time in the shower before leaving and had put on a simple white blouse and pale green skirt to go home in. The skirt was one of her old ones— something she'd picked up in a thrift store before Ike met her. She didn't pack a suitcase. Everything else, the newer clothes that Hound had bought for her, her toilet articles, her pictures, the plants, it all stayed. "Junk," she had said when Ike asked her about it, and had walked through the door without looking back.

Now they sat on a long wooden bench, their backs against a brick wall, their faces turned toward a pale sun. He held her hand, but there was something sad and rather distant, he thought, in her face, and in the silence between them. He could think of things he wanted to say, but he was not sure how to begin, and then Michelle spoke. Her voice was soft and the question was asked in a tentative sort of way, as if she wanted to get the question out but found it difficult. "Ike," she said. "What do you think would have happened?"

"I don't know."

She started to say something else. He could see it in her face, but then she didn't. He guessed it was going to be something about Ellen. He could see the bus now, waiting at the intersection of Walnut and Main. In a few minutes it would be time for her to leave. "I want to tell you something," he began. "I'm not sure why. I just want you to know it. That night in your room. After the movie. That was the first time for me."

She turned and looked at him, the sunlight bright on one

side of her face, the other in shadow. "What about your girl in the desert?"

"There wasn't any. Just Ellen."

She looked back into the street. "Was Ellen the girl?"

"No. Not the way I told you. You were the first." He stopped and looked back toward the bus. He was looking into the street as he spoke. "Ellen and I came close once. I think we would have made it together if she hadn't stopped. I wanted to —or thought I did. I didn't know what I wanted, actually. It was all mixed up. But I sure as hell used to drive myself crazy thinking about it. Then one day the old lady caught us together in the cellar. Ellen was naked because she was washing out this dress she'd been out all night in with some guy—didn't want our grandmother to see it, but the old lady thought it was me. She thought we'd been down there fucking our brains out or some damn thing, and for the rest of the time I spent there I kept having to listen to how perverse I was. The funny part was, I never tried to tell her different. You know, I thought it was like that passage in the Bible where Jesus says if somebody keeps on looking at a woman so as to have passion for her—it's like they have already sinned in their heart. I figured that was the way it was. I'd wanted it and I was guilty as hell."

Michelle had been watching him as he spoke, without expression. She waited for a moment when he was done. "I went to school for a while with this girl who used to fuck her brother all the time," she said. "She thought it was a joke. They both did. I mean, they would both tell their friends about it. Like it was supposed to be funny. It seemed a little weird to me at the time, but not really that big a deal. Maybe it would've been a big deal if she'd gotten knocked up. Or maybe I was just too dumb to know what to think." Then she shrugged and looked into the street, but when she looked back at him there was a bit of a smile on her face—the first he'd seen in a long time. "But I can just see you," she said. "Out there in the desert, driving yourself crazy over something that never even happened."

"Yeah, well." He shook his head and let his breath out

slowly. "It sure seems like a long time ago right now. Sometimes it's hard to imagine that it was even me out there—more like it was some other dumb hick."

"I don't think you were dumb. You were just raised by assholes, people you couldn't talk to. I was too."

"Yeah, that's part of it. But I think you've got to be careful of laying too much off on other people." The bus was pulling into the lot now, and Ike hurried on. "I do think that some of what happened this summer—all that shit at Hound's—had something to do with the picture I had of myself when I came. It's like if someone keeps telling you you're really fucked up all the time, you finally start buying it. You know what I mean? And then all of a sudden you find out that you really are fucking up and there's this temptation to say, 'Yeah, well, fuck it. You think I'm bad? You haven't seen shit yet, man. Watch my smoke.' You know what I'm saying?" He paused, looking rather desperately for a way to finish as Michelle watched the bus. "But that's just part of it, Michelle. I mean, part of me wanted what was happening here. I just wanted it without any responsibility for it. I thought I could slip out from under it by blaming it on other things—that I was raised by jerks, that I was fucked over by my old lady—whatever." Now that he was started, he was finding it hard to stop.

Michelle stood up. "I have to go, Ike. The bus."

He stood up with her. He drew a breath and when he spoke again, it was more slowly. "It's just that I've been thinking about this stuff lately. I wanted you to understand."

"I do," she said. She put her hand on his arm. "Anybody can blow it."

He walked with her to the door. Her hair was soft and golden in the sun, lifted slightly on a breeze. Her face seemed paler than he had ever seen it. "It was my fault, too," she said. "I thought the whole thing with Hound was going to be a real trip. He even told me he was going to let me have a horse and keep it at the ranch, that some of those cowboys would teach me to train it." She shrugged and then she went up the steps and into the bus. He watched her go. He watched through the dark glass until she had found a seat, until the bus had pulled away, then he walked alone back to the Sea View apartments. His room was cool and dark, the shades still drawn. He slept again, for a long time. And he was not troubled by dreams.

44

The stories began appearing in the papers the next day. Most of them focused on Milo Trax, the fact that he was the only son of a famous Hollywood film maker. They noted his early promise as a film maker in his own right and his subsequent demise, his involvement with drugs and pornography—possibly ritual murder, that being a subject still under investigation—and finally his violent death on the grounds of his father's estate.

Ike read some of the stories. But the reports on the incident itself never seemed to make the right kind of sense to him. Preston Marsh and Hound Adams were mentioned only in passing. Preston was depicted as some dope-crazed biker, a psychotic Vietnam casualty. The killings, they thought, were drug-related, Preston perhaps the victim of a burn. Ike finally stopped reading them altogether. There was really only one item that interested him, that captured his attention. Hound Adams, it seemed, was survived by a single relative—a sister and father being now deceased—his mother, a Mrs. Hazel Adams of Huntington Beach. He read that notice numerous times. Once he even made the walk back down to Ocean Avenue and sat one more time on the stone wall that bordered the school. It was where he had sat at the beginning of the summer, and that he should be back here now was a kind of mystery to him. It was like a piece of something, some pattern that he could not quite grasp.

He did not see the old woman that day. He watched the faded stucco walls, the neatly trimmed shrubbery, the empty windows, and he imagined her in there, muttering beneath her breath, baking bread for visitors who did not arrive, waiting for phone calls that were not to be. He stayed there until a nearly unbearable sadness descended upon him. Then he rose and left.

PART
FIVE

45

They buried what they had been able to find of Preston Marsh on the twenty-fifth day of September. The funeral was held somewhere back of Long Beach in a desolate wasteland he had long ago put behind him. Ike made the trip alone, on a bus. He got off at the appropriate street and walked the remaining blocks to the cemetery. When it was over, he walked back again, boarded another bus and left without ever knowing for sure exactly which town he had been in. The towns all ran together out there, as near as he could tell, a labyrinth of bare stucco homes, train yards, and weedy lots. It was a land of shopping centers and billboards—a place so colorless and bleak that Ike wondered what he had ever found so tiresome about the desert.

It was Barbara who had phoned to tell him about the funeral. She had called the evening he'd come home from Mrs. Adams's house. Her voice had sounded tinny and very far away over the phone. They had not talked for long. She had been in touch with Preston's parents, and she thought Ike might want to know. When he asked her if she would come, there had been a pause, and then she had said that she didn't know. He had looked for her upon reaching the cemetery but had not seen her. He could not say that he was surprised.

The funeral was not held in a church. It was a simple graveside service. Ike felt hot and uncomfortable in a suit he had purchased for twelve dollars in a Huntington Beach thrift store. There was little shade among the flat polished stones and bare grass. The sun was high in a gray sky, the silence occasionally shattered by a passing plane. This seemed to happen at fairly regular intervals, as if the graveyard lay beneath the traffic pattern of some nearby airport.

Ike had wondered about what to expect. There were fewer people than he had imagined. The great popularity Barbara had spoken of, that he had seen evidence of in the magazines, seemed to have faded with time. There were only a few, less than half a dozen, guys who looked to be about Preston's age, who may have remembered another Preston, the young man who had put these wastelands behind him to carve out a new name for himself in the shadows of the old Huntington Beach pier. There were also a few older people— friends, Ike guessed, of Preston's parents. The rest of the mourners were bikers, perhaps a dozen of them. Morris was among them and not once that afternoon did he or Ike get around to looking one another in the eye. The bikers had come with their colors flying and their machines sat behind them along the narrow gravel road that skirted the grass, chrome burning and hard to look at in the light of midday.

It was Preston's father who spoke the words. And the first thing that struck Ike about the man was his voice. It wasn't a preacher's voice. At least it bore no resemblance to the voices of the preachers his grandmother used to listen to on the radio, and those were the only preachers he had ever heard. It was just an ordinary voice, and it was a tired voice. He was a big old man, taller even than Preston, though not as thick, but there was a hardness there, and a hardness in his voice, and when Ike looked at him, he could see the son.

The old man was dressed in a cheap-looking blue suit. He wore a dark tie and black shoes. His hair was thin and gray, mussed by the occasional gusts of wind that wafted over the hot squares of grass. He held a Bible in one hand. Both arms hung straight at his sides. He faced his ragged flock across the open grave of his son, and near his side the sleek gray casket caught fire, like the bikes on the road. "I feel it is my duty," the old man said, and his voice cut through the grayness and the heat, "before God, to say some words. I will not judge my son now. Judgment belongs to the One who can read hearts. But I could not stand here today without a word to those of you who have come, his friends." He stared into the blasted eyes of the mourners, and they stared back, with earrings sparkling and bearded faces pouring sweat, and Ike did not imagine that many of them had stood still for a sermon in quite some time.

"I do not mean to say much," the old man went on. His hair rose with a fresh breeze and overhead a jet plane rumbled through the sky. He paused, waiting for the noise to subside. "I would only remind you of the words of John: 'For God so loved the world that He gave His only begotten Son, that whosoever believeth in Him should not perish but have everlasting life.' Now this is the basis for judgment, that the Light has come into the world but men have loved the darkness." He looked across the open grave at the Sons of Satan sweating on the grass. "We have been given a choice. I have put life and death before you, the blessing and the malediction." The old man's voice wavered for the first time. He bowed his head and stared into the chasm at his feet. Ike squirmed in his suit. The sweat dampened his collar and ran down his back. He was moved with a sudden pity for this old man. Preston had been his only son, and Ike wondered if the old man knew there had been a difference between that son and the ragged flock that stood before him now, if he knew that the wake of destruction left in Preston's death had not been born of some simpleminded desire to fly in the face of convention, some loser's desire to rule or ruin. Instead, it was born of a far deeper discontent, of a desire for something more like penance; Preston had worn those colors and tattoos like sackcloth and ashes. And Ike wondered as well if there had not perhaps been more of the father in Preston than either of them had ever known.

The old man spoke the last words with his head down, and the words were harder to hear. "Lord, Thou hast been our place of dwelling. Thou has set our iniquities before Thee, our secret sins in the light of Thy countenance. For all our days are passed away in Thy wrath. . . ." There were other words too, but they were lost in the roar of another jet plane and in the screaming of a flock of crows chased from the trees.

When it was over, no one seemed to know exactly what to do. Preston's father remained by the open grave. The small crowd stood on the grass, milling about. There was one guy Ike had seen earlier, some guy in his early twenties with a camera case over his shoulder and a camera in his hand, who was sort of standing around by himself and looking a little sheepish about taking pictures. Ike guessed maybe he was from one of the newspapers that had been covering the story. When the old man stopped talking and the skies were silent overhead, Ike could hear the soft click of the camera. There was something embarrassing in that sound and then one of the bikers threw a beer can. It came whistling and spraying foam, flashing momentarily in the sun as it missed the photographer's head by a foot. Ike watched the young man holster his camera and walk quickly away across the grass. He tried, craning his neck against the itchy collar, to get a better look at the bikers. He had this idea that it was Morris who had thrown the can, but he could not be sure. He liked to think that it was, and had they been on speaking terms, Ike would have thanked him.

He continued to stand there, with the others, sweating and itching, before working up enough nerve to approach Preston's father. It was something he wanted to do, for Preston. He wanted to tell the old man what he had been thinking, to put it into words. It didn't work very well, though. It was not an easy thing to say, and he found himself stammering around as the old man looked down on him, a slightly puzzled look in his gray hawk eyes. And later, he wasn't even sure exactly what he had said, something about how Preston had been different from the others, and something about how Preston had done some good there at the end, had saved a life, maybe two. He wasn't sure how it came out, or even if he was glad that he had said it. He finally decided that he was. The old man had not spoken. He had stood by, patiently waiting for him to finish, then he had nodded and walked away. The last Ike saw of him, he was walking across the grass, his Bible still in one hand, his arm over the shoulders of a short, gray-haired woman Ike took to be Preston's mother. There was a stiff breeze just then and Ike could see the old man's cuffs snap about his ankles, his thin gray hair rise on his head. Ike stood alone near the grave and watched him go. He watched until still one more plane had passed in the sky. This one, however, passed silently, the sound of its distant engines lost in the roar of a dozen chopped hogs coming to life in the silence of the windswept cemetery.

46

It was the beginning of October when he came back to Huntington Beach. Michelle was gone. There had been a letter waiting for him at the Sea View. She had gone to live with her father; he had sent money. Somewhere up north, along the coast. There was the name of a town, an address. He could come, she said, if he wanted to. He folded the letter and slipped it into the hip pocket of his jeans. She was, after all, one of the reasons he had come back. There was also that business of loose ends. He would find Frank Baker and they would talk one last time.

He moved out of the Sea View and took a room in a small motel near the corner of Main and Pacific Coast Highway. It was a newer building than the Sea View, a low white stucco affair with small square rooms done in turquoise and orange. A small kidney-shaped pool remained deserted, sunk forlornly into a barren rectangle of concrete. From a window he could see the highway, and beyond that the beach. The tourist season was over now with schools back in session and though there were still crowds of surfers in the early mornings and evenings, the beach had taken on a different character. It was cleaner and emptier, sometimes almost deserted in the afternoons with a brisk onshore wind kicking across the sand, turning the surf to junk.

He was without a board and he did not bother with a new one. He would surf later, he knew, in other places, but not here. It was just that there was something to be finished here and when it was, he could leave. He would be done with Huntington Beach, as he was done with San Arco. That was where he had gone after the funeral, back to the desert. The way he figured it, no one in his family had ever left that place without running, or taking the time to say good-bye. He wanted to be the first. And so he had gone. He had spoken to Gordon and they had stood in the ever-present heat of the gravel lot and he had told Gordon as much as he knew, the old man taking the news in his customary stoic fashion. And Ike had shaken hands with him, and thanked him, and he had looked, once, across the town toward the house, toward that cool, rotting porch, the great halo of dust-choked ivy, and there had been no reason to go there.

He stayed in San Arco for another couple of days, sleeping in the back of the market, working a few cobwebs out of the Harley, then getting on it and riding it, practicing, up and down the town's main drag, blowing past the old woman's house like an empty freight blowing out of King City on a downhill run. And when he figured he'd practiced enough to feel comfortable riding into King City, he went to the market for a pair of scissors and cut the sleeves out of one of those damned long-sleeved T-shirts. He'd put on a good fifteen pounds over the summer, and what with all that paddling and swimming, the weight seemed to have found its way mostly into his arms and shoulders. He still wasn't what you could call big, but he wasn't so much the runt anymore either. And then he had gone back outside and he had ridden the Knuckle clear to King City, a new pair of aviator shades giving back the sunlight, and he had walked into Jerry's shop and told them the bike was for sale, because Jerry had asked him numerous times about selling it, and he had stuck to his price and gotten it and he was finished.

The last look he got of San Arco was from the bus bound for Los Angeles, from the freeway, and from there the place was no more than a reflection—like some bit of glass or metal catching sunlight somewhere far back among the dry hills—and then he had closed his eyes, rested his head back against the seat and remembered the look on Gordon's face when he'd seen that damn tattoo, and remembered as well how the old men had stared after him, watching him blow past them forever while the tattered sleeves of his T-shirt beat time in the wind.

47

He stayed in the white motel for a week. He spent time on the streets. He even asked around a bit, after Frank Baker. No one had seen him, or at least would not say so to Ike. But the shop was still there, locked and dark. And it was Ike's guess that Frank would have to deal with it, sooner or later, that he would be back. In the afternoons Ike walked on the beach, long walks from the pier out to the cliffs and the oil wells and back along the edge of the sand where it was wet and steep.

It was strange talking to people. He realized that here, as in the desert, he had not made many friends. Michelle, Preston, Barbara, they had been his friends and they were gone. Even Morris, he had heard, had packed it in and moved inland, all the way to San Bernardino or some such place. And the others, those closer to his own age who he had seen often enough in the water to nod at, did not seem eager for conversation, or even to meet his eye. But then he had, he supposed, been Hound Adams's boy—at least to them, and so he did not really blame them.

A young girl came up to him one afternoon on the pier. He did not recognize her. She was small and dark, not unattractive in a small washed-out sort of way. She claimed to remember him from some party and she wanted to know if he had any dope. He stared at her for what he guessed was too long a time, forcing from her a rather nervous bit of laughter. When he told her that he didn't have any dope, however, and that he didn't know who did, her smile turned cynical and made it plain that she did not believe him. But she didn't push it—a small favor for which he was grateful. She hugged herself against the wind as if she had noticed it for the first time, then she shrugged and started away. He watched her go, down along the empty boardwalk with the wind at her heels, her thin summer dress whipping about her legs. He stared after her until she was gone, lost in the distant blur of sunlight where the pier joined the town.

One more day passed, and then another. It was toward evening of the second day that he saw Frank Baker. Frank was standing in the parking lot of one of Huntington Beach's few expensive bars, a large glass and concrete structure that had recently been built near the entrance to the pier. He was standing in the lot talking to two other men. All three were standing near the side of a low-slung yellow sports car.

Ike was on the sidewalk that ran along the edge of the highway, above the parking lots that extended down into the sand, not far from the lot in which Hound Adams had once fought the bikers. There were palm trees along the sidewalk and Ike stood close to one, slightly behind it and down off the curb. He stayed there for what felt like a long time but what in reality was probably not more than four or five minutes. At last he saw the three men shake hands. Two of them got into the car. Frank watched them go and then started away himself, alone and on foot.

Ike followed. He was certain Frank was on his way to the shop, and Frank did not disappoint him. They went up Main Street, made a left at Walnut, and then another right at the alley.

From the mouth of the alley Ike could see Frank's van at the back of the shop and for a moment he worried that Frank had only parked there for convenience, that he would now just get in and drive away before Ike could reach him, but he did not stop at the truck. He crossed behind it and moved along the right-hand side, toward the rear door of the building.

Ike was in the alley now himself, moving quietly, hugging the backs of the buildings as a fat, pale moon rose in the sky. He listened as Frank moved across the gravel. He could hear the sounds of keys hitting a lock. A yellow wedge of light fanned out from beneath the van and he knew that Frank was inside, alone, and that it was what he had waited for. He moved very quickly now, and in what felt like almost a single step he was there, at the back door, facing Frank Baker for the first time since the ranch.

The shop was almost exactly as he had last seen it. Toward the front he could see that some of the boards had been taken from the wall, that the old brick had gotten a new coat of white paint. But aside from that it was the same and there was an odd, almost eerie quality in that sameness he had not counted on. Most of the old photographs were still on the walls, though a few had been taken down and were now scattered across the top of the glass counter at the main desk. Frank was at the counter, head bent, looking over the photographs, when Ike entered the shop. He jerked at the sound of Ike's boots on the concrete.

Frank looked a bit thinner than Ike had remembered, and his tan seemed to have faded. Still, he looked fresh and neat in what looked to be a new set of clothes—white cord pants, striped pullover sweater, a pair of softly shining boat shoes. And Ike was suddenly aware of his own appearance—the greasy pair of jeans he had worked on the Harley in, the thick black boots that had been waiting for him in the desert and were now the only ones he had, the dirty T-shirt with missing sleeves. And then there was a week-old beard, and hair down to the collar of his shirt. The boots made him a good inch taller than Frank and he could not help wondering for a moment what Frank must have thought in that first instant his head jerked up from the counter—that perhaps some small version of Preston Marsh had come back to haunt him.

For a moment they just stood there watching each other. Then Frank looked back at the photographs. He was looking at them when he spoke. "You go to the funeral?" he asked. He spoke softly and his voice was only barely audible, even in the silent shop.

Ike said that he had gone.

Frank nodded, still watching the counter. "Crowded?"

"No. His folks. A few bikers."

Frank looked at him now for the second time. "There was a time when half this town would have been there. His old man say the words?"

Ike said that he had, then he crossed the floor until he was even with the end of the counter. He'd been working on an idea since that moment on the driveway at the ranch when he'd seen Frank in the van, watched him leaving, remembering that it was Frank Baker he'd once seen talking to Preston, before the first trip, before the shit hit the fan. "You set him up," Ike said. "The first time. You sent him to the ranch and then you told them."

Frank shook his head, but his eyes stayed on Ike now. "No," he said. "I didn't."

"Bullshit."

Frank shrugged. "Maybe you're just lucky to be alive, Jack. Maybe you should leave it at that." He moved as if he was going to step away from the counter, but Ike moved with him, blocking his path.

"You're a fucking liar," Ike said. And he could feel his throat tighten around the words, and the blood going hot in his face.

For a moment Frank's eyes flashed with anger, but then

the anger was gone and he was looking the way Ike had found him—more tired than angry, and beaten in a way Ike had not seen him before. So maybe that was why Ike was surprised when Frank hit him. He'd come ready to fight, if that was what it came down to, but somehow he had expected a different buildup. As it was, Frank just took about one-half step to his side and hooked hard with his left hand. It was a solid punch, but then Ike had been hit a good deal harder since coming to Huntington Beach. He rolled away from it, felt the counter at his back, and came off swinging, head down, rushing wildly in the way Gordon had tried to teach him not to. But it was like he was letting go of something, frustration, anger—something he had held inside of himself too long. He felt himself land solidly on his own, a blow that sent shock waves and slender ribbons of pain from his hand up into his shoulder. But he continued to charge, getting lower, taking another good shot on the back of the head and a knee in the face, but managing to grab the leg and to come up with it, hard, and in a twisting motion that was enough to throw the other man off-balance and into the wall. He could hear Frank's back and head slap the freshly painted brick. But he didn't slow down, he went right after him, digging to the body now, beneath the ribs, and he could hear Frank fighting for wind.

They moved together along the wall, Ike punching, Frank alternately trying to punch and then to hold. At last they stumbled into a rack of wet suits and went down together, their feet tangled in the debris. Ike managed to keep his man turned, however, to come down hard on top of him, and when they landed he could feel Frank lose what was left of his wind. Ike rolled away. He kicked his legs free of the suits and then sat back on his haunches, his hands on his thighs. It had all happened more quickly than he had expected—short but intense. And yet there had been a kind of release in that intensity. Now he waited to see if Frank wanted it to go on.

Frank stayed on the floor a moment longer, then rolled away in the opposite direction, finally winding up in a seated position, his arms out behind him. The funny thing was, he still didn't look angry. He brought one hand up to his face and touched his lip, which was cut and beginning to swell. "Shit, you're still a fucking punk," he said. He was breathing hard, talking in short bursts. "And yeah, I told him some things about the ranch." He paused for breath, shaking his head. "But I didn't set him up. I didn't know he was going up there until after it happened." He stopped and spit some blood on the floor.

Ike was still breathing hard himself. He leaned forward now, on his knees in the fine gray dust that covered the floor, his hands still on his legs. "So what did you tell him?"

"Come on, man. What the fuck is this? You're trying to tell me you don't know? You were with him, the way I heard it."

"Just tell me what you told Preston."

"Shit." Frank shook his head once more. "Let's just say Preston and I traded stories. He showed up one night, out there, in the alley." He nodded toward the back of the shop. "Christ, I hadn't talked to the guy in years. Scared the shit out of me, if you want to know. He claimed he was trying to find out something about this chick, Ellen, and he wanted to trade stories with me. What happened to Ellen in exchange for his version of what happened to Janet Adams."

Ike was silent for a moment. "But you were with them," he said. "You told me that. You took the damn picture. Remember."

"The day before I split." He paused, watching Ike, and Ike could see that he was trying to decide on something. He turned his head and looked at the far wall of the shop and when he looked back at Ike there was a slightly altered expression on his face, as if he had thought it over and made up his mind.

"I was the youngest," Frank said. "Younger than Hound or Preston, a year younger than Janet. I never did dig Milo. The trip began to get weird. Just kinky sort of stuff. And drugs. I got scared and split. I pretended to get this phone call from home. Preston knew I hadn't, but he went along with it, even told them that he was onshore with me when I got the call. I tried later to get Janet to come with me. She stayed. I came back and waited. I saw them come back without her." He paused. "You didn't know her," he said. "She was something special. I never did know what really happened. I mean, I'd heard Hound's version. But somehow I always knew Preston's would be different, if he talked. After the trip he'd just packed it in, joined the Marines and split."

But Ike was having a hard time concentrating on Frank's story at the moment. There was something else, some long, slow tremor of recognition snaking through his consciousness. Suddenly he knew why Preston had looked so strange the first time Ike had repeated what the kid in the white Camaro had told him, and why Preston had never believed the kid's story, and why, too, he had gone to Frank Baker. It was not just, as Ike had once believed, that the two stories were similar. It was that they were the same.

"It was your story," Ike said. For a moment Frank looked puzzled. Then he smiled. His swollen lip made the smile a crooked one. "Preston came to you because he wanted to know why some kid in the desert was telling your story."

Frank touched his lip once more. "Funny how that worked out, isn't it? But it wasn't really my story. It just came out sounding that way."

"And the kid?"

Frank shrugged. "He had the hots for that sister of yours. When she split for a weekend with Hound and didn't come back, he got upset. Hound told him the chick had split on her own, that the subject was closed. He didn't buy it, finally got this wild hair up his ass to go get Ellen's brother. I was the one who told him they went to Mexico. I also told him that what he was thinking about was dumb, but that if he went through with it, he'd better plan on staying gone for a while."

"You told him?"

Frank spread his hands. "What could I do? The asshole was my brother."

"But he said you were one of the ones she went with."

"Like I said, he's an asshole. He was also in love. Know

what I mean? He thought I was putting him off like everyone
else."

"But why your name and not Milo's?"

"Jesus, don't you see? He didn't know a fucking thing
about Milo Trax, or the ranch, or anything else. He was better
off that way. Let him think it was Terry and Hound, me even.
Let him go get Ellen's brother. Who gives a shit? Hound could
have handled that."

Okay, Ike thought, but they had come full circle, back to
what Frank had told Preston. Still, there was a dull ache in his
stomach when he asked again what Frank had known about
Ellen.

Frank met his stare. "You were there," he said.

"Just tell me what you told him."

"I told him there were graves at the ranch."

"Graves." Ike repeated the word slowly, his voice scarcely
above a whisper.

"Rumors," Frank said, but he suddenly seemed angry now
for the first time. "Who knows what to believe about that shit. I
didn't know for sure what was going on up there and I didn't
want to know. I'd just heard things."

"Like?"

"Like Milo having gotten in with some cult—rich fuckers,
people into some very weird shit who were willing to lay down
bread for the use of his land. Milo didn't have that much left,
you know. He'd done some time. He'd pissed away most of his
old man's money."

"What about the movies?"

"Hound's?" Frank shrugged. "Hound made those things
around the house to sell to the greasers, but he had his eye out,
too, looking for people he could turn Milo and his friends on to,
as near as I could tell."

"But Milo was filming that shit at the ranch, too."

"I told you, man, I wouldn't know about that. I wouldn't
want to. Maybe it was just something his friends could use to
get their rocks off with between sessions. Or maybe he'd found
some twisted buyer for them. Who knows? It's over now."

Ike was silent for a moment. "And you told Preston."

"Yeah," Frank said. "I told him." And there was something defensive in the way he said it. "I told the asshole and I laid it on thick, and it wasn't because I was scared—not really —and it wasn't even because I wanted to know about Janet. I just wanted him to hear it, man. I wanted him to know." He stopped and shook his head and when he spoke again there was a note of urgency in his voice Ike had not heard before. "I was here," Frank said. "In the beginning," and he pointed at the concrete beneath them, a quick, jabbing motion. "Those two guys had something, man. Not just bread. A goddamn lifestyle—that was what it was about then. And those two dumb fuckers had it. They didn't need Milo Trax. But they blew it, and no one knew that any better than Preston. Shit, he could never handle what happened to Janet. I wanted him to see just how far it had gone. I didn't tell him because I wanted to set him up. I told him because he deserved to hear it. I wasn't even sure if he was going to believe me." Frank paused. "But then, that was before I heard his version of Mexico."

Ike waited. He wondered if he would have to ask about that, too, but Frank was talking now; he was letting it out. "He said Milo killed some cunt down there. Some Mexican whore he'd gotten down on the beach with them. They were all stoned and Milo just pulled out this blade and did it, before anyone even knew what was happening. Janet saw it. She OD'd that same night." Frank stopped. "But then he never did tell you any of this shit, did he? So tell me something. What the fuck did you think you were doing at the ranch when you went up there with him?"

Ike was suddenly feeling very beat-up. His head was starting to feel swollen and slightly misshapen. "Surfing," he said. The word had an odd ring to it in the emptiness of the shop.

"Surfing? You mean you two actually surfed up there? Preston surfed?"

"It was the end of that good swell. He never said a damn thing about any graves. He said he wanted to show me what it could be like. He wanted to talk me out of hanging around Huntington Beach."

Frank shook his head once more. He tested his bad lip with his finger. "What it could be like, huh? Tapping the old source. Was that it?" But he went on before Ike could reply. "Yeah, well, that's cool. It's cool. But you want to know what's funny about it, about all of that tapping-the-source shit? It wasn't either Hound or Preston who thought that one up. It was Janet. And it was dope. That was the only source she had in mind, brother. Righteous grass, shrooms, pure cocaine. Some good shit. And with Milo pulling the strings, a goddamn endless supply and they were plugged into it. See, Hound and Preston had started out on their own, just a little business on the side—running a little grass back across the border in their cars. It was Milo who turned it into a big operation. And it was Janet who coined the phrase. Tapping the Source. Hound and Preston could dig it. They could see how people would take it and how it would be this in-joke. They only used it on the boards for about a year. Then Janet died and Preston split and I guess even Hound didn't think it was so funny after that." He paused for a moment, then went on, his voice a bit softer. "Don't kid yourself, man. Hound may have been full of horse-shit, but he knew they'd blown it too. I don't care what he said. They both knew. They just went crazy in different ways."

They stared at each other in silence for what seemed like a long time after that. It didn't seem to Ike that there was much left to say. What he kept thinking about was Hound Adams working his way up that damn ravine to open the gate for Preston Marsh. "So how did Preston know about Milo's party?" Ike asked at last. "Did you tell him about that, too?"

Frank smiled. "I sent him an invitation."

"And that's why you split?"

Frank's lip finally came apart on him and began to bleed. He did nothing to stop it and the blood colored his smile. "I told you, man. I always split. But that night, I had a hunch."

48

He didn't know how long they stayed in the shop—only that he had this feeling there was something between them, that they had been a part of something that had ended, and that when this, the talking, was ended too, it would be over and it would not be spoken of by either of them in just the same way again. And in a funny sort of way, he had the idea that Frank felt it too. He hadn't beaten anything out of him. It had all been there, waiting to come out for a long time. It had just been hard stuff to let go of. Somehow the fight had been part of the letting go. And who was there besides Ike to tell it to?

It was finally Frank who pulled himself off the floor. He made a rather halfhearted attempt at brushing some of the dirt from his pants, then he walked to the register and picked up one of the photographs that lay there. He held it up and Ike saw that it was the shot of Hound, Preston, and Janet. "New owners are coming in tomorrow," Frank told him. "Fucking punks from down the street. I didn't want them to have it."

"What about all the others?"

Frank shrugged. "Ghosts," he said. "If there's anything in here you want, take it. Just lock the door on your way out."

Ike was standing now, moving his legs to work out the cramps. He spoke to Frank once more as Frank moved past him, toward the door. "Will you tell anyone else, about the graves?"

"I don't know. Cop considerations aside, and that doesn't really mean shit to me anymore, I'm not sure people really want to know that kind of stuff. Your sister might be up there. Do you want to know?"

"I don't know."

"There you are." He went to the door and stopped. "See you around?"

"I don't think so."

"Got any plans?"

"Not really, just leaving."

Frank nodded. "What I should have done," he said. "A long time ago." He moved his shoulders. "Time flies." He turned his back to Ike and went out into the alley. Ike could hear the door slam shut on the van. He could hear the engine turn over and at last fade into the night. Then he was alone in the empty shop, with just the occasional sound of a passing car, and in the distance, the muted crack of the surf.

He stayed there for a long time, walking and thinking, looking over the memorabilia that still graced the walls. The boards he and Preston had used at the ranch were still in the racks. He pulled them out and placed them on the floor. Funny how he had thought you could be done with a thing, with the desert, with Huntington Beach. He thought about those green hills above the point, as silent as the desert at first light. He thought about Frank Baker, hanging on for so long. Perhaps there was more he should have asked. But in the end, he supposed, he knew enough.

In a way, he would have liked to take one of the boards. In another way, it seemed right not to. He wound up deciding on a single item—the photograph he had often admired of Preston Marsh carving his backside bottom turn from the dark face of a large Huntington Beach wall. As he lifted the picture from the counter, however, he noticed another picture just beneath it, one that he had seen before but that he had never paid particular attention to. It was a photograph of a wave, riderless and dark. The most interesting aspect of the picture was the way the sunlight had been caught in the lip and how it seemed to hang there, to spread and light up the fine white mist that rose along the top of the wave. What caught his attention just now was that the frame which held the photograph was coming apart and that a bit of the cardboard backing had begun to slide out and that between the backing and the picture there was another piece of paper. He tucked the photograph of Preston beneath his arm and worked the slip of paper—which was yellowed and frail—out from behind the print.

There was writing on the paper, writing and a series of small sketches done in black ink. There was something rather elegant and decidedly feminine, he thought, about the work, and then he realized with a quickening of the heart that certainly the work was hers. And he saw her as she had been that day in Mexico, her arms over their shoulders, her fine pale hair riding a wind, and he remembered how that picture had made him feel the first time he saw it, how having to settle for just looking at it had made him feel lonesome and left out of something. And he saw suddenly how it was all there, in that picture, all of it. The promise. The rush. And he guessed he could see how Frank Baker had hung around so long, how there had just been nowhere else to go. And it seemed to him, in the silence of the shop, that a ghostlike wind rattled the alley door, a wind not from the sea, but one that was both hot and dry, laced with sand and blown from across the salt flats of San Arco. And there were names in the wind. Janet Adams. Ellen Tucker. And how many more in between? In his mind's eye he saw the cool green hills of the ranch as they broke and spilled into the Pacific, folding their secret in the earth. The yellowed paper trembled slightly between his fingers as he studied her drawings—the small thumbnail sketches of waves that became increasingly more stylized as they moved across the page, ending at last with the looping silhouette of a wave enclosed in a circle, the wave's crest turning to flame.

He was going to take the paper with him but then on a sudden impulse began looking for matches. He found a book in the drawer by the register. He held the frail yellow sheet as it burned, holding it above the glass counter until the flames reached his fingers. What was left of it burned on the glass until there was only a crumpled bit of ash and when he blew on it, it broke and fell to the floor. Then he took the photograph of Preston and went into the alley.

He must have stayed in the shop much longer than he had
imagined, for as he reached the mouth of the alley he saw that
the streets were black and empty and spoke in their silent way
of that hour just before the first light. Far away, at the dark end
of Main Street, he could still see the yellow pinpoints of light
that marked the pier. The rest of the town had shut down.
Even the purple neon above the Club Tahiti looked dark and
cold against the sky. It was a strange moment, and yet familiar,
dominated by an overpowering stillness and shot through with
the scent of the sea where before there had been the scent of
the desert, and then he could see what it was, how it was
working up to that special time, building toward a silence so
complete the ground itself would have to break it, to speak in
some secret voice of a secret thing. Or perhaps it had already
done so, he thought, many times over, had given up its secret
time and again, but people had forgotten how to listen. And
for the first time he was not inclined to run. Because that
secret was what there was, he thought. And the pursuit of it
was all that mattered.

He tucked the picture beneath his arm and walked back
down the alley once more, entered the shop one last time. He
remembered the shop's original design from the pictures he'd
seen in Barbara's scrapbook, how the brick wall now separat-
ing the two rooms had once been the front of the building, and
he remembered what had been painted there. He found some
cubes of colored wax beneath the counter and he went to work
on the white brick, wondering how many layers of paint separated him from the original, knowing that his was not as polished as hers had been, but working it out anyway for himself,
in his own crude style—giving the new owners something to
think about. He had to bear down hard to get the line he
wanted and his hand trembled with the effort. He drew a
rough circle and within it the outline of a hollow, pitching
wave, its crest on fire, and beneath it the words: *Tapping the
Source.*